# Shooting
# To
# Kill

# SHOOTING
# TO
# KILL

# SUSAN SCHREYER

## WHITEHORSE MOUNTAIN PRESS

"Shooting To Kill"

Published by Whitehorse Mountain Press
Copyright © 2013 by Susan Schreyer
® Susan Schreyer
www.susanschreyer.com

This book is a work of fiction. Characters, incidents, and dialog are drawn from the author's imagination. Any resemblance to actual persons or events is coincidental, except in instances where permission has been granted.

Cover design by Tracy Hayes
www.pastiche-studios.com
Cover photograph by Susan Schreyer

*For*

# *Sally*

*-- my sister –*
*enough said.*

# Acknowledgments

This book was the most difficult of the series for me to write -- not because of any problems with the plot or the characters, but because, part way into the first draft, my mother then, two months later, my father passed away. The shock and the aftermath, as anyone who has experienced the same knows, throw your world off kilter and a good deal of time and energy is spent trying to put it all to rights.

I have many friends and family to thank for their support and understanding. You've all given me a deeper knowledge of how very important, even essential, that network is.

For the nitty and gritty work of building a story, I must once again thank my editors; Mary Buckham, Lisa Stowe, MK Windham and Anne Christensen. I depend relentlessly upon each of you.

For all things veterinary, my thanks goes out to Jennifer Sparks, DVM. You are not only an excellent equine veterinarian, but a patient and creative source of information.

To the many fans of Thea, Paul and crew; thank you for your patience. I have, as they say, opened a vein and bled love, laughter, tears and fears all over the pages. The result pleases me and I hope this adventure will sweep you up as you read.

*Susan Schreyer*
*June 30, 2013*

# Chapter One

Agnes Fulton giggled. The forty-something year old woman, known for issuing directives in a voice so husky as to be unsuitable for levity of any sort, sounded like a thirteen-year-old girl flirting with a fifteen-year-old boy. Two stalls away in Copper Creek Equestrian Center's Big Barn, I stopped brushing my Hanoverian gelding, Blackie, and gently banged my forehead against his dark bay, muscular shoulder. Agnes had been monopolizing veterinarian Don Archterkamp's time for over half an hour.

As if agreeing with my exasperation, my horse tossed his head causing the lead rope I'd tied him with to rattle the metal tie-ring like a door knocker. I gave Blackie a thank-you pat with my unencumbered hand. At least I could act out my frustration unobserved by anyone but him -- such small recompense for having to listen to Agnes babble about her new imported jumper while waiting for Dr. Don to get around to administering the routine West Nile, flu and tetanus vaccinations each horse got in the spring.

"You know my trainer Max is going to be showing Rum Runner on the grand prix jumper circuit in California this year. We all expect them to be spectacularly successful, since Runner was so highly placed in Europe last fall. He competed against some of the best Warmbloods the Germans had in their 'small tour.' With a little more training he'll be an international star -- and Max is the one who can do it." Agnes twittered again.

Blech.

Maybe she was flirting with Dr. Don.

More likely tossing her enormous wealth and hoped-for prestige into the face of someone she wanted to impress, or whose friendship she expected to buy. Definitely not flirting. Why would she if barn gossip was as dead-on correct as usual and she was having an affair with her much younger trainer?

"If you saw Runner jump you'd understand why I spent a small fortune on him," she continued. "He's handy, fast and, Max tells me, a dream to ride – but I haven't been on him yet."

That didn't surprise me -- the blatant reference to gobs of money or the fact she hadn't ridden her horse yet. She probably never would. Despite Max's haranguing, she clung persistently to the round-shouldered and loose-leg technique most beginners abandon as they progress in their training. She was better off riding one of her other, easier horses. It was unlikely she'd ever be able to stick to the saddle when Rum Runner powered himself off the ground.

All of us at the barn, and probably the UPS delivery man as well, knew the imported Warmblood gelding could jump the moon, thanks to repeated demonstrations of his prowess during the entire first month after he'd arrived in Snohomish, Washington, and made his home at Copper Creek Equestrian Center.

Yes, Rum Runner, the big, flashy chestnut Warmblood, was the star of our huge equestrian facility's jumper contingent: one of those elite equine athletes who spent several months of the year traveling from show to show in the

U.S. and Canada defying gravity by flying over enormous jumps for enormous sums of prize money.

Or he would be a star if his training ever got back on track.

Don replied to Agnes' boast with a noncommittal, "Really."

"Max said once we get Runner tuned up properly I can pop him over some small fences." She giggled, again, before rattling on about what special veterinary treatment her horse required.

Good grief.

I'd had about all I could take. It was time to interrupt. I had to get back to my office. Thea Campbell Accounting wasn't going to run itself, particularly with April's tax season breathing down my neck.

I placed my brush into my grooming kit, but before I reached Blackie's stall door, Agnes let loose with a frustrated huff, stopping me like a slap. Her conversation with Dr. Don made an abrupt change of direction and she discarded her vacuous performance.

"Dr. Archterkamp." With the shock of a whip cracking, her two-pack-a-day voice carried up and over the eight-foot-high stall walls, shot through the hay-drop ceiling holes, zoomed out between the bars on the front of her horse's stall, and reverberated on every surface it touched. "I said, inject my horse's joints. Today. And after you've done that, you'll need to give him one of those tranquilizers that lasts for several days."

"Now, Agnes, there's no point in getting yourself worked up. I already told you my professional opinion. It hasn't changed and I'm not going to do it."

I braced for her rebuttal. Unfortunately, she didn't disappoint.

"You're not listening to me, Dr. Archterkamp. I need you to listen to me." She pronounced each word distinctly.

I'd wager my warm barn jacket she was hanging onto eye contact with him in the same imperious manner she used when giving instructions to Miguel, our barn manager, whom she incorrectly assumed had a poor command of English.

"I am listening, Agnes. I've heard every word you've said." Dr. Don's tone held an untypical, icy edge that chilled me more than the damp March wind blowing down the barn aisle.

I returned to Blackie, retrieved the body brush from my grooming kit and leaned into the next sweep. On an impulse, I turned from my horse and raised my voice a few decibels higher than strictly necessary. "I've got Blackie in his stall, Dr. Don."

"He'll be with you when I'm done with him," Agnes shouted. When she spoke again, her voice pitched lower. "I doubt you've understood me, Dr. Archterkamp. I'm giving you instructions."

She was an idiot. Everyone understood her. She routinely leveraged her sizable bank account to assure everyone's cooperation. It worked well enough on most occasions. But not this time. She was as wrong about Dr. Don as she was about Miguel. It was she who wasn't listening.

"I'm not changing my mind. You may as well quit pestering me about it. Injecting Rum Runner's joints again, so soon after the last round, is not only inadvisable but potentially destructive. Shooting him full of Resurpine to control an attitude that is due to physical pain is unethical. The horse needs time off and treatment."

Poor horse. I'd mentioned to both Miguel and Delores, Copper Creek's owner, that I thought there was something wrong with Runner -- in addition to the cloddish manner in which he was being ridden. Miguel agreed, but Delores had been pretty tight-lipped at the time.

"I didn't pay four-hundred and twenty-five thousand dollars, plus thousands in transportation fees, to have him sit in a stall for the duration of the competition season. Runner needs the injections. Max said so."

Of course he did. Max Deniau, Rum Runner's trainer and

one of the jumper trainers at our barn, always had a trick "guaranteed" to solve his problems. Lately, Runner was quitting at the big fences and objecting, with athletic bucks, to Max's strong, disciplinary thumps with his whip. A few of us had even witnessed Max's less than graceful, emergency dismount – and thought his bath in the outdoor arena's single puddle well deserved. Apparently, pharmaceuticals were Max's latest trick to ensure equine cooperation.

"Additional injections," Don said, with so much patience I squirmed, "won't solve the physical issue –"

"*Physical* issue?" Agnes' screech made me wince and Blackie jerk his head up with a snort. "I keep telling you, there's nothing physically wrong with the horse. Max said it's an *attitude* issue. Rum Runner's not lame. He needs the joint injections to be competitive, and Resurpine to keep him in a calm, receptive state. Otherwise it's difficult for him to progress. Max says everyone does it -- that it'll *prevent* future problems. Give him the dose of tranquilizer. Inject the coffin joints in the front feet, plus the hocks and stifles. I'll pay your exorbitant fees, if that's what you're worried about. After all I've already paid you to ultrasound and x-ray him for no reason whatsoever. You'll remember you found nothing. Therefore, the horse isn't lame."

"The horse is not right. I told you he needs additional diagnostics. If a bone scan or MRI show nothing, then I'll agree the horse is ready to compete and we can consider other reasons for his behavior problems, but I will not inject the joints again. Maybe you need a new trainer. Now, if you'll excuse me, I've got fifteen more horses to inoculate and I haven't scheduled the time to rehash this argument."

Agnes' disgusted grumble preceded her barked, "Max! Max, where are you!"

A horse bumped his bulk into a stall wall. Probably Rum Runner, judging from Dr. Don's "whoa, son."

"Max!" Agnes bellowed. "I want you here. Now!"

Light steps hustled down the aisle from the wide barn

door closest to me and the tall, lean form of Max Deniau, Copper Creek's premier equestrian-couture fashion model/jumper trainer, flashed past Blackie's stall. My horse blew a sneeze and shook his head.

"Yeah, I agree," I breathed, running the soft bristle body brush down my horse's sable neck for the hundredth time. "He was probably hiding so Agnes could work on Don. Too much drama for me, too, buddy." I flipped a portion of Blackie's short black mane back to the right side of his neck where it belonged.

Two stalls down, where Rum Runner lived, Max's footsteps came to a halt. There was no rattle of a stall door opening. Evidently, he had no intention of going into the stall with the horse he was at odds with. Good. Maybe Max wouldn't stay long. As it was, if they didn't wind this difference of opinion up soon, I'd have to leave and go back to my office. Not that my departure would cause a problem for Don, I just always liked to be present for Blackie's check-ups and shots. Now, thanks to Agnes, my lunch hour was already stretching beyond the time I'd allotted.

Max cleared his throat. "Since you're insisting on an uninformed and outdated approach to caring for an upper-level competition horse, we'll get another vet to give him the injections. I want all of Rum Runner's records as well as those of Agnes' other two horses sent to me immediately. Come on, Agnes." The stall door rattled, rolled and slammed. "We *will* be taking your horse to California to compete."

"You'll cripple him for life," Don said, his voice rising to a near shout.

"You've lost our business, Dr. Archterkamp. Max knows what he's talking about," Agnes said. "A vet who understands what a top-level horse needs will do it."

"You take him to California, and I'll personally make sure he's drug tested before he steps off the trailer. You'll find yourself suspended from showing."

The air in the barn stilled with the threat. Even the horses seemed to be waiting without so much as taking a breath.

"Let's go, Agnes," Max said. There were three or four rapid steps and a shuffled stop. "You don't know who you're dealing with, Don."

I stifled a snort. Right. Oh, so frightening. The only thing scary about Max was how much he charged his clients for training and lessons.

As the two sets of footsteps stamped off toward the other end of the barn I mouthed a silent cheer. In just a few moments Blackie would get his spring shots and I could go back to my office. I listened, waiting to hear the sounds of Don entering in the stall next to Blackie to vaccinate that horse.

Nothing.

The "nothing" continued until I began to worry. I dropped the brush I'd been using into my grooming kit and moved toward the aisle to investigate, but a stall door slid softly and a latch rattled into place.

"Who've we got next, Michelle?" Don asked.

I hadn't realized Don's tech-assistant had been present. Michelle, a good friend of my twenty-four-year-old sister's, was a striking, exotic-looking girl. Her long, straight dark brown hair contrasted with my sister's long, golden brown curls, but they were similar in height and gracefully curving body type. The two of them monopolized male attention when they went out together. That they both loved a good time worried me on occasion. However, unlike my sister, Michelle was focusing on a career. She had a huge soft spot in her heart for animals of all sorts and had quite a zoo at her parents' home. She couldn't have had a better mentor than Don Archterkamp.

"Um, uh, Agnes' other horse Moody Blue. I think. Then Blackie. Are we going to do Moody? You know, after ...." Her voice squeaked.

Who could blame her for being unnerved?

"Agnes didn't say not to. The horse needs all the shots, too. Won't do him any good to skip them, since he'll be going to

California with the rest of the crew. Don't need her suing me because her horse didn't get the proper inoculations for the horse show."

Moody's stall door slid and bumped closed with a little clang. I picked up a brush and went back to grooming Blackie.

"Hand me that West Nile vaccine, Michelle. Don't fret about this nonsense. Losing a client isn't the end of the world. We're plenty busy anyway."

"Are you really going to report Max if he takes Rum Runner to the show?"

There was enough of a pause that I could imagine Don's slow smile.

"Said I'd do it, didn't I? Here you go. Put this in the sharps container and hand me the tetanus. I'd bet my monthly gasoline bill that Agnes' superhorse has a suspensory injury. It's probably up high. Hurts enough to keep him from wanting to jump, but doesn't make him limp -- just looks like something's not right. If you're going to be a vet, pay attention to your gut. Won't steer you wrong."

Michelle murmured something, and Don chuckled.

"Me, too. It's long past lunchtime. When we're done here how about we go back to the office? Alice made some of her excellent chili and corn bread for dinner last night and I brought in enough leftovers for all of us to share. I'll take the intranasal flu vaccination now." Moody's sneeze was followed by the slap of a hearty pat. "There you go, son. That wasn't so bad, now, was it?"

Moody's door opened and closed again with a clatter of the wheels in their metal track obscuring Michelle's comment.

"Ah, there's our next patient, tied to the wall and getting a rub down. Wish all my clients were as Johnny-on-the-spot as you." Don slid Blackie's door open and came in. He was tall, a good bit over six feet, and wiry, with sandy, though graying, hair. His lean face always had a quick smile and today was no exception, although there was an understandable weariness to it. As usual, he wore tan chinos over well-worn cowboy boots.

His brown canvas barn jacket was unzipped, and I recognized the green plaid flannel shirt from the last few times I'd seen him. When the weather warmed, he'd exchange the flannel for lightweight cotton, in the same plaid. "Thanks for waiting, Thea. How's our boy?"

"Good," I said. "Couldn't be better."

"Vi and Henry holding up?" He was referring to my great aunt and uncle, whose farm was a short distance from Copper Creek, but he continued before I had a chance to answer. "Haven't seen them in a while. And how about that young man of yours? He still treating you well?"

I grinned. "If he didn't Delores would straighten him out." My fiancé, Paul, was Copper Creek owner Delores Salatini's nephew. And three years ago, Delores had been the first client for my nascent accounting business. "My aunt and uncle are well. Uncle Henry said he was having you out next week for Duke's spring shots."

"Glad to hear it. I'll have Willa schedule in a little extra time, just in case Vi has any pie she's hoping to have eaten up."

I laughed. My aunt would feed them, all right. She fed everyone. I expected a comment from Michelle as she came in loaded down with a carryall, still holding a good number of pre-filled vaccine syringes, a sharps container and a canvas bag of supplies. She said nothing, only slid the door closed behind her, set her paraphernalia down in the clean shavings, and didn't look at me. In contrast to Don, she was bundled up with a knit hat pulled down over long dark hair and a zipped-up-to-her-chin, dark blue ski parka. She'd tucked her jeans into mid-calf-high snow boots. Despite all the warm clothing, the end of her nose was red and she sniffed.

"Any health issues I should know about since I saw him last?" Don asked.

"Nope."

"No 'meltdowns'?"

"Not since January." I grinned. Don had been called each

time Blackie exhibited what could only be described as a temper tantrum. My Aunt Vi believed from the very first that the only reason he got hysterically upset on the odd occasion was because he knew I was in danger. The timing of the tantrums and my imminent peril correlated perfectly. Even I believed her now. Don didn't, although he had no other explanation.

"Well, that's good to know." His gray eyes twinkled. "Guess you've been leading a quiet life."

"You know it. What could be more quiet than sitting at a computer working on other people's taxes and books?" I didn't think I'd mention the couple of clients I'd dealt with this morning whose necks I would have gladly wrung.

"Not veterinary work, that's for certain." He glanced in the direction of Rum Runner's stall and frowned. Michelle handed him two syringes. One filled with a light pink fluid, the other a clear. He held the one with the clear liquid between his teeth like a pencil. With a quiet, smooth motion, he injected the pink into Blackie's neck, replaced the needle cap and handed it off to Michelle to dispose of. "That was West Nile." I followed him around to Blackie's right side. "I'm putting the tetanus on the right here. If he has a reaction, put a hot compress on it and give me a holler. You got any Bute on hand?"

"No, but I'm pretty sure Delores does. By the way," I said, lowering my voice, "I think you're right about Rum Runner. Max has been trying to work him through his 'behavior problems' and it's been pretty ugly. In fact Runner's getting progressively worse."

"Doesn't surprise me. Max is chasing prestige and money, so an injury that will sideline the horse for months is not something he wants to consider. He's not thinking about the good of the horse and that chafes me something fierce."

"Delores caught him beating the poor thing through a three-foot course last night."

Don's eyes tightened with disapproval. "I imagine she had

one or two things to say to him about that."

"She did. It ended with her telling Max if she ever caught him treating a horse like that again he could pack up and get out. He yanked the tack off Runner, threw the poor horse in a stall and peeled out of the parking lot."

The vet cocked a sideways look at me. A tiny smile pulled at a corner of his mouth. "Funny, didn't notice any sweat marks on him."

"I kind of rinsed him off and walked him until he was cool enough to put away."

The amusement made it to Don's eyes. "Brushed him a bit, too?"

I shrugged. "Maybe a little. No one else was here to do it."

"That's so nice of you," Michelle said, touching my arm.

I smiled a thank you at her. Her lashes were spiky, as if clumped together by dried tears. Agnes and Max had upset her a good deal.

"Maybe a little risky, if Max had come back." Dr. Don said. "I don't think he would've appreciated the gesture, and if something happened while you were cleaning up after him he'd probably sue you. You can't save them all."

Michelle's jaw tensed. "I think she did the right thing."

"But he's right," I said to her with a small shrug. "Don't think I wasn't really careful about who was around and saw me with Runner. I didn't want to give Max another reason to harass Delores. He's blaming her for every little thing that has gone wrong lately."

"What do you mean? What's going wrong?" Don asked.

"Everything from his clients' horse halters missing and ending up on the school horses, to supplements mysteriously disappearing, and equipment wearing out. He really needs to check the stitching on his girths when he cleans them."

"Max doesn't clean his own equipment," Michelle said. "My boyfriend, Bobby, does. He'd notice if something was worn and tell Max. I'm sure of it."

I wasn't, but made a noncommittal noise. I knew Bobby

only slightly and wanted to know him slightly less. He was an idiot with some illegal habits. Michelle deserved someone better. Someone you didn't have to watch like a hawk just to make sure he didn't "borrow" something and trade it for something more important -- like money or drugs. If things were missing from Max's tack room and there reportedly were, if you believed his clients -- then Bobby was responsible. Unfortunately, Max blamed Delores. Didn't make a lick of sense to me why he thought she could be at fault, but blame her he did.

The clatter and skid of shod horse feet on the concrete aisle interrupted our conversation.

"Whoa, now. Easy." Copper Creek's barn manager Miguel had just brought a horse into the barn. None of us moved to help. He'd have the situation under control shortly.

The door on the stall next to Blackie's slid open and the sharp clap of iron shoes became a thudding scramble as the appropriately named Sudden Squall rocketed into her stall. Miguel continued with the soothing baritone patter, and the flighty mare began to settle down. When the churning of movement slowed to a stop Miguel, without raising his voice, addressed the humans he knew were nearby.

"Are you and Michelle ready for this one, Don?"

"Yeah, we'll be right there."

"She is a bit spooked today -- more than usual. I think it was Mrs. Fulton's little white dog jumping out of her car window that set her off this time."

Great. I'd been hoping Agnes had left already with Max and cringed at the thought they'd overheard anything I'd said.

Don shook his head and sighed. "You might want to stay out of the stall, Michelle. Just give me all the syringes and I'll make quick work of it."

She looked like she was about to protest, but bit her lip instead and gathered up the carryalls and sharps container. Don gave Blackie a quick rub on his face as I untied the lead rope from the wall ring. My horse shoved his head against

Don's chest, forcing him against the wall.

"Hey, now, big guy. You know better than to rub on people."

Blackie pricked his ears at Don's mild reproof and pushed his nose into his stomach. Don scratched my horse's face again then tried to step around the big, dark brown head, but Blackie had managed to take hold of the vet's unzipped jacket in his teeth and held on.

Dr. Don snorted a small laugh. "Usually they can't wait to see me go." He pried at the edge of Blackie's mouth with his thumb. Blackie relinquished his hold for a moment, only to grab hold again. Don pried a second time. "I may have to leave my jacket here if you don't let go, and it's a mite too chilly yet to be running around in my shirt sleeves."

All at once, the hairs on the back of my neck stood at attention. I opened my mouth to speak, but my inhale didn't seem to draw any air. "Don," I choked.

He turned a quick glance at me then doubled back with a hard look. "What's wrong? Your lips just turned white. Sit down before you pass out." He took a solid hold of my upper arm.

"No. Don, it's not me. I'm okay. It's you --"

"The only thing wrong with me is your horse thinks my jacket is a chew toy. Sit down and put your head between your knees. Last time I saw anybody as pale as you was a million years ago in vet school at our first surgery."

I ignored his request to sit.

"Is there something wrong with Thea?" Miguel called from the other stall. "Do you need help?"

"She's just looking a mite pale. You go ahead and keep that filly out of trouble. I'll be there in a minute."

"Don, Blackie doesn't want you to leave. He's trying to warn you. Don, please. Wait."

Blackie's eyes and ears followed the conversation as if he understood. However, he did not release his hold on Don's jacket.

"Are you telling me you believe your aunt's nonsense about this fella having psychic powers? Now, Thea --"

"Actually, I am. There've been too many instances where his behavior and bad things that happen --"

"To you, not me or anyone else. If I understand correctly. Now, off hand, I'd say if that were the case, then he wants me to stay right here because you're about to keel over." He turned his attention to my clingy horse and scratched the blob of white on his forehead. "Don't worry, Blackie. I'm right here. If she falls over, I'll help her back up again."

Blackie, as if he understood, huffled softly. In doing so, he relaxed his hold on Don's jacket, and the vet slipped out the door. Blackie lunged, mouth open, but missed. Barely. Don cocked his head at my horse.

"Watch your manners, son."

"Don, be careful." My voice trembled. I wanted him to stop. But stop what? "Please. Blackie ...." I had no idea what to say to him next.

Don chuckled and shook his head, then followed Michelle to Sudden Squall's stall. Blackie put his head against my side and shoved me toward the stall door. I stumbled a couple of steps and bumped the water bucket hanging on the stall wall, sloshing water down my hip and leg.

"Damn." Before I had a chance to assess my degree of wetness, Blackie brushed past me, whinnying plaintively, and knocked me against the bucket again. More water jumped the rim and soaked my other leg. I grabbed at the dragging lead rope to stop my horse from circling his stall just as Sudden Squall revisited her nervous shuffling. Someone, perhaps the horse, thudded against the wall between Blackie and his fractious neighbor.

"Whoa, now." Miguel's croonings, repeated in an almost melodious manner, should have rocked the animal to sleep. The churning settled.

"Oh, shit," Don said.

My breath stopped on the inhale and my face went cold,

despite his almost casual tone. In all the years I'd known him, I'd never heard Don swear.

"What's wrong? Did you stick yourself?" Michelle asked.

"Oh … damn …."

# Chapter Two

A thud and a scramble preceded a crash that shook the barn walls. Miguel no longer spoke to the horse but hollered Don's name over and over. I flew out Blackie's stall door only to see Michelle, standing in the aisle, bug-eyed, with her hands clasped over her mouth, staring into Sudden Squall's stall. She backed a step and tripped over the carryall, sending the contents skittering across the aisle floor.

"What happened? Don? What happened?" I yanked open the stall door and dodged Miguel hurrying backwards, dragging Don by the armpits away from the frenzied gray mare intent on climbing the far wall.

"Michelle!" Miguel barked. "911! Call 911! Do it now!" She didn't move. He jerked an angry look over his shoulder and saw me. "Thea! Get her phone."

Michelle shook her head over and over. "I don't - I don't have a phone."

"I'm on it," I blurted and sprinted for mine in my car. Just outside the barn door I caught sight of Delores leaving the office, her keys in her hand. "Delores!" I screamed. She snapped around like I'd thrown a rock at her. "Don's down. He's collapsed. Call 911!"

Thank God for her clear head. She ran back toward the office and I spun back to the barn. Miguel had Don on his back in the aisle, his face inches from the vet's, yelling his name, tapping his face. Don's blank stare didn't change; he didn't flinch. I did.

Miguel tore his own jacket off, then his shirt and threw it at me. I caught it, confused as to why he'd stripped to his T-shirt.

"Get down here." He pointed next to Don's head. "You do the breaths."

"I --"

"I will tell you what to do."

My knees buckled and I landed hard next to Miguel. He snatched his light cotton shirt from my hands, tipped Don's head back so his mouth fell open and flicked the garment over Don's face.

"I will count to five then stop. Pinch his nose closed, put your mouth on his and blow."

My own jaw went slack. I made a desperate search of Miguel's face for an alternative instruction. He was dead serious. He meant for me to help. I couldn't do this.

"If he vomits grab his shoulder and pull him toward you so you don't have to look."

Panic closed my throat and I nodded reflexively. But I couldn't do this.

Miguel pushed Don's jacket open, laced his fingers together and placed the heels of his hands on Don's sternum. Shoulders rounded and elbows stiff he rocked his considerable weight forward onto his hands.

I had to do this.

"One. Two."

A gunshot-like crack came from Don's chest. I yelped and grabbed at Miguel. He rocked back. "Stop! Stop! You're crushing him!"

Miguel rocked forward a third time. "Can't be helped. Three."

A snap, followed by another sickening crack of bone and at least two more gut-wrenching snaps followed.

"Miguel!" I begged, pulling at his arm. "Stop!"

He glanced at me. "Broken ribs happen. It is that or death."

I whimpered. Miguel didn't look at me again, but rocked forward once more.

"Four." Only one rib gave under the pressure and snapped this time. "Thea," Miguel's voice was quiet, his accent heavier than usual. "I need your help. Don needs you."

I swallowed, my mouth sour, and nodded. I stared at the shirt covering Don's face. Blood pounded in my ears.

"Five. Now, Thea. Pinch his nose closed."

I pulled in a deep breath, found his nose, and pinched his nostrils.

"Hold his chin."

My shaking hand held his chin delicately through the fabric.

"You cannot hurt him. Mouth on his. Blow through the fabric. Now."

I forced all thoughts from my mind, stared at the concrete floor as I leaned over and blew for all I was worth.

"Again. His chest must rise."

Swallowing, I sucked in a lungful of air and put my mouth over Don's.

"No air escaping out the sides. Push against his mouth," Miguel growled.

I fought my instinct to pull back. Forced my concentration on the checked pattern of the shirt and blew again.

"Good. One."

As Miguel leaned into the compression the unmistakable stench of vomit hit my nostrils and my own stomach convulsed. Miguel grabbed Don's shoulder and pulled him toward us, snatching the shirt from his face. A small amount of bile pooled next to my knee. The memory of Don's comment earlier about not having eaten lunch came to mind, followed closely by the assertion he would not be eating his wife's chili and cornbread any time soon. I shuddered at the cold, inappropriate turn my thoughts had taken. The man's life was on the line, not his food preferences.

"Two." Miguel had rolled Don to his back again and resumed his stiff-armed compressions.

I picked up Miguel's shirt, placed it over Don's face and drilled my focus onto Miguel's voice. At "five" I sucked a lungful of air, covered Don's mouth with my own and blew through the fabric into his lungs. Miguel's barked numbers became my lifeline -- Don's lifeline.

Where was the ambulance, the EMTs? I scanned the area. A few people hung back at the barn door, identical horrified expressions on their faces. Michelle sat pressed against the front of a stall, hugging her knees to her chest, mouth agape, eyes wide like frozen blue pools -- like Don's.

"Five." Sweat trickled from Miguel's brow, down his neck. The stink of urine distracted me. My gaze roved, then stuck to the large dark stain on the front of Don's pants. "Thea."

I snapped to action, blew air into Don, waited to hear Miguel's "good" before releasing Don's nose and chin. Again, a sour taste spread on my tongue. I leaped to my feet and ran. At the barn door the contents of my stomach hurled from my mouth over and over until there was nothing left. Only peripherally did I notice Jorge, Miguel's teenage son, and several other people I knew dodge away. Doubled over, I panted, wiping at my mouth with the back of my hand. Cold March wind slapped my face and guilt did the same. What was wrong with me? Don needed me. Miguel needed my help. I couldn't be puking my guts out. I drew a ragged couple of breaths, straightened and jogged back to Don and Miguel. My post.

More compressions.

More breaths.

The numbers ran together. I listened for "five."

The ambulance -- where was it? Why weren't they here? Had Delores not called?

"Four."

I looked at Miguel as he rocked back. The US Navy anchor tattoo on his forearm trembled. Sweat dripped from his chin and his T-shirt clung damp on his barrel chest.

"Five."

Another breath. Another "good" from Miguel. How did he keep going? He seemed so sure of himself, so rational, so resolute. Thank God. The numbers he spoke secured me to a rhythm that seemed like it wouldn't end.

I felt the rumble of the diesel engine first. It came up through the ground, growing to a growl, intruding on my concentration. At the slam of doors and male voices I looked up, seeking the disturbance. The red and white EMT vehicle backed up to the barn door. Four men in blue trousers and shirts flung doors opened, unloading equipment, a gurney.

"Five. Thea. Breathe."

"They're here, Miguel --"

"We can't stop. Not until they tell us. Breathe."

I bent over Don and blew another of the endless breaths. Activity swarmed around us. Words of reassurance were scarce. Miguel gave them a brief explanation of what had happened -- the accidental needle stick, Don's sudden collapse. The EMTs spoke to each other in checklists, as metal clattered and paper ripped. They circled us, stepped over us, and finally took over from us, stripping Don's shirt, exposing his bare chest, removing his belt and loosening his pants. They moved with a speed that spoke of orchestrated practice, each man making a running commentary of his actions that both confused and reassured me. The compressions Miguel has started were continued without a break, my breathing efforts were replaced with an apparatus that I was certain would choke Don. Refuse from IV bags, syringes, needles, littered the aisle before one EMT knelt next to Don, stuck electrodes onto the sides of his chest and shouted "Clear!" A hum and a thump preceded a reflexive jerk from Don.

I stepped forward, but Miguel's big hand restrained me. I shot a questioning look at him, and when I turned back one EMT counted to three and all four men lifted Don onto the gurney. With an efficient couple of pushes the gurney disappeared into the back of the ambulance and the doors shut. One of the men approached.

"Thanks," he said. "Good job. You'll want this." He handed each of us a bottle of Gatorade.

I waved it off.

He pushed it into my hand. "You *will* need this. Drink it." And he left, climbing into the driver's side of the emergency vehicle.

Miguel unscrewed the top of his drink and poured half of it down his throat. The progress the EMTs were making on Don was more important to me, and I wasn't thirsty. There was a good chance I could look through a window. They weren't going anywhere just yet. I took a step toward the ambulance and my knees buckled. Miguel caught my arm and eased me down. He unscrewed the cap of my drink and handed it back to me. Nauseated and dizzy, I pushed it away.

"Sip this. You need it." He finished his off.

I took a swallow, barely keeping it down.

"More," Miguel said.

I obeyed. At least I didn't feel any worse.

The ambulance rolled away from the barn, and the crowd that had somehow gathered moved quickly out of the way.

"Wait!" I struggled to my feet and took a step toward the departing ambulance, toward Don, then spun toward Miguel. "They're leaving. We -- I -- Don ... is he going to be okay?"

"I do not know." He regarded me steadily, his bandito moustache emphasizing the frown in his eyes. "I do not hold out much hope."

I swallowed hard on the lump in my throat, catching a glimpse of the emergency vehicle as it turned onto the road in front of the equestrian center and accelerated. The strobe lights suddenly activated along with the siren. They'd waited until they were away from the horses. My respect for the men caring for Don jumped a few notches and, along with it, my conviction they would save him. My distress receded, but nothing took its place.

"Thea, come on." An arm settled across my shoulders, nudging me into motion.

Delores Salatini, the barn's owner, urged me away from the scene of all the previously frantic activity. We followed some steps behind Maria, Miguel's petite wife, as she walked her husband toward their house, a hand on his back, rubbing small circles like one would do for an upset child. Of course, Miguel had to be feeling the same emptiness as me.

Jorge, Maria and Miguel's son who worked part time at the barn while attending community college, glanced at his mom and dad before going back to picking up the debris left behind by the emergency crew. Paper and plastic wrapper seemed to be scattered everywhere. I entertained the idea of helping Jorge, but exhaustion kept me from detaching from Delores' firm arm across my shoulders.

Miguel and Maria's tidy, two-story white house was at the far side of Copper Creek's parking lot. Delores ushered me inside, pointed to the sofa and told me to sit. Arguing with her didn't even enter my reeling mind. I sat. Maria had already parked Miguel in his easy chair, and had wrapped a blue fleece blanket around his shoulders. She hustled to the kitchen and Delores joined her. Their hushed conversation lasted only as long as it took to bring mugs of hot chocolate out for me and Miguel. I took my cup and curled over it, alternately sipping then breathing in the sweet steam. I couldn't remember what I'd done with the bottle of Gatorade, or even if I'd finished it. For half a moment it seemed terribly important, but I could summon no energy to find out.

By the time I'd finished half of my drink, I was beginning to rouse from my fog. I straightened a bit and found Delores, perched on the arm of a chair, watching me.

"Better?" she asked.

"Yes. Thanks." I looked around. "Where's Michelle?"

"Your sister took her home," Delores said.

I nodded. Made sense, since she worked in Copper Creek's office. "We need to find out how Don's doing."

She hesitated, flicking a glance at Maria.

"Delores and I will take care of calling the hospital. I will take you home to your aunt and uncle. You stay there until Paul comes home."

"I can drive myself. Paul may be home already." I pulled my sleeve back and looked at my watch then glanced out the window at the dull March sky. It was impossible to make any assessment. "What time is it? I think my watch stopped."

Delores consulted her own watch. "One-ten."

"That can't be right."

"It is." Miguel rose from his chair and handed his mug and the blanket to his wife. "It only seems a long time has passed. I'm going to get a clean shirt and go back to work."

Maria's scowl was as effective as a hand on his arm. "You will not. Jorge can work harder for a change."

Miguel touched Maria's cheek -- a tender, intimate gesture. I looked away. "This is not new to me. You know that. Work will help me forget."

"Come on," Delores said to me. "Give Maria your keys. She'll drive you over to Henry and Vi's in your car, and I'll follow in a minute and pick her up."

"But what about Don? I want to go to the hospital and find out how he's doing."

"Maria and I will go." She raised a hand as I opened my mouth to protest. "If you're at your aunt and uncle's house I won't have to call all over the county to report any updates."

I closed my mouth and gnawed my lip for a moment. There was some practicality to what she said, and Delores was nothing if not practical. "Fine. But I'll drive myself." I dug my car keys from my jacket pocket.

"You will not." Maria plucked the keys from my hand and marched to the kitchen, returning in a moment with her purse. "Now. We will go."

I gave up.

To be honest, it was a good thing Maria drove. I barely saw the streets of Snohomish, with its small businesses and many Victorian homes, as we made the short trip to my aunt and uncle's farm on the other side of town. The scene in the barn, with Don laid out on the concrete aisle, Miguel working at compressions and my own poor performance played itself out from beginning to end in a continuous loop. I didn't even realize we'd arrived at my aunt and uncle's until Maria turned my car off.

I looked around, startled.

Aunt Vi, wearing a cheerful pink cardigan over one of her flower-print house dresses, stood in the kitchen doorway of her steep-roofed, brick house. Worry compressed her lips and knotted her brow. She already knew.

A smatter of cold rain blew against my cheek when I got out of the car and I hurried toward the house. The cold blew through my jacket and damp jeans, still wet from my collision with Blackie's water bucket, chilling me as if I had nothing on at all. My teeth chattered.

"Come in, come in. I just got off the phone with Delores," my aunt said, pulling me into her softness and warmth. "She told me about Don, poor soul, and what you and Miguel did to help. Brave little love. Bless you both."

My throat constricted and I nodded, fast and brief, while looking for some way to force down the emotion I'd thought under control. The teakettle whistled. Aunt Vi released me and I breathed relief as the threatening tears receded.

"Have some tea, both of you. Delores will be here in a shake."

With a sigh and a tsk, Maria settled herself at the big country kitchen table. I pulled out my usual chair and sat, tense, on the edge of the seat while Aunt Vi bustled around, pouring boiling water in the big delft blue teapot then getting the cups and saucers. She poured the water that had warmed the pot down the drain, spooned in some loose tea, then filled the pot with more water. She chatted with Maria about a recipe she wanted to try.

I half listened, adrift and useless, with nothing to contribute.

The footsteps behind me had to be my uncle Henry, since I hadn't heard a door open. I turned and looked up at him as he settled his hand on my shoulder. His solemn nod acknowledged my small smile.

"I've just rung up Paul and told him he could find you here."

"Thanks," I said, relieved I didn't have to call my fiancé to fill him in. I'd have sniffled my way through the details, for sure, then he'd feel he needed to leave early from the University of Washington, where he taught paleontology, and maybe cancel a class to come and comfort me. I didn't need him to do that. I wasn't the one who'd collapsed and been taken to the hospital.

Uncle Henry brought the sugar and milk to the table and Aunt Vi brought the teapot and cups. As she poured, Uncle Henry chatted with Maria, at first about Don. She seemed to know very little, but my uncle didn't press her for information. Instead, they moved on to a different topic and my attention drifted.

I sipped my tea, fussing with the edge of the paper napkin, examining the embossed detail, wondering about how it was done and alternately folding and rolling it until bits began to break off.

The honk of a car horn diverted my awareness out the kitchen window. Delores, in her pickup truck, waved energetically. Maria hopped up, thanked Aunt Vi for the tea and gave me a quick hug. I returned it, pleased when her gesture of support did not tip me to the edge of a crying jag. She bustled through the kitchen door, pulling on her coat. We three watched as she climbed into Delores' truck. Once they disappeared down the driveway, we returned to sipping our tea.

"What happened?" Uncle Henry asked after some time.

I shook my head. "I was in Blackie's stall. Don had just given him his vaccinations and went into the stall next door. Miguel was holding Sudden Squall for Don. I think the horse was fussing a bit, but it didn't sound too bad. The next thing I knew Miguel was yelling Don's name and dragging him out of the stall. Miguel was the hero. He knew what he was doing. I just did a little to help." Guilt washed over me. I hadn't even wanted to do the little bit I had. Miguel bullied me into it, and I'd been frightened, repulsed and incompetent.

"A 'little help,'" Aunt Vi said with a snort. "You did a good job of it. That's what I know." She reached across the table to me, but I was too far away to receive her touch. I extended my hand and we twined our fingers. "It'll be all right, you'll see," she said and patted my hand before releasing me and going back to her tea.

We sat in silence for some time until the phone rang, shrill and insistent, sending my heart into a panicked lick. Aunt Vi and I exchanged an anticipatory look as Uncle Henry rose from the table and answered.

"… I see …. Yes …. I'll tell them." He hung the phone up carefully and I held my breath. As he faced us, expression solemn, he shook his head slightly, and in doing so, the bottom dropped out from under any hope I'd held. "He's gone. They pronounced him when they arrived at the hospital. His wife just arrived. Delores and Maria are with her."

The breath I took sounded more like a sob. I stifled it with a hand over my mouth, but I couldn't stop the tears. Uncle Henry pulled out the chair next to me and scooted close, wrapped a strong arm around my shoulders. Aunt Vi dabbed at the corners of her eyes with a napkin.

How could this happen? It was so unfair. He was alive and then, suddenly and for no good reason, he wasn't. I'd spoken with him, he'd talked to my horse, Michelle was getting ready to have his wife's chili for lunch. We wanted him to be okay. It was so unfair.

"Here," Uncle Henry handed me my cup of tea. "Have a few swallows."

The now lukewarm tea soothed the constriction in my throat. He refilled my cup, then Aunt Vi's and finally his own.

"What do we do now?" I asked. Misery flooded through me, dragging at my heart and weighing down my shoulders. Don had been a friend of the family since my aunt and uncle had moved from their home in England to Snohomish to breed and raise dressage horses. Blackie was the last foal Don had delivered for them, before they retired from the demanding breeding business. We all had a long history together with Don, and it was over. We hadn't been able to save him, despite how hard Miguel worked. If only I'd gotten there faster, done better, if only .... "Blackie tried to warn him." I searched Aunt Vi's face. Uncle Henry cleared his throat.

"Now, Thea --"

"He did," I said, cutting him off. "Blackie didn't want him to leave his stall. He held on to Don's jacket. He was trying to warn us."

This time when Aunt Vi reached her hand across the table I did the same with both of mine and held on. "You wouldn't have been able to stop Don. You know that, duck," she said.

I could have tried harder. The guilt clung with the tenacity of truth.

I released my aunt and sank against the back of my chair.

For a long time we sat, my aunt and uncle sipping their tea, me staring at mine. We each held our thoughts close, until my uncle sighed a little. "I remember when we first moved here, and bought the first broodmare --"

"Pansy." Aunt Vi smiled a little into her cup. "Don came and took a look at her, to check her for breeding. Wasn't too impressed, as I recall -- hated her name. He liked her babies, though. Remember the discussions the two of you used to have right here at this kitchen table?"

Uncle Henry nodded. "And he was right more often than not. Good mind on that man. I learned a lot from him."

My aunt and uncle continued to reminisce. Most of what they spoke about was before I knew Don. I hadn't had much need for a vet until Blackie was born eight years ago. Even though I'd been the one who managed the constant care he'd required for the first year of his life, it was Don who was right there advising, prescribing, supporting. I'd learned to trust Don back then. So had Blackie.

Now he was gone, and it seemed all we could do was bring up the past and drink more tea. Deep sadness pulled at my heart, and shame. Blackie's warning had been so clear. If only I'd tried harder to stop Don, if only I'd acted faster, not held back because of squeamishness, maybe Don would still be alive.

The crunch of tires traveling faster than normal on the gravel driveway stayed my hand as I reached for the teapot. I rose slightly from my chair to be able to see more easily who'd just pulled up in such a hurry. Paul swung out of his gray Honda and strode across the grass to the house. The tweed sport coat he wore blew open and his tie flapped over his shoulder. He vaulted onto the back porch without bothering with the two steps. I had the kitchen door open for him before I realized I was out of my chair.

"I thought you had a meeting," I said, closing the door behind him.

"Cancelled." His dark brows tented above luminous blue eyes. He was thirty-five, fit and handsome in a don't-mess-with-me-way when his expression was serious – like now. Almost a year ago he'd captured my heart with that look and not let it go. He nodded an acknowledgment to my aunt and uncle before catching my eye. "Henry told me there was an accident with Don."

I nodded, but that wasn't the reason for his speedy return

home. Uncle Henry'd told him I needed him, I'd bet real money on it.

"Thea ...." He leaned toward me and, although at five-eleven he towered over me by a good nine inches, I was reminded of Don's height and how he'd almost made Paul appear short when they stood next to each other. I'd never have the opportunity to make that comparison again. My chin began to quiver. I attempted to turn away, but Paul gently took my upper arm. I opened my mouth to tell him Don didn't make it, but nothing came out. He walked me into an embrace and I found my way inside his jacket, pressed against the warmth of his body. He wrapped his arms around me.

"The news isn't good?"

I shook my head, a lump stuck in my throat and grew.

"I'm sorry," he said, and kissed my hair.

The storm building in my chest burst with a suddenness that evaded any control and blew tears out my eyes. I clutched at Paul and sobbed into his shirt.

"It's okay," he murmured, rubbing my back with a hand. "I understand."

"No, no, you don't," I wailed, unable to hold down the horrible guilt any longer. "Blackie tried to save him and I didn't help. And then I didn't want to help Miguel. I didn't know what I was do-o-o-ing. I wanted Miguel to do it all. It wa-a-a-s disgusting and aw-w-w-ful."

"Shh ...." He stroked my head. "It's okay."

"No, it's not. I thr-r-r-ew up. Oh, Paul, Don was dying and I threw up." Words I'd never intended to voice tumbled out as if a switch flipped. Every word of self-reproach, every horrible thought I'd dammed up let loose, turning my mouth into a major spillway. I could not stop.

He tucked me closer and shifted a bit, wrapping his jacket around me like a cocoon as I shivered. It startled me less than it should have to realize I was sitting on his lap. I hadn't noticed we'd moved from the door.

"Shh ... it's okay, everybody feels like that. You weren't

prepared, it's okay." He smoothed my hair and when he lifted his hand from my head an unwelcomed coolness filled the space. "She's shocky. The tea's a good idea. How about adding a splash of the whisky?"

He was obviously addressing my aunt or uncle -- making excuses for me. I cried harder.

"Here." He peeled me away a bit from his chest, and held a mug near my mouth. The aroma of Earl Grey wafted up my nostrils backed by a weaker, smokey, Band-Aid scent that had to be scotch. Probably.

"Drink some of this."

I did. The tea seemed a little over-sweet. Someone had added honey. Although the scotch lingered at the back of my throat, it lacked its typical burn. At last I could breathe without an accompanying sob.

"I'm so sorry." I stared miserably into the now empty mug.

"Nothing to be sorry for." Paul's voice was soft as he took the cup from my hand and set it on the table.

"My goodness, no," my aunt said. "That was a very tough situation you went through, and you did an admirable job. No one can fault you for reacting like so many other people have when faced with the same thing for the first time, isn't that right, Paul?"

He snugged me close again and his chin bumped against the top of my head. "Including the puking. Happens to most everyone, even if they're trained. The guilt for not having saved the victim, the sense of loss, the anger – it's all normal."

"I feel terrible." I plucked at a button on his light blue Oxford shirt. How did he know?

"Miguel probably feels the same," he said, "but I expect he's had some prior experience with CPR."

My uncle cleared his throat. "He has. In the service, same as you, I expect."

Agreement from Paul came in the form of a half-supressed chuckle and a slight shifting that I'd bet had nothing to do with my weight and everything to do with my presence.

More things he'd never told me about.

Oh, I knew he'd been in the Army, done a tour of duty overseas and seen some pretty awful stuff. He didn't like to talk about it, so I never pressed him. However, it was part of a dance we maintained between telling each other all about our pasts and keeping the dust under the rug.

He knew all about me. I knew a lot about him -- but not everything. When one has had a varied, if somewhat checkered past, a few things were bound to fall through the cracks. I wasn't going to come unstuck over every little thing. After all, early on in our now almost-year-old relationship he'd told me how, at fourteen, he'd stolen his parents' car, about dropping out of high school at sixteen, and lying about his age in order to join the Army.

However, he'd also deliberately attempted to keep from me those few items he thought might upset me, like some of the trauma he'd experienced while on active duty, his participation in a Seattle police sting operation ... and his ex-wife.

She slipped his mind, he'd said.

Evidently the CPR training slipped his mind, too. I sighed. Aunt Vi seemed to take it as a signal. She pushed her chair away from the kitchen table.

"Why don't you two go get comfortable in the living room? I'm going to start dinner. We'll eat early. Make tea-time dinner. Then you can go home and rest."

While I mulled over the proposal, Paul agreed and hoisted me off his lap. If I had this much trouble making a decision about food then maybe I was still reacting to ... what had happened earlier.

I made use of the powder room, rinsing my face with cool water, trying to calm the puffiness that passed for my eyes. After a bit I gave up, dried my face, went to look for Paul and found him in the living room, as instructed, slouched on the sofa and already engrossed in a magazine. I curled next to him, tucking my feet under me as I leaned against him and closed my eyes.

Snapshot images of Don, as vivid as the scenes in real life, flashed rapid-fire in my mind: his limp body as Miguel dragged him from the stall, the vacant stare from his eyes, the sounds of ribs snapping like gunshots, the stench of vomit, urine. My eyes flew wide and my heart slammed against my ribs as I flung into a sideways escape. In an instant, Paul had me by the shoulders, pinned to the sofa, his face inches from mine.

"Look at me, Thea. Focus. Look at me."

I struggled first against Paul then, at his repeated command, against the hold of the visions. When his face, his eyes came into focus he blinked once and I was free, sagging in his grip.

He let out a breath and offered an encouraging smile. "You'll be okay. You just need some distance – time and emotional. You'll be fine." He glanced around, snagged the magazine he'd been leafing through and put it in my hands. *The Chronicle of the Horse*. Uncle Henry's. "Read this. Out loud if you have to."

I opened the magazine and stared at a page until I could make out words, until my mind quit looking for images in the middle distance. This must be how guys did it – kept from losing themselves in the emotion-of-the-moment -- change the subject until it could be safely approached. I wasn't entirely sure I agreed with this tactic. At some point one had to grapple with one's demons.

My aunt and uncle both stood in the kitchen doorway, watching me, as if holding their breath. Not wanting to distress them any further, I sat a little straighter and followed Paul's instructions, muttering the words on the page before me.

The ringing phone provided another source of distraction -- this time for my aunt. She answered in the kitchen. I assumed it was Delores. In a moment she popped her head into the living room.

"It's Andrea, duck."

My mental gears churned, ground and came to a halt. Andrea had tracked me down here? Why? My pause was all Paul needed to spring to his feet. "I'll talk to her. Keep reading." The last part was a direct order to me. I opened my mouth to tell him that for women, talking to their good friends about what was bothering them was a better way to deal with trauma. All I got out was "Ah --" before he disappeared into the kitchen. How long could he talk to Andrea, anyway? Not long.

In a longer while than it should have taken him to tell her "she's feeling a bit emotional and will call you back," he returned to the living room. I couldn't read his expression.

"Is Andrea okay?" I asked.

He glanced at me as he sat and twitched a smile. "Yeah, fine."

"Didn't she want to talk to me?"

He picked up another issue of *The Chronicle of the Horse*, opened it and pretended interest in an article. "Oh, um, yeah. But thought maybe she'd touch base with you tomorrow sometime."

"Is there anything wrong?"

"No, not a thing." Another twitchy smile at me and he returned to his "reading."

I didn't have the energy to start a debate over what he was or wasn't telling me so I went back to the dressage article I'd actually had some interest in. Paul turned the page of his issue right after I turned mine. I'd completed another couple of paragraphs when he cleared his throat.

"Say, how about we take a long weekend? Go someplace completely different."

A vacation? Now? It had been a while since we'd gone anywhere. We'd both been busy with work. It was tax season, duh. Although, thanks to my nagging (as one or two clients mentioned), I wasn't so slammed I'd had to skip my midday rides. That would have made me really crabby. "When?"

"I was thinking next weekend. Maybe leave Friday. Come back Sunday."

I weighed his suggestion against my work load. It was the middle of March, not quite "the eleventh hour," so it was doable. Probably. If I got up early and worked evenings. "I'll have to work longer hours before we go, though."

"That's fine, if you don't mind."

"And I don't want to miss Don's funeral."

"No, of course not. We'll go after."

I studied him for a moment. Something was up -- or he was being thoughtful. He was generally pretty thoughtful -- for a guy.

He flipped a couple of pages, then tossed the magazine aside, slouched against the sofa back and closed his eyes. The corner of his mouth rose briefly.

"Okay. We'll go." I went back to my article. I'd find out later what he was up to.

# Chapter Three

I didn't find out. And I forgot about Andrea's phone call. After Paul and I finished dinner with Aunt Vi and Uncle Henry we went home to our little gray and white Craftsman-style cottage, ten minutes from their farm and just a couple of blocks from downtown Snohomish.

Our house had had some remodel work done, thanks to damage from an arson fire in November. We'd moved back in barely three weeks ago, and the restoration and remodel was still like a toy to me. New maple cabinets, built-in storage and granite counter tops graced the kitchen, along with brand-new appliances. The bathroom remained essentially the same (I'd have hated to lose the big, claw-footed tub), and our old bedroom was rebuilt the way it had been, but with new materials -- including windows and flooring -- and became a guest room. The big difference was what had been the attic. It was no longer a dark, dusty home for creepy little spiders, but our bright, spacious bedroom suite with a sitting room that spanned the width of the house. Our builder had added two dormers facing the back yard to match the two that had always been there, but faced the front. A narrow staircase accessed the large room from the hallway on the main floor, ascending in an easy curve through what had been an inefficient pantry. The addition of a built-in dresser along one wall made resourceful use of the space and gave us more room than we'd ever need; the clothes closets were cleverly tucked alongside the dormers, and cozy window seats invited lounging. We'd hauled a sofa up the stairs and the TV, and splurged on a new mattress and box spring. The new headboard we agreed on had a distinct Craftsman look to it. I'd decorated the whole area in earth tones with splashes of red. It was a masculine look without being a man-cave. It was our sanctuary and we loved it.

It was to this area we retreated when we got home. But I couldn't sit still. I brought up snacks from the kitchen, vacuumed during commercials as Paul watched TV, dusted and ran a couple of loads of laundry. Paul stayed out of my way, but I noticed him scrutinizing me from time to time. Unfortunately, I wore myself out. If I lay down, I might sleep. If I slept I knew I'd dream of Don and how he died. Therefore, I kept moving.

Paul finally begged me to stop cleaning and sit with him to watch TV. With arms, legs and back aching, I couldn't refuse. After one of the late-night talk shows was over, he yawned, stretched until his T-shirt rode up his stomach, then hauled himself to his feet and dragged me by the arm toward the bedroom.

"I don't want to go to bed yet," I whimpered.

He powered off the TV. "Yes, you do. Okay, mostly, I do. I can't stay awake any longer and you shake me every time I doze off."

The little tickle of panic in my chest started up, just like it did each time he nodded off. "I'm not tired yet."

He cupped my face in his free hand and ran his thumb

over my cheek. "Then let's play."

He bent to kiss me and I backed away, a vision of other, paler lips startling me. "I don't think I should. I mean, I mean … I don't think I should."

Paul rubbed his chin, considering me for a long moment. Finally, he sighed. "Okay. Let's go turn the TV on again. I'll try to stay awake."

Relief washed through me. "Thanks." I stood on my toes and gave him a quick kiss, and then another -- because he was so sweet -- and one more, because his lips were soft and warm and alive and I had to linger to wipe out the other memory of lips that didn't respond. My hands on his chest rose and fell with his breaths, measured the beat of his heart, sought the heat of his body.

I slid my arms around him and, with no hesitation, he wrapped me in his strength, becoming my refuge. This was what I needed and I didn't want to let go.

On a deep level, where survival kept watch, I knew exactly where the kiss, the embrace were going. In order to find lasting calm, to heal the trauma, I had to take him to me. It didn't take a psychic to read my mind, and for half a moment I worried he'd object to the way my desire had boomeranged. But he didn't. With utmost tenderness he undressed me, shed his own clothes and took me to bed. What began as gentle love-making quickly turned to consuming need.

Afterwards, as the breathlessness of passion slowed to deep breathing, as sweat began to cool, I snuggled into his warmth and, listening to the thump of his heart, drifted to sleep.

Morning found me feeling a bit more like my old, emotionally stable self. I sat in my robe at the kitchen table, sipping coffee and wrangling to get out of the early run Paul had instituted for us to get *him* fit for soccer season.

"I don't like running," I said, making an effort to sound as un-whiny as possible.

He pulled his sweatshirt over his head. "It's good for you."

"I went running with you a couple of days ago. You don't need me every time."

"Sure I do. I'm more apt to stick to a routine and, ultimately, avoid injuries if you go along. Besides, I enjoy your company." He tossed my sweatshirt and pants at me. I thought I'd left them in the dirty clothes hamper.

"You run a quarter of a mile ahead of me. How is that enjoying my company?" I sniffed the sweatshirt. Yup, not clean.

"Did you happen to notice how many guys on my team last year didn't make it the full season?"

"No, I can't honestly say I did." I got up from the table and took the stinky sweats back to the laundry closet. He followed me.

"We were barely able field a full team. It was tragic. By your refusing to come with me I might not get the exercise I need because I'd turn around and come home just to be with you."

I patted his cheek. "That's so sweet. Every woman should be so lucky."

"Do you want to be responsible for the Snohomish Bobcats not making it to the play-offs because their most valuable forward didn't have the stamina to get the job done?"

"That would be you?"

"And it will be, if you don't come running with me."

Male logic. And they scoff when we women go with each other to the restroom.

He wore a triumphant smirk by the time we jogged back up the steps to the front porch, and thoroughly deserved the locker-room swat to his butt I delivered when he edged me out for the shower. I scampered out of his reach when he attempted to pull me in with him, sweats and all.

I shucked my damp exercise duds and pulled on my robe, then started a fresh pot of coffee before checking my voice mail. Miguel hadn't called while we'd been out – not that I expected him to. I picked up the handset and started to dial his number, thought better of it and disconnected. Halfway to the bathroom I turned back, snatched the handset up and came within one digit of completing dialing before I hung up again. Miguel would know I'd be worried. He'd have checked Blackie twice by now.

After I had my shot at the shower and saw Paul off for an early class, I dressed to ride and drove out to Copper Creek.

Before going to the barn I decided to check in at the office and lend my support to everyone else who'd been shocked by Don's death. The additional truth was I needed to face the scene I'd left the previous day -- a decade ago -- to reassure myself of its ordinariness.

Besides my sister Juliet's bright yellow motorcycle and Delores' green truck, there were few cars in the Copper Creek parking lot. There should have been the usual early morning lesson students. The small, sour knot, hiding behind the cereal and coffee sloshing in my stomach, barged forward and elbowed my breakfast aside like a bully. Could something else have gone wrong?

I parked my elderly red Ford Escort and hurried to the office, rapped quickly and went inside without waiting for a "come in." The change from the usual lively mood was palpable. Delores, in her standard working attire of a cotton turtleneck under a flannel shirt, (both blue today), jeans and lace-up work boots, looked up from her paperwork, her usually ruddy complexion pale and haggard.

"Cancelled lessons today out of respect," she said before I could ask. "Juliet's been here for over an hour calling and emailing people. Would have closed the barn, too, but the logistics got away from me."

Juliet, seated at her desk near the office window, didn't even pause in her typing. I took a longer look at my customarily brightly clothed sister. Today she'd dressed completely in black: pants, sweater, scarf, ankle boots. I didn't know she even owned anything in that color. In addition, her long hair, typically cascading freely down her back in loose curls, had been pulled and twisted tightly into a bun at the nape of her neck. She had to have a headache.

She slid a pencil from behind her ear, made a check mark on a list and started another e-mail. "If the door was unlocked, it wasn't my fault. I wasn't there last night." Juliet's standard knee-jerk defense of my anticipated "did you lock the door when you left my office" question lacked its usual enthusiasm.

"I haven't stopped by my office yet, but thanks for letting me know if I should call the cops or not," I snapped, instantly irritated she'd assumed I was tracking her down to be critical instead of realizing I was concerned with how everyone at the barn was coping with the tragedy. I knew better than to think she'd be concerned with how I was faring.

"How are you?" Delores asked. "Did you get any sleep last night?"

The anger at my sister slipped away and I managed a small smile. "Some. And Paul made me go running with him this morning, so I guess I'm okay. How about you?"

"Fine. Got a lot of cleaning done last night and barn work this morning. Better than having some man whipping my sorry old ass down the Centennial Trail at the crack of dawn."

"I think he takes that flight response to stress literally. How's Alice doing?" Uncle Henry mentioned Delores had been with Alice, Don's wife, at the hospital.

"She's holding up fairly well, under the circumstances. I stayed with her until her kids arrived."

"Did they say how Don died?"

"God, you're morbid," Juliet snapped.

I shot my sister a snarl, then ignored her. After all, she'd been in a bitchy mood since January when her fiancé high-tailed it for parts unknown. Don was a more immediate concern for me. I had to know if I'd screwed up, done my part so poorly that I'd contributed to his death.

Delores' sharp brown eyes skipped from my sister to me. She knew what I was asking. "Heart attack, I think.

Personally, I blame that damn Max. All that arguing and the threats probably pushed his blood pressure over the top." Her eyes narrowed. "Neither one of you heard me say that, by the way."

"I don't hear a lot of the things you say, Delores," Juliet said, hitting send on another e-mail.

"I heard them arguing," I said. "I'd have thought if anyone was going to have a heart attack it would have been Max."

"He wouldn't dare," Juliet said, not taking her eyes from the screen. "He's going to win big and become rich and famous competing on Rummy. Just ask Agnes."

Delores raised an eyebrow at my sister. "That's putting it succinctly."

"Well, it's true," Juliet said, finally turning from her computer to face us. "Max told me all about his plans in January when he got back from Europe with Mrs. Moneybags. He was all excited, went on and on about this great horse he'd bought at some big, la-de-da sale over in Germany."

I snorted. A horse *he'd* bought? In his dreams -- which were apparently delusional as well as grandiose.

Juliet took a swig of her diet pop before she continued. "Then the weasel stuck me with the check for dinner. 'I'll make it up to you after my first grand prix win.'" She imitated Max's accent. It sounded fake -- Max's. My sister's was a good imitation. No one could figure out his accent. The general, snarky opinion was he'd picked it up from watching Masterpiece Theater.

It wasn't her parody that got my attention, however. "You *date* him?"

"Are you kidding? That asshole? Only once. I'm no fool. Not anymore. I had to have a rebound date after he-who-will-not-be-named dumped me. To be accurate, I was creating 'distance.' I refused to go out with Max the second time he asked." She opened the Copper Creek Lesson program "he-who-would-not-be-named" created for her and clicked on a schedule date. I wondered how long it would be before she'd put enough distance between herself and the man she'd been crazy in love with. I had to commend my sister for trying to recover, even if it meant dating Max -- and who knew how many other idiots.

Eric had been the barn manager at Copper Creek and my flighty sister's fiancé. He'd always struck me as sensible and stable, someone Juliet could depend on, and Juliet adored him. But Eric had run. Packed up and left in the middle of the night, six weeks before their wedding.

I wasn't privy to the reasons he had decamped so quickly, although I couldn't entirely blame Eric. The closer their wedding got, the bitchier my sister's disposition became. Responsibility in relationship disintegration is never one-sided. I was sure Eric bore some of the blame. I just didn't know what it was. If Juliet did, she wasn't talking. Best, and safest, to keep the conversation on Max and his many faults.

"It's not easy to make a living as a trainer," I said, parroting my Uncle's oft-mentioned declaration. "Success in the show ring is almost essential if they're going to keep getting clients." Uncle Henry didn't have to worry about that issue. He'd ridden for Great Britain in two Olympic Games, winning a Bronze in dressage, and placed well in several World Championships.

"Duh," Juliet said, and went back to her schedule revisions. "He's still an asshole."

"Frankly, I'm about ready to kick him out," Delores said.

I nodded. Frankly, I wished she would. She played a balancing act with the four trainers who operated out of Copper Creek, including my uncle. With the exception of my uncle, they could be demanding and moody, and took any change in barn procedure as an infringement on their potential income. Even a good percentage of the owners played the diva from time to time. But it was Delores' world. She'd grown up in it and lived in it for her sixty-some years and knew when to be difficult to find and unavailable to complaining clients. Juliet, surprisingly, did an admirable job of soothing ruffled feathers and putting smiles on people's faces. I guess she refused to work her magic with Max.

"I can't remember you ever kicking anyone out before," I said.

"Oh, it's happened. Most recently eight years ago. Booted that whiny Cynthia out to the curb."

"Oh, so that's what happened to her."

"Max complains worse than she did. There's always something wrong: the jumps are moved, the feed is wrong, blankets are damaged. He comes storming in here at least once a week accusing me of all manner of crimes and misdemeanors. Ever since Agnes brought that new horse of hers here in January you'd think he's the prince of grand prix jumping and needs to be treated like royalty. I'm sick of it and the accusations."

I hadn't realized Max had been going head to head with Delores on a regular basis. "He sounds kind of desperate," I said.

"He sure is. He's down to eight clients. If it wasn't for Agnes' three horses in training he'd be working at McDonalds to supplement his hobby income."

I squirmed, surprised by the vehemence in her tone. Generally a straight-talking woman, Delores never minced words, but rarely got this catty and never this worked up.

And, not to say I approved, but because I now knew he was losing clients I had a little better understanding of why he'd been pushing Rum Runner.

I cleared my throat. "Where's Miguel this morning?"

"Back at work. He's probably finishing up the watering in the New Barn, if you want to talk to him."

I nodded, started toward the door and stopped. "By the way, Juliet, how's Michelle? Didn't you take her home yesterday?"

"And I stayed with her last night," my sister said. "I know she's upset, but she's acting really weird. She finished off an entire six-pack by herself, and she hardly ever finishes even one beer an evening. I guess you never know how you're going to react in that kind of situation. I'm going to run over to her place at lunch and check on her again. With any luck she'll have such a raging hangover she'll still be in bed."

What did Paul call that? Self-administered anesthesia? Guess I could understand.

"Thea," Delores called as I opened the office door. "Don's funeral is Friday at ten, at the Presbyterian Church. His secretary asked if I could round up some help calling people to let them know."

Guilt twanged my conscience. I hadn't even thought about Willa Weaver, the secretary in Don's practice. Yet another person adversely affected by Don's death. "Sure. I'll be happy to give a hand."

"Run by this afternoon and get a list from her. I'll call and tell her to expect you."

I left to look for Miguel, and as Delores predicted, he was in the New Barn filling up the last of the newly cleaned water buckets. His bandito moustache budged only a little from its customary downward turn. His eyes remained solemn.

"How are you?" he asked.

"Okay." I nodded in a trembling kind of way and exhaled the breath I'd been holding. "You?"

"Fine." He turned off the spigot on the hose, shook the droplets off the end. "We tried. It does not always help, but we tried. You did a good job."

"I --" The sudden lump in my throat kept me from saying more. I swallowed it down. "Thanks." Impulsively, I hugged him and he returned the gesture with one arm, patting my back. "I'm glad I know you, Miguel."

One side of the moustache lifted and the lines around his eyes deepened. "You go ride your Blackie now. He is in his paddock."

Blackie met me at his paddock gate. I slipped his halter over his ears and he marched alongside me into the Big Barn as he always did. Inside, nothing looked different. That, in itself, was unsettling, almost like what happened less than twenty-four hours earlier had been a bad dream, the kind that leaves you feeling vaguely disoriented and jumpy.

It didn't take me long to dust off Blackie's coat and toss my saddle on him. Concentrating on any kind of dressage work was out of the question so I took him on a short trail ride, following the twenty-minute walking loop the lesson instructors used.

When I returned a few people had arrived at the barn, including Agnes. If her immaculately dressed presence meant Max was going to work Rum Runner, she'd have a bit of a wait. Max hadn't arrived at the barn yet. His vintage, cream-colored Mercedes sports coupe wasn't parked in its usual spot beside the barn.

However, Agnes' husband had accompanied her, so perhaps Max wouldn't show up until later -- if the hanky-panky rumors were true. I'd seen Bart around, but never been introduced, and all I knew about him was that he was politically "very important" -- whatever that meant.

I led Blackie to the grooming stall next to where Agnes had cross-tied her second horse, Moody Blue. He was similar to Blackie in size, dark bay color and the single blotch of a white star marking the middle of their foreheads. The resemblance ended there. Blackie possessed not only better physical proportion and significantly better muscling, but had an elegance and presence the other horse couldn't touch. And while Blackie powered himself forward with elastic, ground-covering strides, Moody displayed the stiff-legged, daisy-cutting gaits of an amateur-owner hunter. I suspected it was no challenge to follow his movement, which was precisely what Agnes needed.

I nodded a hello to both Agnes and her husband as Agnes led Moody into the aisle. All three of them ignored me, which relieved me of any necessity to smile or listen to any insincere, sympathetic remarks. Agnes was every bit as responsible for Don's heart attack as Max. There was little chance I'd be able to cough up any kind word to ease the guilt she should be feeling. I took a soft brush to Blackie's coat, leaning into each stroke as much to smooth the saddle marks as to channel my temper.

Two sets of footsteps approached from behind. No way could I dredge up any friendly chit-chat. Seeing Agnes had stoked my anger, and I ignored the sound. Blackie didn't, but then he's interested in everyone. I ignored his antsy push forward against the cross-ties, too.

"Delores said you'd be here."

Surprised, I turned at the sound of my friend Andrea Anderson Paalmann's voice. Detective Dave Ross stood next to her, a friendly look on his face, despite the absence of an actual smile. They'd been dating, so I knew she wasn't in trouble -- again.

"Hey, you guys! I didn't know you'd be stopping by." I tossed Blackie's brush back into my bucket and joined them in the aisle.

"We thought we'd surprise you. Paul told us what happened yesterday. I'm so sorry." Her lips compressed into a worried frown and her hand reached for mine. "Are you okay?"

I nodded and squeezed her hand. "Yeah, I'm fine. It was tough, though."

She released me and stroked Blackie's face with both hands. "How about you, big guy?" His ears pricked so far forward the tips practically touched. "Aww, look at you, precious. Are you the most handsome boy? You are, yes you are. Look at those brown eyes and long lashes. Give me a little smoochie-pie." Blackie pushed his muzzle forward and Andrea kissed his nose. "Aww, you know your auntie loves you."

Dave and I exchanged a quick look. He shifted, straightening his shoulders, and I had a flash of Andrea talking to him like she talked to Blackie. I caught the laugh in my throat.

"If you even ask, I'll find something to arrest you for," he said.

"Don't have to now," I returned, and grinned.

Andrea cast a questioning look at Dave, and his eyes widened.

"Do you want to ask her or shall I?" she said.

Dave visibly relaxed. "You go ahead."

Andrea shivered a little and grabbed my hands. "We were thinking," she said to me, "that maybe you might want to get away for a couple of days."

I didn't want to mess up Paul's plans, but he and Dave were friends and this might be a nice opportunity. "Paul mentioned the same thing last night. We were thinking about going somewhere for the weekend."

"I know." Andrea's eager smile gave me the answer to what Paul had been talking to her about at my aunt and uncle's. She'd wanted the four of us to do something together. Obviously, Paul thought it was a good enough idea that he'd decided to wait until I wasn't too shocky to mention it. "So," she continued, "come with us. In fact, I really want you to. We have something special planned." She glanced at Dave again, whose friendly expression now stretched toward a smile.

"Well, sure," I said. "That'd be fine. What did you have in mind?"

She grinned. "Las Vegas."

"You're kidding. That's special? Isn't that like slumming for you?"

She shook her head and laughed. "We're getting married!"

"We? You and who?"

She slugged my shoulder. "Dave! Who else have I been spending all my time with lately?"

"Oh! Oh! Holy cow! Sure, yes, of course we'll come!"

She bounced a couple of times and threw her arm around me. Blackie snorted in an alarmed manner and we moderated our rollicking. I released Andrea and turned to Dave. "I guess this means I get to hug you, too."

He mirrored Andrea's grin. "Just don't tell Paul." He wrapped me in a tight hug, lifted me off my feet and kissed my cheek. Blackie snorted again and he put me down.

I laughed. "You work fast, Dave."

"Not really, just smart. I was assigned an art theft case that promised to bore me into a coma, so I decided to take some vacation and let someone else investigate. Then Andrea proposed --"

She feigned shock and shoved his shoulder. "You are a tease and a liar."

He corralled her with one arm, kissed her forehead and winked at me. "I had to accept. My time off wouldn't have been approved if I hadn't mentioned I might be getting married."

"He threw himself at my feet, Thea. Threatened to camp out on my front porch until I said 'yes.' When it started to rain really hard and then hail I felt sorry for him and caved."

"Now who's the liar," he said, smiling into her eyes.

She raised her chin. "I could have held out if it only drizzled."

"I'd have worn you down one way or another."

My friend sighed dramatically. "I expect. A good attorney can sense the lay of the land and plan accordingly."

"A good cop always get his man, or in my case, his woman."

Blackie tossed his head and whinnied. Neither Dave nor Andrea looked at him. They were busy gazing sappily into each other's eyes.

I patted my horse's neck. "This is almost embarrassing, Blackie. I think they need to get married as soon as possible if only to save the rest of us from having to put up with such blatant displays of mush."

Andrea grinned, but never broke eye contact with Dave. "Then you'll come with us this weekend?"

"Oh, I suppose." I tried hard to sound resigned, but a laugh popped out.

"How pleasant to see smiling faces after yesterday's tragedy," Bart Fulton said, joining our group.

All three of us jerked in his direction. We'd all lost our smiles. Dave's eyes narrowed to the expression he wore when fully immersed in his detective mode.

Bart inclined his head at me. "Miss Campbell, is it?"

I nodded. "You're Agnes' husband?" I knew he was, but couldn't think of what else to say since he hadn't jumped right into an introduction.

He bowed slightly. "That's right. Bartholomew Fulton. I understand you are to be commended for your efforts to resuscitate Dr. Archterkamp yesterday. Such an unfortunate event. My wife was devastated."

I doubted Agnes was all that upset. In fact, she'd looked just fine to me a few minutes ago. A sudden, acute wave of sadness washed over me and, along with it, guilt for so easily focusing on my friends' good news.

"It was awful," I said, struggling to keep my voice from cracking.

Bart turned to Andrea, his expression turning intensely charming. "You are Mrs. Paalmann, are you not?"

Andrea smiled coolly, almost like she was prepared for his intrusion. "Nice to meet you, Mr. Fulton."

Dave took a step closer to his fiancée, but his gaze stayed glued to Bart. I hoped he didn't act this possessive of her each time a man introduced himself. She'd grow tired of the unnecessary shielding almost as fast as I would.

Bart extended his hand as if to shake Andrea's, but when she accepted the gesture, he grasped her finger lightly and hovered over them in a half bow. Her jaw slackened ever so slightly. I wasn't sure if he meant to kiss the backs of her fingers or was about to drop to a knee and swear allegiance.

Dave frowned. He had a point.

Andrea slid her hand from Bart's light grasp and made a small gesture to Dave before taking his arm. "Mr. Fulton, this is my fiancé, David Ross."

"Nice to meet you, Mr. Ross." Bart inclined his head then returned his attention to Andrea. "I apologize for intruding you while you're visiting with your friends, but I saw you arrive and, in my zeal, seized an opportunity."

Andrea looked like she might laugh. Dave did not. Bart reached into his jacket pocket, extracted a business card and proffered it to my friend. She glanced at it then tried to return it. Bart waved it off.

"I have a modest social welfare organization," he said, dipping his head in a self-deprecating manner. I half expected him to add "aw shucks," but he didn't. "We exist to lend assistance to children who deal with challenges the rest of us aren't burdened with, so they can learn how to best move forward in their lives, build self-esteem so they can be successful in business or whatever field they choose without feeling the daily struggle a handicap might impose upon them."

"How generous and thoughtful," Andrea said, her tone neutral.

Bart seemed to mistake her lack of enthusiasm for interest. "Thank you. I'm hoping I might have the opportunity to secure an appointment with you in the near future and show you some of the literature about our program. Perhaps give you a personal tour?"

Andrea smiled and pocketed his card. "I'll have my assistant get in touch."

"Thank you, and I beg your pardon for interrupting your private time."

"Not a problem." Andrea's smile was cool.

Bart bowed to all of us, and we watched in silence, as he walked quickly away, in his rigid and somewhat rolling gait, down the barn aisle and out the big double doors.

"What an odd little man," Andrea said.

"What an asshole," Dave said.

Andrea signed. "Get used to it, my love. I had to when I married Sig, and it got worse after he died. People will be hitting you up for donations all the time once they find out you have money."

He put an arm around her shoulders and hugged her close. "Do you mind if I tell them to take a hike?"

"No, but you'll probably get tired of wasting the energy." She wrapped her arms around his middle and grinned at me. He took the opportunity to nuzzle her sleek blonde hair. "Isn't he adorable?" she purred. Dave raised an eyebrow. "I love having him protect me."

"It beats the heck out of having him arrest you, again." I snorted at the snarl he shot me. "When are you planning on leaving for Las Vegas?"

Dave nestled Andrea closer, if that was possible. "We're going to go down Thursday," he said.

I bit my lip. "Wow, that's soon. Don's funeral is Friday. I don't really want to miss it."

"What time?" Dave asked.

"Morning. At ten, I think. Yes, ten."

"No problem," Dave said, and dropped a light kiss on Andrea's forehead. "We'll get you tickets for Friday evening."

"We're planning on Saturday afternoon for the ceremony and then flying out Saturday evening for Hawaii." Andrea cuddled her fiancé, turned her face up and was rewarded with a rather passionate lip-lock.

"Well, okay then," I said rather too loud, just in case they forgot I was standing right in front of them.

"Great," Andrea said, moistening her lips like she was gearing up for another go.

"Perfect," Dave said, and kissed the end of Andrea's nose before dipping to her mouth.

I chose to believe they were referring to my plans.

# Chapter Four

Don's funeral was a touching tribute to his life, without being maudlin. Of course, having spent every waking moment in the previous days immersed in other people's taxes allowed me to conquer the overwhelming emotions I'd experienced when he died. I made it through the entire service and reception talking to people I'd not seen in ages, about a man we all admired, without pulling out the Kleenex I'd stuffed into my purse and pockets.

Of course I wasn't totally unaffected. One of the sobering aspects about funerals is the realization that life simply continues on despite someone's absence. Another is the dawning awareness that, while time is marching along, maybe one ought to quit talking about things and do them.

I continued to turn this notion over in my mind even as we returned home and began packing for Vegas. I hung Paul's tuxedo with my green gown in the garment bag and smoothed the lapels, not thinking so much about the jacket as

I was about the man who wore it. Last time he'd put it on was New Year's. I smiled at the memory. He spiffed up better than Bond – better than any of them. Of course the excellent raw material helped. Even in a T-shirt, jeans and running shoes, he made my heart rate giddy-up just by breathing. I was incredibly lucky to have a family who loved us enough to have orchestrated our meeting.

I let my gaze linger on him as he packed his few items in the other carry-on we'd be taking with us. "We should set a date for our wedding," I said, then caught sight of the clothes he'd chosen and sighed.

His incandescent blue eyes met mine and a corner of his mouth curved upward. He stuffed the sweats into the bag. "So, when do you have in mind?"

"August maybe. Don't you have a break from the university then? It's March now, so that will give us plenty of time to put some plans together. By the way, we won't be doing any running."

"August will be fine. First part. And yes, we might have a chance to run. I packed your sweats, too, since you didn't."

"You're so thoughtful. We can look at a calendar on the flight to Vegas."

"What's made you give up your firm stance on procrastination?"

I laughed. "Despite your obsession with making me run with you, I love you, and after Don --" A wave of unexpected sadness hit me, stopping my voice in my throat. I tried to push it away, force a smile, but my lips trembled. Concern drew a line between Paul's brows and he took a step toward me. I held a hand up, stopping him, and took a breath. "After what happened with Don I just -- I just --" Damn. Tears filled my eyes and spilled one by one down my face. And my nose ran. I sniffed.

He shook his head, tossed the socks and underwear he'd taken from the dresser onto the bed and came to me, pulling me into a gentle hug. "It's okay. It'll ambush you from time to time." I nodded against his chest. After a moment he raised my chin and looked into my eyes. "Hey, I'm glad you want to set a date. That's a good thing for us, don't you think?" I nodded against the support of his fingers. "I'm getting a little tired of 'fiancée' -- makes some guys think they still might have a chance with you." He peered into my face and wiggled his eyebrows. I made a sincere attempt at a laugh.

"It'll always be you and only you," I said. The declaration of devotion I'd meant to sound steady and upbeat dissolved into a whimper. How long had Alice thought she'd have Don? How many missed opportunities to say "I love you" was she counting before she fell asleep now?

We finished packing and, dressed in traveling clothes of blue jeans, sneakers, a lightweight green sweater for me and a gray Henley for Paul, made it to SeaTac airport and parked without me having another emotional meltdown. In fact, we'd even snapped at each other debating which floor of the parking garage had the shortest walk to the terminal. That had to be good. At least it was more normal. Once we made it through security and found our gate, the excitement about our mini vacation took over. I clung to Paul's hand as best I could while toting my purse and the garment bag. He squeezed my hand frequently. No doubt he was feeling the thrill of getting away together, too.

At last, the flight boarded and we settled into our seats, our carry-ons stowed. I pulled a notepad from my purse.

"All right." I flipped pages until I found a blank one. "Where shall we start? Location?"

"Sure, whatever you want," Paul said, shifting his legs around, trying to find a place where he could stretch them out. After a moment he gave up. I shouldn't have insisted on economy when Andrea offered first class, but last minute was expensive enough.

"Let's list a bunch of different places and narrow it down later."

"Okay."

"Should we have the ceremony one place and the reception another?" With pen poised over paper, I looked up, waiting for an opinion.

"Whatever you want."

"Let's consider both."

"Okay."

"Since we're just brainstorming right now, let's not limit ourselves."

"Fine."

I bent my attention to the page, and wrote, "the farm."

"You know Aunt Vi is going to offer her home and, since we're planning on an August wedding, outdoors is an option.

"Sounds good to me."

"There's the event hall on Avenue D and one just outside of town on Westwick Road, too."

"Okay."

"Minister or justice-of-the-peace?"

"I'll be happy with whoever."

Could there be a pass-the-buck pattern developing? I gnawed lightly on my lip, studying him for a moment. He studied me back. He looked interested. At least he wasn't making any overt move toward the airline's in-flight magazine. "We can always do a traditional church wedding."

"If that's what you want."

Now I knew he'd rolled over and totally abandoned any thought of participating in the planning. He didn't go to church. At all. Yes, he was raised Catholic, but it hadn't stuck -- even a little. At least our family gave some lip service to religion at Christmas and Easter.

"You can have an opinion on this, Paul. It's actually encouraged in some cultures. Like ours."

He grimaced. "I just --"

"Make a suggestion."

"All right then. The library."

I opened my mouth to request he quit fooling around, but he stopped me with a raised eyebrow.

"The Suzzallo Library at the University. It's beautiful. Collegiate gothic. And people have been known to have weddings there in the rotunda."

I shut my mouth and wrote "library."

After the plane backed away from the gate, taxied to the runway and finally climbed to cruising altitude, we continued listing locations that ranged all the way to our not-so-grand living room. It became apparent that to decide on a location would require we know how many people would come. I turned to another blank page and started a guest list, which Paul contributed to with an avalanche of names. I didn't complain. At least he was making an effort. When we ran out of names, I flipped the pages, reviewing the list. The absence of several names jumped out at me right away, since they were almost all of Paul's immediate family members. I began to correct the omission.

"Uh. No."

I stopped. "Paul, we have to invite them. They're your family."

He scratched his head. "It's only going to be unpleasant."

"Well, I know, but I really don't think your mother will call me a whore and a heathen again for coming between you and your ex. Particularly when there are a bunch of people around – and especially my family. I'm sure she's gotten used to the idea of us being engaged by now."

"Don't count on it. And you know my brother will prod her into a mood, and my father will tune them out or annoy everyone with his superior attitude."

"Paul, we can't not invite them."

"They'll probably bring Jan along and convince her she can win me back."

"She can't be that dumb. Or that much of a masochist. Who would attend their ex's wedding?"

He didn't answer, just kept looking at me.

"Well, crap." I sighed, crossed their names out, added Jan's and crossed it out, too – just so I wouldn't forget. "Cake. What about cake? And food. Buffet or sit-down?"

He rubbed both hands over his face and sighed. "Is all this really necessary?"

"Paul, it's what people expect."

He raked his fingers through his hair. "It's so involved. And at this rate we aren't going to have any money left to go on a honeymoon."

"We will if we budget."

"When your mother gets involved any budget we come up with will get blown to bits. She'll be pounding on our front door the day after you tell them we have a date, dismiss every word I say and you'll end up with a battle on your hands trying to keep her from hijacking our wedding like she did last summer when Eric and Juliet were planning theirs."

He had a point. Mother had just returned home to San Francisco after spending six weeks taking care of Aunt Vi, whose mending broken wrist and collarbone limited her activities. Paul and Mother kept a polite distance by avoiding each other, but it was a toss-up as to which of the rest of us would be tying Mother to the railroad tracks first. The lineup was rather long and included the most tolerant of people, Uncle Henry.

"If we don't make plans, we'll lose control. You know that," I said.

Paul grumbled before retreating into acquiescence. I ignored his attitude and nipped away at our wedding to-do list until the flight attendant came on the PA system and instructed us all to return our seats and tray tables to their upright and locked positions. I stuffed the notebook back into my purse and pushed it under the seat in front of me.

The reality of what we were facing stripped the romance right out of our wedding plans. "Let's talk about a budget," I said, as the plane taxied to the terminal. "Before we narrow down the list, let's hammer out the budget."

"Pardon me for eavesdropping," said the woman who'd quietly occupied the window seat next to me for the previous two plus hours. "But what you need is to get married in Las Vegas. It's simple, fast and cheap. I should know. I've done it four times, and was pleased as punch each time. Even having Elvis marry me and Fred, God rest his soul -- Fred, not Elvis because of course he's not the real one -- didn't cost but a few dollars more. They operate by volume so they can afford to keep the price down."

Neither Paul nor I said a word. I slid a look at Paul and found him watching me. The corner of his mouth twitched. Not funny. I refused to allow Elvis (or a replica) to bind Paul and me together for life.

Then the reality of where we were and why we were here hit me. Surely Andrea would have better taste than to hire a celebrity impersonator for her ceremony. I made an attempt to cover my apprehension with a polite "thank you," retrieved my purse and nudged Paul. All we needed was advice from a stranger. I wanted off the plane.

McCarran International Airport was a maze of concourses, moving walkways, elevators, gift shops and people. Hordes of people. And not only did all of them seem to know where they were going, but they were in a hurry to get there, too.

Wall-sized promotions for hotels, casinos and shows were everywhere. The Blue Man Group was hard to miss. I couldn't help but wonder how those men managed to cover themselves so thoroughly with blue. Not a single square millimeter escaped. They must have submerged in vats of whatever the stuff was. No way could that be good for one's skin.

We passed restaurants of all types. Some enticed passersby with elegant settings and dim lighting. Others promised fast, familiar fare, from coffee to cookies to burgers. All of them reminded me I was hungry, but the banks upon banks of slot machines everywhere I looked chased me along. They clanged, rang and were thoroughly exercised by people dead set on losing money. This town worked hard to part each and every visitor from their cash – whether they were coming or going. The sensory extravaganza made SeaTac, the airport we'd left just two hours earlier, look sadly provincial.

Andrea and Dave met us on the general public side of security. How they managed to determine where to intercept us was beyond me. Probably had something to do with all of Dave's years as a detective. The milling crowds didn't seem to faze either one of them. They both waved when they spotted us. Andrea glowed with happiness and Dave's grin made him downright handsome -- not that he wasn't attractive in the first place. However, I had a habit of comparing all men to Paul, even my sister's ex-fiancé Eric who, although movie-star handsome, had become less so in my eyes when he dumped her.

"How was your flight?" Andrea asked after hugging me and then Paul.

"Good." I said. "How are the wedding plans coming?"

"Perfect," Andrea said. "There's almost nothing for us to do but relax and enjoy ourselves."

Paul shot me a meaningful glance. I pretended not to notice. "So," Paul said, abandoning me and clapping Dave on the back as we headed off to who knew where. "Does that mean you've manage to secure Elvis for the ceremony?"

Dave laughed and wrapped an arm around his soon-to-be wife. "I suggested it, but someone else vetoed it."

Andrea play-slapped his chest and he grunted. "That's not true. Elvis wasn't part of the package we bought -- something, I might add, you made darned sure of."

"Package?" I asked.

"Yeah. The hotel has a bunch of wedding packages to choose from," Andrea said. "It's all very professional, tasteful. Incredibly easy."

"Easy?" Paul asked, wistfully.

I ignored him; there was no way we'd be able to pull off easy. Why even entertain the notion?

Dave nodded. "They do all the work, you schedule the date and time and show up with the license. Pretty slick.

You'd think they'd done all this before."

A limo waited for us outside the airport and took us to the hotel. I'm fairly certain the driver took the long way, just so we could see The Strip in all its neon glory. In honesty, I gawked. The place glowed, sparkled and was spotlighted enough to rival daylight. There were icons from every corner of the world lining our route: the Sphinx, the Great Pyramid, the Eiffel Tower, New York, Venice, castles, architecture of every sort. Each hotel and casino outdid the previous. The electric bill for a single hotel's exterior display had to cost more on a monthly basis than what I was likely to earn in a lifetime at my accounting business.

I expected to see crowds of beautiful people strolling the sidewalks in evening clothes, resplendent in sequins and dripping diamonds. Instead, the crowds were tourists, in shorts and blue jeans and polyester. The contrast between assumption and reality jarred.

The Bellagio, a towering Italian Renaissance structure where Andrea had booked rooms, dazzled the eye. Once you got past the massive "dancing" fountains in the lake in front of the hotel, the lobby itself gave one pause. It was a good thing I was being led along. Everywhere I looked there was something to distract -- from the Chihuly art glass suspended from the eighteen-foot ceiling, to gardens, pools, and an art gallery currently exhibiting the works of Monet.

Our suite, which I was quite certain topped the square footage of our home even after the recently completed remodel, was done in soothing earth tones and white, and looked out over the Strip -- from the king-sized bed. There were even separate his and her bathrooms and, Andrea warned, twice-a-day maid service.

We changed from our traveling clothes into something more appropriate to wear to dinner in one of the resort's restaurants, which is to say we swapped the blue jeans for slacks and sneakers for less casual footwear. Because I gave him a frowning once-over, Paul exchanged the Henley for a dress shirt. I didn't suggest a tie, and hoped the restaurant wouldn't either.

Dinner (no tie required) was excellent, particularly the company, and we finished in time to make use of the tickets Andrea and Dave got for us all to see the Cirque du Soleil. This particular one (there are several, apparently) was not only acrobatic and artistic with fabulous costumes, but was done on water. Dave said there were divers stationed in the pool during the show to assist the performers. Considering the risks they took, I certainly hoped so.

I half expected the women in the acts to be topless -- such is the reputation of Las Vegas. However, they weren't. I wouldn't put it past Andrea to have double-checked the attire before getting the tickets. She could be a bit of a prude at times.

It was after midnight when Paul and I got back to our suite. The lights from The Strip made turning on any room lights unnecessary. I kicked off my shoes and went to the large window, marveling at the view of the Eiffel Tower as well as the Statue of Liberty farther down the street. Paul joined me similarly unshod and shirt unbuttoned. He wrapped me in his arms and kissed the top of my head.

"I'm glad we came," I said. "I'm so happy for Andrea and Dave. I really think they're making the right choice."

"Umm humm," he said, kissing the side of my head this time. "If they got married in Seattle, the media hype would be more than Dave could stand."

"Andrea would hate it, too. At least they'll have some privacy for a while before they get back to headlines that will read 'Heiress to Paal Toys Fortune Marries Cop Who Arrested Her for Husband's Murder.' I'm glad neither one of us is wealthy."

Paul chuckled. "The worst they can say about us is, 'Why is he marrying a woman who has a horse?' or 'Hasn't he noticed how his medical expenses have escalated since he's known her?'"

I jabbed him lightly with my elbow. "Comedian." But his comment about Blackie nudged forward the memory of how my horse had tried to prevent Don from leaving his stall. Sadness, but not consuming sorrow, over Don's sudden death wound through my mind along with the useless speculation over whether Blackie's warning, if heeded, could have prevented the tragedy.

No. Surely not.

Paul turned me to face him and delivered a soft kiss to my lips. I sighed and pushed his shirt aside to snuggle against his bare chest. "How are you feeling?" he asked, too carefully.

"In love," I said, sincerely. "And better. You're right about needing distance. I'll tell you, though, I meant it when I said I didn't want to put things off. I'm done procrastinating. We need to make a budget, plan our wedding and make sure we negotiate some kind of peace with your family."

"I'll do my best, but let's not hold things up waiting for their blessing. They're a stubborn bunch when they don't get their way."

I stood on my toes to kiss him and worked his belt loose.

"Hey," he said, a little breathy from my insistent pursuit of his lips. "You trying to get me naked?"

"Subtlety doesn't escape your keen eye, does it?"

"Neither does fumbling."

He scooped me up, dropped me on the bed and finished the job I'd started. With the drapes still wide open, the colored light coming through the window added a touch of naughtiness to the efficient revealing of his toned body. If I'd had a hundred dollar bill and he'd been wearing a g-string, I'd have tipped him. His was the best show I'd seen all evening. Of course, anticipated participation from this audience of one may have influenced my opinion.

"I can't believe you're getting married this afternoon and

picking up your dress this morning," I said to Andrea, as the limo's door closed softly beside me.

"I picked it out yesterday before you guys got here. They only had to do minor adjustments. Believe me, they've got this wedding thing down to a science. I think it's a bigger industry here than gambling."

"Must be." I looked out the window as we pulled away from the front of the hotel. The sparkling fantasy that was The Strip had faded with daylight. To my eye it looked massively overbuilt, and more than a little garish. it wouldn't have hurt to sweep up some of the litter, either. And yet, here Andrea and I were, on our way to Neiman Marcus, the most expensive department store on the planet. Haute couture side by side with the tasteless and gaudy. I grimaced. "You're not -- are you ...?"

"Am I what?"

"You know."

"Pregnant? No. The doctor advised I wait a while because of the miscarriage."

"No, no, that's not what I meant. Who's officiating at your wedding?"

She cracked a devilish smile. "Elvis? You still think we're going to have an Elvis impersonator?"

"Um, are you?"

"You're really worried about this, aren't you?"

"Say," the driver called over his shoulder. "You need an Elvis, my brother-in-law does a good one. He'll even sing *Blue Suede Shoes*."

"Thank you," Andrea said. "But we've already got things lined up."

"Okay. You take my card when you get out and give me a call if you change your mind. Or maybe your friend might be in need. Larry's an ordained minister, too, so it'd be all official."

The staff at Neiman Marcus treated Andrea like royalty. Her dress, a strapless white silk, fitted to the waist, flared to a pleated, A-line skirt that floated down to brush the floor. Over it, a light netting strewn with sequins and styled the same as the white silk, but with a high neck and three quarter sleeves, gave the impression both she and the dress had been sprinkled with fairy dust. Andrea would take Dave's breath away -- she certainly did mine.

With the gown boxed up, and set for delivery along with veil, shoes and some very expensive underwear, we returned to the hotel and her room. She'd had my dress brought up to her suite so we could get ready together and had requested a stylist, provided by the hotel, to help with her hair and makeup. The woman arrived promptly, did an artist's job on Andrea, then had a little fun with my makeup and hair as well.

After the stylist left, we lazed around Andrea's gigantic bedroom in comfy chairs, wrapped in cozy robes and sipping mineral water while waiting for our nails to dry. A silly romantic comedy we'd seen together several times played on the big flat-screen TV. We poked fun at the characters and the plot, providing alternate dialog and suggesting more disastrous plot lines. I hadn't had so much girl-fun since we'd had sleep-overs in junior high school. Laughing, I turned to her, about to mention a remembered escapade, when a tear traced a path down her cheek. She whimpered and ducked her head.

"Andrea." I touched her arm. "Andrea, what's wrong?"

She faced me, chin trembling. "What if I'm making a mistake?"

I checked a sigh. *Now it occurs to her.* "You don't have to get married."

"But I love him."

This time I quashed an eye roll. "Just because you love him doesn't mean you have to marry him."

"But I want to get married. You know that."

"Yes, I know. And you want children. And you want the kind of family your mother didn't think was particularly necessary after your dad died. I know. None of that means you have to get married right now. And if you're worried about the arrangements being cancelled, I'm sure the hotel has had to handle the situation once or twice before." I gave her an encouraging smile and a "there, there" pat on her fluffy-bathrobed shoulder.

"But what's Dave going to think if I bail now? He'll never speak to me again."

Good God. When did my sensible attorney best-friend who'd toughed out an arrest for murder at the same time as a miscarriage turn into such a wuss? "If it makes you feel any better, he's probably feeling a bit shaky right now, too."

"Will you call him and find out what he thinks?"

Was she joking? "Andrea, no. You should talk to him."

"Talk to Paul then. Please? Oh, please? I can't ask him if the fact that I have so much money emasculates him."

*And I could?* "I thought you guys talked this through."

"We did. But …. Please, call Paul. Please?"

I got up from the bed and went to the suite's living room, finally finding my purse under the sofa, where I'd kicked it earlier while pulling off my sneakers, and dug out my phone. I walked to the far side of the living room, glancing at Andrea's bedroom door to make sure she wasn't hovering. With a push of a button, I speed-dialed Paul and waited. It was half a ring from voice mail when he answered.

"What."

I stared in surprise at the gruff, impatient tone. He knew it was me calling.

"Thea, are you there?"

"Yes, I'm here. What's going on? Are you okay?"

"Of course I'm okay. Why shouldn't I be?"

"No reason, unless Dave is chewing on the ropes you've tied him down with."

He grumbled a short laugh. "Now what makes you ask that?"

I started to fist my hair, then remembered how much time

the stylist had taken on it and pinned my hand under my arm. "Seriously, Paul. Is this looking like a terrible idea? Andrea wants to know if Dave is having second thoughts."

"Second thoughts? He's been triple and quadruple guessing himself and Andrea since I met him for breakfast, and probably before that. I want to punch him in the face, but he'd punch me back harder."

Splendid. He'd resorted to planning a brawl. "I'm for stopping this whole thing -- via peaceful means. Andrea's a mess. She's not making any sense when I try to talk to her."

"Ha. There's your mistake. Don't try to talk to her. Do what I've been doing with Dave. Pretend she's mentally incompetent and they deserve each other."

"Dammit, Paul, this isn't fun--"

"Thea, I could use your help with my dress."

I pivoted on my heel, and gaped at Andrea. She seemed perfectly composed, except for the fact she was struggling to keep her dress from falling off with one hand and waving my deep green gown around by the hanger with the other.

"Damn right this isn't fun," Paul growled in my ear.

"Give my love to Paul and come do my zipper. You need to get dressed, too, or we'll be late. Are the boys ready?"

"Oh, yeah," I said with the phone close to my mouth. "The *boys* are ready and waiting impatiently. Let's get this show on the road."

"Crap," Paul said.

The wedding coordinator arrived as I, literally, gave Andrea a hand, keeping her gown out of the way so she could put her shoes on. The middle-aged, business-suited woman gave us some simple instructions, along with bouquets of roses, and ran interference for us as we negotiated the hallways and elevators downstairs to a softly lit foyer in front of the wedding chapel.

My stomach buzzed with so many hyperactive butterflies I felt the vibration all the way to my toes. I squeezed Andrea's ice-cold hand and we gave each other air kisses before allowing the woman to position me for my entrance into the chapel. "Wait for the music," she said.

Noiselessly, the double doors swung open to an intimate room in pale blues and white, decked in flowers along each pew and glowing with candlelight. Dave waited to the right of a white-robed minister and Paul stood beside him, both men in tuxes and both with smiles. A tsunami of relief washed over me. They'd made it and they looked calm. What a freaking miracle.

A chamber music group, unobtrusively positioned in an alcove off to the side, took their cue and began the wedding march. My knees wobbled and, much to my surprise, my chin quivered.

"You can go in now," the wedding coordinator prompted me in a stage whisper.

I squared my shoulders, summoned my dignity and began a stately walk down the twenty-foot aisle, my footsteps silent on the Dresden blue carpet. Paul held my gaze the whole way.

When I got to my position at the front of the chapel I turned and waited. After a moment that stretched to a worrying degree, Andrea glided to the doorway and stopped. She looked like a misty painting of an angel, glistening in ethereal lighting. Her large blue eyes focused on Dave and her smile trembled.

Dave appeared to have forgotten to breathe.

And ... Andrea appeared rooted in place.

Was this supposed to happen? How long was she supposed to stand there? Should I be waving her forward? Were there instructions I'd missed?

Or had she really been looking to me earlier to give her an excuse to not go through with their wedding? I shot a concerned glance at Dave. Alarm was widening his eyes. Then, jaw set with determination, he was in motion and striding down the aisle.

Paul's startled expression told me this was unplanned. The minister's mouth opened and closed a couple of time. Safe bet this didn't happen often. With a worried look at my friend I shifted, ready to dash to her side at the drop of a tear.

Dave halted in front of Andrea. Her expression didn't change as he spoke to her in a tone too low for me to make out words. She responded -- or at least her lips moved. Counter to my expectations and with a gentleness that seemed reverent he then cupped her face in his hands and kissed her lips. A tear slid down her cheek sending a shot of panic straight to my heart.

Oh crap. My dear friend who, I knew, loved this man with a fierceness she thought she'd never have the good fortune to experience, was going to get dumped at the altar. I was going to kill him.

But, instead of making a hasty exit, Dave turned, jogged back to his place and held his hand out to Andrea. I wobbled with the reversal of my assumption. Radiant, she stood a bit taller and walked with her usual, unhurried grace down the aisle, foregoing the hesitation step the wedding coordinator had suggested. When she reached the base of the dais, she passed me her bouquet, took Dave's hand and didn't let go even after he'd assisted her up the two low steps.

The rest of the ceremony proceeded as planned, at least I believed so. I hardly paid attention. The emotion singing in the air between bride and groom held me captive. I had no recollection of passing Dave's ring to Andrea, but I must have because the minister blessed them. Dave slid Andrea's ring onto her finger and, with a husky voice, repeated the minister's words of commitment. Andrea's voice was near a whisper. Although I didn't see, I'm sure her face was damp with emotion.

Then the ceremony was over. Dave kissed his wife and together they fairly flew down the aisle. Paul's touch on my arm reminded me we should be following. As I took his arm he handed me a Kleenex.

"You came prepared," I said, sniffing.

"But not nearly well enough, from the way those two are

carrying on."

I laughed. "What did he say to her? I thought he was going to ditch the whole thing."

"I could see you were getting ready to leap on him and beat him senseless. I have no idea. Maybe she'll tell you later."

She did. After we'd had a lovely dinner in a private dining room, gone dancing in the ballroom and had several glasses of champagne that none of us bought ourselves because other happy people helped us celebrate, Andrea and I made a trip to the ladies room.

"I have to tell you," I said tossing the paper towel into the trash basket. "I was really afraid Dave was backing out of your wedding when he hopped off the dais and ran down the aisle before the ceremony started."

Andrea half smiled and pressed a hand to the base of her throat. "He thought I'd changed my mind."

"He did?"

She nodded. "I can see why. I got so nervous and didn't know when to start in, and then when I did and saw how shocked Dave looked, I thought he was having raging second thoughts and I couldn't move."

Oh, if she only knew. But then maybe one day they'd confess to each other. "Second thoughts? I thought he was so overwhelmed with how beautiful you looked and how lucky he was that he'd stopped breathing. *Then* I thought he was having second thoughts. What did he say to you?"

"He proposed all over again, he said …." She swallowed. Her fingers trembled, tracing the high neckline of the netting of her dress, and she laughed a little. "He said the best mistake he ever made was arresting me last November and, although I may believe he saved my life, the truth was I really saved his because without me, his life had no meaning." Her chin her quivered. "He said, 'I swear to you I will work every day to make you happy. Please don't leave. Please marry me.'"

Her eyes brimmed with tears.

Mine just spilled.

# Chapter Five

We didn't go with Dave and Andrea to the airport to see them off on their evening flight to Hawaii. It just wasn't fun anymore with all the security in place, so we hugged goodbye in the hotel lobby. Our reservations included another night in Vegas. With no reason to remain dressed to the nines, we decided to change clothes and take in what the town had to offer.

Andrea's and my earlier conversations, in the ladies room and before the wedding in her suite, played back to me as we returned to our suite. As we exited the elevator Paul settled his hand on the back of my neck and steered me closer to his side, gently massaging away the tension left over from the day.

"You're awfully quiet. What's up?"

"Just thinking," I said, leaning into the unrequested neck rub.

"About ...?"

"Andrea and Dave. I hope this is the right choice for them, getting married so quickly after, well …."

Paul kissed the top of my head. "You worry too much. They love each other, and they both know how tough things can be. The intention to make a life together is there, so I expect they'll do fine."

I hugged him and studied his calm features as he slid the key card into the slot on the door. "What about us?"

He cut me a quizzical look as he shoved the door open and nudged me inside. "What do you mean?"

I kicked off my shoes, losing three inches in height and several degrees of cool sophistication in the process. "Are we going to be okay? We've got a huge hurdle of a wedding in front of us. It'd be one thing if we only had to figure out all the details, scrape the money together and deal with my mother, but I don't want to start off having to overcome all that bad juju from your family, not to mention your ex. I have nightmares about her tagging along with your parents, robbing a skuzzy pawn shop for an assault rifle and trying to take me out right in the middle of 'do you take this man.'"

"Well, that would be memorable, although I wouldn't put money on her success. You're tougher than you look."

"I'm serious, Paul. Maybe we should just skip the wedding. Go for the never-ending engagement."

"Maybe we should get married while we're here and apologize later."

We stared at each other. Then the corner of his mouth twitched upward. A little thrill danced its way up my spine. I pressed my lips together to hold back a smile.

"That's a terrible idea," I said, then snorted a laugh.

Paul nodded, his lips contorting in an effort to hold in the laughter that danced in his eyes. "Awful," he said and started to laugh. "Especially if we hang the picture of us with Elvis on the living room wall."

"Oh, God! Can you imagine? My mother --" I dissolved into guffaws, wiping tears from the corners of my eyes.

"Let's do it," Paul said.

"No!" Then I laughed again.

"Why not?"

"No Elvis, I told you."

"Okay, no Elvis. Dave and Andrea's wedding was perfectly respectable. We can do this. Think of the headaches we'll avoid."

"True."

"Come on. We'll get married here, and when we get home we'll plan a reception. It'll be perfect. No nightmares of Jan with automatic weapons."

Within half an hour the ever-so-helpful concierge at the hotel had us in a limo and on our way to the Marriage License Bureau. Having completed the application for the license online at the hotel, all we had to do was retrieve it at an Express Window (a concept that seemed redundant since there was no waiting time and few other regulations in the state of Nevada) and get it notarized, if we wanted. I wasn't sure if it would be a legal necessity in Washington state, but better safe than sorry.

Even though it was ten o'clock on a Saturday night, limousines were parked three deep in front of the brick, multi-story Clark Street building. The driver let us off and told us not to worry, he'd find us when we came out. With the skirt of my green gown clutched in one hand, to avoid tripping, and Paul's hand securely in the other, we trotted up the steps, through the heavy glass doors, and hauled up short. The huge foyer was not empty, or even lightly populated. Not by any stretch. A long queue of couples in all manner of dress snaked around the lobby. There were a few white dresses and black tuxedos, but it was far from the norm. A costume party couldn't have been more diverse, although many appeared not to have bothered to change from touristy outfits or blue jeans and T-shirts. Hawaiian print shirts had an undisputed following among the men present. At least two couples were dressed in identical cowboy/cowgirl outfits. The couple with the white Stetsons also sported yards of swinging fringe -- his turquoise, hers pink. Silver conches weighed down the black-hatted couple. Near the head of the queue was a couple in grass skirts and orchid leis. I suspected they wore bathing suits under it all, but I wasn't going to look too hard. Behind them, black motorcycle leathers had a run of popularity. It wouldn't have surprised me if they were going to do a group wedding.

Paul poked my ribs with an elbow. "Hey, I should have worn my kilt."

He gestured to his right. Sure enough, next to a blonde in a kimono stood a gentleman sporting his plaid, and all the additional accoutrements down to voluminous quantities of lace exploding from the ends of his sleeves and around his neck.

"You don't own a kilt and you're not a Scot," I said. "Although I think we could set you up with a Campbell tartan. Oh!" I tugged on his arm.

"What?" He turned away from surveying the kaleidoscopic flock around us and his eyebrows tented. "Don't tell me you've changed your mind."

"What am I going to do about my name? I can't believe I haven't given this any thought whatsoever."

"Change it if you want."

I gnawed my lip.

"Or don't." He frowned. "Or hyphenate it. Whatever you want. It doesn't matter to me."

"You're sure?"

"Of course I'm sure."

I hugged his arm. "Okay then. I'll keep my name."

He frowned. "What's wrong with 'Hudson'?"

"Nothing. There's nothing wrong with 'Campbell' either. I've always been 'Campbell' and that's how everyone knows me. This bothers you."

"No, it doesn't."

"Yes, it does. I'll change it.

"No, don't."

"Okay. I'll keep 'Campbell.' Are you sure it doesn't bother you?"

He sucked a long breath in through his nostrils and exhaled an extremely patient, "Yes."

My eyes stung with tears. I was going to cry. Crap-a-doodle. "No, you're not, you're scowling. I'm going to change it."

"You don't have to for me. I'd love you if your name was …." He shrugged expressively and shook his head once. "I don't know … Priscilla Fenwinkle."

A round woman, likely in her fifties, edging past us ground to a halt. She regarded Paul with a confused expression. "It's 'Farnsworth' and I'm sorry, but I don't think I know you."

"Uh," Paul said, blinking rapidly, "I don't see why you should."

"You just said --"

"I was being hypothetical."

She narrowed her eyes. The large man who was evidently with her doubled back, his florid face deepening to a darker red, his right hand flexing into a fist. "Hey, buddy --"

Looked like everyone's emotions ran high in this place. I grabbed Paul's arm and dragged him in the direction of the Express Line. "Excuse us." I wiggled my fingers while smiling idiotically, which beat the living daylights out of the crying jag I'd inexplicably teetered toward. "We need to get this done before the baby's born. Nice to finally meet you, Priscilla."

The couple gaped at me as I hauled Paul into motion.

"'Nice to finally meet you'? You know I can't possibly know her."

"Of course you can't. Come on."

His momentum ceased abruptly, spinning me around to face him. He'd gone pasty pale. "And what baby?"

"Kidding. I was kidding."

Color snuck back into his complexion. "Not funny. And

for future reference, not how I want to find out."

"Oh, for heaven's sake. You needed to move before that guy decided to take a swing at you and it was the best I could do on short notice. Besides, think of the story they'll have to tell when they get home. Now please, come on. Let's get in the Express Lane. We have fewer than ten items, and I don't have to make a decision about my name until after the ceremony."

He still appeared vaguely bewildered, but at least he moved.

The Express Lane, as I called it, was shorter than the long queue we'd encountered on our way in and it moved along at a good clip -- for a line. The clerk at the window asked for our names, searched her computer program and within a minute handed us our marriage license, notarized (for an extra five dollars), in an envelope and in our hands. I stared at it as Paul moved us toward the exit, a little bubble of excitement building in my chest. I kept peeking inside to see if our names were still there, the date was correct and the official signature in place.

"You're laughing," Paul said, grinning down at me.

"I am." At the top of the steps leading to the sidewalk I flung my arms around his neck. He picked me off my feet, spun us in a wide circle and kissed me.

"Let's celebrate," I said when we came up for air.

"Great idea. Let's have a wedding."

"Let's see if we can get the same room Andrea and Dave had. That was so pretty."

"Yo! Hudson and Campbell!"

We looked toward the shout of our names. Our limo driver, a grin on his face, had just pulled up to the curb and was holding the door open. We jogged down the steps. Paul handed me into the backseat then slid in as I tucked the skirt of my gown out of the way.

"Where to, folks?" he asked, pulling away from the curb.

"Back to the hotel," Paul said. "We'll have the ceremony there."

The driver pulled back over to the curb. "No can do," he said, turning in his seat to face us more directly. "You got to have a reservation for Saturdays and Sundays."

"But …." My heart sank. "Paul …?"

"I thought people got married around here all the time without a reservation," Paul said, a growl in his voice.

"They do, sir. Just not at the hotels on the weekends. Lots of places to choose from. I can take you to any of them. You have any particular theme in mind? Any religious preference?"

Paul and I exchanged a consulting look. He shrugged.

"Something tasteful and pretty. No religious preference," I said.

"You got it." He straightened in his seat, flipped on his blinker and pulled away from the curb. "Anybody you want to bring along? Need to change clothes?"

"No, we're fine as we are. And it's just us," Paul said.

"Got your rings?"

This time the look Paul and I exchanged was shock mixed with panic.

"Hey, don't worry. The Little Snowbird Chapel has some nice rings right there. Makes it real convenient."

Paul expressed some enthusiasm. I was disappointed. I'd been looking forward to spending some leisurely time shopping for rings. However, I told myself, in the grand scheme of things it wasn't all that important. Really.

The Little Snowbird Chapel was a smallish, steepled, church-like building, unsurprisingly painted white and drenched in spotlights. However, unlike most of the commercial businesses I'd seen in Las Vegas so far, this one was not festooned with neon. My mood lifted.

Two other limos were parked out front. As we approached the front door swung wide and a couple dressed in business suits emerged, hand in hand, smiles on their faces. Not very dressy for a wedding, but not been-too-long-without-oxygen whacky, either.

A smiling, gray-suited, egg-shaped man greeted us when we walked in. Even his head was egg-shaped. Thick brown hair occupied only the back half of his skull, his shiny wide forehead dominating his face and continuing right up to the top of his head. I giggled.

"I see we have pre-wedding nerves," he said, clasping his hands as if about to applaud. The multitude of rings on each and every finger must have made any sort of dexterity a challenge for him. They reminded me what we were lacking.

"Rings," I blurted. "We need rings."

"And we have an excellent selection." He gestured toward a small table off to our right. It barely had enough room for the cash register. I didn't see any rings. "You'll want one of the nuptial packages that includes the symbol of your eternal love, then."

"Package?" Paul asked.

"Yes, they're listed in the brochures we have distributed to the hotels and the different license locations in the city. We can accommodate most religious preferences with any package. Number five includes rings, flowers for the bride," he tipped his head in a courtly gesture to me, "a boutonniere for the groom, a five by seven photograph and the ceremony performed by our special celebrity official --"

"We'll take it. Nondenominational," Paul said, reaching inside his jacket for his wallet. "How much?"

"We have other packages, as well with more options -- live music, a video of your vows along with an album of photographs, a honeymoon package at any of a number of lovely hotels on the Strip."

Paul's hand stayed inside his jacket, like he was reaching for a gun. "How much for number five?"

Egg-man lifted his chin. "Three hundred."

Paul's eyes narrowed. "Let's see the rings."

Muttering something that sounded like "Saturday nights are always the worst," the man fished a key from his pocket, unlocked a drawer below the cash register and emerged with two velvet trays of wedding rings lined up in neat rows. He balanced them on the tiny counter. "For Package Five you can take your pick from the bottom two rows."

I scrutinized the meager selection, picked a plain white gold band and slipped it on my finger. It fit well enough against my engagement ring, but the little pang of disappointment over the lost opportunity to shop resurfaced. "This is good."

Paul tried on a narrow gold band. "Are you okay with this?" he asked me.

At the sight of a wedding ring on his finger a flock of little butterflies took flight in my chest. As I touched the ring the flutter bloomed into a heady flood of emotion.

He was mine. I looked into his vivid blue eyes and tried to work some sort of sound around the lump in my throat.

"Not good?"

I shook my head. "It's good, I --" My chin trembled.

He touched my face and dropped a soft kiss on my lips. "We'll take them," he said without looking at Egg-man. I surrendered the envelope with our license application.

"Very good," he said, tucking the envelope under his arm. The trays disappeared and a receipt book and a clipboard with a form took their place. "Package number five. Master Card or Visa?"

Paul handed him his Visa card at the same time the door to the chapel opened. Strains of the wedding march flowed out, followed closely by a middle-aged couple. A woman in a lavender print skirt and matching jacket was on the arm of a portly man in dungarees. Their huge smiles made me want to smile as well.

The woman looked our way and did a small double take. "I remember you two! Twenty-three D and E!"

The woman from the flight down from Seattle -- the married-by-Elvis-four-times woman.

The quintessential romantic, an example for us all.

"Oh, of course!".

"Congratulations," Paul said, echoing my good will.

Twenty-three F hustled over with her new husband, Number Five.

"Why, thank you, and congratulations to you, too. I see you're taking my advice." She hugged her husband's arm, leaning into him. "I told them this was a great place to get married. They were planning a sure-fire disaster." She flapped a hand at me. "Don't worry about his family. They'll come around eventually."

"Don't live down the street from them, and you'll be fine," Number Five said, then hugged his wife and gave her a big smooch on the cheek. "My Lois knows how to plan the best wedding. This is our second time to each other -- we're a couple of two-timers. Ha!" They both guffawed at the joke. He caught his breath and gently patted her cheek. "Same chapel, but upgraded the plan for better results -- right, honey-pie?"

"Countin' on it, snookums." She winked broadly at us and hustled Number Five out the front door.

"Mr. Hudson, Miss Campbell," said Egg-man. "I believe we are ready for you. Let me introduce our celebrity officiate."

I turned and my gaze crashed solidly onto a large photograph of an Elvis impersonator, in the white sparkly suit, gold chains and errant forelock. The poor imitation of that famous lip curl mocked me. I spun toward Paul, stuttering his name. His eyes widened.

"What? What's wrong?"

"Elvis," I choked and pointed.

His gaze jumped to the photograph then to Egg-man. My almost-husband wrapped a protective arm around me. "Elvis performs the ceremony?"

Egg-man looked slightly abashed. "Sorry folks. If you were counting on having an Elvis wedding you're going to have a hard time finding one tonight. There's a big Elvis review and competition over in Henderson. That's why there isn't much of a crowd here this evening.

"Oh now, Wally." A tiny blonde with a softly drawling,

down-home accent sauntered toward us from the wide-open door to the chapel. Her ankle-length white robe brought to mind a church choir. "You're gonna make these nice folks think we can't get them hitched up the way they want."

She kept coming as though intending to insert herself between Paul and me. Stunned, I made room and she took us each by the arm. Wally, aka Egg-man, handed her the form he'd filled out from our license application when we'd settled on a package. She took it without releasing my arm.

"Come on, darlins'." She waved the paper, looked up at Paul then me with a dazzling smile and, prodigious chest authoritatively leading the way, set us into motion. "Dolly'll get you married to this big hunk 'o good lookin' man quicker'n you can go scootin' down the road."

I looked over the top of the mass of intricately curled, blond hair to Paul, unsure of … well, several things. He shrugged. I, however, had to know at least the answer to one question.

"You look so much like -- you're not really …?"

"Dolly Parton? No, I truly wish I was, but that's so sweet of you to say. I can almost sing like her." She winked, and I swear I felt the breeze from her false eyelashes.

"I'll just bet you can," I said, falling into the rhythm of her speech.

The genuine delight in her laugh warmed my heart. I raised my gaze to Paul. "Let's do this."

She gave us some brief instructions, never once slipping out of character, and collected our rings since we had no attendants. Out of a slim, refrigerated display case, she selected a lovely fresh bouquet of white and pink roses that worked with my green dress, and a white rose she pinned to Paul's lapel.

"Come on, handsome," she said to Paul. "Let's go on in. And darlin'," this was addressed to me, "when you hear the music, Wally'll open those big ol' doors and you just sashay right on down the aisle."

Paul took two steps to accompany her, then stopped and came back to me, rubbing a hand over his mouth. "I have an alternative. If you don't like it, I understand," he said.

My jaw dropped. He couldn't be backing out. "An alternative?"

His eyes softened and he touched my cheek. "No, listen to me for a moment. What I mean is we've been through so much together, more than most people, and we've worked hard to become a team. There've been times when I'm sure you could have left me and never looked back, but you didn't. You've stuck by my side when I didn't deserve it, and I hope you know I've been there for you, because you always deserve it. We've had each other's backs from the beginning. Let's walk down the aisle together."

In that moment I could not have loved him more, and I could not trust my voice to utter a word. I only hoped the happiness on my face and the nod of my head gave him the answer I couldn't say. He held his arm out and I stepped forward to claim it. Dolly beamed at us, hands pressed over her stunning bosom, then she turned and hurried to her place at the front of the chapel. With a nod from her, the music began.

Paul hugged my arm securely to his side and we walked up the aisle, never taking our eyes from each other.

Dolly glanced at the form Wally'd handed her as Paul and I stepped up onto the dais, then tucked it into a pocket in the folds of her robe. "We're off to a good start, here, folks." Her smile was so warm it wouldn't have surprised me if she'd added an invitation to join her for a drink afterwards.

"We all are gathered here today to witness the joining of Theodora Bernadette Campbell and Paul Anthony Hudson in marriage." She made eye contact with each of us as she said our names. "Darlin's, the possibilities and potentials of your married life are truly great and the story of your life together is yours to write. For true marriage is more than a joining of two individuals, it is the union of two hearts." She reached a hand to each of us, and it occurred to me then that she wasn't reading from a book. When we each took the hand she offered, she continued. "May you always need one another, not to fill an emptiness but to help each other know fullness. May you always want one another, but not out of lack. May you have happiness and may you find it in making one another happy. May you always have love and find it in loving one another." She moved our hands together and Paul took mine tenderly in his.

"Do you, Paul, take Theodora to be your wife, in sickness and health, richer or poorer until death do you part?"

He never took his eyes from mine. "I do."

"And do you, Theodora, take Paul to be your husband, in sickness and health, richer or poorer, until death do you part?"

I nodded and my lips trembled. "I do."

She produced our rings from the hidden pocket. "Paul, take this ring as a symbol of your love for Theodora, put it on her finger and repeat after me."

He took the ring she handed him.

"With this ring I thee wed," she said.

"I love you with all my heart, Thea." He slid the hastily purchased item onto my finger with far more care than I'd taken in choosing it. Happiness built inside my chest so fast I feared the only out would be through tears. "With this ring I thee wed and commit my life and soul to you. I will always be at your side. You will always be my love."

"Weren't those words the most heartfelt you've ever had the pleasure of listenin' to?" Dolly said, before reaching Paul's ring to me. "Here you go, darlin'. Put this ring on Paul's finger and repeat after me, or add your own. With this ring I thee wed ..."

"With this ring I thee wed," I repeated, finding my voice. "Paul, I love you more than you can ever know, and commit my life and soul to you as well. I will always be at your side."

"Well, hallelujah, that's just so beautiful I may cry, too."

She fanned at moist eyes with one hand and laughed. "Now, y'all, by the power vested in me by the great state of Nevada, I pronounce you husband and wife. Kiss your bride, honey."

Paul folded me in his arms and kissed me long and soft and with a tenderness that filled me with more happiness than I could have imagined. He hugged me closer and rocked us back and forth before we stepped back. Laughing like giddy teens, we wiped tears off our cheeks.

With pictures taken, license signed, and repeated hugs and congratulations from Dolly, we left the Little Snowbird Chapel and returned to the hotel.

An hour and a half later, our good clothes strewn from the suite's door to the bed, we lay on our backs in a tangle of sheets, our rapturously fatigued bodies damp with cooling sweat. I held my left hand aloft, taking in the new sight. The diamond on my engagement ring flashed multicolor sparks, caught from the neon lights from The Strip. Evidently it was pleased with the company of the plain band snuggled next to it. Paul shifted, captured my hand in his and brought my palm to his lips.

"My wife," he said.

My heart swelled. And, as he folded his fingers around mine, the glint of his wedding ring stirred the fire I'd thought we'd temporarily quenched. I scooted closer, brushed my lips over his muscular shoulder and giggled. "I'm afraid, my husband, I've become one of those women who becomes wildly aroused at the sight of a wedding ring on a man's finger."

"Is that right?" he asked, his fingertips drifting over my stomach. "And when did you notice this proclivity to such wanton behavior, madam?"

"Why, just now, truthfully. I'm afraid, sir, that you aren't safe. You really must take steps to protect yourself."

"You have me concerned. I'm not sure I know what to do." His hand drifted lower.

I purred. "Umm ... yes, I believe you're on the right track

… just … lower." My breath came in a pant.

"Here?" He caressed the top of my thigh.

"You're a tease." I moved his hand between my legs, and he obliged my desire.

He rolled onto his side, nearly covering me. His breath tickled my ear. "And you're insatiable."

"I want … you." I arched to him, feeling I was begging, and ran my hand forward from his hip, hoping I'd find he wasn't as spent as the previous hour or so of activity might render him. Lucky me. Heart pounding and my mind laser focused on my need to feel him inside me, I threw my leg over him and pushed him onto his back. Time for more of that joining Dolly had referred to in our marriage vows.

"Darlin', I'm gonna ride y'all like a pony."

"Stallion," he corrected, quite correctly.

I grinned. "Stud."

After the desperate, frantic grasping and pounding to become one, after the explosions that racked my body, I lay limp on top of him sucking air with the desperation of someone nearly drowned.

"Oh my God," I said.

Paul chuckled through his own panting. I pushed myself weakly with one arm, sliding off him and rolling onto my back.

"Oh my God," I repeated. "I'm an addict." I turned my head enough to study his beautiful features. I loved this man so much, the emotion consumed me. What was more, I couldn't have been more joyous about losing myself so completely. "I'm never going to be able to keep my hands off you. Do you realize that? Every time I lay eyes on you all I'll be able to think about is making love to you. We won't be able to go out in public without me embarrassing us both. I'll be all over you, yowling like a cat in heat." I flung an arm out, encountering acres more bed. An excellent place to be. "Who knew getting married would do this to me? It won't just be your family who's upset we got married, everyone will wish --

oh, my God." I sprang up, scrambled to my knees and clutched the sheets to me. I'd been shot dead on, and at long last, with a conscience. "Paul, what have we done?"

# Chapter Six

When Paul mentioned getting a divorce I'd wept so hard I thought I'd throw up. He'd carried me to the shower and held me there, in his arms, under the spray of the four shower heads, apologizing for ever bringing up the "d" word until I calmed down. We agreed we had to have an alternative plan. The only one that made sense was a second wedding, and very soon. Who knew how long we'd be able to keep our secret -- well, okay, he could keep his mouth shut, but I was the one who might let something slip.

By the time we'd boarded the flight back to Seattle the plans for our second wedding were falling into place -- enough so that I felt we could afford to relax and take a casual approach to the affair. He said if I seemed too relaxed everyone would know something was up. He had a point. Then again, if we got Mother involved -- which would be impossible to avoid -- she'd stress me out every time she opened her mouth, anyway. Our subterfuge was safe with me.

We dilly-dallied around Seattle, having dinner and strolling through the stores and galleries, before heading back to Snohomish. The later we got back, the less chance there was of running into anyone. I wanted one more evening of not pretending -- a few more hours to wear my wedding ring and see Paul wearing his.

Unfortunately, whenever I thought about removing our rings, heartache I hadn't anticipated snuck in and threatened to reduce me to tears. I told myself I was being ridiculous. We weren't any less married. It was simply a secret.

And none of the rationalizations made me feel any better.

When we arrived home our wedding license and the picture with Dolly went into a manila envelope. The rings would join them in the morning, then I'd put them in my office safe when I went to work.

The alarm went off early enough for us to go for a morning run, but Paul didn't even suggest it. Neither of us made a move to get out of bed until the clock made it clear we'd both be late for work.

After a hurried shower and half a bowl of cereal, Paul filled his thermos with coffee and secured the lid. Then he walked to the kitchen table, picked up the envelope with the evidence of our elopement and pulled off his ring.

My throat constricted.

The little thud it made when he dropped it in nearly turned on my tears. He held the envelope out to me. I gnawed my lip, straightened and, with the speed you'd rip off a Band-Aid to shorten the pain, removed my ring as well and dropped it into its temporary hiding place. The rings found each other with a tiny, muffled, metallic kiss.

Tears streamed down my cheeks. He sealed the envelope and set it on the table.

"Hey, my wife," he said wrapping me in a tight embrace. "Nothing's changed. We're still married, I still love you."

I nodded, hugging him hard. "I wish you could stay home today. I don't want to be without you."

"I know. I won't be late, I promise." He stroked my hair, then peeled my arms from around his waist and kissed me good-bye.

My chin started to tremble as the door closed behind him. I ran to it and yanked it open. "Paul!"

Already half way to his car, he turned.

"I love you," I said, fighting back tears. Again.

One side of his mouth turned up. "I love you, too."

I trotted down the steps and across the rough concrete walkway in my bare feet and bathrobe to kiss him good-bye a second time. He obliged with prolonged passion then, patting my butt, released me.

"Go get dressed and go to work before I can't control myself. See you tonight." Instead of turning him loose, I clung to his arm and walked with him to his car. He unlocked the door, kissed me once more before tossing his briefcase on the passenger seat and sliding behind the wheel. I watched from the end of the walkway as he drove down the street and waved as he approached the corner. He lifted his hand in acknowledgment before he made the turn.

Gravel crunched behind me, and I glanced over my shoulder. Mrs. Baron, my neighbor, and her new puppy were out for their morning walk. I crouched and called the little fluff ball to me. He hopped, in that ungainly happy-puppy way, at the end of his leash until he and Mrs. Baron reached me. Then I received an enthusiastic few licks before he tripped over his feet.

"Oscar, you're a clown," I said, scratching his soft curly head. There had to be some poodle in his background, but who knew what the rest was.

"That he is," my neighbor said. "Even Mr. Baron is enjoying him now."

I laughed and stood, sniffing and wiping at my eyes. "Darned allergies," I said. "I knew he'd win your husband over in no time."

She chuckled. Her husband had been adamantly opposed

to having a pet. Oscar was supposed to be a "foster." I believed he'd transitioned to "permanent."

"Kind of cold this morning," I said, folding my arms in a tight hug.

"A little chilly, but I'd trade my coat and shoes in a minute for kisses like the ones you just got. I noticed the two of you weren't home this last weekend. You must have had a fine time to come home and behave like newlyweds."

Heat flooded my cheeks. Well, crap. I'd been right. We really had to watch it. "It was a lovely weekend, thanks. Our friends Andrea and Dave got married."

"Nothing like a little romance to stoke the fire."

"You must be right. Paul's been very attentive. We've even started to plan our own wedding."

"Oh, well, congratulations! I'm so pleased for the two of you. Have you settled on a date and place?"

The date! What had we settled on? I shot from the hip in the mental scramble. "We're thinking around the beginning of August, but we're still looking into locations. I need to put a budget together." Crap. That was the first date we'd talked about before we'd left on Friday.

"A budget is the best way to start, but you know that. You're always so sensible."

If she only knew. I shivered, said goodbye to Mrs. Baron and hurried back to the warmth of the house. If I were sensible, I'd get dressed, walk to the office and, after getting caught up on work for my clients, make some command decisions about my wedding. It wasn't going to plan itself, and if I left it off too long Mother would have the whole thing mapped out and choreographed. Now that I'd blabbed to Mrs. Baron, also not a sensible decision, news would spread quickly to my aunt and sister. By Friday Mother would be taking over.

I had to get cracking.

<><><>

My cell phone rang before I left for lunch and it was not Paul, like it had been the first four times. My caller ID said it was Aunt Vi. Sure, I'd talked to her last night when we got back to Seattle, but I hadn't mentioned a word about putting together wedding plans. I braced for the hurt feelings she'd surely have, hearing it second hand from Mrs. Baron, and answered before the call went to voice mail.

"Aunt Vi! Hi! Had to dig in my purse for my phone." Was that over the top?

"Hello, love. Goodness, you sound very chipper today."

The perfect opening. "I sure am. Paul and I are finally setting a wedding date."

"Now there's a bit of news that makes me happy."

She didn't sound all that thrilled. My hands broke out in a sweat, and the little warning bell clanging in my head jarred my nerves. "Yeah, I guess Andrea and Dave kind of inspired us." Andrea and Dave and some other things.

"We can't wait to hear all about their wedding. I am sorry we couldn't make it, but we're still planning on a little party for them when they get back from their honeymoon."

"They'll like that."

"Thea." She paused, the dead air lasting long enough for me to squirm. "Thea, I have some bad news."

My heart halted for a moment. I reeled back my line of thinking like Mrs. Baron had done with the determined little Oscar. My aunt wouldn't say she had "bad news" if the "bad news" was me. She'd have just started in with the lecture and let me figure out the "bad news" heading. Something had happened while we were gone. I took a small breath.

"What's wrong?"

"Detective Thurman rang us up a short while ago. He needs to talk to you again. He said the medical examiner told him Don had been murdered."

Blood drained from my head, and the room wobbled. "Are you telling me I killed Don? Aunt Vi I was trying to help. I --"

"No, no, dear. I'm sorry. Someone killed Don, and Detective Thurman wants to go over your statement with you again to see if you recall anything else that might be of some help. He asked me to let you know he'd be in his office this afternoon and to please stop over."

The floor quit shifting under me, but sweat trickled from my arm pits. "I don't -- of course. Yes. I'll go see him. Why didn't he call me directly?"

"He tried, but you didn't answer your home phone. I guess he didn't have your cell number and doesn't realize you have a new office."

"I'll go see him this afternoon."

"You and Paul come to dinner. Then you can tell me what he has to say."

She disconnected. Only after I left my office and walked back to the house for lunch did I realize she hadn't revisited any mention of my wedding plans. There was more she wasn't telling me.

# Chapter Seven

I unlocked the door to the old two-story Victorian that housed my office on the first floor. It was February when I signed the lease and moved in. The small, tasteful "Campbell Accounting, Inc." sign on a little post by the sidewalk in front of the freshly painted, Delft blue and white building still thrilled me. I habitually paused to drink in the sight. This time, preoccupied with what I hadn't learned from Detective Thurman, I barely paid attention.

I'd gone directly over after a quick lunch, seen the detective right away, reviewed my statement and answered more questions -- mostly about what other people were doing when Miguel and I were administering CPR, and what had preceded. I still had a hard time remembering anything but my own activities once Don collapsed. Thurman gave nothing of his investigation away as he questioned me. It was impossible for me to determine what his theories were or who he suspected.

When he told me I could go, I'd hesitated so long he invited me to stay.

"Something's on your mind. Want to tell me what it is?" he said.

I swallowed, felt my skin heat and the prickle of forming sweat. I met his inquiring gaze and my words rushed out. "Do you think Miguel and I botched the CPR and killed Don? Because if you do, I'll tell you right away I may have done things wrong, but Miguel had training in the Navy and he knows what he's doing and believe me neither one of us had any reason to want to hurt Don. He was a good friend."

Thurman regarded me for a moment, eyebrows raised, before a small smile tugged at the corners of his mouth. "Thea, even if you two did botch the CPR -- which you didn't, by the way -- we couldn't arrest you and you can't be held liable for your assistance. Washington's had a Good Samaritan Law in place since nineteen eighty-five. You and Miguel didn't kill Dr. Archterkamp, you just didn't save him."

"Could we have saved him? If … if we'd done something different?"

Thurman pursed his lips and shifted in his chair. Finally he exhaled. "You are in no way to construe what I am about to say as any kind of evidence or any encouragement to lend your assistance."

I leaned forward.

"No," he said.

"'No' what?"

"No, you could not have saved him."

That was all he'd say.

Now, hanging my parka in my office's tiny coat closet, I pondered over, examined and rejected reasons for someone to kill Don. Murder was a deliberate act. Not an accident. It meant someone wanted him dead, needed him dead. The thought prompted me to turn up the office heat. Then, checking the time, I reached for my phone. Paul should be in his office and not in class.

"Are you in a meeting?" I asked when he answered.

"You mean, am I alone and can you talk dirty?"

I didn't laugh. "Half of that. The 'are you alone?' half."

There was a pause. "Yes. What's wrong?"

I told him, and finished with, "I don't know what to do," although I knew he was going to say "nothing, butt out," which, of course, was reasonable.

"Just make sure whatever you discover you give to Thurman."

It was my turn to pause. "I'm sure I won't find anything out, but if I do …."

There was a small chuckle. "I miss you, my wife. I might be home early."

"I miss you, too, husband. We're having dinner at Aunt Vi and Uncle Henry's."

"Dessert at home then."

"Dessert. At home." If the mood over dinner wasn't so morose it killed the desire.

We had dessert first – call it "comfort" but not necessarily "food" -- and arrived at the farm a little after six. Thanks to my morning conversation with Mrs. Baron, we got our story straight about what to tell Aunt Vi and Uncle Henry about our wedding plans and agreed to put a tight rein on our energized libido so as not to arouse any additional suspicion.

We hung our jackets on the coat pegs in the little mud room off Aunt Vi's big country kitchen. The mouthwatering aroma of pork roast and apple pie had me kicking off my boots and heading for the stove to peek into the oven. Paul headed for the living room as we heard Uncle Henry's uncharacteristic, snappish grumbling. "Blasted high-bloody-tech record player" was likely not praise for his new sound system.

"Hungry?" Aunt Vi asked. She took great pleasure in tempting anyone within sniffing distance with her irresistible use of seasonings.

"Starved. It smells so good. What did you put on it?"

"Salt, pepper, a little of this, a little of that."

" Are you ever going to give me your recipes?"

"When did you get so interested in cooking?"

"Oh, well --"

Paul strode in with two glasses of wine and handed me one. "Here you go."

"Thanks." I smiled, politely. My fingers brushed his as I took the glass and his gaze locked with mine for a brief, lust-filled moment before he beat a somewhat panicked retreat for the living room.

"I suppose," Aunt Vi said, drawing my attention from Paul's backside, "it's more fun cooking for two."

"Oh, um, right. Yes, of course. I mean ...."

The microwave dinged and Aunt Vi turned away to open its door, but not before I noticed the silent laugh she was doing a poor job of suppressing. Obviously, Paul and I were doing a poor job of acting normal.

"Anything I can help you with?" I asked. "Set the table? Stir something?"

"No, we're all set, once your sister decides to show up."

On cue, the back door opened with a whoosh and bounced off the door stop. Juliet caught it on the rebound, shut it with more authority than necessary and threw her backpack to the mudroom floor. Both Aunt Vi and I stared at her. I hadn't heard my sister's motorcycle roar up the driveway, otherwise I would have expected her entrance -- although not such a dramatic one.

"Dammit." She glared at us from the doorway to the mud room, huffing like she'd just run a sprint. Half of her long golden brown curls escaped her knit hat and the protection of her jacket and frizzed wildly from the drizzle we'd endured all afternoon. With a couple of angry jerks she removed her hat and jacket and shoved them at the coat pegs. Only the jacket found purchase. The hat dropped to the floor. "It's probably your fault," she snarled, directly at me.

"Where's your motorcycle? And how could anything that

happened to your precious bike be even close to my fault?"

Uncle Henry and Paul came into the kitchen and Paul's arm went across my shoulder. I leaned away. His arm dropped to his side and he increased the space between us. Juliet cut him a narrow look before returning her disdain to me.

"Nothing happened to my bike. It's raining, in case you didn't notice, and I forgot my rain suit at home. Bobby dropped me off at the end of the driveway and I walked up."

Bobby, Michelle's boyfriend, proved once again how thoughtless he was. "Wow, how nice of him. He couldn't have bothered to get you any closer?"

"His car doesn't have reverse, for your information. Besides, he was on his way to try and get Michelle out of jail, so there."

I expected her to stick her tongue out. She didn't. However, everyone was looking at me as if I could explain what Michelle was doing in jail. I set my wine on the counter and crossed my arms. Just because I'd been talking to Detective Thurman earlier didn't mean I was privy to local police activity. "What are you talking about? What did Michelle do that would get her arrested?"

"Yeah, like you don't know. They're saying she substituted euthanasia solution for the vaccines Dr. Don was giving, so she's responsible for his murder."

# Chapter Eight

Shocked silence hung in my aunt's kitchen. I rubbed at my temples and stared hard at my sister. "Are you saying there was euthanasia solution in the vaccination syringes?"

"That's exactly what I'm saying. And the police think Michelle put it there. On purpose."

"Every single syringe?"

"Yes, every single syringe."

"But ...." My face went cold. "She was trying to kill horses? Why would she do that?"

Juliet's face went scarlet, her fists clenched. "She didn't! Michelle wouldn't try to kill any animal! But you told the police Michelle filled the syringes for Dr. Don."

I groped for support from a chair. I had told him that. "Oh my God." He'd asked who filled the syringes, if Don didn't do it. Of course Michelle would, since she was his tech assistant. The question had been so casual, so much a part of a larger conversation, that I hadn't made any connection with the accidental stick and Don's death. Someone had targeted the horses, including Blackie. But only Don was dead.

"Thea," Uncle Henry said, his strong hand on my shoulder, demanding my attention. "The amount of euthanasia solution in a vaccine syringe would be only a small fraction of what it would take to kill a horse. It wouldn't even be enough to slow its pulse."

I clung to his gaze. My uncle could surely make sense of this. "So she figured the horses would be okay and was hoping Don would stick himself by accident? That doesn't make any sense. It must have been a mistake."

"Well, duh." My sister's shout, so near my ear, backed me into the kitchen table. Uncle Henry held her away with a grip on her arm. She leaned forward as far as she could manage. "Why do you think Bobby's trying to spring her from jail? He's going to try to talk sense into the cops."

Oh, I could imagine that. Bobby, the guy who learned the hard way that a hubcap wouldn't hold a tire on a car, who thought the "do not jump from bridge" sign at the Pilchuck River was a dare and ended up in the hospital with multiple fractures and a concussion, who Michelle took pity on when his parents kicked him out for "borrowing" their car and their credit card. "You must be joking. He'll probably convince them it was an evil plot and get himself arrested as an accessory."

"He's not that stupid." Juliet sneered and crossed her arms.

It was some small relief that she wasn't winding up to throw a punch. "Yes he is. He's an intelligence black hole. I feel I.Q. points being sucked away every time I have to talk to him. I can only imagine the adverse effect he's had on Michelle."

Paul strangled a chuckle with a sip of wine.

"Girls, girls!" Aunt Vi said.

Uncle Henry cleared his throat. "Is this the same young man Max hired to clean tack?"

Juliet nodded. "Michelle helped him get that job."

Uncle Henry frowned. He knew all about Bobby. Probably stuff I didn't know.

"Were you with Michelle when she was arrested?" Paul asked Juliet.

"Well, no. Bobby called me right after they took her away. He said he thought they were coming to get him for, um, something else, and he hid in the closet until they left."

"What might that 'something else' be?" Aunt Vi asked.

"Uh ...."

"Drugs," I said, based on nothing but pure intuition. You had to be stupid *and* high to even try some of the crap Bobby pulled.

"Pot," Juliet said. "Just pot. I'm pretty sure."

I snorted. Paul rubbed a hand over his mouth and studied the floor. Uncle Henry opened his mouth to speak, but Aunt Vi beat him to it.

"Young lady, you are under no circumstances to accept another ride anywhere from that young man. I don't care if it's the middle of the night. You call one of us and we will come and get you. Is that understood?"

Juliet's gray eyes had gone wide. "Yes, ma'am."

"Now," Aunt Vi said, addressing all of us with a sweeping glance. "Dinner is ready. And I want to hear about Andrea and Dave's wedding. Michelle's parents are capable of handling their daughter's problem." She turned on her heel and marched to the stove.

While we five ate dinner, I gushed about Andrea and Dave's wedding, described her dress, all she and I had done on our shopping trip to Neiman Marcus, described the food we'd had and the shows we'd seen. The meals at the restaurants reminded me of my aunt's superb cooking, so I commented on that, as well. Her roast pork, herb seasoned wild rice, dinner rolls she'd made from scratch, and beans they'd grown in their garden last summer were the equal to or better than anything we'd had in Vegas.

Flushed pink with pride, she insisted we try a new dessert recipe she'd run across -- an incredibly smooth vanilla custard drizzled with caramel and topped with whipped cream. If I could cook like my aunt, Paul and I would get fat.

At long last, I pushed away from the table stifling an urge to reach a hand to my husband's shoulder, to feel his warmth and solid muscle through the soft flannel of his shirt.

"I don't know how you keep so trim, Uncle Henry," I said, gathering empty plates and silverware. He laughed and stretched.

"Balanced meals, exercise and no junk food," Aunt Vi said. "And a metabolism I wish I had."

"You're not heavy, auntie," Juliet said, helping to clear the table.

"I'm not the trim girl I was, I can tell you. But that's what happens to us women. You reach an age and your body turns on you. Just remember that."

I carried a stack of dished to the kitchen and turned on the tap. Aunt Vi washed her good china and silver by hand, and she always used them for dinner. We couldn't talk her out of it, so we did the dishes for her. Juliet was silent until we were halfway through the stack of plates.

"What's with you and Paul?" she asked.

My stomach made a half twist. I could have sworn we kept our hands off each other. In fact, we'd hardly exchanged a glance the entire evening and I hadn't said one word directly to him. In fact, he hadn't spoken to me either. "Nothing's 'with' us. I don't know what you're talking about."

"Jeez, if you'd been leaning any farther away from each other you'd have fallen out of your chairs. What are you fighting about?"

"We're not fighting."

"Oh, so the silent treatment is now considered not fighting? I guess since I don't have a boyfriend anymore I've gotten out of the hang of relationships."

"Maybe you should find another boyfriend, then. Go back

to having men as a hobby."

"Sorry, I have another, more fulfilling, interest."

I dove at the opportunity to change the subject. "I noticed how you've filled up that spare room across from my office. Looks like you're taking that class seriously." I rented the entire first floor, although I didn't need it -- I didn't really have a choice. It was all or none. It took Juliet less than twenty-four hours before she was begging for space where she could set up a worktable for her clothing design class projects. I saw no reason to say no. She had a history of flitting from one interest to another, so I doubted she'd be there too long after the class was done -- too bad, since she had a flair for clothing construction. Her ideas concerning style were a little wacky, but no one could say she didn't grasp the tailoring skills.

My only condition in lending her the space was that if she ever left the place unlocked I'd kick her out faster than she could change her outfit. So far, there hadn't been a problem. In fact I hardly knew she was there. The door to her workroom was shut most of the time.

"Of course I'm taking it seriously. I'm good at it. In fact, I'm better than good. I'm a rare talent. But that's not what I'm talking about. I've got something else I'm going to do, and I was hoping you'd help." She tipped her head and smiled at me.

Talk about a deliberate suck-up. At least she hadn't brought up Paul and my odd behavior again. I handed her the last plate to rinse. "Okay, I'll bite. What do you need my help with?"

She took her time, dried the plate and stacked it with the others before answering. "Bobby isn't going to be able to help Michelle. He's not smart enough. I'm going to investigate Dr. Don's murder and prove Michelle didn't have anything to do with it."

I would have almost preferred she insist Paul and I were fighting. "Juliet, that's a stupid idea. In fact that's the worst idea I've heard in a long time." Unless I counted my impulsive wedding.

"What makes me conducting an investigation any different from all the times you have?"

I pulled the plug out of the sink's drain and watched the still sudsy water level drop. "The only reason I have in the past is because I had no choice."

"Did you know what you were doing the first time?"

"No. Or any of the other times." I wiped my hands on my apron and untied it.

"That's not true, you've gotten better at it. You know stuff. Maybe I'll ask Paul for some advice. He'll help me."

Ha. "Go ahead. Good luck."

She dried her hands with a dish towel and went to the living room. In less than a minute she was back. It surprised me she didn't take more time to try and wheedle a deal.

"Well?" I asked.

"He said 'no.' Uncle Henry said, 'absolutely not,' and Aunt Vi said over her own dead body. Looks like you're it. That's okay. You probably know more than you think you do."

Obviously, she'd been allowed to harbor this idea too long. One of us should have realized where she was headed and cut her off before she started. Now we had to battle the laws of physics: Juliet in motion tended to stay in motion.

"Your mistake," Paul said on the drive home, "is you try to reason with her. Her mind is like the Escher illusion from hell. She charms you into following her logic and you get yourself turned around and in worse trouble than when you started."

I snarled at Mr. Know-it-all. Sisterly concern rather than an inability to resist her charm, like some, kept me stubbornly looking out for her well being. However, he had a point. "Maybe that's why Eric left her. Maybe he couldn't take her brand of logic anymore."

"Doubt it, that's one of the things he liked about her. She has a certain creative twist he's lacking."

"Then why did he leave? He just took off in the dead of

night and hasn't shown his face around here since -- unless he's been talking to you."

He shot me an annoyed glance and slowed to turn onto Second Street. "No, he hasn't been talking to me. And I don't know why he left. It was out of character for him. I can only imagine he was pushed past some point of toleration. We'd all have seen it coming if we'd been paying attention -- and none of us were."

I mulled this over. "Whatever happened is beyond fixing now, I suppose. I'm not sure I like the change in Juliet, though. She seems to have lost that joy she always had. At least she's found an outlet in the design class -- for as long as that will last. After that, I'm going to be worried."

"She's growing up. She'll work it out."

"I wish she wouldn't do it by defending Bobby and taking on local law enforcement. For all her wildness before, she'd never have believed Bobby. He's the kind of scum she always avoided, until Michelle hooked up with him. And it seems to be his influence that has her running to Michelle's rescue. This isn't going to turn out well, even if I can keep tabs on her while she's across from my office. What's going to happen when she gives up this hobby and moves her stuff out?"

"Give her a chance to grow up, get her feet under her. You're her anchor, along with Vi and Henry and everyone else who cares about her. She won't stray far, she'll be okay."

I worried my lower lip while we waited at a light on Second. By the time the light changed I'd made up my mind. "I'm going in to see Thurman tomorrow morning. The information Juliet got from Bobby has to be wrong. There couldn't have been euthanasia solution in those syringes. Something else had to have come up for them to have arrested Michelle. Maybe Juliet will give up her crusade if she gets hold of the facts."

<><><>

I knocked on the detective's door jamb. Thurman, seated at his desk wearing the same (or similar) brown suit I always saw him in, looked up from his two-fingered typing on the computer keyboard.

"Thea, I did expect to see you back here, but not quite so soon. Have you solved the case?"

I chose to ignore the good-natured mocking, but briefly entertained the notion of suggesting to my sister she make it a project to convince him to upgrade his wardrobe, as a way to divert her from her current obsession with Michelle's arrest. "I'm afraid I'm here just to clear up a rumor."

Thurman nodded. "What rumor might that be?"

"I understand you arrested Michelle Martin yesterday."

He motioned me to the orange, molded plastic chair next to his desk. "I can verify that rumor."

I perched on the edge of the chair, my purse in my lap. "And I'm told that Don died from accidentally injecting himself with euthanasia solution."

"Not so accidentally. The euthanasia solution was in all the syringes that should have contained the West Nile Virus vaccine. Both liquids are pale pink. Miss Martin had knowledge and access, plus opportunity. We're lacking a motive, but we're working on it. I'd say it was a deliberate set up. Eventually, Dr. Archterkamp was bound to be in a situation where a little nudge and …." He shrugged.

"So it definitely was euthanasia solution?"

Thurman leaned back in his chair. It squeaked a painful protest. "Yes, ma'am."

"But …."

"It was deliberate. There was no way it couldn't have been. Knowledge, opportunity and her fingerprints all over the syringes and vials. Premeditated murder."

"Don couldn't have filled those syringes himself?"

"Could have, but he typically didn't. And he didn't this time. That's what he used his tech for."

"But …."

"Any other rumors I can put to rest for you?"

"No." Juliet was right. Unfortunately, it looked like she was getting more and more wrong in her ability to pick her friends. I stood, thanked him for his time and left.

The shock of knowing Michelle had committed such a heinous crime climbed in the car and rode with me all the way back to my office.

Somehow I had to convince my sister to give up her quixotic pursuit of Michelle's innocence.

The morning dragged, providing little opportunity for me to steer my thoughts completely away from what Michelle had done to Don. I made a point to double check my work. Paul called after his last morning class and the sound of his voice cheered me enough to think I'd be able to get in a ride on Blackie at noon without being overly distracted. When I hung up from his call, I locked up the office, drove home to change into my boots and breeches and then drove out to Copper Creek. I avoided the barn's office, where I knew I'd find my sister working.

Generally, the barn was pretty quiet until shortly after two o'clock in the afternoon, and today proved no exception. Uncle Henry was in the middle of a lesson when I led Blackie into the arena. He waved to me, barely taking his eyes off his student. Polly, a thirty-something, intermediate-level rider, was apparently not having a lot of success with Jeremiah, her chestnut Morgan gelding. Incessant kicking, on the horse or rider's part, is never a sign of accomplishment. She tickled him with her whip, also with no positive result. My uncle cut her no slack -- but that's why he's so good.

"Tell me what happened when you used your whip," he said.

"Nothing happened," Polly said. The exasperation in her voice as she hauled her horse to a halt made me cringe.

"What should have happened?"

"He should have gone forward." From the flat tone of her voice I knew this was not the first time around on this particular topic. I pulled Blackie's girth up a hole.

"Very good. Now, tell me what you just taught him."

"To ignore my whip."

"Correct. Is that what you want?"

"No. I should have tapped him again?"

"Yes --"

Polly cocked her long dressage whip as I stepped onto the mounting block.

"Wait." My uncle's tone didn't change, but Polly froze. "If you tap him now, what do you teach him?"

"That my whip is random?"

I smiled to myself as I settled onto the saddle. Use your head before you act. Be persistent, but with correct timing. Otherwise you will confuse your horse and no progress will be made. Those were lessons we all learned over and over.

I sympathized, but didn't want to stick around to find out if she'd succeed. I rode Blackie out of the arena and to the trail that looped through the woods behind Copper Creek's property. A brisk trot along the less muddy of the paths would help clear my head.

By the time we returned to the barn half an hour later, somewhat damp from the light drizzle, the anxiety I'd carried with me all morning had resolved into determination to talk to my sister when she came to her studio after work. I hosed mud off Blackie's feet, legs, tail and belly, wiped him down with a towel and tossed his stable blanket on him before taking him back to his stall.

Agnes, chin up and looking her usual queenly self in her immaculate riding togs, walked by leading Rum Runner. I removed Blackie's halter and fed him a treat listening carefully to the metallic clop of Runner's footfalls. One scuffed slightly instead of being solidly placed. I peered out of Blackie's stall to watch, but from my angle couldn't see anything untoward in the way the horse moved. She led him into the grooming stalls. Perhaps she was planning on riding him. Her unbalanced, heavy handed flat-work technique wouldn't be good for him, but at least she wouldn't be jumping.

"Put my dark brown Pessoa on him, and check the stitching on the girth," Max called from the far end of the barn. "I'll be there as soon as I can."

Oh. Max was going to ride. Poor Rummy. He was going to have his "attitude" adjusted. Quite a different style of communication from the one my uncle advocated.

Blackie nudged me and I dug around in my pocket for another treat. "Yeah, I know," I said and scratched his head. "I'll tell Delores. Maybe she can prevent a disaster."

The aisle-way was empty as I exited Blackie's stall. I hung his halter on its hook and left the Big Barn via the end where Max's office/tack room was located – the quickest way to get to the Copper Creek office and Delores. Despite the door being closed, Max's impatient, raised voice was clear. I assumed he was on the phone until I heard another male voice, lower pitched and calm – and one I recognized as Detective Thurman's. I slowed my pace as I approached.

"So you know Michelle Martin, too, then?"

"Yeah, I know her. So what? It's a small community. Most of us horse people know each other." Max's clipped response seemed too aggressive for the question.

"I expect being as charming as you are, she's willing to do favors for you."

Whoa. This was a line of questioning I hadn't considered. I wanted to hear more. With a burst of inventiveness, I stopped abruptly to retie the laces on my paddock boot. Before I'd even touched them, a kick in the butt knocked me on my face.

Agnes hopped over the top of me in an ungainly lurch, the heel of her shiny black field boot narrowly missing my fingers. "What did you stop like that for?" she shrieked. "I nearly broke my neck."

I struggled up off the concrete floor. "Dammit, Agnes." The palm of one of my hands stung, as did one cheekbone. "What the hell were you doing on my heels in the first place?"

She sneered and marched toward Max's office.

So much for snooping. I didn't wait to see if she went in, although I'd have loved to hear Thurman put her in her place. At least there was no rush to get to Delores since Thurman would have Max busy for a little while.

After my customary, short rap on the Copper Creek office door I walked in. Delores and my sister glanced up then did simultaneous double-takes.

Juliet turned in her chair, tugging her black skirt an inch lower. I don't know why she bothered. She wore black leggings with her black boots. At least she was back to wearing bright colors for tops, although the fuchsia and yellow were a bit much.

"Did Paul hit you, 'cuz if he did I'm going to take him out."

Delores' look of concern shifted to annoyance -- and to my sister. She shook her head.

"Agnes fell over me and knocked me on my face," I said.

"Cripes." Juliet rolled her eyes. "We've got people *and* mirrors falling down around here. How'd she manage to fall over you? You're short, but not *that* short."

"I stopped to fake-tie my boot in front of Max's tack room door. And what do you mean? A mirror fell down? In the arena? I was in there a little while ago, everything looked fine to me." The indoor arena had large mirrors, strategically placed so riders could get a visual bead on their dressage work. It was useful to check on how square your halt was, if your shoulders-in was truly on three tracks and other things a rider can't see because they're sitting on the horse.

"Just happened," Delores said. "It was the one at the end of the long side farthest from the gate. All the anchors were loose. The bottom support gave way first, of course, and it slid behind the kickboards. Made quite a racket. Nobody got hurt and there isn't any glass in the footing."

"Thank goodness for that. Any idea how the anchors got loose?"

"Nope."

"I think someone loosened them deliberately," my sister said. "Do you have any idea how much those stupid mirrors cost? I've been checking online for a replacement and, holy crap, its highway robbery. Plus we've got to hire someone to install the new one. It's going to cost a fortune. Glad I'm not paying for it."

Delores regarded Juliet for a patient moment before casting a curious look at me. "Why were you 'fake-tying' your boot?"

"Yeah, Thea. What were you trying to do, trip Agnes on purpose? Jeez."

"Very funny, Juliet. For your information, I didn't even realize she was behind me." I turned to Delores. "Detective Thurman is interviewing Max and I wanted to listen."

"So you *are* investigating," Juliet said, sitting back in her chair with an annoyingly triumphant grin on her face. "I knew you'd do it."

"No, I'm not --"

"Investigating what? Or do I want to know?" Delores asked.

"Last night I asked her to help me prove Michelle had nothing to do with filling those vaccination syringes with poison and she refused. Now she's doing it."

"I am not. I was just curious, is all. The reason I stopped by here was to tell you Max is taking Rum Runner out. I'm pretty certain he's planning on jumping him."

"Poor Rummy," my sister said.

Delores shook her head. "That boy's an idiot. I should let him get himself hurt, but then he'd probably turn around and sue me since he seems to believe all the accidents around here lately are my fault anyway." She rolled her chair away from her desk, rose and pulled on her red, down vest. "Maybe I can catch him before Phil leaves, then I'll have an official police witness to what I have to say. Lord knows if Agnes is there she'll just twist every word I say."

"She's there," I said, then pointed to my face. "Don't let her sneak up on you."

"Go home and clean that up. You don't want it getting infected." My friend's expression softened a bit and she flashed a small, cunning smile. "I understand the wedding was very nice."

Panic grabbed me by the throat. I swallowed on my intended response to the first aid treatment and coughed so hard my sister jumped up and delivered a vigorous thump to my back. I fended off her second attempt.

"Hey, I'm only trying to help," she snapped. "You weren't this choked up about their wedding last night."

Oh. Right. Andrea and Dave. "Breathed wrong. Sorry. Yes, it was very nice."

"Did anyone attend but you and Paul?" Delores asked.

I forced my breathing back to normal and dabbed at the tears my coughing fit produced. "No, not even her mother. But they didn't mind. They gave short notice to avoid any problems with publicity or interference. Aunt Vi wants to do a reception for them when they get back. I think she's planning it with Carmella." Carmella, Andrea's full-time cook at her estate, had always dreamed of owning her own restaurant. When Andrea's first husband died, my friend decided to divide as much of the estate as possible between employees and relatives. She didn't want any of it. One major reason was that the enormous amount of wealth she'd inherited was a huge issue for Dave. Another major reason was she simply didn't want it. However, because Carmella wouldn't accept Andrea's gift of cash, they struck a deal. They would be partners in a restaurant. "I'm pretty sure the reception will be downtown Seattle at their restaurant. It's getting rave reviews, by the way."

"I'm not surprised. That's one party I certainly don't want to miss," Delores said.

"If Eric and I --" Juliet cut herself short and turned away.

Delores shook her head a little. "And," she said to me, "I

understand you and my nephew have finally made a decision."

Damn. She shouldn't have had to ask. I should have told her myself. Or Paul should have, since she was his aunt. "I'm so sorry. Did Aunt Vi call you?"

"Yesterday afternoon. 'Bout time you two set a date."

"It is. After Don --"

A draft of cool air cut off my comment and I turned, hoping I wouldn't see Max or Agnes. But the door was closing softly and my sister was gone.

# Chapter Nine

I examined the scrape on my cheek in my bathroom mirror. It wasn't nearly as bad as I anticipated, and once I'd cleaned off the dirt you could barely tell I'd landed on my face. With a little antibiotic ointment on it I was good to go.

However, one item wasn't good. The fact that I'd been neglecting to relay the news about my wedding plans to the people I'd normally tell was decidedly worrisome. Someone was bound to get suspicious since the first thing one normally did, as far as I knew, was call everyone you knew, unless you were in Andrea's position and wanted to avoid publicity -- definitely not my situation. I needed to approach our upcoming "nuptials" with appropriate excitement or someone would figure out our secret. We had five months to go and in less than a week I was making mistakes.

Just to make sure I didn't get into any further trouble, I called my parents to tell them Paul and I had set a date in August for our wedding. Much to my relief they weren't home. I left a message, changed from riding clothes into work clothes of blue jeans and my favorite dark green sweater, donned my parka with the hood, in case it rained, and walked the three blocks to my office. I intended to spend the remainder of the afternoon working on clients' taxes, but the phone was ringing when I unlocked my office door. I should have checked the caller id instead of rushing to pick up before the call went to voice mail.

Mother's joyous reception of my news at least reassured me no one else had found it their duty to call her first. She told me to take notes while she talked, and proceeded to dictate instructions.

"Use Mrs. Cunningham, the wedding planner I picked out last summer for Juliet. I have her number here -- hold on." The sound of a drawer sliding and the brief rustling of paper indicated the extent of her search. "Here it is. Now write this down."

For some reason I grabbed a pen and pad from my desk drawer and obeyed.

"Call her right away. Invitations will have to be ordered, addressed and mailed. Do you have a guest list yet?"

"We started --"

"Really, Theodora. I expect you to be more organized than your sister. You need to get this done immediately. People make plans, you know, and can't wait while you 'get around to it.' Now, where will the wedding take place? Paul's family is Catholic, so you'll not want to offend them with your choice. I'm sure Mrs. Cunningham will have suggestions, but including them right from the start will not only be the polite thing to do, but will prevent any future ill will."

No way was I going to tell her about the "ill will" already blowing my way. "Right."

"That brings to mind the ceremony. It may be a little touchy. Oh, dear. These inter-faith marriages can be so delicate to manage. At least the reception shouldn't be a problem."

I didn't bother to mention neither Paul nor I had a problem with religious preference. She would have insisted we should. The reception, despite not being a "problem," received a thorough analysis of possible pitfalls before we moved on to what style dress would look best on me. She didn't notice that I failed to respond when she suggested I go try on dresses and send her pictures via my cell phone for her immediate input, because she'd moved on to her dress and didn't want to clash with my "colors" (although if I wanted her advice, I should pick a nice, gender-neutral teal). There was a brief pause while she consulted a handy etiquette book regarding how many attendants I'd need and, finally, she revisited Paul's family.

"I suppose you haven't contacted Sofia and Robert yet."

I took a breath to respond, but didn't get an opportunity to utter a single lying syllable.

"No, I hadn't thought so, but I can't fault you for telling me first. I'll call them this afternoon and smooth the way for you."

Beads of sweat popped out on my forehead. "No, Mother. I really think Paul should talk to them before anyone else."

"Well, of course he can tell them about the wedding date, but since they've known about your engagement for ages, I can call and welcome them to the family. I should have telephoned last November when you two got engaged but something distracted me … oh, that's right, poor Andrea's husband was murdered. I remember now. Poor dear. How is she doing? I expect she's still having a difficult time."

She'd changed the subject all by herself. Thank God. I made soothing sounds. "Oh, no, no, no. Don't worry about her. She's fine, really. She just got married." Whoops.

"What? Oh dear. Who did she marry? Some fortune-hunting cad talked her into a quickie wedding, I suppose."

That remark would draw a laugh from the two them -- in about ten years. "They did get married in Las Vegas, but Dave Ross isn't a 'fortune-hunting cad'."

"David Ross … Ross …. Didn't I meet him? Oh yes, the

police detective. Broad shoulders, scar through an eyebrow, rather sexy. Huh. Nevertheless. Las Vegas. This won't end well."

I held back an amused snort. Mother and Dad had married in Reno, and against her parents' wishes. One way or another, they'd managed to hold it together for more than thirty years.

"Well, never mind. Andrea's mistake is water under the bridge, and nothing to do with you. Give me Paul's parents' phone number so I don't have to look it up. I'll call them this afternoon."

My pulse slammed into a panicked lick and I leaped to my feet. My chair rocketed backwards, bounced off a file cabinet and crashed into the wall. "No. Mother, please don't. Let Paul call them first."

"Theodora, calm down and don't be ridiculous. I've been remiss enough already -- although, I would have thought Sofia could have remembered to call me. Never mind. I'll correct my oversight right away."

Sweat dripped from my armpits. The phone turned slick where my hand gripped it. "No. No, you can't --"

"Theodora --"

I threw the first coherent thought I had at her, and it happened to contain more truth than lie. "If you call them, I'll cancel the wedding and get married in Las Vegas."

Silence met my ear. It was an awful, searing silence that kept me from breathing. A silence that taunted me with the dire possibility of having to confess to my mother that I'd married into a family who considered me a whore and a heathen. This was not going to go well in much the same manner as the assassination of Archduke Ferdinand of Austria did not go well.

"I don't know what your problem is, young lady, but since you seem so determined to have your way I'll put off calling Sofia and Robert until this weekend. Then, like it or not, I will call them and let them know that someone in this family has manners – despite the way I tried to raise you."

When she disconnected I collapsed into my chair, eased my head down on my desk and tried to remember if I had stocked any ibuprofen in the office bathroom. I didn't think so. Two minutes later I verified my oversight. Head throbbing, I dumped my purse onto my desk and found a lone brown pill that I was fairly certain was my drug of choice. I wiped the lint off and swallowed it, then soaked a paper towel from the bathroom in cold water and applied it to my forehead before sending Paul a text message requesting he bring dinner home because I'd be working late to catch up. I didn't tell him he wouldn't feel like cooking or eating once he found out he had four days to convince his parents to happily accept me into the family.

At ten after five the front door to my building blew open and my sister, not Paul, stormed in, passing my office door without so much as a glance. She disappeared into her studio and after a bit of banging around strode into my office.

"Max," she said. "You need to investigate Max."

I sighed, my headache stirring to life. "It seems to me Detective Thurman is already doing that."

"Well, you're in a better position to do it. I tell you it has to be Max."

I drummed my pencil on the edge of my desk keeping time with the thumping in my temples. "It wouldn't surprise me if Detective Thurman thinks Max and Michelle were in it together. However, it seems to me he's looking into all possibilities and in all likelihood has the investigation under control."

My sister shook back her mane and crossed her arms. "Michelle doesn't like Max. She wouldn't buy him a beer, much less plot a murder with him."

"All right, if you've got this all figured out, then tell me how Max managed to fill those syringes with euthanasia solution."

She thought for a moment and her face fell. "I don't know."

"And," I jabbed my pencil at her for emphasis, "if Max wanted to kill Don there are far more reliable methods of doing so. All he has to do is watch prime time TV for a week and he'd have at least a dozen inventive plots for murder."

"Well, see, there you go. Michelle couldn't have been trying to kill Don. It was too inefficient, and she watches lots of TV."

My headache came back with a rush. I stood, rubbed at my temples and glared at my sister. "So what was she trying to do, kill a bunch of horses with three cc's of euthanasia solution? You do realize, don't you, that Blackie was one of the horses injected. Furthermore, Don Archterkamp is dead, his wife, his family and his friends are grieving. The horse community has lost someone important. If Michelle is guilty, she deserves to be punished. Phil Thurman is a good detective. He will get to the bottom of this without your help -- or mine."

Juliet flung her arms wide. "How can you think Michelle would want to kill anyone? This was an accident, pure and simple, if she was involved. And because she wasn't, then my money is on Max being the bad guy." She leaned across my desk, her hands clasped in supplication. "Please, I'm begging you. Investigate this with me. I don't know what to do. Please."

"I'll tell you what you can do. Talk to Detective Thurman if you have any information. And leave me the hell out of this."

Juliet straightened and glared. Her chest heaved with each breath she took. "Why is it that when someone is important to you, you jump in, investigate like hell and leave a trail of bodies in your wake, but when I need some help you go all 'not me, I don't have any idea how to do this'? Huh? Is 'talk to the cops' really the best you can do?".

We stared each other down for several beats.

"Yes, it is. And for your information, I do not leave a 'trail of bodies' in my wake or anywhere else."

With a growl of frustration, Juliet spun on her heel and

stalked out, slamming the door behind her hard enough to rattle the windows and make me wince.

I sank back into my chair, hoping my police-phobic sister would take my advice and talk to Thurman. The only times I'd ever gotten involved in solving a murder were when I had no choice. It was dangerous territory. She should know that. All she had to do was look at the narrow escapes I and the people I cared about had had over the past year or so.

If she gave it a minute of thought, my impulsive sister would realize I wanted to keep her safe, not thwart her. No good would come of trying to do Detective Thurman's job. I didn't know what Michelle's motive could possibly be, but he would find out. As for Max, I could understand and even applaud my sister's suspicions. However, I wasn't sure if I was convinced he'd had a part in it, or if I was just hoping he had so we'd all be rid of him.

The bone he continually picked with Delores over things that should have been non-issues kept most of us on edge lately. It seemed he continually ranted about something that had nothing to do with the running of Copper Creek, and could be directly traced to one of his own client's errors. He'd gotten particularly diva-ish since Agnes had bought Rum Runner in January. And Agnes, who seemed to yearn for the status of being a high-level performance-horse owner, had virtually turned into his assistant.

I sighed, rolled my neck and woke up my computer. I had work to finish before I could call it quits for the evening.

Shortly after six the front door opened, and although from my office I couldn't see who entered, I knew immediately the footsteps in the front hall were Paul's. The weariness from the day's battles slipped away, and when he walked through my office door carrying three white plastic grocery bags my stomach growled.

"Chinese okay?"

"Perfect. Pull up a chair. Let's eat here. I still have a bit of work to do before I can go home. How was your day?"

He tipped his head focusing on the scrape on my cheek. "Better than yours, apparently. What happened?"

I related my encounter with Agnes and what I'd heard between Max and Thurman while Paul unpacked the white take-out boxes. As I shared Juliet's whacky ideas about investigating, he pulled out a package of paper plates, utensils, a stack of plastic cups, a short, fat candle, a bottle of wine and a vase with a single rose. My explanation of Juliet's demands petered away as he set the rose in the middle of my desk and lit the candle. The flame grew then flickered briefly while, with a tiny upturn of the corner of his mouth, he opened the wine bottle with the corkscrew from his pocket knife and poured some of the golden liquid into the plastic cups. I moistened my lips and a smile grew.

"White with Chinese, don't you think?" His black-lash-framed blue eyes flicked me a smoldering look that heated my belly and weakened my knees. He picked up both cups, rounded my desk with a saunter that drew my attention directly to the fit of his jeans, and handed me my wine. "Here you go, wife." Before I had a chance to raise the cup to my lips, he leaned and kissed my neck. Every erogenous zone on my body sang the Hallelujah Chorus. To hell with working late.

I ran a slow, appreciative gaze over my spouse's fine form while I sipped the wine. Its sweetness trickled a warm path down my throat. "Thank you, husband."

He took a swallow of his, then put his cup on my desk and turned my chair so my back was to him. Standing behind me, he laid warm hands on my shoulders and with strong, sensitive fingers began to massage my neck. My eyes closed and I melted under his touch.

"You're awfully tight," he said, his voice a low hum.

"I'll be quite loose in a minute." I'm sure I didn't have to tell him. His soft, lingering kiss on my neck told me he understood the double entendre. "Have I told you yet today how happy I am I married you?"

"Um," he said, sliding my sweater off my shoulder. His hand drifted forward to caress my breast. "A couple of times."

I purred at his touch. "Then I should tell you --"

"Can I take some of that food that's getting cold while you two are heating up?"

I spun in my chair knocking into Paul. He staggered and I grabbed at his arm only to be deflected by his grab at my chair back.

I gaped as my sister. "Why the hell didn't you knock? I didn't hear you come in."

She smirked. "Yeah, that doesn't surprise me. You were watching the hunky professor pour wine like he was doing a strip tease."

Paul shifted. I glanced at him in time to see him rub a hand over his mouth, and I straightened my sweater. I didn't see the humor.

"You were going to stay and watch?" I snapped at my sister.

"I was going to stay and eat. You have enough food here for a party." She advanced on the cartons and peeked inside one. "What'd you guys do, decide to elope and use Andrea and Dave as a cover?"

"No." I shot a desperate look at Paul. He shook his head slightly.

"Oh," she said, "so they really did get married and you, just on a whim, decided it looked like a good idea."

"Pretty much," Paul said, then shrugged at my shut-the-hell-up expression.

"I don't get why you didn't tell anybody," Juliet said, opening the package of paper plates and pulling one out. "I, for one, have hurt feelings."

The perfect opening. "That's exactly it. There would be hurt feelings all around, even though our intention was to save everyone a lot of stress and conflict like that nonsense you went through. Now we have to go ahead with the August wedding date as if it was the real deal. I don't know what else we can do, and I'd appreciate it if you'd play along."

She spooned a mound of fried rice onto her plate and opened another container. Paul and I exchanged a hopeful look while we waited for her response.

"I don't know --"

"Juliet!"

She opened another container and considered the contents for a moment before moving to the next. "No, seriously. It seems to me you've been getting things your way an awful lot. You're the perfect Campbell daughter, always doing the smart thing. Successful, mature -- not like me." She laughed, but there was no humor in it. "You know something? I was trying to do all the right stuff planning Eric and my wedding the way everyone wanted --"

"Ha," I said.

"I was doing so to the best of my ability. And then when he cut and ran everyone immediately blamed me. Now you two go and do something Mother will have a screaming fit over and will reduce Aunt Vi to tears and I'm just supposed to suck it up and not point out that Dr. and Mrs. Perfect aren't so perfect after all."

"Well, since you put it that way," I said, "yes."

Juliet's eyes narrowed and a tiny, calculating upturn of her lips -- which I would never call a smile -- worried me.

"You know what? I'm going to do just that. Pretty much. However, my silence, if you want it, has a price."

"This'll be different," I snarled. "I usually don't have a heads up on what you're going to steal from me since you habitually take whatever you want."

"True, but what I have in mind is a little out of my usual scope."

I snorted. Paul raked a hand through his hair and gripped the back of his neck. The addition of a pained squint had me worried. While I'd been standing at the gate, so to speak, trading insults with my sister, he'd probably followed her maze-like thought process and knew where she was going. I studied Juliet with growing suspicion. What new little monster had she become?

Her gaze shifted between Paul and me and a certain smugness joined forces with her calculating expression. "In exchange for me keeping your most damning of secrets, you will investigate Don's murder."

"Okay, we'll do it," Paul said.

# Chapter Ten

Juliet grinned while I struggled to process the words that sounded exactly like my husband, my partner for life, had just jumped the fence and joined forces with the enemy.

I pointed at my sister and spoke to Paul. "Did you actually pay attention to what that person who claims she swims in my gene pool just said? She's *blackmailing* us. And you," I thrust the same finger at him, "just rolled over and gave up."

"I know it's a fine line, but she's not so much blackmailing us as she is using coercion to get what she wants."

"Same freaking thing. God." I emphatically implored the ceiling for some kind of divine intervention.

Juliet pumped an arm and did a little dance. "Whoo-hoo, I got you both when I was originally only trying for the short one! Let's not fight, Dr. and Mrs. Perfect -- whoops, excuse me. That's Dr. Perfect and Ms. Pain-in-the-ass."

Paul turned from his patient observation of my sister to me. "I don't see where we have a lot of choice. Have you got a better idea?"

"Short of murdering my sister? No."

"Well, then." He nodded as if the whole thing had been his idea. "Pack up some food and go home, Juliet. Thea and I have some planning to do."

My effusively happy sister made short work of packing up a good portion of Paul's and my dinner, skipped to her studio to grab her notebook -- her reason for returning in the first place -- and waltzed out the front door with a "report in soon!"

Arms crossed and still steaming, I confronted Paul.

"I'm waiting, start talking."

"Like I said, we didn't have a choice. We had to agree with her. However," he raised a finger and paused like he'd come to an important point in a lecture, "She didn't tell us how long or how hard we had to work at this investigation. In fact, she gave us no requirements whatsoever."

My anger faded. Sly man. I should have guessed. "So we're just paying this investigation lip service?"

"Pretty much. We'll have to do something."

I frowned.

"Hey, a man needs a little adventure in his life."

"Huh." I tightened the hug on my body, drumming my fingers against my ribs.

He stepped closer, unpinioned my arms from their tight cross and repositioned them around his waist. "You love me, admit it. And secretly you're looking forward to snooping around and finding out why Michelle did something so stupid."

I curled a lip. "Funny, I thought you were the one who volunteered to be Sherlock."

"I did. And I will. But you may have an easier time of it. I doubt Sherlock could have done so well if he didn't have Watson doing so much leg-work."

I snorted. He chuckled then turned serious.

"Listen to me. You have been in some grave danger in the

past and I have no intention of allowing anything remotely similar to happen again. We'll put on a show for Juliet and if by some fluke we find something useful, we'll turn it over to Thurman." He shuffled backwards to my chair, dragging me along, sat and, in a couple of deft moves, put me on his lap. "Now come on, don't be mad. I'll bet if you liked the way I poured the wine a little bit ago, you'll really like the way I can dish up the food."

"Oh, you can dish it, all right." I crossed my arms again, but maybe not quite as tightly as before.

He patted my hip, then reached around me for the cartons of food, dragged everything -- including the candle and flower -- closer. "Here." He held an egg roll to my lips. "Let's eat and make up."

I skinny-eyed him and ignored the egg roll.

"Okay then, you can be Sherlock. But you still have to do the leg work." He nudged the egg roll against my teeth.

I took a bite so he wouldn't see the laugh forming. "Fine, Watson."

The sesame chicken, fried rice, broccoli beef, shrimp egg rolls and wine went a long way to restoring my mood to a reasonable state. We packed up what was left over, and got our coats.

"You don't have to stay?" Paul asked.

"I do, but I'm so worn out from all the drama with Juliet and --" I clasped a hand over my mouth.

"What's wrong?"

"Oh, God. Paul, I forgot to tell you I talked to my mother."

He shrugged. "You knew you'd have to, right? If Vi or your sister got to her before you she'd be throwing a fit and charging admission."

"Paul ..." I grabbed his hands. "She wants to talk to your parents and welcome them to the family."

The humor disappeared from his expression. "What did you say?"

"I threatened to cancel the wedding and get married in Las

Vegas."

His lip twitched. "Good one."

"Not so good in the end. I was only able to delay her. You've got four days, at most, to talk your mother down from the top of the tower where she howls like a banshee when she hears my name."

"Four days?"

"At the most. Probably closer to three."

"Christ." He searched his pockets until he found his phone. "I wish I hadn't eaten." He scrolled through his contacts and paused when he found his parents' phone number. His finger hovered over the green icon and his blue eyes met mine with a small wince. "I apologize ahead of time for everything you are about to hear. This has nothing to do with you, and everything to do with my dumb-ass mistake years ago … and them. It has to do with their closed-mindedness, too." He pressed the icon and put his phone to his ear.

I paced to the other side of the room, turned and watched every nuanced blink of his eyes waiting for his conversation to begin. A muscle twitched in his jaw before he launched into a friendly greeting. Voice mail. He'd gotten their voice mail. My dinner settle back into "digest" mode.

He stared at the floor as he spoke. "So, uh, just wanted to say hi. Give my love to everyone, especially Katie and Three."

His ten-year-old niece, Katie, and eight-year-old nephew, Robert the third, adored Paul, much to his brother's annoyance. Paul had given his nephew the nickname "Three" and the kid insisted even his teachers call him by it.

"Talk to you soon. Oh, and uh, Thea and I set a date in August. Hope you can all make it out. The wedding will be here." He disconnected, raised his eyes to mine and swallowed.

My heart thudded against my ribs. "You're not going to leave it at that, are you? You have to call them back."

"They aren't home."

"I'm not going to be able to sleep until you call them back."

He looked at his watch. "It's still early. I'll try again later. Don't worry, I'll talk to them before this weekend. Of course it might be best if your mother just called and dealt with my mother."

"No. Not best. Really really really not best." My shoulders had hitched up to my ears again.

I shut down my computer and secured the file cabinets while Paul checked to make sure the windows and back door were locked. We secured the front door and, since I walked to the office, I got in his car for the short drive home. No sooner had he pulled up in front of our house behind my Ford Escort than his phone rang. He fished it out of his pocket, looked at the caller id and answered without looking in my direction.

"Hi Mom. No, I'm not driving. Just pulled up in front of the house." He turned the key, shutting down the engine, and flicked a glance at me. "Her name is Thea and no, she isn't home yet ... Mom ... yes, I'm sure ... no ... no ...."

Paul winced and held the phone away from his ear. I didn't need bat ears to hear the crying mixed with things like "you're breaking my heart" and "you will not marry that woman." At least she hadn't called me a whore -- yet. I chewed my lip. Paul reached his free hand to me. I took it and hung on.

Finally, Paul took a deep breath. "Enough, Mom. Your opinion has been noted." His voice carried the same stern authority I'd heard him use once with a student who had crossed the line. "Now you're going to hear mine .... No, you will listen. Thea is the woman I will spend the rest of my life with. I love her. You will make an effort to be civil to her, or you won't see me again. Am I making myself clear?"

More of Sophia's sobbing followed. He didn't even need to hold the phone away from his ear for me to hear. Then there was quiet.

"Hi Dad." He sighed, squeezed my hand and repeated

what he'd told his mother -- the part about us getting married in August -- then waited. A low pitched, calm voice reached my ears, but I couldn't quite make out the words. Paul slid a look at me, and shook his head once. "Yes, I told her that, and yes, I meant it. Frankly, I'm having a hard time understanding what the problem is here …. Dad, Jan and I are divorced. We've been divorced for more than fifteen years …. That's not even a consideration … I love her, I'm going to spend the rest of my life with her. We'd like you to come to our wedding, but if you're only coming to be disruptive -- " He released my hand and raked his though his hair. "Right. Fine. I'll talk to you later." He disconnected the call and let his head drop back against the headrest. After a long moment he turned enough to look at me. "I'll give them a day or two then call back."

I touched his face and he turned a bit more to kiss my fingers. "I'm so sorry, Paul."

"Like I said, it's not your fault. I don't know why there is such a problem, but I'm not going to spend any time trying to figure it out. They'll either come to our wedding or they won't. We're already married and there's nothing they can do about it. Now, come on." He unsnapped his seatbelt and opened his door. "Your sister ate most of my dinner. I'm still hungry."

# Chapter Eleven

A sheet of notebook paper taped to my office door fluttered in the breeze when I opened the building's front door early the next morning. I snatched it off, read it and wadded it into a ball. My sister obviously felt she needed to remind me of our deal, and instructed me to "report in" when I went to Copper Creek for my weekly lesson with Uncle Henry. I didn't need this irritation when the situation with Paul's family was far from resolved and my mother was about to waltz right into the middle of it.

He'd harped so much on our morning run about having no reason to worry that I had to believe he didn't believe it himself. I mentioned this to him along with the certainty that unless his family did a convincing one-eighty in their opinion of me, Mother would suss it out. In her opinion it was fine for her to be critical and stir up discontent. After all, she had everyone's best interests in mind. But, woe be to an outsider who did the same thing.

He finally shut up and jogged on ahead of me as if he were annoyed and trying to run off some frustration. Mother had that effect on people.

I needed to talk to Aunt Vi and Delores. My aunt might have some ideas on how to handle my mother. Delores, Paul's aunt, had been married to Sophia's brother for forty plus years, until his death. Surely she had a clue as to how to handle her sister-in-law. I'd stop in her office at Copper Creek before my lesson.

Delores leaned back in her desk chair, shaking her head. "Sophia's always been like a little Jack Russell Terrier, but without the joy. Gets all worked up about things, grabs onto an opinion and won't let go. I expect she'll come around eventually, although it may be that Jan will have to be the one to change her mind and quit mooning over Paul."

"So there's nothing I can do, then."

"Well," my sister said, drawing out the word while she adjusted the sleeves of her blue and green top. She should have adjusted the neckline. It was dipping dangerously low. Delores and I waited. Having claimed center stage, she continued. "You can talk to Jan. Explain she's too late."

I narrowed my eyes at her.

She shrugged. "Tell her she had him once, kicked his butt out of her life for someone else, and no self-respecting guy is going to go back into a situation where he's always wondering when the same shoe is going to kick his butt to the curb a second time."

"I'd say you have a point," Delores said. "However, that logic shouldn't be coming from Thea. Or Paul, for that matter. It'd be like throwing down a challenge."

Juliet's expression turned thoughtful.

"And it shouldn't come from you, either," Delores said. "Someone she trusts has to talk to her."

"Like Paul's sister," I said, and the idea blossomed into a tactic worth pursuing -- if I could get Paul's cooperation.

"Thea." Delores' voice held disapproval.

"Aw, come on," Juliet said. "It'd work, unless his sister is like mine and you have to coerce her into any kind of cooperation." He smile had a certain smug quality to it that worried me. She was getting entirely too pointed in her remarks.

"Leave it," Delores said.

I looked at my watch. I'd already wasted too much time. I needed to get Blackie tacked up for our lesson. I left Delores' office promising to let Paul handle his family, and headed out to the Big Barn where Blackie was stabled.

Michelle's boyfriend Bobby was coming out of Max's office. When he saw me a smile lit his otherwise vacant face.

"Oh, hey, tiny dudette."

I slowed my pace a little. "Hi, Bobby. Done cleaning tack?"

"No, haven't done those yet. Just finished up the saddles and bridles, though."

I stifled a comment about them being the same thing. He'd never remember, anyway. "Good for you. Where are you off to now?"

"Gotta sign-waving gig for that taco restaurant, um, Ring-A-Ding Tacos." He held up a large mound of reinforced fabric in banana yellow. I tipped my head and looked at it. There were even brown stripes.

"That looks like a banana costume."

"Dudette, you are correct." His grin widened. "Makes people look twice. Much better than the taco outfit. Easier to hold the sign, too."

His logic made an odd amount of sense. And I had to hand it to him, the guy worked wherever he could. Of course, he probably had few options. I nodded. "So, how do you like working for Max?"

"Oh, man, the dude's much better now that Dr. Don is out of the picture – sorry, don't mean to disrespect his memory, but Max was like way hyper tense and a real downer to be around."

"So he found another vet already?"

"Yeah, and hey, he hooked up with Dr. Don's partner. How cool is that? He even got ol' Rummy's joints all greased up, just like he wanted. What a name, huh? Rummy. Makes him sound all, you know," Bobby crossed his eyes and staggered, then laughed.

Don's partner Rick was a nice enough guy and probably a good vet, but he didn't have Don's depth of knowledge. They always seemed like an odd pairing to me. The younger man's manner around the horses had always struck me as tense. I wondered if he even liked them.

"Hey, can I bum a ride into town? If you're going that way, anyways."

"Sorry, I just got here."

"No worries. Oh yeah, thanks for lending a hand to spring Michelle. Juliet says your old man's helping out, too. Awesome."

"Sure, no problem." I smiled, kind of. Juliet was broadcasting to the world that I was investigating Don's death. Great. Just flipping great. There was an irate call from Detective Thurman in my future.

Juliet strolled up while I was doing up the last of the buckles on Blackie's bridle. His low huffle alerted me to her presence. My horse loves my sister. I'm not sure why, but you can see it in his soft expression whenever she's in his vicinity. She patted his forehead, but otherwise directed her attention to me.

"Have you learned anything so far?" she asked in a stage whisper.

"Yes."

Her eyes lit up.

"I've learned you should keep your big mouth shut. Quit telling people like Bobby I'm investigating – although now that he knows, I expect the entire county will find out -- and for God's sake quit making 'oblique' references to our 'deal'. People will put two and two together and hit four right on the head."

She rolled her eyes. "Fine. I just thought you could use some help."

"I don't need help. Especially from Bobby." I led Blackie out of the grooming stall, past my sister and to the arena.

A good while later Uncle Henry's ever patient voice came through the headset I wore.

"Renvers, Thea – not travers. And allow him to go forward to your hand. You're carrying unnecessary tension in your back."

The fact I'd gotten the command for haunches-out confused with haunches-in attested to the fact that I was paying only half attention to my lesson. I grimaced, straightened Blackie from my error, half-halted and made an effort to release the knot between my shoulder blades. With the restriction telegraphing from my arms now eased, his shoulders lifted and his trot softened. I asked for the correct movement -- the haunches-out, or renvers -- and, finally properly balanced and unencumbered by my tension, my horse made the change easily.

"Good. Shoulders-in at B," Uncle Henry said.

As Blackie and I approached the midpoint of the arena's long side I stretched a little taller and exhaled. After a step of straightness I switched my position to that of shoulders-in, and visualized the perfection of what I expected. There was no neck bobble, only an improvement in the cadence of the trot as Blackie stepped toward the middle of his body with his inside hind leg. I smiled. This was a trot I could sit all day: soft, yet with a powerful swing.

"Good. Better. Walk at C," Uncle Henry said.

I straightened my horse before the corner, and transitioned

to walk by the midpoint of the arena's short side.

"It's taken you …" he consulted the clock on the arena wall, "forty minutes to get your head in the game. That's what they say these days, isn't it?"

I nodded and let my reins slide through my fingers. Blackie stretched his neck out, taking up the slack. I made a quick decision to tell him about Paul's family, as opposed to Juliet's plea to play detective. He'd only want to know why I didn't just shut her down. Besides, he'd find out about the Hudson family objections to me fairly soon anyway, since I intended to seek Aunt Vi's advice.

I turned Blackie toward my uncle and halted when we were close enough to carry on a quiet conversation.

"Sorry," I said. "We told Paul's family last night that we'd set a date and let's just say they weren't thrilled."

Uncle Henry's brow knotted. "Haven't they known for some time now you two were engaged?"

"Yes, but I think they were hoping Paul would come to his senses."

One hand rested on his hip while he covered a severe frown with the other. After a couple of beats he spoke. "What's the objection?"

I took a deep breath and gave him the short version of how Paul's family, claiming religious reasons, thought Paul's divorce from Jan was meaningless.

"Are you thinking Paul will change his mind? Is that why you've been distracted?"

"No! Of course not. It's just that Mother is hell-bent on calling them and welcoming them to the family and she doesn't know …."

One corner of my uncle's mouth turned up. "Ah. You haven't worked up the nerve to tell her they're opposed to the marriage."

"Or that Paul's mother keeps forgetting my name and calling me 'that heathen' and 'that whore.'".

The half smile made a full transition to a frown. "That's

bloody rude." He thought for a moment. "Maybe Vi will have a different suggestion, but I think you'll do best to stay out of the turmoil -- let Paul handle it. If they come to your wedding, fine. If they don't, I expect they'll reconcile themselves to it later."

"What about Mother?"

His eyes twinkled, which surprised me. "Give her a bit of a heads up, enough so she won't be blindsided. Somehow I don't believe Paul's mum will take on Rebecca."

He had a point.

However, the nervous twisting in my gut was still there.

Uncle Henry patted Blackie's shoulder and my horse curved his long dark neck and rubbed his eye against my uncle's shoulder. "Why don't you and Paul come for dinner tonight? Take this big fellow back to his stall and I'll give Vi a call." He patted my knee in much the same manner he'd patted my horse. "You're getting some running in these days, I understand."

I managed a smile. "Paul's idea. He says I'll need it for stamina when I go to the horse shows."

"He's right. Keep it up. We'll work something out with his family. Try not to worry."

I agreed to try, and rode Blackie back to the barn contemplating different approaches to tell Paul I'd just unloaded his family's bad behavior onto my uncle and aunt. Blackie halted of his own accord outside the big open doorway to the barn, looked briefly over his shoulder at me and sighed, clanking his bits together. I dropped my stirrups and leaned forward to swing a leg over Blackie's back to dismount. Unexpectedly, he pinned his ears and skittered sideways a couple of steps. I grabbed mane.

"Whoa. Hey now, I can get off without your help."

"My fault, I'm afraid. I do apologize," said a male voice from behind me.

I turned to look. Agnes Fulton's husband Bart, decked out in tweed and ascot with his tan Burberry trench coat flapping open, stood near where Blackie's hindquarters had been, a hand frozen in mid-reach. He'd walked up behind a horse without announcing his presence and had meant to pat his butt. Unbelievable.

"You can get yourself kicked doing that."

Bart's lips tightened briefly before he donned what could have been a contrite smile and bowed slightly in that odd, courtly manner of his. If he'd click the heels of his polished brown loafers together I wouldn't have been surprised. "You're right, of course. Forgive me."

Blackie shook his head, rattling his bridle. I slid off his back. "No problem. For your own safety you should approach a horse's shoulder -- especially one you don't know." I ran my stirrup up, thinking he was simply passing by.

"Say, Miss Campbell -- it is Campbell, isn't it?"

I shot him a look, before deciding he was just being certain he'd remembered my name and hadn't heard a "rumor" I'd gotten married. "Yes."

"I was wondering if I might procure Mrs. Paalmann's phone number from you. Last week she and I had discussed an investment opportunity in a social welfare group I manage. She said she'd get back to me, but I haven't heard from her yet. I'd like to keep the situation as simple as possible."

Right. "How about I take your card and let her know you were asking about her when she gets back from her trip."

"She's on vacation?"

"Yes."

"I had no idea. She would be pleased to know that for a fraction of what her vacation costs she could sponsor a deserving child at our camp. We do excellent work with helping the children learn how to manage their special challenges, and we have a strong lobby locally and at the state level where important decisions are made."

I searched for some kind of appropriate response before I nodded in a vague kind of way. "Fascinating."

He nodded like a salute before executing his trademark

almost-bow. "Thank you for looking out for my well-being, Miss Campbell."

"Sure thing," I said.

Evidently satisfied he'd completed his task, he turned and left, passing close enough to Blackie's back end to be a problem if my horse decided to kick. He didn't, though, but swung his tail instead, swatting Bart across the back. I turned a narrow look on Blackie. He clanked his bits around with his tongue and blew a sneeze before turning an inquiring, liquid brown gaze on me. I led him into the barn.

"You're not funny," I whispered to him.

"Sure he is," Juliet said.

I looked under Blackie's neck. My sister leaned against a stall door, one blue jeaned and booted leg crossed over the other, thumbs hooked in her front pockets.

"That Bartie Fulton is one weird dude. You'd think he was rehearsing every day to meet the queen."

I couldn't disagree with her. His mannerisms struck me as peculiarly formal, but I'd also seen people positively preen over his deference to them. I lead Blackie down the aisle to the grooming stall where I'd left his blanket and brushes earlier. "I have to assume you're here to talk about something other than Bart," I said keeping my voice low.

Juliet scampered around Blackie, trusting him not to bolt or kick. I took a breath to warn her of what she was doing, but Blackie was watching her with adoration in his eyes. I bagged the lecture.

"So what can I do to help?" she whispered.

I should have guessed. "Nothing. Yet." I added the qualifier to appease her in case she felt the need to exert more persuasion. "I'll let you know. Just keep your ears open. I'm in the information gathering stage right now." That had a nice ring to it, so I added, "everyone's a suspect." I slid Blackie's bridle off and replaced it with his halter.

She nodded, wisely. "Do you want me to come over tonight?"

No. "Give me a couple of days."

"No prob. I'm going to be working on my class project in my studio later, so don't get all freaked out if you see the light on."

"No prob," I said, and watched her stride away back toward the office, the handkerchief hem of her blue and green top swinging rhythmically across her butt. It had to be one of her own creations. It screamed carefree, sexy and "Juliet."

I pulled Blackie's saddle off and took a brush to his coat to scrub out the saddle mark.

"Hey, Thea." It was Max.

Wasn't I the popular girl in school today. Everybody wanted to talk to me. I slid a glance at him, then had to look again. His hair was mussed up. Even riding without a helmet didn't make him look like he'd just rolled out of bed. "Hi Max. How's it going?"

"Good. Say, you haven't seen Bart, have you?" He stuffed his hands in his riding parka's pockets and rocked nervously on his booted feet.

Okay, I was feeling like the *friend* of the popular girl in school. "Yeah, actually. He went that way." I pointed with the body brush.

"Thanks." He walked quickly back toward his tack room/office -- the opposite direction I'd indicated.

I took a breath to correct him, but he was so rushed I watched instead, puzzled. He didn't go into his office, but opened the door and motioned for someone to come out. Agnes, dressed in black slacks and spiky red heels, dashed out, her head down while she zipped her jacket. The two of them left the barn together.

"Well, that's a surprise," I said to Blackie. "I guess the rumors were right."

He swiveled his ears and turned his head toward me as much as the cross-ties allowed.

"I didn't believe the rumors because I never figured her for a cougar. And did you know I used to think he was gay?"

Blackie blew a long breath and tossed his head.

"Don't be so smug. You're here twenty-four seven. I'm not."

I wasn't so immersed in my clients' taxes that I missed the creak of the front door opening and the heavier-than-Juliet's footsteps in the hallway. My heart did a happy jump and I followed suit by abandoning my desk. I knew it was Paul even before my office door opened.

"Hey, how's my ...." He closed the door behind him and scanned the room. "Wife."

I scampered over, slid my arms under his sport coat and hugged an "ooof" out of him. "So much better now that my husband is here."

"Bad day?" he asked and kissed me.

"No," I stood on my toes for another. "Fine day. Just got better."

He chuckled and put a little more passion into the next kiss. I sighed when it ended and released him, wrinkling my nose with my next inhale. A damp wool smell had replaced the scent of the cologne he'd splashed on this morning. Under the bright over-head light his dark hair sparkled with rain drops.

"You're wet."

"Yeah, just started coming down hard as I drove into town. I had to park a block away. Are you ready to go home, or do you have more to do?"

"A bit more."

"Do you want me to stay or shall I go home and start dinner?"

How many guys would make that offer? He was so sweet. And he so wasn't going to like the fact that our invitation to have dinner with my aunt and uncle was because I couldn't keep my mouth shut. I winced. "We can go now, actually. In fact, I'd rather. We're going to Aunt Vi and Uncle Henry's."

He raised an eyebrow. "You don't look happy. How

come?"

I moved his tie aside, ran a finger down the button placket on his shirt and grimaced. "I told Uncle Henry your family wasn't very happy about our wedding." In slightly more detail.

"Ah." He waited, the eyebrow remained quirked, and there was a telltale tightening around his eyes.

"I was kind of distracted at my lesson today," I said, evaluating the tension in his expression to determine how much more I needed to explain. "So, I figured it was better I tell him about that than trying to explain why I was cooperating with Juliet. He suggested we come to dinner and discuss it with Aunt Vi."

He nodded, shifting his gaze past the top of my head. "I see."

I stopped myself on the verge of a pout. What was wrong with me? I never pussy-footed around him. "You're mad."

"No, I'm not." Now something off to my right required his visual inspection. "I just don't know why you had to tell Henry something that would only create more tension when our families finally get together."

"I only told him there were religious reasons your parents wouldn't accept your divorce." Damn. I did it again. Pussyfooted. But no way was I fixing my error by telling him I'd also talked the situation over with Delores … and Juliet.

"Humph." He fixed his eyes on my shoulder. "Okay. We'll smooth things out over dinner. I want to lose the tie. I'll come back and pick you up." He gave me a quick kiss and left in what I'd call a hurry.

I remained where he'd left me, sifting through our conversation. Hadn't I said we could leave now? And, "lose the tie?" What was that all about? He'd normally pull it off and stuff it in his jacket pocket or briefcase. Something was up. I returned to my desk, fairly certain I'd find out later.

Less than fifteen minutes later the front door opened. Clompy and lighter-than-Paul's footsteps hurried to my office door. I barely had time to register Juliet as the creator of the noise before the door flew open. My sister stood in the doorway shaking out her long curls, motorcycle helmet in hand. She'd already unzipped her rain-suit.

"Whew. It's really coming down out there."

"You're dripping all over my floor. Do you mind?"

She backed a step into the hallway, dropped her helmet and wiggled out of the wet rain gear. Much to my amazement she wore a pink, flouncy skirt and short, orange jacket with a stylish, off-center zipper underneath it all.

"Sorry." She pulled her last foot out of the pants leg, kicked the wet mass away from her then retrieved the black high-top sneaker she'd lost in the heap, "So, any more information?"

"No." Then I thought better of shutting her down. Who knew what she'd do? "Except that Max and Agnes seem to have something going on and barely escaped an encounter with Bart."

Juliet's eyes widened and she grinned. "No shit? Bart's finally on to them? What a hoot."

I shrugged. "I'm not sure it's of any use in solving the case." Again, I thought better of my dismissal. "I never figured Agnes for someone who'd play around. Guess I was wrong. Maybe this will somehow play into figuring things out."

"Max is an opportunist. I told you that. And a cheapskate. Didn't realize how cheap until after I dated him. Do you know he's never paid Delores directly for his office space or arena fees? I've never seen a check with his name on it cross my desk. He has all his clients write a separate check every month to Copper Creek for shit he should pay for directly. It's a bookkeeping nightmare."

The irony of my sister and I having something in common didn't escape me. Neither did Max's peculiar way to do business, but it didn't make him a criminal. I couldn't resist a poke at my sister's logic. "Is that why you think I should investigate Max, because he's cheap and makes more work for you?"

"No, of course not." She bent and scooped up her helmet and wet rain suit. "I've got to get working on my class project."

"Aren't you going to Aunt Vi's for dinner?" *Please say "no."*

"Nope, gotta work." She disappeared from my line of sight, and her key rattled in the lock to her studio.

Thank God she was busy. I didn't want to talk about Paul's family in front of her, like I'd already done. She'd let something not-so-subtle slip, again, about our marriage just to add to the discussion and our secret would be a secret no longer. I didn't know how we were going to keep her mouth shut for five months. We needed to move the wedding up.

In a moment the radio was on and blaring something unmusical I could barely stand. I got up to insist she turn it down, but her door closed muffling the noise.

Moments after I went back to work, flipping through my client's poorly organized box of paperwork for legitimate deductions, the front door opened again, letting a cold, damp gust of wind through my still opened office door. It had to be Paul, although the footsteps coming my way seemed less sure than what I expected of him. When they ceased in my doorway I looked up from my work. The darkly handsome, blue jeaned and leather-jacketed man standing framed by the dim hallway lighting was not Paul, but Eric Fuentes, my sister's ex-fiancé.

Eric: the man who'd been missing for the last two and a half months.

Shock stopped my breath and I stood abruptly, dropping the box of receipts on the floor and sending my chair rolling backwards at a rate rapid enough to crash loudly into the metal filing cabinets. He winced, pressing his lips together. All I could do was stare. He looked weary, damp and bedraggled, but as movie-star-drool-worthy as he always had – maybe more so, since he wore misery with the same effect some men wear a good haircut and expensive cologne. He also appeared apprehensive, his gaze taking in my spilled receipts for a fraction of a moment before returning to my face, as if he was trying to determine how my astonishment was going to play out.

Poor Eric --

Oh lord, if I wanted to run and comfort him with just one look, my sister was surely doomed. She'd be throwing herself into his arms and not letting go.

He cleared his throat. "Where --"

With zero hesitation, my arm flung sideways, a finger pointing toward Juliet's studio.

He ducked his head briefly, then looked up with a more determined expression on his face. "Thanks. And I'm sorry." He turned and disappeared.

I couldn't move. Or breathe.

His soft knock on her studio door was barely audible, but she obviously heard it.

"I'll turn it down!" she shouted, annoyed and obviously believing it was me.

He knocked again.

"Good-freaking-grief, Thea. Turn the round thing and push. It's not locked."

The floor boards creaked under her stomp and the door complained as she yanked it open. Then nothing. I half expected to hear the thud of her body hitting the floor, but there was nothing. Not a sound. For a very long time. Then ....

"What do you want?" The threat in her tone was unmistakable and unrooted me from where I stood. If she was going to go after him with a pair of scissors I should probably do something to stop her. I crept across the room and hid behind my open door, pressing my eye to the crack by the hinges. All I could see was Eric's shoulder. That was probably enough.

"Juliet," Eric said.

The floor creaked and he disappeared from my sight.

"Don't touch me."

"I'm sorry."

"Really? That's rich."

"I need to apologize, to explain to you --"

"You left me without so much as a 'go to hell'. There's nothing to explain."

"There is, please --"

She cut him off with a harsh laugh that ended too high pitched. I made a move to leave my hiding place and rush to her aid, push Eric out the front door if necessary, but her determined growl stopped me.

"Do not for one minute think you can waltz back into my life and mend everything with an 'I'm sorry.' I have a life, and you're not part of it anymore. Get out."

"Juliet, please, can we talk?"

"More than this? Absolutely not. Get out. I mean it."

"I still love you."

"And I'm not a fool. You've got 'Juliet's broken heart and smashed dreams' written all over you and I've got too much self-respect to let you have at it again. Get out."

Her studio door slammed. I wanted to cheer for my sister's gutsy response, but hadn't heard Eric leave. After a pause the floor creaked under his footsteps as he retreated to the front door.

I waited until it closed then peaked into the hallway to be sure he'd actually left. Empty. I took the couple of steps to Juliet's door and tried the knob. Locked. I knocked.

"Go away."

"It's me. Eric is gone."

"Go away."

I dropped my forehead against the door. "Juliet, please. Let me in."

"No. I need to be alone right now."

"Are you okay?"

She stomped to the door and flung it open. Tears washed

down her face and her nose was red. "No. I'm not okay. That's a stupid question." She spun to walk away, but I grabbed her arm. She held herself together for half a beat and then crumpled, sobbing. I wrapped my arms around her, my heart breaking into tiny pieces.

I doubt she felt the cool breeze from the front door opening, but I did. I craned to see who had just come in, half expecting Eric again, but it was Paul. He stayed in the studio's doorway, his expression wary.

"So that was Eric I saw," he said.

I nodded.

Juliet pulled away from me and looked up, scrubbing at her eyes and sniffing. "What's wrong with you men?"

Paul's eyes widened and he licked his lips. "Well, for starters, we're all short-sighted, self-centered pigs with shit for brains. But in our defense it's not because we don't mean well."

I held down a smile.

"You're an asshole, Paul," my sister snapped. "You're no more sincere than Eric."

I had to disagree. They were both sincere. However, that wasn't a debate I wanted to start at the moment.

Paul caught my gaze. "Maybe I should wait for you in the car?"

I nodded. As he retreated I turned my attention to my sister. "Come to Aunt Vi and Uncle Henry's with us for dinner. You know she always makes enough."

"No ...." She looked over her work table, littered with fabric, sheets of paper and pattern pieces. "I have so much to do ...."

"You need to come with us. Have something to eat, unload on Aunt Vi, you know she'll make you feel better. Then come back and work. It can't go well when you're this upset."

"I'm not upset."

"Of course you're not. You're doing a good job of handling it, though. Anyone else would be a wreck." I rubbed her back, urging her along to where she'd hung her jacket then helped her into it.

"I don't think I should go," she said, zipping it up.

"Okay, that's fine. Where's your purse. There it is." I snagged it from under her work table and handed it off. "Here you go. I'll lock up."

I grabbed my coat, purse and keys, locked the doors and led her to where Paul waited in his car. I opened the back door and she climbed in.

"Oh, hi Paul," she said, as if she hadn't just lambasted him. "Are you ever an inconsiderate jerk?"

He glanced into the rearview mirror. "Frequently. I don't know how Thea puts up with me. Guess I'm just lucky she's got a forgiving nature."

"Huh," Juliet said. She rested her head against the window and stared out. I wasn't sure if it was tears running down her face or shadows from the rain streaming down the window.

"I called Vi and told her to expect three," Paul said to me in a low tone.

"Good."

"You and I have to talk. As soon as possible. Before we answer any of their questions about my family."

# Chapter Twelve

Dinner was ready when we arrived, but Juliet broke into fresh sobs when she saw Aunt Vi and, obviously because Paul had told her why to "expect three," Aunt Vi had tea ready. She sat Juliet down at her big kitchen table to nurse her into coherence while Paul and I went to the living room with Uncle Henry.

"I gather you saw Eric," Uncle Henry said, pouring us each a glass of wine.

"He stopped by my office. I didn't get a chance to talk to him, though."

Paul took two of the glasses and handed me one. "You spoke with him, Henry? I only saw him leaving Thea's building. Surprised the heck out of me."

My uncle took a slow sip from his glass, and nodded. "He stopped here before he went to find Juliet."

Oh, so that's how he knew where she was. "Had he been to see Delores?"

"No, I think he wanted to go later, and talk to Miguel and Maria at the same time."

"Makes sense," Paul said, although it didn't to me. Must be a guy thing. "Did he tell you where he'd been?"

"Not precisely," my uncle said. "I was more interested in why he left in January."

Count me in on that one. "What did he say?"

"Apparently, the reality of living a married life was hitting home for him --"

"What do you mean?" That was ominous and gave me more than a little pause. Had I failed to consider something important in my own decision making?

"Providing for his wife, children -- when they came along -- the financial issues, mostly. He was going to school part time, following a dream while working full time at a job that didn't pay him all that much -- or as much as he would need if he was married. I'm afraid your sister's little trick of telling your mother and father he was well off backfired. They expected him to perform at a level he couldn't finance. Juliet was buying into it -- or so he thought -- and in the end, he couldn't bear up under the pressure."

Paul nodded like he understood, which concerned me. He'd need to explain to me later. I was still confused on a point with Eric, though.

"Why didn't he say something?"

"I'll bet he did, as best he could, but the people who mattered didn't listen," Paul said.

Uncle Henry nodded. I didn't.

"What do you mean, 'as best he could'?" Were men really so obtuse?

"Henry," Aunt Vi called from the kitchen. "I could use you here for a minute."

"Excuse me," my uncle said and gave Paul a brief pat on the shoulder.

Paul sighed, and scratched the back of his head. "He probably dug his heels in on a number of issues without explaining in much detail. Plus, I'm guessing he saw the gap between what was being expected of him and what he was capable of getting wider and wider. Therefore, the likelihood of people's opinions of him as a husband, father, and provider would be diving right into that gap as well. Take into consideration his background, where respect from his family and friends is important, and you can understand his difficulty. He wanted Juliet to see how impossible the situation was for him. Probably couldn't understand why she didn't."

"I think she did, but just handled it differently. My mother sure didn't help, did she?" I sipped my wine, contemplating his insight into Eric. Now mildly worried, I studied my husband. "So is this man-as-provider-thing just as important to you, too? You know, you don't make that much more than me right now and, with my business growing, that's bound to change eventually --"

The sudden scowl on his face as he glanced toward the kitchen derailed my train of thought. He leaned closer to me, his expression intense. "Don't bring up my family." His voice was a bare whisper.

"That's why we're here. Remember?"

"Just don't. I'll explain later."

Aunt Vi bustled into the dining room carrying a platter of carved, roast chicken. "Let's eat, dears. If we wait any longer this will all be dried out, and the world is so much easier to deal with when there's food in one's tummy. Isn't that right, Juliet?"

My sister emerged from the kitchen with a bowl of veggies and put them on the table.

"I suppose."

"Of course it is. Come along Henry, and bring those potatoes with you."

The chat at the table was circumspect and couldn't seem to find the right balance between happy and otherwise until my uncle began discussing Blackie's training schedule to prepare him for our first show of the season. He wanted us to show at Prix St. Georges level, the first of the FEI, or international, levels. This scared me a bit. Yes, we'd done well at Fourth Level, but he was talking about going up against bigger fish in a bigger pond. I was okay with the small pond scenario. Certainly, Blackie was capable, but I didn't have a lot of confidence in my ability to pull off an entire FEI test. Paul contributed his ideas to help, which mostly had to do with accompanying him on his morning runs so I'd be fit enough. Aunt Vi reminded me to have confidence in my horse. It was a good diversionary discussion for everyone but Juliet, apparently. When the laughter died down from my horrified look at Paul's suggestion to imagine the judge naked, Juliet sighed deeply.

"It's Mother's fault. I only ever wanted a small, intimate wedding like Thea and Paul."

Paul and I darted panicked looks at each other.

"Is that what you two are planning?" Aunt Vi asked, with a shrewd, assessing look across the rim of her tea cup, first at me and then Paul.

"Um, well, yes actually. I think that's what we want, isn't it, sweetheart?" I said.

"Right. Right. The smaller the better." He laughed a little, high-pitched noise. I could have thumped him one.

"Well, not huge, anyway," I said feeling a flush creep up my cheeks.

"But small," Paul said and reaching over, he grabbed my hand and squeezed it painfully.

A hint. An obvious, clumsy hint. "Right." I smiled at him and then my aunt. "Small."

"In fact, we were thinking about moving it up a bit from August." He nodded encouragement at me.

"Oh, right!" I laughed, sort of. Not a totally bad idea since my sister was having so much trouble keeping her mouth shut. "We were thinking, you know, maybe July --"

"April," Paul said, simultaneously.

"Or June, after the show," I said, appalled.

"April would be better," he said, with an intense look.

"I think we need to talk about this," I said, through gritted teeth.

"Yes," Aunt Vi said, setting her teacup carefully in its saucer. "I really think you should. Does this have something to do with Paul's family? Henry said --"

I shook my head as subtly as I could then added a couple of jerky nods toward Juliet. Aunt Vi's rosebud lips compressed to nothing and she skinny-eyed me. There was little doubt she'd corner me later. If I let her.

We drove in tense silence back to my office to drop Juliet off. She slid out of the back seat, started to close the door, then changed her mind.

"By the way, you guys, thanks to your little nervous Nellie act over dinner, Aunt Vi now thinks Thea's got a bun in the oven. She mentioned it just before I went out to the car, and she wants me to find out for certain. After all, we're family and can support one another through a crisis." She slammed the door and strode up the walk.

Not a single word found its way out of my gaping mouth. What an ever-increasing, complicated, knotted mess we were creating.

Paul waited until the light went on in her studio before putting the car in gear. He hadn't said a word, either. Probably because he was trying to figure out how this was not his fault.

I glared at him for the three remaining blocks home, got out of the car before he turned it off and stalked into the house. I yanked off my jacket and threw it and my purse onto a living room chair just as he came inside.

"What in God's name are you trying to do? Have you completely lost your mind? Dammit, Paul, you'd better have some kind of decent explanation because I'm going to have more than a little trouble straightening out what is rapidly becoming a mountain range of misconceptions, pardon the pun, thanks to you and my ever-so-helpful sister."

"Thea --"

"I'm not done yet." I slammed my fists onto my hips. "I was just drawing another breath so I can continue without passing out from lack of oxygen. How the hell am I supposed to investigate Don's death, so my sister will keep her mouth shut, while simultaneously dealing with Eric being back and obviously wanting Juliet -- which in case you didn't notice makes her an unstable, blabbering fool -- plus my Mother, wedding-planner-in-absentia, and now Aunt Vi who, thanks to you, thinks I'm pregnant, *plus* your family who wants nothing to do with me and will likely boycott our wedding and drive my mother to unusual lengths to convince them of the error of their ways? Huh? Answer me that." Advancing on him, I poked his chest with my finger. Man, I was so glad I'd gotten over that pussy-footing crap.

"Thea."

He didn't look or sound the least bit contrite, which pissed me off further. "Oh, and let's not forget the horseshow Uncle Henry wants me to go to in Oregon in June. I'm supposed to travel, with my horse, to a strange place and do something that scares the crap out of me? And don't you dare even tell me not to worry about that."

"Thea ...." He waited for a moment, hands slid into his back pockets, while I panted, catching my breath. "Are you done?"

I crossed my arms. "Probably not, but go ahead. I'll interrupt if the need arises."

His nostrils flared a bit like he'd gotten a whiff of milk just gone bad. "You're not going to like this."

I threw my arms in the air and paced a couple more steps away from him. He was still wearing the same nauseous expression when I faced him again with crossed arms. "Well, don't keep me in suspense."

"The phone call today, this evening, that I told you about?"

"Yeah?"

"My father said he's coming out to stop our wedding."

"Little late for that. Let them come."

"I'd rather not. He's bringing Jan and --"

"Holy Mother of God. Doesn't she ever give the fuck up? Does she realize -- well, of course not. Shit."

"Sit down. And watch your mouth. You sound like me."

I sneered and dropped ungracefully onto the sofa. "Yes, your royal husband-ness."

He should have sneered back at me. That he didn't was worrisome.

"My father is planning on bringing Jan and my alleged son."

I drew a breath to say something, but either the breath wasn't enough or the words weren't showing up for duty. A wrecking ball was making multiple passes through my life and there was nothing I could do but watch the carnage. I blinked and tried to focus on Paul so I wouldn't tip over. He sat next to me and put his hand on the back of my neck forcing my head toward my lap.

"Put your head between your knees before you pass out," he said, with a gentleness that was nearly lost in the ringing of my ears. "First, I've known about this for approximately two and a half hours longer than you, so while I'm still in shock, I've also had a bit of time to do some math. Jan's boy isn't mine. I don't know whose he is, but he just turned fifteen and that's not even close to the timing of when we were together last."

I turned my head without lifting it and trained one eye on the man who was a constant, unnerving, surprise to me. "Then why are they saying he's your son? I thought Jan got married to someone else after she dumped you. I'd think whoever that was would be the father."

"Don't think I didn't mention that very fact. The boy's

conception coincides approximately with an instance of me setting eyes on her and saying hello in passing. Since her father and mine are in practice together, that has happened fairly frequently. Last time I checked, however, it was insufficient contact required for pregnancy. Nevertheless, my father is dead set on heading out here just as soon as the boy is out of school in June to make me 'do the right thing'."

I struggled to sit up and finally had to take his hand off my neck to accomplish it. I sank back against the cushions and exhaled. My head only spun a tiny bit. "No wonder you pushed for April. You didn't have to do it in front of my aunt and uncle, though."

"No, sorry. I panicked."

I snorted a laugh. Paul eased back, propped his feet on the coffee table and wrapped an arm around me.

"Maybe we should forget trying to keep our marriage a secret and tell everyone what we did and forget about the second wedding entirely," he said, a little too upbeat.

A bit of panic of my own zinged its way to my fingertips as visions of my mother arriving on my doorstep with blood in her eye, my aunt crying and my uncle cutting me off from lessons for betraying all the love and trust they'd showered me with through the years swam through my mind. I put my head back between my knees. "No."

Paul patted my back for a moment. "Then we have to arrange our second wedding as soon as possible."

Some tension left my shoulders and I sat up again and sagged against his side. "It's probably all for the best, anyway. Juliet will never be able to keep her mouth shut, and I'm not at all certain I could find any information that might help to clear Michelle. I hope Aunt Vi doesn't tell Mother we're moving the date. I'll never hear the end of it."

"Ask her to keep it under wraps. First thing in the morning -- although I'll bet if she thinks you're pregnant, running to your mother won't be the first thing she does. She'd let you do it." He hugged me and kissed the side of my head. "As far as

Juliet is concerned, I think we should still make an effort -- just to keep up appearances."

"I suppose." I told him about Max and Agnes, and how Juliet was pushing me to investigate Max.

"Let's find out who else has access to all those drugs. Don's office is still open during regular business hours, right?"

"Yeah, I'll bet his partner Rick is hopping like mad to cover all the appointments. I can go in and chat with Willa. She's the office person. She might have an idea or two."

Paul nodded. "Don't give her the third degree, just get a bit chatty -- mention it must be difficult to get work done when you're a one-person office and have clients popping in and out all the time. That sort of thing."

"Don't worry, I'm not always straightforward." I patted his thigh and let my hand linger slightly higher where I knew I'd get his attention. "I know how to be artful."

He nestled me closer, breathing a rumbled chuckle into my ear. "I'm quite aware of that talent. It's the talking to potentially guilty parties I'm cautioning you about."

I woke up shortly after two in the morning, freezing, with the bed sheet twisted around my leg, the blankets on the floor and the pillows nowhere to be found. I liberated myself from the sheet, careful not to wake Paul, who laid spread eagle, in all his glory on his back, taking up most of the mattress, and tip-toed around the bedroom gathering blankets and pillows, trying not to trip over shoes and piles of discarded clothes. I crawled back into bed, plumped a pillow then covered myself and part of Paul with the blanket. Then I stared into the darkness wondering what in the hell I was going to do.

How was I going to keep my mother from calling Paul's family, how was I going to throw a wedding together in less than a month and how was I going to investigate Don's death?

And then I thought about this young boy, Paul's alleged son, who was being forced forward into a mess that was none of his making. I felt sorry for him. He didn't deserve whatever drama was being foisted on him, and I had to imagine he was none too keen on any of it.

First things first. Paul and I needed to plan a strategy. I needed help and that would entail pulling in some trustworthy people who could help me out. That would be Andrea. Did I care that Aunt Vi thought I was pregnant? No, it likely distracted her from coming up with any other theories, so I'd just dodge any questions about why I wanted to keep the April wedding date from Mother and let her assume what she wanted. We all knew Mother would be moving back in with Aunt Vi and Uncle Henry to oversee wedding plans the minute she found out about the April date. It was a given that she'd drive everyone nuts like she had when she took care of Aunt Vi as she recovered from her broken wrist. Adding any warning to Aunt Vi about a potential war if Mother learned about Paul or his family was overkill.

Of course someone else might tell Mother, since she had so many friends still living in Snohomish. That meant no one at all could know about the new date until the last minute. Then, even if Mother did call Paul's family, they probably wouldn't have time to pull the alleged son out of school, descend upon Snohomish and become front-page news. Disaster could be averted by precise timing.

The thought of disaster brought me to Eric. With him back in town, Juliet may (hopefully) be sufficiently distracted to pose no problem for us, which brought me to her "deal."

Did I want whoever killed Don brought to justice? Definitely. And I definitely thought Michelle was guilty, although it was probably an accident and should be treated as such. I'd have to dig up enough evidence to show it wasn't premeditated and hand it over to Detective Thurman in as timely a manner as possible.

In a nutshell, with the exception of begging Aunt Vi to keep the new date under wraps, I was putting off a bunch of people and focusing on the investigation. That would work – provided I could deal with Mother's harping about getting things lined up for August.

I pulled the covers over my head. The only solution would be to never ever again answer my phone.

Paul shifted to his side and felt around until he discovered the lump that was me, hiding in a blanket.

"There you are." He groped under the warmth, pulled me closer and threw a leg over me. "Go to sleep, wife, and quit muttering. We'll talk about it in the morning."

I snuggled close, pressing my face into his neck, breathed in his warm scent and thanked God for the comfort of his naked body pressed against mine. He belonged to me, no one could change that. So why did I feel the tiniest twinge of fear that he'd be snatched away?

We did talk in the morning, or he did. He paused in detailing his plan when he took my coffee mug out of my hand to fill it up again.

I laid my head on my arm on the kitchen table. His silence lulled my eyelids into a more restful position and my mind wandered toward that fuzzy, half-conscious state right before sleep. A thump near my head opened my eyes with a start. My stoneware mug sat within a couple of inches of my nose, radiating heat.

"You shouldn't have stayed awake worrying last night," he said.

I sat up, wrapped my hands around the mug and stared at it. "I had to work on a plan."

"You were worrying. If you'd slept, you'd be arguing with me instead of trying to figure out how to get the coffee to your mouth."

He had a point. I chose the gravity-assisted method, lowered my face to the mug and sipped.

"Once again, this is what we're going to do," he said. "And try not to fall asleep while I'm talking. I get enough of that in my early-morning classes.

"Go to Don's office and talk to Willa. Find out what you can from her -- who knows enough to be able to switch out the euthanasia solution for the West Nile, who has been coming in and out of her office that she might not keep a close eye on, things of that nature. Let her know you sympathize with her work load and how tough it must be to get anything done with people coming in and out all the time -- even though that's just what you're doing. If you bring her a Starbucks, she'll probably count you among the non-annoying."

I sighed, or groaned. Even I couldn't be sure.

"Forget about trying to convince your aunt you're not pregnant, forget about your mother, my family, Eric, Juliet and, for that matter, put our wedding aside."

I groaned. Definitely groaned.

"Because we can only do one thing at a time, and if I'm not mistaken you have taxes to work on."

I sighed.

"Since getting information to Thurman is important, let's do that first. Call me around ten forty-five and we'll plan the afternoon." He stroked my hair then patted my back. "I'd take you out for a run, but you'd probably fall asleep mid-stride. Try to stay awake while you drink your coffee. I'm going to take a shower."

I sighed once again and sipped coffee as instructed. At some point I'd wake up enough to figure out if his plan was a good one or not. At that moment everything seemed unreasonable.

I knew Willa opened Don and Rick's office in the little strip mall just north of town at eight in the morning. I figured I'd give her twenty minutes or so to put out any fires. It took a touch longer since the line at the espresso stand had been longer than I expected. At eight thirty, juggling a tall mocha in each hand, I opened the door to Don's office. Willa stood in front of a file drawer at the rear of the office, a stack of file folders balanced in her right arm. She wore blue jeans and a large, white Washington State University sweat shirt long enough to completely cover her amazingly broad bottom. Combined with her narrow shoulders, wide mouth, long ski-jump nose and receding chin she resembled a duck. Her medium length, white-blonde hair, slicked back and gathered in a low pony tail, only reinforced the unfortunate image. I waved one of the coffee cups in her direction and her doleful eyes lit up.

"Bless you, Thea," she said, waddling across the room to take the drink from my hands.

"Thought you might be able to use something. How are you holding up?"

"I --" She clamped down on her lower lip and looked away. After a breath that seemed a struggle, she faced me with a half smile. "It's day to day, you know. Rick is running himself ragged, and we're losing some clients. I guess that can't be helped."

"Will he be looking for another partner?"

"He'll put the word out when he gets a chance. Life goes on, huh?"

I nodded and took a swig from my own cup. "How's Alice? Have you seen her since the funeral?"

"She's come in a couple of times to sort through his desk." She gestured with the coffee cup to a back room. "There's a lot of years of accumulation of stuff. It's going to take a while. I want to help, but I don't know what she wants to toss or keep." She swallowed some coffee and sighed. "She's been a real trouper, no doubt about it, but no one can be prepared for … for that."

"Do you really think Michelle had anything to do with Don's death?"

"I -- I don't know." She shook her head vigorously before

taking another, longer sip. "I always thought she was such a sweet girl. Partied a bit with your sister, I believe, but they're not wild -- if you know what I mean."

Not really, but I nodded in agreement anyway and leaned on the counter before I spoke again. "Some people have been saying Max might have held a grudge. You know he'd been after Don to inject Rum Runner's joints and Don wanted to do an MRI. I think Don believed the horse had a suspensory injury."

"I know, I know. Don came in the office fuming about it often enough. He just didn't see the logic behind not doing everything you could to keep the horse sound. You can't reach the level Max was aiming at with a lame horse."

"And Agnes put her foot down, too. I thought that was strange. It's not like she and her husband can't afford it. They've got more money than dirt. You'd have thought they'd go ahead and get the diagnostic work done." I cringed inwardly. The gossip-approach made me uncomfortable.

"I know. I told … well, never mind. It's neither here nor there."

I considered pressing her for whatever it was she'd told someone, but she began to turn away from me and I didn't want the conversation to end just yet. "What do you know about Bobby? He's such an idiot. Did you know he's working for Max?"

She faced me with an eyebrow raised. "Now that's a youngster I believe is into drugs."

"Do you think he could have substituted the euthanasia solution for the West Nile vaccine? Even accidentally, if he was trying to help Michelle?"

"Oh, you mean Bobby? I would think he'd be smart enough to read the label. But who knows? No telling who was in helping her out."

I'd have thought she would know who'd been working here even casually, since the vets loaded their trucks from the stockroom. "I wonder if Max put him up to it? Bobby'd probably do anything if it meant he'd get paid."

Willa shrugged. "I hate to see Michelle in this position. I have to believe it was an accident. Just about everyone liked Don, except ..."

"Max," I finished.

She swallowed some coffee, watching me the whole while. "And maybe Sybil."

"Sybil? Who's that?"

"Not sure. Someone who was involved with him a few years ago. I overheard a phone conversation a couple of weeks ago. Sounded, hmmm, personal. Definitely upset him."

An affair? Don? "Do you think Alice knew? Was Sybil a client?"

"If she was I'd have no easy way of finding out. I can't do a search by first name on our computer system, and we've got over eight thousand records, so paging through is not something I'd feel like doing. As for Alice, well, if she did know, she didn't let on to me." The phone rang as Willa pulled her purse out of a desk drawer. "What do I owe you for the mocha?"

"Nothing, it's on me."

She protested, but I shook my head as her phone rang again. She picked it up, greeting the caller, smooth and professional, took a quick note and hung up.

"Must be hard for you to get any work done with people popping in and out of the office," I said, remembering Paul's suggested subtle approach.

She shrugged. "Not really."

With no clue what to say next, I shrugged, too. God, I'd sounded like an idiot. This was the last time I'd let Paul suggest interrogation techniques. "I need to get to my office. Just wanted to stop by and say hi."

"Thanks for the coffee."

I waved good-bye and left. On the short drive to my office I reviewed the information she'd let slip about Sybil. The name rang a bell, but it was so faint as to be useless.

I told Paul what I'd learned when I called.

"Okay. This is something. Forget about Sybil for now, though. Get in touch with that wedding planner your mother forced on Juliet last summer."

I grumbled before I spoke her name. "Mrs. Cunningham."

"Yeah, her," he said. "Unless you think you have time to do whatever needs to be done by April sixteenth."

"If I had nothing else to do, I could manage. Though, I don't know if I can convince her."

"You won't know if you don't ask."

I weighed the risks of telling someone who knew Mother against everything else I needed to do. Obviously, by Paul's exasperated sigh, I'd paused too long.

"I don't think there's anything I can do to help, but I'll try."

He'd been the one to insist on April sixteenth, the day after tax-day, despite the fact I'd be exhausted. According to him it was better for me to be dragging my butt than have to go right back to work after the ceremony. "I think you've done enough already," I said, dryly. "I'll call her. Then maybe in my spare time I can find out something about Sybil's identity to pass along to Thurman."

"Forget about Sybil."

"We can't forget about her, Paul," I complained. "She may be a key to this investigation."

"I'm just asking you to put her aside for a day. We've got too much to do --"

"You mean I do," I snapped.

"We both do. We can only do one thing at a time."

I cleared my throat at the comment.

"Okay, I can only do one thing at a time. You can multi-task. Give your sister the information about Sybil. That should keep her happy for the short term. We have to get this wedding in place, and the sooner the better. I don't want to take any chances with my family. I don't want them waltzing out here with Jan and the alleged heir-to-the-spare before we've got all the troops on our side."

Visions of banners, bugles and flashing sabers marched through my head. "You make this sound like a military operation."

"It is."

"You're so romantic."

"So I've been told." There was no chuckle. His tone was so dry I couldn't even imagine a twitch of a smile.

I sighed.

"Thea ...."

"Okay, okay. I'll call Mrs. Cunningham this afternoon, sir." I saluted despite the fact he wouldn't see, disconnected, and glanced at the wall clock. Great. I was going to be late for my lesson with Uncle Henry at Copper Creek. There weren't enough hours in the day to get ready for a horse show, do people's taxes, plan a wedding and investigate a murder.

By the time I arrived at the stable, completed a slapdash tacking up job and got my butt into the saddle, Uncle Henry had finished his previous lesson and was waiting for me to pick up the miniature two-way radio headset from him.

"Running a little late," I said, adjusting the earpiece and rebuckling my helmet. I could have been later if Juliet had waylaid me. Her motorcycle was parked by the office and I'd half expected her to tackle me and demand information. Fortunately, she'd left me alone.

"That's fine," my uncle said. "Go ahead and work through your warm up. Let's see where you are today."

Uncle Henry's typical willingness to work with exactly what the horse and rider presented on any given day did little to ease my disorganized and overburdened mind. I'd ridden for enough years to be able to focus on the here and now -- a vital requirement when one works with a horse -- but I still rushed. I should have arrived at the barn, tacked up and been working through our warm-up for at least twenty minutes prior to our lesson. Not wanting to waste my uncle's time, I hurried my horse through the preliminary stretching exercises.

However, Blackie's back was not loosening into its customary swing. Instead of feeling the soft pulse of his footfalls through the reins, the contact I had with his mouth alternated between leaving my fingers feeling empty or like I was holding up a block of concrete.

Frustrated, I pushed him forward in the trot with a stronger drive from my seat, hoping to gain a longer stride. Unfortunately, Blackie's speed increased instead of his stride length, and so did the weight in my hands.

"You seem to be having some problems." My uncle's voice was soft in my ear.

I let my ankles relax and settled my weight into my legs. Blackie dropped into a walk and we turned toward the corner where Uncle Henry sat, leaning back in his chair, one leg crossed over the other.

"It won't do to rush the warm-up. You know that," he said.

"Yes, I know. Sorry."

"Let's start over again and stay in the walk until he tells you he's ready to move on. Pay attention to your own balance and tension, too. I believe today you need this warm-up more than he does. Slow down and focus on one thing at a time."

He was right. I'd been bullying my horse through the warm-up, not waiting until he'd accomplished what each exercise was for, but hoping I could just lump it all together and get it all done at once. Not only did this not do my horse any good, but it changed his routine. The mistakes I made were compounded by his mistakes, which made me make more mistakes. I had to be the one to break the cycle, not him, and I was half surprised my uncle let it go on as long as it did. On the other hand, the lesson was very clear to me.

Within ten minutes of doing one warm-up exercise at a time at the walk, we were ready to trot. Blackie's trot was exponentially better from the beginning, but I didn't rush. Knowing my uncle watched every muscle twitch, I concentrated on the single objective of the exercise and kept close tabs on my own balance and position, repeating my mantra du jour: first things first, one step at a time.

The lesson, as it applied to my current situation outside of my riding, was not lost on me, either. As I untacked Blackie, it occurred to me that Paul was right. I could put Sybil aside. The police were handling the investigation into Don's death, the bit of information I'd dug up about a possible liaison between him and whoever she was should keep my sister happy for a little while. We needed to be sure we got our wedding under way now in order to cut off the potential interference from Paul's family.

"I'm calling Mrs. Cunningham the minute I get home," I said to Blackie as I returned him to his stall and slid his halter off.

He blew a long sneeze while shaking his head. Cold, moist droplets sprayed my face and the front of my jacket. He watched, ears pricked, as I wiped a gloved hand across my cheek.

"You're really expecting another treat?" He tossed his head and I dug into my pocket, found one and passed it to him. He plucked it from my fingers, chewed, swallowed and shook his head again. "I'm serious. This really is my biggest issue at the moment, so stop looking at me like you don't believe me. I'll talk to Willa again later."

"Hey, little dudette, do you always talk to your horse?"

I turned so fast I bumped Blackie's nose with my shoulder. "Bobby, you startled me."

He grinned while rocking back and forth on his sneakered feet, hands stuffed deep into the pockets of his baggy black jeans. He wore no jacket, just a black, short-sleeved T-shirt. He ought to have been cold, but seemed perfectly comfortable.

"You've got big issues, so have I. I've gotta spring Michelle from prison. Her folks won't let me even though I got the money for her bail. Harsh. Really harsh."

I didn't really know Mr. and Mrs. Martin, having met them

only a couple of times, but they didn't strike me as the "tough love" type. He couldn't be right. "They won't let their daughter get bailed out? You're kidding."

He shook his head emphatically while continuing to rock. I half expected him to topple over. "Kid you not, short stuff. But Bobby, here, has plans to be stealthy, like those little drone-bots the Army dudes use." He put his arms out like an airplane and tipped from side to side. I suppose he was imitating a drone. "Little dudette, Bobby's going forward with Plan A, like the hero he is. Could use an amigo in this mission, though. How about you take the bail money in for me. Don't want to spoil my chances of success just because of the one or two legal-type issues I need to avoid for awhile."

Right. Issues with arrest warrants, no doubt. No way was I going to explain how I ended up with a wad of cash that Bobby probably came by via one illegal means or other. "Sorry. I'd like to help you out, but I have appointments that will keep me busy all afternoon."

"Oh, hey, that's cool. I'll get your sister to help."

Crap. "I don't think she can," I lied, frantically searching my mental files for a plausible excuse. "Um, Eric is back and I think she's seeing him after work."

"Wow, really? Eric-the-man is back in town? Don't want to bust up that reunion. Besides, I don't think he likes Bobby too much. Thanks for the heads-up." He stopped rocking suddenly and straightened. "Hey, did you catch that? I used a horse expression I learned from Max. Maybe the dude will help me and Michelle out."

"Maybe you should let Michelle's parents handle this, Bobby."

The rocking started up again. "No way, little dudette. I gotta prove to my woman I can take care of her."

Oh, yeah. Every woman's dream: Bobby on a white horse.

He wandered away without saying goodbye – just kind of switched universes. I took a few quick minutes to put my saddle and other equipment away, then hurried to the parking lot. As I started my car, my line of sight settled on the spot where Juliet generally parked her bright yellow Kawasaki Ninja motorcycle. It wasn't there. I thumped my fist on the steering wheel. Crap. That damn Bobby hadn't taken but two seconds to convince my idiot sister to run his errand for him. "I am going to kick her ass. And then I'm telling Aunt Vi." I'd see Juliet tonight. She'd likely stop by her studio after she got off work at Copper Creek.

Back in my office, I took a bite of the hamburger I'd picked up at Pilchuck Drive-In, the local hamburger drive-through, and dialed Mrs. Cunningham's number. I swallowed the small mouthful when she answered, and eyed the crispy French fries as I introduced myself and explained what I needed and when.

"April sixteenth," she said with enough hesitancy to get me worried. "That doesn't give me much time. Let me get a check list so we don't miss anything ...." There was a rustle and she cleared her throat. "Now, the printer will need –"

"We'll send e-vites," I said.

"Oh, okay. Considering the time constraints, that makes sense. I assume you have your dress?"

"Umm, no -- yes -- no, not really." Wearing the dark green gown I'd worn at our Las Vegas wedding probably wasn't going to go over well. "Paul has a tux, though."

"Well, good for him. Are you planning on shopping for yourself soon? I'd suggest it, because if alterations need to be done you'll need all the time you can get."

"I was hoping to get something off the rack." I grimaced, waiting for a lecture, but didn't get one. "I'll see what I can find this week."

"Not a bad idea. Shall we move on to some other, possibly more important, items? Have you thought about the location? If you want a church wedding we'll have to get busy."

"Oh, well, I guess I hadn't really thought about it."

"Reception? Food? Cake? Bridesmaids, groomsmen?"

"Uh …. I was thinking we could just rustle things together pretty quickly … you know?"

"No rehearsal?"

My hand hovered over the French fries. "Rehearsal?"

"You want me to just slap it all together in less than a month?"

"Um, yeah. There's one more thing." I could tell, already, she was going to balk.

"What would that be?"

"You can't tell anyone."

The silence that followed held a distinct amount of hostility and made me very glad she wasn't sitting across the desk from me.

She cleared her throat. "Are you actually expecting anyone to show up?"

I forced a laugh, although it was plain she wasn't trying to be funny. "Well, sure. We, um, just want to surprise everyone -- tell them a few days ahead of time."

"If you're going for non-traditional, you've certainly hit it out of the park. At least when I did that New Age wedding on Beltane last year I had some vague pagan rituals to go by -- and enough time."

I wasn't sure if she expected me to respond. "Well, um, it's just that -- you're right. I'm asking too much. I can see how this would be too much trouble." I expected to hear a "good-bye" and moved to disconnect the call.

"No, no, I can help you out, but I don't think it's going to end up being the memorable affair you envision."

A memorable affair was exactly what I wanted to avoid, but not for the reasons she was likely thinking. "I don't really envision anything elaborate. We just want some family and friends to help us celebrate."

Mrs. Cunningham laughed like she'd been off her medication for too long. "I'll see what I can do. If nothing else, we'll wing it. Tell you what. I'll keep all this planning under wraps if you promise never to tell anyone I helped with it."

By the time I'd gotten off the phone with her, I'd agreed to have the ceremony at my tiny house, the reception wherever she could get room on short notice, any cake she could get her hands on, and whatever food trays the local grocery stores could provide.

I was fairly certain my sister and Andrea would agree to be bridesmaids and probably Dave would be Paul's best man, but with Eric out of the picture I wasn't sure who else Paul would ask to even things out. I took two ibuprofen, called Paul and left a voice mail telling him we could go back to investigating with a clear conscience. Then I went to work on my clients' taxes.

Juliet did not stop by her studio after work. I called the Copper Creek office and got the voice mail. I called her cell phone and got the same result. I left non-specific messages asking her to call me and waited. When the phone rang it was Paul, not Juliet.

"Did you lose track of time?" he asked.

"No, I'm waiting for Juliet to show up."

"If she wants a report she knows where to find you. I'm hungry and we --"

"Eat something." Good God. The man knew how to cook. "Juliet's screwed up big time today. I feel the need to tear her a new one before I hand her over to Aunt Vi." I launched into a hurried synopsis of my conversation with Bobby and what could only be Juliet's poorly thought-out complicity with him. I added the fact that I'd called Mrs. Cunningham, just so he wouldn't think I was shirking my assignments.

"Come home. I put a frozen lasagna in the oven while you were talking. And, by the way, Mrs. Cunningham called and left a message. She was able to book the bed and breakfast down the street from us for the reception. Apparently they aren't busy mid-week and have a large living room -- or something. Also, Eric's here."

My elation at the fast procurement of a reception site met the same fate as a balloon when intimately introduced to a pin. "At our house?"

"Yes."

Anger, the same I'd felt in January when he walked out on my sister, filled the emotional vacuum with a vengeance. Yes, the other day I'd forgiven him with one look in those soulful brown eyes, but this was different. He was in my home, probably wanting to figure out how to use us to get my sister back. That made me mad.

"Are you still there?" Paul asked. "Do you want me to come get you?"

"I'll be home soon." I hung up with care, then kicked my waste basket across the room.

# Chapter Thirteen

My wipers created blurry arcs on my windshield the whole drizzly three blocks home. Except for an offhand mental note to get the blades replaced, I hardly noticed, being too busy building a good head of steam to unleash on Eric.

Juliet deserved credit for not caving in and throwing herself into his arms when he showed up unexpectedly at her studio, but she'd obviously been so shocked it was affecting her thinking. Otherwise she would not have gone against Aunt Vi and Uncle Henry's specific instructions to stay away from Bobby. Who knew what she'd do if Eric stayed in town? He had to leave. And I had to have a talk with her immediately, so I wouldn't end up trying to explain her alliance with Bobby to Detective Thurman.

Paul met me at the front door as I walked in and dropped a quick kiss on my lips that I didn't return. For some reason he seemed puzzled. Evidently, we'd have to discuss later what part of get-Eric-away-from-my-sister he didn't understand.

"Eric's in the kitchen," he said.

I hung up my jacket in the front closet and kicked my shoes off, pretending to aim each at a sensitive part of Eric's anatomy. I set my jaw and advanced to the kitchen. This was war.

"Are you leaving?" I asked striding in.

Eric stood abruptly and the chair skittered on the hardwood floor. "If you want me to."

Paul's spoke from behind me. "I asked him to stay for dinner. In fact, I'd like him to stay so we can hear what he has to say."

I made an abrupt about face and glared at my husband. "Oh, is that right?"

For a couple of very long seconds we stared each other down. It was the slight lowering of his chin that told me I needed to change my tactic unless I wanted a screaming fight right here in front of Eric. The low growl in my throat fought briefly with the insincere smile I managed to put on before turning back to Eric.

"Since my hu -- fiancé extended the invitation, please have a seat."

Eric's return smile wouldn't stay in place. He tentatively returned to his seat, appearing ready to make a run for it, if necessary. "Thanks, I appreciate it. I'm actually here to apologize to you."

"To me?"

"And everyone else. For the way I left. Without saying good-bye – without telling anyone why."

Of course he should grovel to everyone. "The only person you need to apologize to is my sister."

He looked at his hands, knotted together on the table in front of him. "I've tried. She won't talk to me."

"Seems to me, you're the one who needs to do the talking."

"She won't listen." He turned his beautiful, dark-lashed brown eyes up at me. The request was totally obvious, sincere and heart wrenching. He wanted me to help him.

I had new respect for my sister's ability to light right into him when he'd ambushed her the other night. The memory of her dazed gray eyes, filled with tears, felt like a blow to my solar plexus.

Paul nudged my shoulder but didn't remove his hand. "Thea."

"I'd have been more than happy to listen to him talk months ago. In fact, I'd have cheered him on." I shrugged away from Paul and stepped toward our guest. "I get why you didn't want to go through with the wedding, Eric. Aunt Vi and Uncle Henry told us. But it sure as hell would have been better to hear it ages ago. You're now well into the classic 'too little, too late' territory. You broke my sister's heart, and I will not sit and listen to your weak apologies now."

Paul stepped from behind me. "For God's sake, the man made a mistake. A more egregious error would have been to follow through with the wedding. How much worse do you think your sister would have felt when their marriage fell apart and they divorced?"

I fully faced my husband and my lip curled. "So you're telling me he did the right thing?"

"I'm telling you it could have been worse. Yes, he did the right thing by backing out of the wedding, but I'm not saying he couldn't have handled it better."

"Isn't that the understatement of the week."

"Christ, Thea. If your sister hadn't started the whole thing off by lying about his financial situation just to get your mother off her back, maybe things wouldn't have gotten so out of hand."

"That's right," I scoffed. "Blame my sister. She's not the one who ran away."

"But she took the easy way out, instead of facing your parents and doing things the right way even if it was harder."

"So now you're an advocate of the difficult path? Seems to me you were pushing for easy just a few days ago."

Paul feigned surprise, barking a short laugh. "Easy? You

think it was easy getting you to marry me? I've never worked so hard to get what I wanted in my life."

I reared back. "Oh, really? 'Hard'? Is that what our relationship has been for you? Hard work? Let me be the first to apologize. On second thought, I take that back. Now that we're mar --"

With my heart rate slamming into overdrive, I cut myself off and jerked a panicked look toward Eric.

The chair he'd occupied was empty.

"Shit," Paul breathed and sprinted to the living room. I matched his pace. "His car's gone. Dammit, Thea."

"Me?" I shrieked. "You're blaming me? You were flapping your jaws every bit as much as I was."

"How could you have forgotten he was here?" he bellowed.

"Excuse me, but you're the one who lost his bearings. Why the hell did you invite him here, anyway? Did you expect me to pat him on the head and say 'poor baby' after the misery he inflicted on my sister?"

"You know as well as I that their break-up wasn't entirely his fault."

"No, it wasn't, but he sure could have prevented the current level of hate and discontent, not to mention Juliet's knee-jerk stupid decisions, by speaking up before he took the easy out by running away."

We stared each other down. He knew I was right. His twitching jaw proved it.

"How much do you think he heard?" he asked.

Would it have killed him to tell me I was right? "I think we'd better assume too much."

Paul rubbed a hand over his mouth and jaw. "Too many people are finding out. I'll track down Eric in the morning and talk to him. Then again, maybe we ought to reconsider and confess. It'll give my family and Jan one less reason to come out here and yours will eventually forgive us. How bad could it be?"

Not this again. "Bad. No. I do not want to see my aunt cry and my uncle angry. And I don't want the whole guilt-trip-with-lecture combo from my mother. My Dad's feelings will be hurt that he didn't get to give me away, and it probably won't stop your family or Jan, so no. Just no."

"Then you've got to do whatever it takes to keep your sister's mouth shut. We've got to get this wedding done and over with as quickly as possible."

I raked him with a seething once over. "Yes, by all means. It's so distasteful."

His smile was like ice. "Maybe you want to forget the whole thing."

Two deep breaths later I found my voice. "If it will make it easier for you, let's *do* forget the whole thing. All of it."

"If that's the way you feel." His words, so quiet, vibrated from deep in his chest.

My chin quivered. "If that's your opinion, then I have no intention of holding you to something you don't want." I spun and stalked to the kitchen.

He didn't follow me.

Wouldn't that make things so much easier if we split up now? His family wouldn't be so hysterical. He could remarry Jan and his not-my-son would have a father. Of course they'd probably move here to the Seattle area because of his job at the university, and I might run into him when he took his new family to visit Delores.

My throat convulsed with the effort of holding back a crying jag. Failing, I ripped a paper towel from the holder and wiped at my eyes before I blew my nose. I nearly slammed the cabinet door where the trash can lived before realizing I probably shouldn't mistreat my new kitchen. Poor kitchen. I loved it and it didn't deserve my temper. Tears leaked again, along with a little "Eep." I tore off another paper towel.

He'd forget about me eventually, but I'd never forget him. My heart would never heal. I was done with men. Forever.

I parked my butt at the kitchen table and dragged a catalog

from the pile of the day's mail, turning the pages and wiping at my eyes when the print became blurry.

The timer on my new oven dinged and I wondered for a moment why before remembering the lasagna. I cut myself a piece and sat at the table to eat. Paul came in when I was nearly done and served himself a healthy portion without looking at me once. I know this because I watched him the entire time.

He left the kitchen with his food. By the sounds of his footsteps and the squeak of his old desk chair, he'd gone to the little room that used to be my office, and now served as a work place for both of us.

My heart ached all the way to my fingertips. We hadn't even gone on a honeymoon yet and we were ready to call it quits.

I cleaned up the kitchen, retrieved the book I'd been reading from my nightstand upstairs and went back down to the living room making sufficient noise getting settled on the sofa so he'd know I was there. Fifteen minutes later, he still hadn't come out of the office. Fifteen minutes after that he walked out of the office with his empty plate and went to the kitchen. I pretended to read when he returned, but he didn't come into the living room. I peeked over the top of my book in time to see him disappear back into the office with a beer in his hand.

This was stupid. We couldn't go on like this. I knew I wouldn't stay angry with him. After all, we'd had fights before -- many times -- and we'd always found our way back to each other. I closed my book, knowing I'd have to go back and reread the pages my eyes had skimmed for the last half hour anyway, and set it on the coffee table. With resolve, but no particular speech planned, I rose and walked to our office to cough up an apology. He didn't look up when I shuffled to a stop in the doorway.

I cleared my throat.

He clicked the mouse and another page of an article he

was reading displayed on the monitor.

"I'm sorry," I said.

He glanced in my direction, then returned his focus to the computer screen.

I gnawed my lip. "I'm not upset with you. I'm mad at Eric because he hurt my sister."

"I understand," he said, without looking my way. Then he clicked his mouse and the article disappeared from his screen. A picture of me, covered in Montana dust and laughing as I held up the first fossil I'd found last summer at his dig, filled the screen. Another two clicks and the picture faded. The computer went to sleep. "What I don't think you understand is the lengths Jan and my family will go to in order to get what they want. They are very determined, as is evidenced by the barrage of emails I've been receiving -- and ignoring. Not to mention the voice mails I've been deleting."

I opened my mouth to say something, but had no words. Paul raised an eyebrow and nodded.

"If Eric and your sister's problems can put us at each other's throats, then we don't stand a chance when the Minnesota Mafia gets here." He held out a hand. "I'm sorry too. I love you. There's no way I want to call it quits now when I've finally gotten the one thing in life that means more to me than anything else. Thea, I want to shout to the world that you're mine, not hide what we've done because we're afraid. The sooner we have our second wedding, the better for us. Okay?"

I walked across the room and took his hand, wishing I hadn't tossed out that last paper towel.

I didn't sleep much, not because we reconciled with passionate abandon, but because plans and tactics ran through my mind most of the night without ever settling into anything even remotely workable, much less intelligent. In the lulls between frantic planning, the words of defeat we'd both uttered in anger echoed back, reminding me just how fragile our union was.

When my alarm went off I hauled myself to the kitchen, measured out coffee and water, and hovered, waiting for my first cup. Paul dragged into the kitchen, his robe loosely knotted, dark circles under his eyes, and took the mug I handed him. He delayed my plod toward the kitchen table, wrapping me in a loose one-armed hug and rested his cheek on the top of my head.

"Don't ever leave me," he said, after a couple of moments. "I don't think my heart could take it."

"I promise." And I would never threaten again. But I couldn't speak for him, and no matter what words came out of his mouth, only he knew the limits of his heart.

However, my two words seemed enough for him. He tipped my chin up, kissed me lightly, and nudged me toward the kitchen table. We sat opposite each other and sipped in silence. Half a mug of coffee later, he stretched and leaned back in his chair.

"Something else is bothering you. What is it?" he asked.

I swallowed more coffee. "Nothing, everything. Mostly I want to run away, but we'd have to take Blackie with us and I don't own a horse trailer."

He reached across the table wrapped his hands around mine as I held my mug. "There's not much I can do about my family except hold them off. Put most of your effort into the plans with Mrs. Cunningham. We'll talk at lunch, but let's concentrate on our wedding."

"What about …?"

"Our investigation? I think we can continue to do what we've been doing. If you find out something give it to Thurman, but there's no point in going out of our way to investigate as long as your sister seems satisfied."

My enthusiasm wasn't overwhelming. "We might be able to keep Juliet satisfied, but to tell the truth, I'm not. There has to be something more we can do. I'm not saying I completely agree with my sister, but ...."

"Trust Thurman."

A twinge visited in my gut.

"Please, Thea."

"If Michelle is involved then she's only guilty of an accident."

"Thea ...."

"Okay, fine. I'll concentrate on our wedding."

# Chapter Fourteen

I spoke with several clients throughout the morning. One asked if I was sick, another wanted to know if I was coming down with the same flu she had, and a third kept the conversation short and thanked me profusely for working on his books when I was feeling under the weather. And those were just the ones who voiced an opinion.

I wasn't sick. I had an emotional hangover, but let them all think it was some unknown, but temporary, bug.

Paul called before I left my office at noon to go to Copper Creek, having just remembered he'd forgotten to stop and talk to Eric and find out how much he'd heard. Despite the certainty of a sweat-producing awkward moment, I volunteered to ask him myself. If the opportunity presented itself, I'd apologize for being a raging bitch too.

My husband did not express overwhelming enthusiasm for the idea. I could relate. While we were on the phone reviewing the pros and cons of me trying to persuade Eric to keep his mouth shut, if indeed he'd stayed long enough to learn our secret, someone came into Paul's office. Whoever he was apologized for interrupting, but needed Paul in a meeting even if he wasn't feeling well.

Apparently, he had the same bug as me.

The moment I drove in the driveway at Copper Creek, I spotted Eric striding up the walk to Miguel and Maria's house on the opposite side of the parking lot from the barns and arenas. Without giving myself a chance to chicken out, I pulled into a space, killed the engine and jogged toward Eric. He turned toward me the second time I called his name, his expression wary.

"Hold up a sec, Eric." Slightly out of breath, I tried a smile. It wasn't easy, but Eric returned my attempted friendly gesture.

"Hi, Thea. I'm sorry about last night. I should have checked with you --"

"No, no. Please. I'm the one who needs to apologize. Juliet's behavior lately has been upsetting me, and I'm afraid I took it out on you. I really am sorry."

"That's okay, I understand ... so, what do you mean? What's she been doing to upset you?"

"Oh, um, worse than usual decisions, you know."

He shook his head. "I thought she was taking clothing design classes. Seems like it's a good use of her talent. How is that a bad decision?"

I grimaced, not wanting to get into the details, but he waited. "It's not the clothing design," I said at last, although I had serious doubts as to any use she'd make of it. "I'm thrilled she's taking the course. What bothers me is how she's been hanging around too many guys with questionable reputations, and trying to clear Michelle of Don's murder. Stuff like that."

His lips tightened when I'd said "hanging around" but at least he seemed to know he had no right to comment. "You're letting her investigate a murder?"

"Of course not. She asked Paul and me to find information

that would help Michelle. She's just being supportive." I think.

He scowled.

"Well, ah, I really am sorry I unloaded on you last night. And sorry Paul and I got into our issues in front of you." I held my breath.

He squinted at me like he was about to ask a personal question and didn't know how to do it. I braced for an "I didn't know you two got married" comment. "You guys argue all the time like that?"

"No!" The word blew out on an exhale. "No, of course not. So, um, we didn't see you leave." Once again, I stopped breathing.

"I figured I'd better leave about the time you finished with me and started in on each other."

"Sorry." His answer was hardly definitive. I waited.

He shrugged. We shared an uncomfortable, silent moment, shuffling and avoiding eye contact.

"Well, I'll see you around, I guess." I started to turn away, but stopped. "Are you back for good?"

He cleared his throat. "No. I'm living with my parents and working for my dad at the Yakima orchards until I earn enough money to go back to school."

"So you'll be leaving soon?"

He smiled, slowly, and looked me straight in the eye. "Depends on how long it takes me to win Juliet back."

He left me with my jaw sagging, and no come-back. When he reached the front door to Miguel and Maria's house he lifted a hand to me in a half salute before disappearing inside. I took a breath and regrouped.

Fine. Good luck to him. Juliet was leaving him behind. He was wasting his energy.

I strode back the way I'd come, gravel jumping from under my heels, peeved at Eric's admission he was once again in hot pursuit of my sister. She didn't need pressure from him that would surely add to her "worse than usual decision-making." I scanned the parking lot for her motorcycle. It wasn't present, and I didn't know whether to be relieved or worried for the lack of opportunity to talk to her. Nevertheless, it was likely I'd see her after work. I could spend whatever time I needed at that point discussing the lack of intelligence she was showing by associating with Bobby and warn her about Eric.

It occurred to me that although I'd gained knowledge of Eric's intent concerning Juliet, I hadn't gained an ounce of feel for whether Eric knew that Paul and I were married. I ground my teeth in frustration and packed a little more hustle into my step. A ride on my horse was just what I needed to shed my sour mood and gain some clear thinking.

I passed Max's tack room, located at the end of the Big Barn closest to the parking lot, and although the door stood open, I didn't see anyone but Agnes inside. She glanced up and I greeted her without slowing my pace. Uncle Henry's advice about not rushing my warm-up did not apply to stepping up the speed at which I got ready. Evidently, my horse felt the same. His impatient whinny as I entered the barn spurred me along as well. He always knew I was on my way before he could see me.

To be efficient I swung through the bay where my locker was located, grabbed my helmet, whip, brush bucket, saddle, pad, and bridle, carted it all to one of the grooming stalls and then went to get Blackie.

Footsteps alternating between a walk and run approached. I ignored them.

But, as much as I wanted to, I couldn't ignore Agnes' breathless, "Thea! Oh, Thea!"

I finished buckling Blackie's halter and turned, mildly annoyed at this latest impediment to my ride. My very social horse didn't seem the least startled by her rush toward us and, in fact, poked his nose past me to greet her. Traitor.

"Here." Agnes pushed a blue plaid stable blanket, still in its original packaging, in my face. I had no choice but to take it from her. "This is a new blanket I bought for Rum Runner. This new one doesn't fit him and I thought you might want it for Blackie."

I didn't want it and tried to hand it back, but she turned away, as if ready to leave. "Agnes, wait --"

"Runner ripped his old blanket on a nail in his stall. I just can't believe the shoddy way maintenance is handled around here ever since Eric was let go."

What was she talking about? "Eric wasn't fired. He left for personal reasons. And the maintenance here isn't shoddy." She wouldn't look at me. If my hands hadn't been full of horse blanket I'd have grabbed her arm.

"Well, Max has been having all kinds of problems. He's here all the time and he sees what's going on. You don't, and you ought to be aware of it. Why, Max had to hunt Miguel down and explain to him how important it is to do more than just shovel up manure. The nail was three inches long and could have caused a lot of damage to Rum Runner." She huffed indignantly. "I tried to get the same blanket from the tack store, since his shoulders are so big, but they didn't have it. They told me this one is similar." She waved her hand at it but, once again, didn't face me. "It's not at all the same. I don't like the way it fits him. If you like it, keep it."

I seethed over her accusation that Copper Creek's barn maintenance was anything but top-notch. Pain-in-the-ass Max was likely exaggerating the nail issue.

"I don't want the blanket, Agnes."

"Don't be silly. Everyone can use another blanket. They get dirty so quickly. You must take it. I insist."

She had a point. Blackie could use another blanket. "If it fits, then I'll pay you for it."

"I won't hear of it."

"Agnes –"

"You're welcome." She glanced quickly at me then turned away, again, but not before I got a good look at her face and the shiner she sported.

"Good grief, what happened?"

Agnes laughed. "Oh, that Rum Runner. When I was

leading him yesterday, after Max rode, something spooked him. He swung his head around and got me. Knocked me flat on my back. My shoulder is stiff, too."

"Maybe you should have it looked at." Agnes was, after all, over forty. All kinds of things could go wrong.

"No, no, I'm fine. Just a little bruised and sore."

If she was as sore as her "little bruise" indicated it was a wonder she'd been able to hand me the stable blanket. "Well, you take care." I stepped around her.

"Aren't you going to try it on Blackie?"

"I will later. I don't have much time and I need to get on and get riding."

"Oh, well ...."

She walked along beside me as I led Blackie to the grooming stall. Something else was on her mind, but I wasn't in the mood to play guessing games. She'd either tell me or not, and it certainly made no difference to me either way.

"So, um, I was wondering if I might ask you a favor."

I clipped the cross-ties to Blackie's halter then bent over my brush bucket and dug around for my hoof pick. "Sure, ask away."

"I wouldn't, except that I'm a little worried and I do feel terrible about Don's death and everyone knows how good you are at detective work."

My hand stilled. Oh, crap. "I'm not, really."

"Oh, you are. Don't deny it. You solved that Parsons girl's murder, and the university professor and Sig Paalmann's. You have a knack."

Hoof pick in hand, I bent over next to Blackie's foreleg. "Up," I said. He obliged, lifting his foot. It was packed with mud and gravel from his morning romp in his paddock. I hung onto his hoof with one hand and, gritting my teeth, pried at the debris with more concentration than necessary. "The police are handling the investigation, Agnes, and I'm almost positive they wouldn't appreciate me playing detective and making a mess of their work."

"But that's just why you have to investigate, Thea. It's the police I'm worried about. They think Max is responsible for Dr. Archterkamp's death."

I straightened and looked her in the eye. Subtlety was wasted on Agnes. I should have said I was one hundred percent certain Detective Thurman would object to even a whiff of meddling from me, and that she was obviously out of the news loop. "They've arrested Michelle."

"Well, I know that," she said, as if I'd offended her. "But they seem to believe she didn't act alone, and that Max used his wiles on her to get her to cooperate with some vile plan."

Wiles. Right. And a conspiracy. Good one. I moved to Blackie's hind leg, and he lifted it without me asking. "Michelle has been dating Bobby. I don't think she has time for Max's 'wiles'." I dug at the mud packed in the bottom of my horse's hoof.

"How do you think Bobby got that silly job? Max did Michelle a favor, after she buttered him up, and now the police are concocting evidence so they can accuse Max of masterminding a murder. It's beyond preposterous and you have to help."

I moved to the other side of Blackie and picked up a third foot. Agnes followed me.

"You know how to investigate. You've done it before with excellent results."

"I've stumbled into investigations and gotten damn lucky."

"I'll pay you. Stop your sister."

Was she threatening Juliet? Heat built in my chest and pumped my pulse. "What do you mean?"

"Money. Not just a horse blanket."

I shook my head. "What do you mean, 'stop my sister'?"

"Your sister is supposedly trying to clear Michelle. What she's trying to do is frame Max. He's a sweet, kind and caring man and had nothing to do with Dr. Archterkamp's death. I'm sorry to have to tell you this, but your sister is a liar. She hates

Max because he went out with her a couple of times then realized how much maturity she lacked and lost interest. Not only are you the perfect person to investigate this crime, but you can also keep your sister from finding herself in considerable legal trouble due to her quest for revenge."

The slow burn that had churned my gut pushed toward outrage. "Agnes, I'm going to tell you this one last time. I refuse to have anything to do with this investigation. And let me tell you something else. Juliet is no threat to Max, so you can just back off of your crusade."

Agnes drew herself up, eyes narrowed. I matched her glare.

"Keep the blanket. You might change your mind."

That was not what I was expecting her to say, and I didn't have an opportunity to recover. She spun on her heel and marched off. I'd return the blanket, untried. There was no chance in hell I'd change my mind.

I finished cleaning out Blackie's feet, tacked him up and led him to the arena. One circuit of big indoor arena convinced me I didn't have the concentration to work. We went on a trail ride in the rain.

Once back in the Big Barn I stripped off Blackie's tack, rubbed him down and put him away with his own stable blanket buckled on. Once I'd taken care of my equipment, I grabbed Agnes' "gift" and headed for Max's tack room. The door was shut, so I knocked. When there was no answer I tried the knob. It opened and, feeling a bit like an intruder, I felt for the light switch on the wall.

I'd never been inside Max's domain before, and when the overhead light went on, I'm disappointed to say I was impressed. Extreme tidiness and the rich scent of well-cared-for leather met my senses. A sofa and overstuffed chair, both with a fox hunting print on a burgundy background, formed an inviting group to my right. A small, dark wood desk and chair nestled against the wall just beyond. The desk's ornate, Tiffany-style lamp had illuminated along with the ceiling fixture when I'd flipped the wall switch. The glow from the multicolored glass shade lent a cozy, almost intimate, feel despite the bright overhead light.

Artfully arranged on the wall behind the sofa were a number of framed photographs. Holding Agnes' bribe against my chest, I strolled over to get a closer look and was surprised to note that, although most showed horses jumping, not all were of Max. In fact, some were of his students and others were prints or paintings of varying quality. Above his desk was displayed a small, expensively framed painting of an old-style, fox hunting scene. Not my taste in artwork, but by its quality I could understand why it occupied a place of its own.

On the opposite side of the room, arranged in a precise four by four grid on the wall, were shiny black saddle racks, each with a saddle -- sixteen in all. Far more saddles than he had horses in training. Next to them, on matching brackets, bridles hung in an orderly line, the throat latch of each twisted in a tidy figure eight around the headstall -- exactly the way Uncle Henry hung his bridles. Again, there were more bridles than horses under Max's care. Further along were hooks for martingales, halters, lunge lines and so on, all clean and glowing. All giving the appearance of being on display.

Toward the back of the long, narrow room was where the work, versus the socializing, was done. A hook hung from the ceiling for cleaning bridles. A stand to hold saddles for cleaning butted against a deep sink. Shelves above the sink held cleaning supplies. Sturdier shelving units flanking the sink held shampoos, medications, supplements, galloping boots and clean, folded blankets.

I could put Agnes' stable blanket on the shelf, but she might not see it and no way did I want her to think I'd kept it. That would imply a possibility of cooperation, and I had no intention of cooperating to that degree. Best to leave the thing on the sofa along with a note where no one would miss it.

I skirted the large chair to get to Max's desk. Although it felt intrusive, I opened drawers, looking for pen and paper, clutching the horse blanket to my chest to keep it out of my way.

"Anything I can help you find, or would you just prefer to rifle through my desk on your own?"

I jerked upright and wheeled to face the voice so close behind me. Max, not more than five feet away, stood with arms crossed and a muscle twitching in his jaw.

My mouth went dry. He'd snuck up on me. How could he sneak up on me with those big heavy riding boots and spurs with rowels? At the very least I should have heard his riding raincoat rustle. "Sorry. I was just looking for something to write a note on." I held the blanket toward him. "Agnes thought this might fit Blackie. It doesn't, so I wanted to return it, but maybe you can give it to her and tell her it doesn't fit, and tell her thank you anyway, but I can't use it, and … here." I shoved it closer, since he hadn't moved to take it from me.

"Really? You know what I think? I think you were stealing that blanket and then got the idea there might be some money to be had in my desk." His gaze shifted past me to the still open desk drawer.

I followed his line of sight and noticed, for the first time, a slightly bulging envelope with the words "receipts from clients" printed near one end.

My face flushed. "No! Seriously, Max, I didn't even notice it. I really was looking for a note pad and pencil, and I really am returning the blanket. I --"

"I believe her."

Max and I turned toward the new presence. Agnes' husband, Bart, stood in the doorway, a mild, almost beatific smile curving his wide mouth. He strolled toward us with a slight swagger, the camel-hair coat he wore over a dark blue suit swaying slightly with each stride. He removed his tweed snap-brim cap and smoothed his thinning hair.

"You know our Miss Campbell, Max. She's an upstanding local business woman. I have no doubt every word she says is true." Despite addressing Max, he was looking at me. Sort of.

His gaze kept darting past me in the direction of the desk. At the envelope? Was he going to suggest Max check the contents of the envelope to prove my innocence? How humiliating.

But he reached a hand toward me. "Let me take the blanket off your hands. Since my wife doesn't care for it, I'll return it to the store on my way home."

I handed it off, not unhappy to be rid of it. Though his smile was friendly, I was not grateful, or impressed. His token intervention smacked of opportunism.

"Run along now," Bart said, as if addressing a child. "I'm sure you have more important things to do than wait here for Max's apology."

He was right, but so was I. Bart wasn't so much concerned with me as he was with the chance to make Max look bad and him good -- in front of a witness.

Max scoffed. "Who said I was going to apologize?"

"I'm sure it's your intention," Bart said.

Each man focused keenly on the other, as if sizing the other up. I didn't wait for what might happen next, but said a quick, "Thank you, Mr. Fulton, but I'm not holding my breath," and left at a swift, but dignified, walk.

Vexation with Bart and indignation with Max had my heart slamming a righteous rhythm against my ribs as I strode across the parking lot to my car. I pulled the door open and slid into the driver's seat, fastened my seat belt and took several deep breaths.

I sincerely hoped the karma fairy nudged Delores into kicking Max and his crowd out of Copper Creek. They were nothing but trouble. All of them. I would have marched into her office and told her so if I hadn't been in a hurry to get back to my own office.

As I turned the key in the ignition, the polite purr of the engine coming to life was accompanied by an odd little knocking. It took me a beat to realize that it wasn't my car developing a new problem, but someone rapping on the side window. Bart flexed a smile and I rolled the window down.

"I wonder if I might ask a favor," he said.

He was going to ask me to drop the blanket off at the tack store. Not happening, if only for the simple reason that I didn't want someone saying I kept it instead. "Sure," I said and returned an identically smarmy smile.

"You have some investigating skills, I understand."

My shoulders sagged. Crap. Here we go again. "Not really."

"Don't be so modest, Miss Campbell. You've had some impressive success in crime investigation."

"Dumb luck."

"I think not. And I believe you could be of some real use to the police investigating Dr. Archterkamp's death."

"And I think they wouldn't appreciate me interfering."

"They would if you put them onto the real culprit. You understand I can't become involved because of my position with the social welfare organization I manage, of course."

"Of course." Not. What an idiot.

"Good. Then you'll want to look closely at Max. I believe he's involved in some way. The police need to know. I did you a favor in there just now." He tipped his head toward the Big Barn. "You might show some reciprocation, show some gratitude for the way I was able to avert a crisis on your behalf."

My temples pulsed with the effort I'd been making to be pleasant. I simply couldn't keep it up. Gratitude? What a self-righteous ass. He was looking for some way to hang Max and not get his own hands dirty – and all the while his wife was trying to buy my help to direct the police away from Max. I was sorely tempted to fill Bart in, but I'd had enough of all of them.

"No, I won't help you. And if you ask me again, I'll advise Andrea against investing in your organization." I shoved my car into gear, backed out of my parking place, jammed the shift into drive and left Bart hopping out of the way of flying gravel.

The triumph of having the last word steadied my pulse a bit. Of course I wouldn't even bring the subject up with Andrea, but he didn't know that. It was none of my business what she spent her considerable fortune on. I should have felt badly about the threat, but I was so sick of being manipulated. He's lucky I didn't sic the cops on him for trying to make me interfere with their investigation.

There was just one thing I wanted to clear up, however, and that was the question of Sybil's identity and what she had to do with Don. Michelle's arrest bothered me for the simple fact that although she had the means and opportunity to kill Don, she had no motive.

I pulled my car up in front of my office and sat, drumming my fingers on the steering wheel. The "accident" theory I'd been so keen on hadn't been sitting well with me since my visit to Don's office either. Willa kept that office tidy and organized. I knew vaccinations were kept refrigerated until they were ready to use and euthanasia solution, a sedative, was not. Besides, I was well aware each vial was clearly marked as "Euthanasia Solution."

Detective Thurman was right. Don's death was murder, but Michelle's arrest sang "set-up" in the most classical manner. I had to go back and talk to Willa -- not for Agnes or Bart, or even for Juliet. I had to do it for Michelle.

# Chapter Fifteen

It was closing in on five. The lights in Don's office were still on and the "Open" sign still hung in view on the door. Don's partner Rick had left his vet-mobile idling at an angle across three parking spaces, driver's door, tailgate and the lid over his equipment all wide open. He must be loading supplies, and was likely going to be running in and out. So much for hoping Willa was alone. I didn't want Rick's presence to stifle our conversation or keep her from taking the time to chat. At least my excuse of discovering that my emergency supply of Banamine paste had expired, and therefore needed replacement, would be a believable reason for showing up again so soon.

Rick, with his cell phone to his ear, slid me a quick look as I approached. I smiled and nodded, but got no acknowledgment in return. I shrugged it off and went inside.

Willa looked up from her desk, pen in hand, where she was making an entry into her phone log. Her eyes went wide.

"What a surprise, Thea." The smile she added did little to ease her startled expression, leaving me with the uneasy feeling of an unwelcomed intruder.

"I see you're busy." I tipped my head toward Rick, still deep in conversation outside the glass door.

"Oh, no, no. He's going to leave soon. A horse with colic, I think." She laughed, high pitched, twisting her hands together. "Always seems to happen on a Friday at closing time."

Colic was no laughing matter. For the horse it was often life or death. "I won't keep you. All I need is some Banamine. I noticed my tube is expired."

She darted another look at Rick, now closing up his truck. "I'll go get some. Be right back." She trotted off to the supply room and disappeared from view for only a moment. "Here you go." She hurried back, set the tube on the counter, grabbed a charge sheet, hand-wrote an invoice and shoved it across the counter at me. I winced a little when I looked at the amount due. "Yeah, it's expensive stuff. Whoever borrowed yours really ought to pay you back."

"I didn't loan it, mine expired," I said, pulling out my checkbook. "Say, when you mentioned Sybil yesterday morning, the name rang a bell. I just can't place it, though. Are you sure you don't know who she is?"

"Nope, 'fraid not." She didn't even hesitate in her answer and rested her hands on the counter near my purse, her fingernails tapping a light, quick skitter.

I paused, pen hovering above the blank check. "Who do I make this out to?"

At that moment, Rick pushed through the door and strode past the counter. Willa dove in his direction.

"The toilet's clogged, Rick, and the floor is flooded."

He made an abrupt about face, rolling his eyes. "Fine. Call the plumber and make sure he gets it fixed this time."

"I was just about to," Willa called as he strode back out the door and to his truck.

"Bummer," I said.

"Yeah, tell me. Make the check out to Don -- as usual. The account is still open. I'll just stamp the back."

"Okay." I wrote in the date and Don's name, taking my time. With Rick gone I had the perfect opportunity to question Willa the way I'd planned. "I'm still having a hard time believing Michelle did that to Don. She just doesn't seem to have a motive."

Willa grunted a response.

"Is there anyone else who might have access to Don's drugs? Someone who might risk the possibility of an accident? Maybe someone who he had help him prepare all the vaccines for the appointment?"

Her mouth tightened to a firm line. "I didn't do it, if that's what you want to know. He's -- he *was* always afraid I'd stick myself with a needle."

"Sorry, I didn't mean to sound like I thought you might have been involved." The only thing I was sorry about was how I'd worded the question. She didn't acknowledge my apology, except to scowl.

I signed the check and ripped it from my check book. Before I could hand it to her, she reached across the counter but pulled up short, grimacing.

"Are you okay?" I asked.

"Yeah. Wrenched my shoulder is all."

I nodded. "Let me know if you remember anything about Sybil."

"Sure."

I put my checkbook away and, grabbing my purse, turned to go.

"Thea …?"

I stopped and looked back. Willa's hand clutched my check like it might fly away. Her gaze held mine in a plea. Prickles shot up my spine.

"Um … Michelle is out of prison. Her parents paid her bail."

"That's good to know." I paused, waiting for her to say the something else I knew was there. When she didn't, I said good bye and left, a small seed of unexplainable dread lodged in my chest.

I puzzled over Willa's odd behavior as I backed out of my parking space in front of a tobacco shop. What had gotten into her? I was fairly certain my presence hadn't set her off. When I'd walked in she'd been distressed and uncharacteristically short tempered -- to a degree I found difficult to attribute to a clogged toilet.

As I waited for a break in traffic on Avenue D, a car pulled into the entrance of the strip mall without the benefit of a turn signal, leaving me with a missed opportunity to pull out. I grumbled until I realized who the other driver was: Alice. She was likely going to her husband's office to work on clearing out more of his personal effects. I could forgive her for the oversight. She'd probably be distracted for some time to come. I hoped Willa pulled herself together. Alice didn't need to deal with the woman's mood.

Returning to my own office, I worked on some clients' 1040s, catching up on what I'd put off, and waited for Juliet to show up. I hadn't seen her since Wednesday and, besides cautioning her about Eric, still had a bone to pick with her about Bobby. If Willa was right, I now knew Michelle's parents fronted the money for her bail, so I had to question what it was my ditsy sister did for the miscreant and why she was making herself so scarce.

Although I got plenty of work done, Juliet was a no-show. Around seven thirty Paul arrived with left-over lasagna, left-over salad and a left-over bottle of wine. We ate at my desk and I filled him in about my most recent visit with Willa. He left for home, and by nine o'clock, tired of working and waiting for my elusive sister, I went home as well. I'd run her to ground eventually, although I feared the longer it took, the more damage there would be to put to rights.

<><><>

Morning broke dull, dreary and punctuated by a sharp pounding on my front door.

"Stay put," Paul said, putting down his coffee and pushing away from the kitchen table. "If it's Juliet and she sees the blood in your eye she'll run."

"It's not Juliet. She never knocks, just comes right in. And, no, I don't know how she keeps getting keys when I keep taking them away."

Paul held up both hands, fending off the implied accusation. "Talk to your aunt." He headed for the front door and our early morning visitor.

"Morning, Paul." Detective Thurman's casual greeting to my husband turned the coffee I'd swallowed degrees more acidic. Coming to our house first thing in the morning could not possibly be a social call. "Is Juliet here?"

My stomach twisted. I was out of my chair and in the hallway before Paul could answer, ten different scenarios, all involving my sister ultimately getting tossed into jail, playing out in their entirety in my mind.

"Good mor --"

I cut off Thurman with a wave. "What did she do?"

Except for a slight cocking of his head, the detective's expression didn't change. "What do you think she did?"

I glared at him. He'd sprung this verbal trap on me too many times for me to fall for it again. "Hard saying with Juliet."

"What did she tell you?"

"I haven't seen her since Wednesday. She hasn't told me anything."

"And yet you seem to think she's done something. Why is that?"

"Because you're here."

Paul's attention had been following Thurman and my "back and forth" without comment. Now he held up a hand.

"Can we stop this, please, and get to the point of your visit, Phil?"

Thurman smiled, but like all his "official" expressions, few of his facial muscles were put to use. Sweat trickled from my armpits. I stepped toward Paul and clutched his arm.

"You went to Don Archterkamp's office yesterday."

"Yes. I needed to pick up some Banamine paste. Why?" It was my official line and I was sticking to it. No doubt he'd spoken with Willa.

"What happened while you were there?"

I shrugged. "Rick left for a colic emergency, I bought the Banamine, wrote Willa a check and left."

"Nothing else?"

"No, Willa didn't have much to say."

Thurman's eyes narrowed. "Why was that?"

"I don't know. She was tense, in a crabby mood. Told Rick the toilet was clogged and the bathroom flooded. That would make me crabby."

"Was anyone else there?"

"No. Why, what's happened?"

"Willa Weaver was found dead this morning. Your check was on her desk."

Paul and I exchanged a startled look. Shock and denial whirled through my mind, producing no words.

"How?" Paul asked.

"Same as Don – injection of euthanasia solution."

"She --" I gulped down the dryness in my throat. "She killed herself?"

"I'm going to have to say we're treating it as a suspicious death. She could have, but it's not sitting right with me."

Sitting seemed like a good idea. I released Paul, went to the living room and perched on the edge of the sofa, clutching my robe closed at my throat – although it wasn't in any danger of falling open. Paul and Thurman followed. Paul sat close, an arm wrapped around my shoulders. Thurman took my coral wing chair.

"Do you think Michelle killed her?" I had to know.

"We've brought her in for questioning, but ...." He shrugged. "How about you two tell me what you've been digging up lately."

I raised my chin. "What do you mean?"

Paul chuckled. Then he leaned back into the sofa's pillows, dragging my rigid self along, and proceeded to spill our guts about our impulsive wedding and how, despite trying to keep it secret so no one would be offended they weren't invited, Juliet found out and was using it to coerce us into helping find evidence to exonerate Michelle.

Thurman laughed and rose from the chair. We stood, too.

"Well, congratulations, once again," Thurman said, shaking Paul's hand at the front door. He twitched a real smile. "That sister of yours certainly has a creative streak."

"Please don't tell anyone," I begged for the hundredth time.

"I won't."

"My aunt would cry, my parents would be furious, and it would be an all-around bad idea."

"You told me that already. I understand. Don't worry." He raised a hand and left, jogging down the porch steps.

Paul shut the door and turned to me. "I'll repeat: don't worry."

"I'm not."

He snorted.

I frowned. Staring at the closed front door, I sucked in my lower lip. "We didn't tell him everything."

"Like what?"

"Like how I saw Alice pulling in to the office when I was leaving."

"Tell him."

"No. I can't believe Alice had anything to do with Willa's death -- or Don's. She just wouldn't."

He opened the door. "He needs to know."

I snarled at my husband, stepped into the doorway and,

with a wave, caught the detective's attention as he opened his car door. "There's something else," I said, probably not loud enough for him to hear.

He seemed to understand just the same and returned to the house.

"One more thing," I said as he mounted the steps. "When I was leaving the strip mall where Don's office is, Alice drove in. I don't think she noticed me. You might want to find out why she was there, although I understand she's been going through Don's personal effects in fits and starts. Can't say I blame her."

"Already talked to her," Thurman said, flicking a glance at Paul. "You're right, she didn't see you. She did, however, see a yellow motorcycle pull in when *she* was leaving."

My jaw sagged. Paul's hand closed on my shoulder. Thurman nodded at the two of us and retraced his steps to his car before I could demand he explain what my sister had to do with all of this. Had she confronted Willa in an effort to pin the blame of Don's death on someone other than Michelle who had access to the drugs and could have filled the vials -- like I had?

"Detective, wait!"

He stopped and turned.

"I asked Willa yesterday about who had access to the drugs besides Michelle. She got defensive with me. I could be the one who got her thinking she was going to be caught. I could be the one who pushed her to suicide."

Thurman shook his head. "I'll talk to everyone, but we'll never know. Rick found her this morning, on the floor by her desk. No note, just the syringe in her right hand."

An image, as he described, swam through my mind and I cringed, taking in the details, such as they were: Willa sprawled on the old linoleum floor, her expression vacant, the syringe in … I gasped.

Thurman stopped and eyed me. I met his gaze.

"Willa wrote out my invoice last night. She was left-handed," I whispered.

# Chapter Sixteen

Detective Thurman nodded, got into his car and left while I stood on my porch in my bathrobe, incapable of moving, horrified at what I'd just discovered. Willa had been murdered the same way as Don. And my sister had quite possibly been one of the last people to see her alive. Paul took my arm, walked me inside and closed the front door with extreme control. I turned desperate eyes to him, but did not see in him the shock I felt. The muscles in is jaw flexed and his blue eyes all but threw fire.

"Goddammit. Your sister --"

My protective reflex came to life in a rush, and at a pitch that would have made dogs howl. "There is no chance in hell my sister killed Willa, so don't even --"

"I'm not saying she killed Willa, but Goddamn, she is involved in this up to the top of her curly head. She was supposed to leave the investigating to us. She didn't, that much is obvious, and now she's going to get hauled in on suspicion of murder." He raked both hands through his hair then paced across the living room, one hand raised in a fist as if to pound something. Instead he turned back to me, rubbing the back of his neck.

Obviously, I'd misjudged. We were on the same page, after all. I voiced the continuation of his thought since he seemed apoplectic. "And, if she's arrested my parents are going to have a stroke. Then they'll hot-foot it up here and Armageddon will look like amateur night."

He closed his eyes and blew out a breath. "It won't be that bad."

What? I sucked a breath, but he waved me off with both hands.

"Okay, okay. Then we'll have to do something. There goes my idea of letting her learn a lesson by getting herself arrested."

Boy, was I wrong. The same page? We hadn't even been in the same book, much less adjacent chapters. "Paul! How could you even think that? This is my sister you're talking about."

"You coddle her too much. She has no incentive to grow up when you save her butt every time she screws up. Christ, Thea, she doesn't even have to buy her own groceries. She practically steals the food off my damn fork."

He couldn't be right, could he? Maybe just a little. "She has been kind of free with access to the pantry lately, but Paul, she's my little sister. I have to help --"

He threw his hands into the air and let loose an exasperated growl. "The point is, I don't want you putting yourself at risk by charging out to save her."

"I'm not putting myself in any danger. And besides, what choice do we have? Even if we could keep the news from my parents, I'd still have to help her. She's my sister."

His chest expanded with the breath he took and his lips compressed to a bloodless slash. "There has been one more murder, in case it slipped your mind. Someone is getting desperate. We don't know who, and I'll be dammed if I'm going to put you in harm's way. Another thing --"

The sound of quick footsteps up the steps to the porch cut him off. The front door flew open and the reply I'd been forming flew out of my mind. My sister, hair flying around her head as if possessing its own personal whirlwind, blasted through the door and into the front hallway. If her eyes had turned red and she'd hopped off a broom I could not have been more stunned.

"How could you?" Juliet shrieked. She bore down on me, rage smoking from flared nostrils. "You told me you were going to clear Michelle. Now you've gotten her arrested again. What'd Thurman want, to congratulate you for your good work so they could lock her up for good? I'm going out that door," she pointed, furiously, "calling Mother and telling her you're already married. Then I'm telling Aunt Vi and Delores." She spun, heading back the way she'd come.

"Juliet, wait--"

"Go ahead," Paul said, arms crossed casually over his chest.

"What?" The word erupted from both my sister and me simultaneously.

He jerked his chin at her. "You heard me. Go ahead. Tell everyone. See what happens."

"No!" I leaped at my sister, grabbing her arm -- needlessly, as it turned out.

She studied Paul like someone who'd been outfoxed once before. I could almost hear the gears grinding in her brain. "Don't think I won't," she said, lifting her lip in a tentative snarl.

"Juliet," I growled, then cast a begging look at my husband. "Paul, please ...."

Without taking his eyes off my sister, he tipped a casual wave in my direction.

"How do you think that's going to play out?" he asked her. "How good are you going to feel when everyone's upset because of what you did? You. Not us. You."

Her mouth gaped like an oxygen-starved fish. I let go of my sister's arm. There was no need for me to restrain her. Paul's method was more effective. Even as much as Juliet and Mother fought, she never gloated about it. In fact, most of the time the conflict reduced her to tears. Now, apparently, she'd made a leap ahead to the consequences of her actions.

"I only want to save Michelle," she whispered.

Paul raised an eyebrow. "And what we want is the person responsible for Don's death, and Willa's, brought to justice."

Juliet sniffed. "It wasn't Michelle."

"Since Thurman only brought her in to ask some questions, and not to arrest her as you erroneously assumed --"

"She wasn't arrested again? Thank God. Then he was wrong."

"He? Bobby?" Paul asked.

Juliet grimaced, pressed her lips together and stayed silent.

Paul's casual stance didn't change, but his frown deepened. "We'll make you a deal."

A little warning bell clanged in the back of my mind. Sure, it *looked* as if Paul had the ball in his court, I just wasn't sure it was *my* court, too. I drew a breath to request a consultation, but he flashed me the same look I'd seen him use to silence rowdy students, and I swallowed my interruption whole.

"Thea and I will keep investigating, provided you quit having anything to do with Bobby and stop nosing around these murder investigations. Also, you tell us what you were doing at Don's office yesterday. It goes without saying you will keep the fact of our marriage to yourself."

I exhaled relief. Yes, that was what I wanted. He could have read my mind. However, irritation replaced the tension in my sister's features. "Of course I won't mention your Las Vegas wedding. And a lot of good your investigating has done up to now. Michelle is still the main suspect. Do you know her parents already put their house up as security in order to bail her out? How are they going to help her if she gets arrested for Willa's murder? There's nothing left. And, by the way, what makes you think I was at Don's office yesterday?"

"Don's wife, Alice, saw your motorcycle pulling in as she was leaving."

Juliet's gray eyes grew wide for a moment before narrowing. "It wasn't me."

"Well, Thurman thinks it was you," I snapped.

"It wasn't. It had to be -- it wasn't me."

"It had to be' what, Juliet?" Paul growled. "Or should I ask, 'it had to be *who*?' If you know something you'd better start talking."

She licked her lips and glanced at me before looking at the floor.

"Oh, please," I said. "Tell me you didn't loan your bike to Bobby."

"I didn't."

"Right."

"I didn't. He stole it."

"When?"

"Thursday. He took it from the Copper Creek parking lot when I wouldn't take his bail money to the jail. Michelle's parents were handling it. They didn't want him involved."

Smart parents. Stupid Bobby. "You reported the theft, of course."

"Uh, no."

Stupid Juliet. "Why not?"

"Uh, because, uh ...."

Paul shook his head. "This is what I'm talking about, Juliet. You're getting in the way of our investigation."

Her lower lip quivered. "I'm trying to help Michelle."

Paul's shoulders sagged and he turned away, rubbing his forehead, before he addressed me. "What are you wearing to our wedding?"

Talk about whiplash. I blinked.

"In April," he said, his tone impatient. "What are you

wearing?"

"I don't know. I haven't bought a dress yet."

Paul smiled. Not a happy smile, more like a "that'll do" smile. He turned to Juliet. "Make Thea's dress, keep your mouth shut about our marriage, tell us everything you know, stay out of our way and we'll keep investigating. Otherwise, we're done. Finished."

"What?" I croaked.

"Okay," my sister said.

I lept at Paul and grabbed his bicep with both hands. "Now wait a minute. You can't be serious. You want me to dress like Juliet at our wedding?"

"I'll approve the design. I've seen her work. She's good. Besides, you wore green sequins to the real thing and didn't seem to mind."

I shook his arm. "*You'll* approve the design?"

"You got married in your green dress?" Juliet let a laugh loose. "I can do way better than that." She stepped around me and stuck her hand out to Paul. "It's a deal. I'll sketch the design and you can give me the money to buy the fabric. I get to use it for my final class project, though."

Despite the fact I hauled at his arm, my husband moved to shake her hand. At the last moment he pulled back. "I want to see the design *before* I spend money on the fabric."

Juliet shrugged. "Sure."

I gasped as he shook her hand to seal the deal. "Hey, now. This isn't right. This isn't the way it's done."

"Sweetheart," Paul said, with a real smile this time. "When have we been doing things the right way?"

Defeated, I released my hold of him.

"Good point," Juliet said and, with a grin on her face, turned to go.

"One more thing," Paul said. Juliet stopped. "Report your bike stolen to Thurman -- along with the reason you didn't mention it earlier. It might help if you can get someone to corroborate your story."

Defiance and then uncertainty darted across her features as she regarded my husband, "I have to?"

Paul raised an eyebrow.

She sighed. "Okay. I'll take Delores with me. She knows."

"I'm not above calling to check on you," he said.

Juliet's jaw jutted for a moment. "You won't have to." She turned on her heel and did an excellent imitation of Mother's regal march to the front door.

"Do you need a ride?" Paul asked.

Juliet paused, a hand on the doorknob. "Jeez. It's not like it hasn't been bad enough having a sister who rides my ass, now I've got a brother, too. No, I don't need a ride. I've actually managed to arrange my own transportation." She flipped her hair over her shoulder and curled her lip at Paul. "Don't worry. It's not Bobby."

The moment the door closed, he strode to the living room and peeked out the window. I would have laughed at Juliet's assessment of having a brother to report to, but I was still steamed about the deal they'd struck. It was presumptuous, not to mention ridiculous, and I had no intention of cooperating.

"What in the name of God possessed you to make that arrangement with my sister?"

He didn't act like he'd heard me, didn't turn away from his spying. "Son of a gun, I was right."

What amounted to self-doubt was coming from a man who believed himself to be correct virtually all of the time. I simply could not let his comment pass. "Right? About what?"

He straightened and caught my eye, hesitating enough to make me suspect he was debating what to say. "Eric brought her over here," he finally said.

I sprinted to the window, but didn't see my sister or any car, other than the ones I already knew, parked on the street.

"They're gone now," he said.

I scoured the street again, anyway, before skinny-eying him. "You knew Eric gave her a ride here?"

"I suspected. She's obviously been getting reliable transportation for a couple of days. She hasn't been calling us and no one else has mentioned having to cart her around."

Oh. Made sense. I'd probably have reached the same conclusion if I hadn't been blindsided by their little deal – speaking of which, I couldn't help but notice how he'd returned to spying out the window. Who was he trying to kid? They wouldn't be coming back. He was avoiding me.

I strolled to the coffee table, picked up one of the paleontology magazines he'd left there, and leafed through.

"So," I said in as close to a casual, nonthreatening tone as I could manage. "Tell me how you got to be such an expert on women's wedding fashion. Not seeing any of it in your usual reading material."

He stuffed his hands into his jeans pockets and kind of faced me. "I'm no expert."

I tossed the magazine onto the coffee table. "And yet?"

The phone rang and we both looked toward our home office. I took a step, remembered it was Saturday and froze, my heart rate ratcheting to workout level.

Oh, my God.

I knew who was calling at this hour and we were in so much trouble. Paul shot me a quizzical look and started toward the office, the closest phone. I grabbed his arm.

"Don't answer that," I whispered.

"Why not?"

The phone rang a second time. I licked my lips and swallowed.

"It's my mother. Unless you've got some excellent plan in mind for keeping her from calling your parents, don't answer it."

He scoffed. "I'll just tell her I've been busy and haven't had a chance to call yet. She'll give me a few more days."

"She won't. She'll call your parents just like she threatened."

He had the decency to pale slightly. The phone rang a

third time.

"We're going to have to face her sooner or later."

"Then you deal with her. And if she asks, I've gone riding."

"Might as well get this over with," he grumbled and strode to the office, grabbing it up before the fourth ring.

I was right, of course. Paul's abruptly straightened posture and shuttered expression told me as much.

"Good morning to you, too," he said.

I listened, straining to hear and yet not wanting to. The conversation, at least from Paul's end, sounded polite and banal. Yes, we were fine, as were Aunt Vi, Uncle Henry and Juliet. Yes, Mrs. Cunningham had been contacted. No, we hadn't made a decision about where the ceremony would be to the best of his knowledge, but he'd let me know what her suggestions were, and yes, they all sounded excellent. Then came the moment I dreaded:

"No, you're right. I haven't had the time .... You did? .... Well, sure I knew. Thea told me you were going to call .... Oh, that's too bad .... I'm sure that will be fine .... Yes, of course .... Happy to .... Sure thing .... Bye." He disconnected the call and looked at the handset for a moment before looking at me. "Somebody is lying besides us this time, and I'm betting it's your mother."

# Chapter Seventeen

"Lying?" I asked, my heart rapping out a nervous two-step against my ribcage. "Mother?" She was always so straightforward. Usually. "I don't understand. What did she say?"

Paul took a breath. "In a very cheerful, even friendly, way she told me she'd called and had a 'lovely' chat with my mother. She'd have spoken with my dad, too, but he wasn't home."

"'Lovely'?" I gulped.

"Yes, her word. There's more. She wanted me to tell you how much it means to her to be helping with our wedding."

"She ...." I sat gingerly on the edge of the sofa. The implication that she was already up to her elbows in assistance left me with the helpless feeling of falling off a cliff with no big fluffy airbag to land on. Maybe he'd misquoted. "She said she's going to help plan our wedding?"

"I guess. Although, she never said 'plan,' only 'with'. And

she never said 'going to.'"

"Oh." I chewed my lip for a moment, staring at nothing, searching for an interpretation other than the obvious, hands-on, in-person, already-in-progress variety.

Paul cleared his throat -- twice. "Are you about to tell me that's code for 'she just took my mother to the mat'?"

My gaze crawled up from intense examination of the carpet to meet his eyes. "Could be."

"Terrific." He tried to run a hand through his hair but was still holding the handset and clonked himself in the forehead. It seemed to jar a thought. He studied the phone for a moment as if trying to remember someone's number. "Maybe it would be simpler if we just confessed."

I sprang to my feet and tripped over the coffee table to get to him. "No! Not yet. Not unless we don't have any choice. This is just a stumbling block with our mothers. Please?"

"You wouldn't have to have Juliet make your dress." He looked so hopeful and the confession theme had become so relentless I could have smacked him.

"Is that why you made that stupid deal? Are you trying to push me into telling everyone we've already done the deed?"

"I made the deal as incentive for her to keep her mouth shut, not undermine you. If we can't find the evidence to clear Michelle, she won't have any reason to keep our secret."

"You mean besides not wanting to upset everyone in our family?" Obviously, he underestimated how well Mother had trained us to respond to guilt -- which, from all appearances, had been sufficient to thwart Juliet's latest threat without the addition of his deal.

He scowled at me as if I were the one being intentionally obtuse. "Look at it as a positive reward. Juliet actually gets something for doing what we want, regardless of the outcome of our investigating. Isn't that what you do with horses? Positive reinforcement?"

"Sure," I grumbled, "but a firm hand is required at times, too. You can't let them walk all over you."

"And what did I do with your sister?" That damn eyebrow went up again and we had a brief stare down.

"Fine. I suppose I'm going to have to wear whatever she concocts."

"Not if we tell everyone we've already done the deed."

I stifled the urge to thump him. "Maybe the dress will be nice."

The phone rang and we both started. Since Paul was holding it, I figured he could answer it.

"Aw, shit," he said, after a quick look.

Then he stuck it so close to my face I had to rock back to read the caller ID on the dim LED screen. I almost uncrossed my arms to take it from him before working out that "MINPOLIS, MN" was not an abbreviation for Mini-Police, Mounted, but for Paul's hometown, Minneapolis, Minnesota.

I reared back, an inhale and exhale trying to occur at the same time.

My husband set the thing gently on the coffee table as if his parents would feel the jostle and know we were backing away.

It rang again.

"Are you going to answer?" I whispered.

He stared at the handset as if it had grown legs. "I about threw my back out to be nice to your mother. Genuflecting to mine will probably cause me an injury my insurance won't cover."

"Maybe it's your sister --"

"Nope. Not risking it. Don't want to deal with them." The phone rang again. "Get moving."

"Huh?"

"Get dressed, we're leaving." He pushed me toward the hallway.

"Where are we going?"

He nudged me along, hard on my heels. "I don't know. Copper Creek. Don't you have to ride Blackie?"

"Well, yeah --" I tripped on the first stair step. The phone rang again. I scrambled and kept going.

"Good. I'll come along. I haven't seen him in a few days."

In the time it took me to change into my riding clothes the phone had gone to voice mail and the house was scary silent. Once we got to the car, and the terror of a narrow escape began to recede, my brain began to function again.

"What are you going to do while I'm riding? Don't you have something you'd rather do than hang around the barn?"

"Nope. I thought I'd talk to Delores and probably Maria to see if they know who Sybil was."

"Who?"

He spared me a look as he checked for traffic at an intersection. "Sybil. The woman *you* told me about. Willa said Don had an affair with her."

"That was a long time ago. I think. I can't see how she'd have any bearing on Don or, especially, Willa's deaths."

"I'm asking anyway."

"Fine."

Familiar scenery rolled past on our way to Copper Creek. Bits of color and new green brightened up what, for months, had been a gray and brown landscape. Yellow daffodils and purple crocus dotted flower beds. Redbud and cherry trees had begun to sprout their pink and white blossoms. In another week or so there'd be masses of pink all over town and a couple weeks past that, about the time of our wedding, cars would be covered with tiny pink petals as leaves replaced the flowers. The thought made me smile. I always liked to think of it as pink rain. A romantic backdrop for a wedding – our wedding.

Despair at the overwhelming complications we'd created washed over me. I turned away from the early signs of spring, of new life, and studied my husband for a moment. He reached for my hand without taking his eyes off the road.

"What's wrong?"

I paused for so long he jiggled my hand.

"Thea?"

I shook my head. "I wish we could start over -- begin again."

Frowning, he flipped his blinker on and slowed to turn into Copper Creek's entrance. "I'm not following you. What do you mean?"

I surveyed the parking lot as we drove in. It wasn't empty. Several people had already arrived. Among the cars was Agnes' tan Mercedes. I groaned. "I don't know if I can do this."

"Do what?"

A lump grew in my throat. I gestured, as wide as the interior of the car would permit. "Everything." My voice cracked.

He pulled into a parking spot near the office and shut the engine off, then shifted in his seat, undoing his seatbelt. "Hey. Come here." He reached for me.

I leaned across the console and parking brake for the comfort of his hug.

He stroked my hair and held me for a long moment. "It'll be okay. We've got each other."

I turned my face into his shirt, breathed in his warmth and drew on his strength. The world faded away to just us -- until there was a sharp tap on the driver's side window.

We drew apart and sighed, not at all startled at being caught in a public cuddle like we'd often been before we married. For a fraction of a moment I considered worrying about giving ourselves away, but it was too much effort.

"You two have an entire house to yourselves," Delores said, loud enough to hear clearly through the closed window.

Paul kissed the end of my nose before releasing me and opened his door. By the time I was out of the car he was already striding after his aunt.

"You're just the person I was hoping to run into," he said, draping an arm over her shoulder.

She stopped and addressed him with a disbelieving snort. "Of course I am. Don't know why that didn't occur to me before I interrupted. I'll be in the office." She strode off without him.

"She's not mad at us, is she?" I asked, trotting up.

"Jealous, maybe," he said, with a laugh and shake of his head before swatting my butt. "Go ride. A horse. I'll go grill the dragon."

His words lightened the load on my shoulders. I arrived at Blackie's stall if not with a spring in my step, then with a calmer attitude. We'd have a good ride and be better prepared for next week's lesson with Uncle Henry. I led my horse to the grooming stall, eager to get him dressed and out to the arena.

Because the indoor arena was busy with lessons and people who minded the occasional bit of drizzle, I chose to work in the vacant outdoor dressage arena. A grassy strip and gravel path flanked one long side. The opposite long side included a stretch of four-tiered bleachers where people could sit to watch the dressage shows our barn hosted in the summers. Beyond the bleachers was the huge outdoor jumping arena, easily three times the size of the dressage arena. Cleverly designed, the plank seating also stepped down on the backside, thus serving as a viewing area for both areas.

Today, both sides of the bleachers were empty. But Agnes riding Elf, a steady and reliable hunter she'd owned for several years, did have an audience. A single person, bundled up for the weather, stood in the shelter of a group of evergreens near the barns.

"Bridge your reins in one hand," Max yelled.

Apparently, Agnes was taking a jumping lesson. Max didn't use a communication device like Uncle Henry, and his clear, exasperated voice carried his instruction easily to me in the dressage arena. Nevertheless, I didn't have any trouble ignoring him, and, apparently, neither did Agnes.

"Did you not hear me?" Max shouted. He always shouted when he taught, even when he didn't need to. "I said, bridge your reins in your right hand."

Agnes continued to canter Elf in a large circle, a rein in

each hand.

I smiled to myself and let Blackie motor along in his big walk, focusing on the swing of his back and the rhythm of his footfalls. He needed no encouragement to go forward when we worked outdoors. His neck was low, relaxed and stretched, his ears flicking occasionally to me when I shifted my seat for a turn, and occasionally to a bird chirping. He ignored Max's barked orders, too. Poor Max. I chuckled. Both of Blackie's ears swiveled to me. I patted his shoulder.

"Good boy."

The words seemed to encourage him and he stepped along smartly. Uncle Henry would be pleased I was allowing my horse the time to warm up properly.

"The reason," Max bellowed, causing both Blackie and me to look in his direction, "I'm asking you to put your reins in your right hand is precisely because your left shoulder hurts. Elf will not run away with you --"

Agnes said something I didn't catch.

"Or take advantage," Max added.

Again Agnes replied, but her tone was too low for me to hear.

"Let him do his job. Enough with the endless circles. You can steer him with one hand. I want to see you put him through that gymnastic line. It is not a jumping lesson if you don't jump."

Agnes booted Elf into a more active canter.

Blackie and I returned to our warm-up. I added some shallow leg yields at the walk, moving Blackie obliquely from a corner of the arena to the center of the opposite short end, all to the background accompaniment of Max's criticism and encouragement of Agnes. She must have been doing okay one handed, since there was no break in Max's yammering.

Silence, which I hoped was the end of Agnes' lesson, coincided with the end of Blackie's walk warm-up and the first half of our twenty meter trot circle. Then all hell broke loose.

"I said jump the damn thing!" Max's shrill shout certainly would have spurred me into an immediate leap.

Agnes must have been inspired – or something.

A crash, like so much lumber being tossed to the ground, snapped my attention to the jumping arena. Through the bleachers I saw Elf heaving himself to his feet, red and white painted four-by-four poles scattered around him like pickup sticks. A bright blue lump that was surely Agnes wheezed painfully from the ground in front of him. Max dashed toward her. The man who'd been sheltering in the evergreen trees ran, as well, although with less grace. It was Bart, of course.

Elf darted wild-eyed glances at the fast-approaching men and trotted away with a pronounced limp, stopping himself when he stepped on a dangling rein.

"Agnes," Max said, his voice high pitched and frantic as he knelt at her side. "Are you all right?"

She wheezed in reply.

"Of course she's not all right, you nincompoop." Bart panted the words and had slowed his jog to a quick walk. "This is your fault. If she's injured I'll sue you."

Agnes wheezed again and croaked, "No!"

Max shot to his feet, red faced. "If anyone is to blame then it's Copper Creek for shoddy maintenance." He stomped to where Elf had apparently attempted to take off for the jump and kicked at the ground. "Look at this," he shrieked. "There's a hole in the Goddamn footing."

Elf retreated several steps, neck up and ears on a swivel. He whinnied, low and pitifully, but no one looked his way.

I patted Blackie's shoulder. "Come on, boy. We need to go rescue Elf.".

"You should have noticed a problem with the footing when you were setting up the jumps," Bart shouted.

"I always check the footing," Max snapped. "I set this course up two days ago and it was fine."

"I doubt you did a thorough job."

Agnes struggled to get to her feet. Both her husband and

trainer jumped to help her. "Leave me be," she said, probably not as forcefully as she intended since her hand flapping was degrees more vigorous than her voice. "I just knocked the wind out."

"It could have been far worse," Bart said. "I want you to stop this dangerous sport immediately."

"Absolutely not," Agnes said.

"And you," he snarled at Max, totally ignoring Agnes' comment, "for the amount of money I pay you each month, you should treat *my wife* as if she were porcelain."

Max's drew himself up and glared. "In which case she would learn nothing. You pay me the going rate and I do my job training and teaching."

"This will end immediately."

Agnes took a step toward Max. "It most certainly will not. Bartholomew Fulton, you will not even suggest taking away the one thing in my life that brings me joy. And I'd like to remind you that it is *my* money."

*Okey doke.* I rode Blackie, as unobtrusively as possible, through the gate Bart had left opened. Elf pricked his ears at Blackie as we approached and nickered. "Max," I called, scooping up Elf's reins with one hand. "I'll take Elf up to the barn."

Intent on snarling at one another, no one even looked in my direction. I shrugged. Elf followed obediently, despite limping on his right foreleg.

I hadn't seen the accident, but as I rode past I did see the hole Max was referring to in the arena's base. Even with my brief and distant examination it appeared as if someone had dug a wide trench, removed the firm ground underneath the sand and then smoothed it all over. When Elf had stepped on it, his foot found no purchase and he'd fallen into the jump. Poor guy. Whoever did that should be drawn and quartered. Delores would never allow the arena to become compromised like that. She would not only be horrified when she found out, but livid that Max would accuse her of deliberate negligence.

Elf insisted on cuddling up against Blackie's left side as we walked to the barn. Before I could figure out how to dismount on the wrong side of my horse, Max rushed up and snatched Elf's reins from my hand. Startled at the abrupt treatment, the unfortunate fellow rolled his eyes and pulled back.

Max jerked the reins a couple of times, intimidating Elf into a halt. "I can take care of my own animals," Max snapped at me and dragged Agnes' horse behind him into the barn.

"Just trying to help," I called and, just to prove I could be every bit as juvenile, stuck my tongue out at his back before turning Blackie toward the dressage arena.

Agnes and Bart left the arena together and appeared to be continuing their arguing. Bart, angled toward his wife, jerked his hands in small, emphatic gestures.

Then, his voice raised to a shout. "You are done with the damn horses. Done." He pounded his fist into his open palm.

Agnes leaned abruptly away. Bart stopped, grabbing her arm with enough force to spin her toward him. She twisted, raising her opposite hand as if she intended to slap him, then, fist clenched, stalked toward the barn -- and me.

I changed direction, choosing a route that wouldn't even remotely be close to theirs.

"Delores must sometimes wonder why she still runs this place. Good thing most people here are nicer than that lot," I commented to my horse. His ears flicked back and he tossed his head. I laughed. "I'll take that as agreement."

Once in the dressage arena, I put Blackie back to work, paying close attention to his progress through the warm-up. With the suppling work at the walk and trot completed, I asked for canter. He bounded forward, not as round and balanced as he would be after a few minutes, but he settled in well, ears tipped toward me in concentration. His back swung with each stride and he blew softly through his big nostrils. The thrill of having such power on tap never dulled. The generosity with which he allowed me, as rider, to direct him left me deeply awed.

The forward flick of Blackie's ears warned me of an impending interruption. I raised my focus from our line of travel to see Bart standing by the low fence. He waved an arm in an energetic manner when we were a couple of strides away. My own back tensed in surprise. Any other horse may have spooked at his unexpected movement, but Blackie simply walked.

"Is Mrs. Paalmann back from her vacation yet?" Bart asked. His features had resumed their usual genial, if stiff, appearance. Not a trace of his previous, red-faced anger remained.

I held his gaze a long moment, hoping to convey my displeasure at the interruption. It was wasted effort. His expression didn't change. "Not that I'm aware of." I set Blackie back into canter.

Bart was still by the rail when we completed the circle. "Tell her I look forward to hearing from her," he called, loud enough to rattle my deliberate concentration.

I sent Blackie into an extended canter down the next long side, away from Bart. When we came around again, he was gone.

Despite all the disturbances, Blackie and I completed our training session well enough to give me confidence we'd show improvement in our next scheduled lesson with Uncle Henry. Completing a series of trot/halt/trot transitions that produced a slower, more cadenced trot, I gave my horse a hearty couple of pats on his neck then, grinning, hugged his neck. Applause came from a single source behind us, and I twisted in the saddle to see Paul lounging on the bleachers. He raised a hand in greeting.

"Nice job."

Blackie changed direction and strolled over with no prompting from me.

"How long have you been sitting there?"

He glanced at his watch and stood, stretching. "Five minutes, maybe. I didn't think you'd mind if I sat and watched until you were done."

"Of course not." I stayed in the saddle, smiling at my husband. How lucky was I to have someone like him and not Bart.

He raised an eyebrow and my silent, pleased appraisal of him. "What?"

"Nothing. Just looking. And admiring."

He chuckled, shaking his head, and stepped over the low arena fence. I leaned and kissed him. His lips were cold, as was the end of his nose. In all likelihood, he'd been sitting on the bleachers for more than the five minutes he admitted to. I handed him my dressage whip and zipped his jacket up higher. Blackie curled his neck and nuzzled Paul's pocket while Paul scratched Blackie's forehead. "I expect the big guy is looking for a treat."

I dug a sugar cube out of my pocket and handed it to my husband. "Here. Give this to him. He deserves it -- and for more than just a good workout."

"Oh?"

"There was some drama earlier that has made me appreciate what I have even more than usual."

"Want to go inside and talk about it?"

I shook my head. "Too many 'ears' inside. It's like a megaphone in there." I slid off Blackie and into my husband's arms, where I proceeded to relate an abridged version of Agnes' fall and the ensuing argument between Max and Bart.

"Interesting," he said and, with an arm around my shoulder, led me, as I led Blackie, toward the barn. "So do you think Agnes is going to take her husband's advice and find another hobby?"

"Doubt it. She was digging her heels in pretty good and, from what she said, it sounded like all their wealth comes from her." I shrugged. "Your turn. Did you find out who Sybil was?"

He nodded. "Like you said, too many ears here. I'll tell you at home over lunch."

We entered the barn and went to the grooming stall where I'd left my brushes earlier. Paul helped me untack Blackie then took him for a cool-down walk around the property while I put my equipment away and cleaned up my mess. In short order we were in the car and headed home.

He dodged my questions on the way home, and my curiosity shifted to impatience over the possibility of solving the case. He continued to put me off until we'd put lunch on the table. By the time he began relating his conversation with Delores about the identity of the elusive Sybil I was tipping off the edge of my chair in exasperation, ignoring my turkey sandwich and broccoli-cheddar soup. The information was far from enlightening. In fact, it was downright disappointing and hardly worth the build up of having to wait so long to hear. Delores either couldn't or wouldn't answer his questions.

However, his smug demeanor over the fact that his aunt stonewalled him had me suspicious.

"I don't understand. What aren't you telling me? Why wouldn't Delores talk to you about her? She knew her, right? At least it seems she must have from the way she kept shutting you down. She *was* shutting you down, wasn't she?"

He swallowed what he was chewing. "Like Stevens Pass in a snow storm. All I got was a lot of 'long time ago,' and 'don't you have something else to do' crap followed by questions about what was going on with my mother and father." He popped the last of his sandwich into his mouth, chewed a couple of times and swallowed. "Henry told her about my mother being so insulting to you, by the way. Delores would like me to believe she's ready to fly out there and kick butt."

"I can't believe she'd get so worked up over your parents' attitude that she'd drop everything to be the family peacemaker. That's so unlike her. Not that she wouldn't help you out if you needed it, but I'm intimately acquainted with her preference for letting people work out their own issues. She was definitely avoiding answering your question about

Sybil. I'd say she was protecting someone."

"Exactly. Which is why I went to talk to Maria when I left Delores' office."

My spoon hovered over my soup. "Did Maria remember her?"

Paul smiled, cat-like. "You going to eat that?" He reached for my sandwich.

"Paul! Come on. What did Maria say? And make yourself another if you're still hungry."

"Maria remembered her, and the whole incident with Frank."

The spoon fell from my hand. "Frank? What do you mean? What kind of incident with Frank?" Frank, Delores' husband, died several years ago, when I was in my last year of college. He was a stand-up kind of a guy, someone everyone respected, a perfect match for Delores.

Paul's little "I know more than you do" smile continued. The pedestal I'd built for Frank began to crumble.

"Oh my God," I blurted. Paul held up a hand but I charged on. "Are you saying he was involved with another woman? We're talking about your mother's brother, here -- the man your parents sent you to when you were a kid because they knew he could straighten you out. I'm sorry, Paul, but I can't believe he would have strayed and, not only that, I can't believe Delores would have taken him back if he had, much less still be covering up for him. In fact, I refuse to believe it." I leaned back in my chair, arms crossed and locked a challenging gaze with my husband.

The whole while I'd been talking, he'd been making moves to interrupt. But I'd been so offended, I hadn't given him the chance. He eyed me as if waiting for me to say more. I didn't.

"Are you done?" When I didn't answer, he continued. "Frank wasn't 'involved' like you're thinking. There was no extra-marital affair. Sybil was a trainer and ran her business out of Copper Creek. Did a lot of showing and a lot of winning. Frank found out she was drugging her horses and told Don, who'd just set up his practice here and become friends with Frank."

"Oh," I said, picked up my spoon and readdressed my soup. "So, the incident was over the drugging?"

"Yes."

"So why was Delores so closed-mouthed? There must be more."

"From what Maria said, they had quite an argument. Don wanted to turn Sybil in. Frank claimed it would ruin her, and Delores wouldn't tolerate what she considered abuse. The compromise was to kick her and her business out of Copper Creek. But it was after she left that Don took action and turned her in to the governing body for the horse shows."

"The 'horse show Gods.' That would have been the American Horse Shows Association. It's now the United States Equestrian Federation." At his puzzled look, I continued. "Think of them like the NFL or the NCAA. They make the rules everyone has to abide by, including rules about drugs and conduct – not just the actual sports. Their word is law. You break the rules, you can be suspended from showing, fined, and everyone knows about it. It can ruin your business. Apparently, it ruined Sybil's if no one seems to remember her. This had to have happened more than ten years ago."

"It did," Paul said. "Not too long after Delores and Frank opened Copper Creek. When they were still competing in the A circuit horse shows, according to Maria."

"So they were afraid of any association with Sybil. That doesn't explain why Delores won't talk to you about it now."

"Oddly enough, I made just that observation to Maria." He paused long enough for me to want to smack him. "She believes Frank may not have been entirely clean, and Delores encouraged Don to turn Sybil in after she left for the sole purpose of taking any focus off Frank."

I could see Delores protecting her own, but this new perspective on Frank was going to take some adjustment of the heretofore God-like image I'd had of him. To me, he'd always been on the same level as Uncle Henry -- completely and utterly above reproach. I sighed and mulled over Paul's discovery as I finished my soup.

Finally, I pushed my bowl away. "Sounds like revenge, sort of. But the timing bothers me. Why would Sybil wait for so many years to go after Don for turning her in to the AHSA, and why kill Willa?"

Paul, sly devil, smiled. "Let's not get ahead of ourselves. There's more."

I picked up half of my sandwich, took a bite and waited. "You sound like a TV ad. Come on, tell me."

He leaned across the table, looking way too satisfied. "Sybil worked for Don, part time. Willa was his other part-timer."

My jaw dropped. "But …. What did he do, hire her out of guilt? And how could Willa not remember who she was?"

"Exactly. Willa lied. I'd bet money on her being involved in some way – either directly, or she found out something that made her a liability. Once Sybil is located we should have some answers." He sat back, the crafty smile still in place. "There's one more thing."

"Well?" I could have grabbed him by the neck and shook it out of him.

"Max is Sybil's son."

I dropped back in my chair. "Holy crap."

Paul nodded. "Looks like we've got some interesting possibilities."

"No kidding." I put my sandwich onto my plate and shoved it away. "Why hasn't Delores spoken up? Max has been at war with her lately."

My husband snatched up my sandwich and took a large bite. "No clue. Remember, she wouldn't talk to me about Sybil. Claimed she had no idea who she was."

"Which brings us full circle. You didn't believe her. Why?"

"Because, if Sybil had anything at all to do with the horse business, Delores would have known her. My aunt knows everyone. Everyone. It's pretty much that simple." He finished the half sandwich.

I nodded. Made sense.

"Therefore, since I couldn't get any information out of Delores, Maria was the logical next step. She and Miguel have been at Copper Creek since the beginning and she makes it her business to know what's going on with everyone."

I couldn't dispute that. "What made you think Maria would be less closed-mouthed?"

He laced his fingers above his head and stretched. "She likes me. I knew she'd be willing to talk to me if she thought she was helping me out. In fact, she'd feed me and do my laundry if I looked like I needed it. I'm her pet."

It was all I could do not to laugh. Maria had quite a number of "pets" and took care of all of them whenever she felt they needed some mothering. Although I knew he was quite fond of her, I had no idea Paul was even mildly aware of his special status.

Even Detective Thurman was "her" detective -- her special "in" with the Snohomish County Sheriff's department. She stopped by his office every now and then to check on him -- and bring him some of her home-made Mexican food specialties that he loved. I had no doubt if she ever needed him, he'd come running.

Paul pushed away from the table and got the pot of soup from the stove. I shook my head as he offered me more before pouring the remainder into his own bowl. I watched him eat, and mulled over the new perspective on Max.

Considering how angry Max had been, a visit to Thurman seemed like a good idea. In addition to suggesting he pay the jumper trainer another visit, maybe he could be convinced to interview Maria instead of putting Delores through old hurts. I told Paul and wasn't surprised to find he'd been thinking the same. Satisfied we had a plan, I went to shower and put on clean clothes while he cleaned up the kitchen.

A knock on our front door interrupted my final swipe of

mascara. I left the bathroom and ran into Paul in the hallway.

"Not Juliet?" he asked.

"Nope -- too polite. But if it is, we've got plenty to tell her."

Just then, the visitor on our porch laughed. I recognized the source immediately, dashed down the short hallway to the front door and flung it wide. "Andrea!"

She scooped me into a hug, laughing. "Surprise!"

"I'm surprised, and in the best way."

We released each other and Paul stepped around me to greet them both, slapping Dave on the shoulder and giving Andrea a kiss on the cheek.

I gave my friend a once over. "You look fabulous, although I expected you to be tanner." I eyed Dave, feigning disapproval.

Dave made a poor job of pretending uncertainty with me. "Do I get a hug?

"Depends." I propped my fists on my hips. "Have you treated my best friend like a queen?"

Dave's mouth twitched with a suppressed grin as he put an arm around Andrea's shoulders. "There's a very good reason we're not all that tan."

Andrea laughed and blushed.

"Sunscreen," Dave said. "I took very good care of her. Personally made sure she had it applied everywhere. What did you expect in an exotic, sunny climate with white sand beaches and swaying palm trees?"

"Oh, all right. I'll give you a hug. I suppose you'll do for a friend-in-law."

I stood on my toes to bestow the favor but he swooped in, lifting me off my feet.

"Oof!" was all I could manage.

"You can't fool me, squirt," Dave said. "You don't do 'tough guy' very well." He lugged me toward the living room.

Paul laughed. "Hey, scumbag, put my wife down."

# Chapter Eighteen

Dave dropped me and Andrea squealed. I made a slow turn, glaring bullets at Paul. He'd gone pale.

"Who needs Juliet to blab secrets when I have you?" I asked.

Andrea grabbed Dave by the shoulders, bounced around like an insane teenager and then hugged him, all the while shrieking, "I was right! I was right!"

Totally un-attorney-like.

I continued to froth anger at Paul. Could he not keep his mouth shut at all? Could he not have checked with me first? Could he not have considered I'd be concerned Andrea's feeling would be hurt, too, along with my family -- although, fortunately, that didn't seem to be the case.

But still. Dammit.

Paul winced, briefly, at me.

Dave's gaze flashed between me and Paul several times before he belly laughed. "No shit. You two really got married?

In Vegas? Andrea was right?"

"Uh," Paul said, sliding another uncomfortable look in my direction.

"Nice work, detective," I snarled. "Yes. And it was totally impulsive and totally without a single thought to the consequences."

Andrea sobered instantly to the point of worry, abandoned Dave and took my shoulders in a firm grip. "It wasn't a mistake. It really wasn't. You're meant for each other." She turned to her husband in an appeal for support. "Isn't that right, honey?"

"Well, yeah, of course they are, kitten." His voice, tender with Andrea, went all cop-like when he addressed me. "So, what's the problem?"

"The problem," I said, more snappishly than I intended, "is that we're trying to keep it a secret."

"Why?" Dave asked and smirked.

I hated that slight, lopsided smile, particularly when he aimed it at me. I felt he knew something he was only partially trying to hide and wanted you to assume he thought the absolute worst. That tiny lift of the corner of his mouth compelled me to blab an endless defense, just to convince him of the truth.

Andrea saved me from making an idiot of myself.

"Oh. Right. Of course. It's okay, really. We won't mention anything."

Dave studied her like he was contemplating a clue in a crossword puzzle then turned that smirk on me again. "What's the deal?"

Not saved, after all. Fine. I didn't bother to look at Paul, but launched into an extremely embellished version of why and when and how we decided to get married. I didn't leave out the couple on the plane, or Priscilla Fenwinkle, Dolly Parton, our narrow escape from Elvis or the annoying Eggman at the Little Snowbird Chapel. He deserved them all for backing me into a corner. Against my intention, Dave seemed to enjoy the entire recitation.

He dabbed at the corner of his eye as his chuckling died down. "This is a great story. I don't get why you're trying to keep it a secret."

"Because our family, and some of our friends, will be upset they weren't invited. Mother and Aunt Vi will be wounded for life, Dad will be upset he didn't get to give me away, Uncle Henry will be upset with us for upsetting Aunt Vi, and ... and I don't even want to think about the rest."

"So, through this all you were worrying about everyone else's hurt feelings and just went ahead and got married anyway?" Dave asked.

"No," I said. "It wasn't until after the ceremony and I saw the ring on Paul's finger. I went on and on about how sexy it was --" Dave and Andrea exchanged a look. "It was! I mean, holy cow, who knew married sex could be --" my face ignited and I looked to Paul for help. He only cocked his head like he wanted to hear what I had to say. Unfortunately, my mouth wouldn't stop. "And, and I said when everyone saw us together -- dressed! Not ... you know ... and just kissing, not, um, and they'd get embarrassed because we, well, mostly me, um ...." I'd hung myself, and Paul hadn't even tried to stop me.

Andrea covered her mouth with both hands, but I distinctly heard a giggle.

"Oh," Dave said, looked as if he was about to say more, then with a glance at Andrea, his face suffused to a sunburned shade and he shut his mouth.

"Now, Thea," Andrea said. "You can't possibly be angry with Paul for telling us. You know we can keep your secret. And besides, look at him." She took me gently by the shoulder and turned me toward the man I'd married. "How can you be mad at that face?"

My funny and less than contrite husband tipped his head and crossed his eyes. I made a face at him.

"Stop it, children." She pushed me at him, but I stopped

short of a collision. "Give each other a hug and say you're sorry. Both of you. Now."

We looked at her. I didn't know what Paul thought, but it seemed to me she was practicing too hard at being a mother.

"Oh, for heaven's sake. A little kiss wouldn't kill either one of you."

"You're asking Thea to demonstrate what she was trying to tell us, kitten? I may have to loan Paul my ring, since his is missing," Dave snarked.

"David," Andrea warned.

Paul reeled me in and bent me backwards. "Pucker up, sweetheart," he purred, but stopped abruptly before delivering the kiss. Cocking an eyebrow at Andrea he said, "I could take her to the bedroom and do a really thorough apology. I have to tell you, though, I've apologized twice today already and no ring was necessary."

Andrea crossed her arms. "How accommodating of you, Paul, but it's not polite to brag."

Dave chuckled.

My husband delivered a quick peck on my lips and stood me upright, my shredded dignity no worse for the command performance.

"So," Dave said, "what's with the comment about Juliet?"

"Shall I tell them the rest?" Paul asked me.

I dropped my forehead against his chest and sighed. "Go ahead, but I want to hear about Hawaii over coffee first."

"It was a dream," Andrea said, strolling back to Dave's side and hugging his arm.

He kissed the side of her head. "The dream was the company I kept. Hawaii was Hawaii -- warm and sunny with flowers and sandy beaches. The rest would either bore you or," he gave Andrea a wink, "make you jealous. That's all *I'm* telling." His self-satisfied gaze returned to Paul. "I want to hear about 'the rest.'"

Paul scratched the back of his head. "Ah … my fault, too, I'm afraid."

I sagged in relief that we were moving past my screw-up and left them to go to the kitchen and start another pot of coffee. My husband launched into a concise summary of how Don's death had been ruled a murder, Michelle arrested and how Juliet decided to investigate. Andrea, apparently uninterested, followed me.

She ran her hand along a granite counter top and sighed. "I'd almost say the fire you had last fall was worth the trouble. I really love the way your house turned out."

She'd had several tours before, so I didn't feel the need to drag her around and point out all the lovely additions upstairs. Besides, I figured she was just nudging me into a better frame of mind. I smiled, filling the carafe with water. "I love it, too. It's perfect for us."

"I'm so happy, Thea. In fact, I never thought this degree of happiness was possible. I want you to be happy, too, and frankly, despite your marriage, you don't look it."

I glanced toward the living room. The back and forth questions, comments and answers between Dave and Paul about Don's and Willa's murders were the sticky in my own wicket of happiness. That and the unmentioned drama with Paul's family. And the fact we could tell only a few people we were married.

"I will be," I said. "There's just a few hurdles in our path." Big hurdles, tricky ones, like the water jumps a horse and rider had to negotiate on a cross-country course, which typically drew crowds of spectators salivating at the possibility of watching a wreck.

She hugged me and helped gather the tray, mugs and other things we'd need. When the coffee maker beeped we took the carafe and tray to the living room. Paul wrapped up what he'd learned about Sybil as we all fixed our coffee.

"And you've turned everything you know, or suspect, over to Phil, right?" Dave asked Paul, then shifted a more pointed look to me.

"Of course we intend to." I sipped my coffee, with as

nonchalant a manner as I could dredge up. "We just haven't gotten to it yet."

I expected some sort of reprimand, but the honeymoon glow seemed to have mellowed him. Dave let out a long breath and chuckled. "I have to say I'm a bit jealous. You two amateurs have dug up quite a bit of good information on two murders and I get to come home to a still missing, dusty old British horse painting. I was hoping someone would have it wrapped up by the time Andrea and I got back, but it seems they've left it for me."

Andrea patted his arm. "Don't worry, darling. I'm sure someone will be murdered soon in Seattle and you'll get to figure out who killed them."

I studied my friend for a moment, waiting for her to crack a teasing smile. She didn't. Jeez. I rolled a "do you believe this?" look at Paul.

"One-hundred percent," he said.

"Of what?" Dave asked.

"Of your marriage succeeding," Paul said. "Unless she starts knocking people off just to give you something to do. Then I'll have to revise my prediction."

"Zero," I said, tossing him a withering glance.

"I was going to say seventy-five, possibly eighty," my husband countered.

"No, 'zero' is my own assessment of how funny you are."

Paul put his mug down and, smiling broadly, reached a hand toward me. I sighed and took it.

"She loves me," he said.

Dave laughed. "You're sure about that?"

"Positive."

We spent the remainder of the afternoon catching up, including confessing the reason why we'd moved our second wedding to April. Andrea's concern was for Jan's son, and cautioned us repeatedly not to add to the cruelty his mother and Paul's family had already heaped on the child by rejecting him the moment we met him. She was tender-hearted where children were concerned. If anyone would make a good mother, it would be my friend, and I wondered how long it would be before I'd have a little "niece" or "nephew" on the way -- and then I worried she'd have another miscarriage. At least she had Dave and wouldn't have to face it alone, like she had last time, but still …. I took the tray and assorted remains of our coffee and snacks back to the kitchen. Paul got up to help, but Andrea waved him off and followed me with a stack of plates.

"So you're coming, right?" Andrea asked, diverting my attention from loading my new dishwasher.

"Coming?"

Her expression turned patient. "To our reception. I knew you weren't paying attention. Our reception is next Saturday at the Arctic Club in Seattle in the Dome Room. It's beautiful, and the last of my extravagances for our wedding."

"Of course we'll be there." I slid a mug onto the top rack then hugged her.

"What had you so preoccupied? Are you worried about Paul's family? Because if you are, don't be. You're already married. You don't need their approval, and Paul has never sought it. And his ex's son will manage because you'll be kind. It'll all work out."

"You read me like a book," I lied, releasing her. It would do her no good to know I'd been fretting over something I had less control over than Paul's family: her well-being. "I will try very hard not to worry." That, at least, was true.

But the worry niggled at me throughout the dinner Dave and Andrea insisted they treat us to and the visit we all had with Aunt Vi and Uncle Henry. No one noticed how quiet I was. Of course with Aunt Vi so excited to hear about Andrea and Dave's reception and Uncle Henry taken up in Dave's police stories I could have passed unnoticed if I'd dyed my hair purple. Suited me fine.

But Paul noticed. He mentioned nothing until we were back home and alone.

"Quite a day," he said, sliding into bed. He leaned across me to turn off the light. I took the opportunity to slide my arms around him and, since his chest hair tickled my nose, kissed the middle of his chest. He propped himself on his arms, hovering above me still within nuzzling distance.

"Umm ... crime-solving, drama, horses, visiting with good friends and family, and now ...." I ran possessive hands down his muscled back and over his very fine butt.

"And now, I get to tell my wife to quit worrying about her best friend. I saw you watching her all afternoon and evening. She's in love. Dave adores her. He'll support her regardless of what happens if and when she gets pregnant. And he's in a better position, as her husband, than anyone else. Even you. And if it makes you feel any better, she is well aware she can depend on you when she needs to."

I cringed and dug my fingers into his back. "Was I that obvious?"

"Only to me."

And then I had to ask, because we'd never met the question head-on. "What about you? How soon do you want kids?"

"Ah. The other shoe just dropped."

"We have so many. Shoes, that is."

He laughed. "Too true. I say we not add to the excitement in our lives just yet. Besides, I don't want to share you for a while. Maybe a couple of years?"

I released a breath and my arms fell to the mattress. "That sounds good. Definitely in a couple of years."

"You don't have to stop, you know."

"Stop what? Worrying? I thought you wanted me to stop worrying."

"No, that thing you were doing with your hands."

A smile snuck onto my lips, and I followed a kiss to his chest with a little nip. "You know, I just don't seem to remember. Why don't you tell me and I'll see what I can do to accommodate you."

He drew a long breath and brushed the length of his body lightly against mine, stirring my awareness and sending my pulse into an anticipatory trot. Tender kisses pressed along my cheek. "'Accommodate.' Mmm ... sexy. I think I'll use that word a lot from now on."

Worry, and every other thought fled my brain.

I woke with a start, my heart racing with the conviction we were too late. I threw off the blankets and I shook Paul's shoulder.

"Wake up. Paul, wake up."

He fended me off, but I grabbed his wrist and pulled.

"Wake up. We've got to get going. They need us. Hurry!"

He groaned, turned toward the alarm clock on his night stand then rolled back and squinted at me. "Why?"

"Thurman arrested Delores and Juliet. But it was Bobby who ran everyone down with Juliet's motorcycle!"

"What?"

"We have to ...." I sat back on my heels, thinking hard. "We, um ... never mind. I was dreaming." I flopped face first into my pillow, groped for the blankets and pulled them over my head.

"About what?"

"About Juliet and Delores and Sybil and I don't know," I said into my pillow. "I was scared we'd be too late to save them." I shivered and scooted closer to my connubial heat source.

"Huh. Well, now that we're awake ...." He slid a hand over my shoulder and ran his fingers, teasing, down my spine to my butt.

"Stop that."

"Stop? Why?"

"Because I'm worried. We have to go talk to Thurman."

"It's seven o'clock on a Sunday morning. I might have mentioned that already. He'll be asleep."

I propped myself on my elbows. "By the time we eat breakfast and get dressed and call, we'll be lucky if he hasn't left for church. We have to get him the information we have as soon as possible. We should have done it yesterday. It's irresponsible of us."

"We can call him later at a decent hour. He won't mind that we didn't wake him up."

"No."

"I'm not calling him right now."

"Eight o'clock." I set my jaw and stared him down.

He groaned, flung the blankets back, swung out of bed, plucked his robe off the floor, threw mine at me and headed downstairs. I found my slippers and trotted down after him, starting the coffee while he monopolized the bathroom. When he came out, I went in, tended to what needed tending and turned on the shower. Before the water warmed up enough for me to even consider stepping in, the door opened. He handed me my sweats and sneakers.

"Get your butt dressed. If you're going to wake me up at seven on a Sunday morning, then you're going to go running with me. We'll call Thurman when we get back."

I sniffed the rich coffee aroma, just beginning to perk, and cast a longing glance at the shower, now sending up billows of steam. While waiting for the civilized hour of eight o'clock to roll around, I could be warm and freshly bathed, sipping a mug of hot coffee with cream and sugar in my beautiful kitchen. Aunt Vi's cinnamon rolls could be warming up in the microwave.

Or I could go outside in the cold and drizzle and trudge my underfed, under-caffeinated self along for a couple of miles in Paul's wake.

"I don't want to go. I don't like running."

"Too bad, whiner."

Additional protesting earned me nothing. I gave up, dressed in my sweats, running shoes, a knit cap and mittens and followed the most stubborn man on the planet out the front door. I wasn't happy. I hadn't even had a sip of coffee.

I hugged my body to keep out the chilly, dismal morning

air as we walked the few short blocks to the beginning of the Centennial Trail. The trail is an old railroad bed that cuts through the town of Snohomish and winds north for thirty miles to the county line. Walkers, joggers, bikers, roller skaters, and anybody but motorized vehicles is free to use it.

It had been way too handy for us, in my opinion.

At the first park bench we reached Paul did some stretches, shamed me into doing the same, then took off at an easy, for him, lope. I grumbled and trudged along behind, allowing the distance between us to open up.

After a bit, he turned and jogged backwards. A gust of damp wind messed with his hair, blowing it onto his forehead. The chill March morning had already turned his cheeks rosy. He was adorable, in a wholly masculine way, and I simply couldn't stay mad at him.

"Come on, slow-poke. This is good for you." He grinned.

I caved, managed a grudging smile, and waved him on. "I'm coming, you don't need to wait."

He faced forward again, continuing his ground-eating jog, increasing his lead. Yes, I was getting used to the running and yes, he was right. Uncle Henry encouraged me to run in order to develop the additional stamina I'd need for riding in the dressage shows. Nerves and adrenalin took a toll when competing. Being fit helped.

Stride by stride I lifted out of my sour mood. Even if I wasn't exactly leaping forward in joyous gratitude for the exercise, at least I was no longer focused on the next piece of asphalt my foot would land on. Furthermore, once I got my eyes off the ground, I noticed that despite it being Sunday, and the hour early, there were a number of people on the trail. We passed some dedicated walkers, huffing along, arms pumping, and several cyclists -- who passed us. Most everyone was friendly, and smiled or nodded an acknowledgment. Without fail, the women took a second look at my husband. One of the walkers coming toward me caught my eye and gestured toward Paul.

"Aren't you lucky this morning to have such a nice view."

"It's keeping me going," I said.

I stepped up my pace a bit, and breathed deep. The drizzle had stopped. Budding leaves and blossoms wanting to burst teased the air with the fresh scent of spring. Birds, returned from their winter vacation spots, sang their little hearts out. I almost laughed. Under a dappled gray sky, wisps of pale clouds skittered, pushed by a stiff breeze. Once in a while it pushed against me like it was in a hurry to get by.

I loved this time of year, loved leaving the cold, wet winter behind. So what if the weather wasn't Hawaii-perfect? Being out in the chilly morning with a playful breeze and the distinct possibility of more rain made me feel alive, and it was certainly less worse than viewing it from indoors.

The distant wail of a police siren reminded me of my intention to call Detective Thurman later, but the thought didn't panic me like it had first thing this morning. The case was all but over for us. Not too much could jar my appreciation of the spring day.

Except for the stuttered brbrbrrrrr waaaa waaaa of a motorcycle approaching from behind.

My initial thought was of Juliet, except I never noticed the stuttering when she rode. Besides, Bobby had absconded with her bike and hadn't been seen for days. With luck it would be several more. I doubted Thurman would need him to solve the case, anyway.

I made an effort to shut out the crescendo of brrrs, waaas and coughs. Shortly, I could go back to listening to the chirping birds. The oncoming motorcycle would likely stagger past on Maple Avenue (the road that paralleled this section of the trail) eventually if the driver didn't give up.

Give up, he didn't.

He flew past, on the path, clipping my arm and spinning me onto the grass. From the corner of my eye I caught a glimpse of a banana riding a bright yellow bike. I hauled myself upright as Juliet's Kawasaki Ninja with Bobby, dressed for work at the taco store, sped unsteadily down the path, the wind blowing back the top third of the banana outfit giving him a partially peeled appearance.

Despite the minimum amount of control he seemed to have over his direction, I had no doubt he was headed straight for Paul.

"Paul! Watch out! Paul! Paul!"

At my shout, he glanced over his shoulder and, wide-eyed, scrambled out of the way in the nick of time.

He stared, chest heaving, after the bike-riding banana. "What the hell?"

"It's Bobby!" I shrieked, launching into a flat-out run. "He's on Juliet's motorcycle." I flew past my husband, arms and legs pumping in hot pursuit of my unsteady but speedy quarry, who'd just disappeared around a bend. If he tipped over, I'd catch him. Maybe.

The police siren grew louder, and I silently thanked whoever had called 911 -- even if it was just to report a motor vehicle on the trail. Nevertheless, I pushed on, my lungs tearing with the effort. That was my sister's bike and I was so going to kick Bobby's stupid banana butt. If I caught him.

Then a dark blue form flashed past me.

Paul, long legs covering more ground than I could ever manage, moved at a speed that fueled my hope we'd cage that oversized, thieving monkey-bait.

Although I hadn't lost sight of Paul, I'd lost sight of Bobby. Worse, the sound of my sister's motorcycle had grown faint, sputtered and disappeared altogether. Gone. With a sinking heart I watched Paul come to a halt and, hands braced on his knees, suck lungfuls of air. I cut my speed to a walk, but when he turned his head in my direction and gestured for me to catch up I attempted to coax a bit of speed from my burning legs.

The Snohomish Police beat me to the rendezvous, lights strobing, and siren silent. The officer got out of the car and joined Paul who pointed off the trail toward a group of houses. Before I could reach them, they were both running off the path, and down a shallow embankment toward a thicket of blackberry bushes and, what I could now see, was my sister's motorcycle buried nose first in the thorny trap. Slightly above and to the right hung a large, unmoving, banana.

As much as I disliked Bobby, I hoped he hadn't killed himself, and wondered how Paul and the police officer were going to extract him without tearing themselves to pieces on the thorns. But the two men, with my husband leading by a good bit, dashed right past the thicket. Only then did I see the fleeing form, with familiar, ratty pony tail flapping against his pale and bare back, disappear around the corner of a house.

Neither Paul nor the officer slowed their pace. They'd spotted him too.

I waited on the path unable to take my eyes from the spot where I'd last seen them, but aware of the crowd gathering around me.

"Is that a banana costume in the bushes?" a woman next to me asked.

I nodded. "And a motorcycle."

"Didn't I tell you?" said a teen to her male companion. "I knew I'd seen a banana on a motorcycle. I wasn't lying, you dweeb."

"Okay, okay, I believe you. Shouldn't we go get him out?"

"Nah, he's not there. The cop and a jogger ran after him."

The teenage boy snorted unattractively. "What'd banana guy do? Is there some city ordinance about fruit riding motorcycles without helmets or something?"

"Funny. Not. Here they come."

Sure enough, Paul and the cop were returning at a walk with a struggling Bobby gripped between them, his hands behind his back and likely handcuffed. The defrocked fruit looked like he was wearing a kilt, but as they got closer I dismissed the notion. He was filthy with mud and bits of plant debris and wore nothing but shredded boxers, one sneaker and enough bleeding scratches to make me think the labor involved in "death by a thousand cuts" could be decreased considerably by simply running the victim through blackberry bushes.

A breeze whipped through the crowd and, when it reached the three approaching men, blew Bobby's shredded shorts apart, giving us all a prolonged and unfortunate view. His privates had not been spared the blackberry thorns. No wonder his gait appeared so odd. Several people groaned.

"Oh, man, that's gotta hurt," a guy behind me said.

"I'm never going to un-see that," the younger woman next to him commented.

But no one looked away.

"Hey, man," Bobby said, addressing the cop. "All those people are staring at my naked self."

"They probably want a good look at the idiot who'd ride a motorcycle dressed up like a banana and run it into the blackberry bushes," the officer said.

"Dude, it was hard to control that bike with the banana suit messing up my line of sight. And it was a total bitch trying to fight that crosswind."

"I'm sure it was," the officer deadpanned.

Paul shot me a grin when they reached the path. He was muddy down the full length of the left side of his body. I hadn't noticed until he'd gotten close.

"Had to tackle the bastard," he said, not at all like it bothered him, and continued to the police cruiser.

"Damn," the officer said. I recognized him, but couldn't recall his name. "I wish I had something to put on the backseat. I'm going to spend the rest of the day cleaning blood and dirt out of there." He sighed, opened the back door and helped Bobby inside. "Try not to bleed all over the upholstery before I get you to the hospital."

"Man, I'm so grateful. I thought you were taking me to jail."

"I am after they patch you up."

"Have a heart, dude. I'm gonna be late for work as it is."

"You know," the officer said, "I think that should have occurred to you earlier."

He got in the cruiser and left. No lights, no siren, and with Bobby slouching out of view.

"We'll need to go to the PD and give them statements," Paul said, after he'd answered a few questions from the crowd and they all went back to what they'd been doing before the excitement.

I gently rubbed the sore spot on my arm where Bobby had clipped me. "I pretty much figured that."

"Let's go home, have some breakfast and get cleaned up first, though. Oh, and Andy said we can take Juliet's bike home." It figured he'd be on a first-name basis with the cop. Male bonding -- if it didn't include drinking, then wounds and blood had to be involved.

"How are we going to get it out of the bushes?"

Paul squinted at the mound of blackberry thicket and shook his head. Together, we jogged down the slope to size up the job. The bike was buried. If you didn't know it was there you might miss it. The banana suit hung in tatters off to the side. Bobby must have had to wriggle out of it to escape. I'd have stayed put and given up, spared myself the injuries and embarrassment. Now, we'd be lucky to escape without getting bloodied ourselves.

Lucky for us, the man whose house Bobby had tried to hide behind, and who'd seen the whole thing, came out with his riding lawn mower and a rope.

He was a big guy, with a bigger laugh. "Nice tackle, young fella. I haven't laughed so hard in a long time. Woo-ee!" He wiped at a corner of his eye then pointed to Juliet's bike. "That yours?"

"Sister-in-law's. The naked guy borrowed it."

"Hope he's not her boyfriend. That ninny's a bubble and a half off plumb."

"No shit."

With a little ingenuity and not a little muscle, he and Paul dragged my sister's motorcycle free of the blackberries. Since it seemed no worse for the wear, except for scratches and mud, Paul rode it home. I was happy to walk.

Detective Thurman blew out a long breath and scanned our statements a second time. "I can't believe I got called in to the office on my day off for this. The kid's an idiot."

"Won't argue that point," Paul said. He leaned back in the orange, molded plastic chair, legs stretched out in front of him, arms crossed loosely over his chest. "What'd you arrest him for?"

Thurman peered over the top of his glasses. "Theft, reckless endangerment, evading arrest, public nudity, and anything else we can dig up to pacify my crabby mood. Wouldn't hurt to get him off the streets for a while."

"I'd been thinking Bobby might somehow be involved in Don's and Willa's deaths," I said. "But now I'm not so sure."

The detective's eyes slid to me and he waited.

I glanced at Paul, giving him a chance to tell our theory, but he tipped an acquiescing nod at me. I explained about Willa's comment about Sybil, inferring she'd had an affair with Don, and claiming not to know her last name or where she was. Then, how Paul had found out Sybil had been the trainer that Delores and Frank kicked out, and who'd subsequently been ruined by Don's report to the AHSA of her doping her horses at shows. Finally, and triumphantly, I added our coup: she was Max's mother. Revenge had to be the motive.

Thurman nodded in the way I hated. It meant either he wasn't taking me seriously, or he knew something I didn't. I suspected the former.

"I wish you wouldn't do that," I said.

Thurman blinked and sat back in his chair. "Do what?"

"Dismiss me off-hand. You know we have a point. That

we've provided you with someone else's motive and opportunity, besides Michelle."

"True. But then I suppose you already know that Sybil is Michelle's mother and Max is her brother."

# Chapter Nineteen

How did we not find out that Sybil was Michelle's mother? How did we not find out Michelle and Max were half siblings? How had we screwed up so badly?

"We did not screw up," Paul snapped, opening the car door for me.

"Was I thinking out loud?"

"Might as well have been. You had that same stunned expression when you decided we screwed up by getting married."

I cut my retort and got into the car. He slammed the door before I had a chance to reach for it, then slid into the driver's side, slammed that door, too, and jammed his key into the ignition.

"You don't have to be so cranky," I said. "You know I'm right."

"Are we talking us getting married or us investigating murder?"

I glared at him. "I am not talking to you if you're going to pick a fight. Bad enough you got in a shouting match with Thurman."

His nostrils flared as he turned the key in the ignition. "I did not shout at Phil, I was making a point regarding motive. And we did not screw up."

Right. In a pig's eye. We screwed up and at least I was willing to accept that we'd jumped to conclusions.

In the less than blissful silence for the drive home I revisited my impulsive assumptions. The fact that the relationship between Michelle, Max and Sybil seemed to have deliberately been kept quiet nagged at me. Could two reasonably intelligent people, meaning Paul and me, have missed that without having been steered away from it? The answer was clear: no one wanted us to know. But why? I rolled different potential reasons around in my brain, but it all stank of too much "conspiracy theory" to make me happy. Besides, I didn't much care for the queasy feeling in my stomach when I poked around the reasons for Delores' silence.

Still, both Don's and Willa's deaths had to have been planned. And if they were, and revenge over Sybil's ruined career the motive, why set it up so Michelle was the logical suspect? Would a mother do that to her daughter? A brother to his sister? Going down that road would require a load of ill will.

As much as I fought with and disagreed with my sister, I could not conceive of setting her up in that manner. As it was, I spent a huge amount of effort protecting her – sometimes from herself.

But passions within families tended to run deep and strong – as was evidenced in Paul's case. It could be possible Max would set Michelle up. After all, hadn't Juliet mentioned that Michelle didn't like him? Yet she'd gone to him and managed to get him to hire Bobby.

So, if not Max, who? Someone who wanted to bring Max down as well? Again, I was uncomfortably close to naming

Delores, and the thought made my stomach twist into a knot.

Paul parked the car in front of our house and got out without a word. I scrambled out my side, slammed the door behind me and hurried to catch up as he strode down the path to the front door.

"Why --?"

"I'm calling Dave."

"Paul, stop."

He didn't even pause, but took the three steps to the porch in one easy leap, unlocked the front door and stormed inside. I jogged after him and shut the door behind me. He couldn't talk to Dave. Dave would reach the same conclusion I had.

"Dammit, listen to me. Don't call him. What's he going to do? He's Seattle P.D., not Snohomish. You're asking him to cross a professional line here."

"I want to bounce some ideas off him, if you must know."

I grabbed his arm. "Yes, I must know. And why can't you bounce them off me?"

"I can't."

I stared him down. He'd reached the same conclusion I had, I knew it. I couldn't stop him and I wanted to throw up. I had to get to Delores first. "You're making a huge mistake. Just so you know, I'm going to the barn to ride my horse." I stomped upstairs to the bedroom, shucked my jeans and sneakers, yanked on my breeches and headed down to the front closet to pull on my boots. I left without saying goodbye.

By the time I turned my car through Copper Creek's main gate I'd gotten a handle on my temper, but the coming confrontation with Delores was giving me a bad case of the shakes. The office was dark, so I knew she wasn't there. I turned my car around and drove over to her house at the far end of the property. Her car was gone.

I returned to the parking lot, found a spot near the office, and locked up. Just to say I had, I peeked in the big indoor arena. A couple of lessons were in progress, but Delores wasn't there. I strolled through the barns. No Delores.

Max's car was parked in its usual spot, but I saw no evidence of him anywhere, riding or on foot. Could they be together? For what purpose? Before I jumped to any panicked conclusions, I decided to hang out for a while and see if she showed up. I'd take Blackie for a trail ride, then, if she hadn't returned I'd call in my uncle and aunt and do an all-out search.

Blackie whinnied as I approached the Big Barn, a predictable habit. He whinnied a second time, not his usual pattern, and I almost missed my name being called.

Bart Fulton stalked toward me, his face slightly flushed and the center of his upper lip jerking downward in the peculiar little twitch that usually precipitated a saccharine smile. No smile followed this time, though. In fact, his pinched nostrils made his already narrow nose knife-like. He sputtered my name again.

"Yes, yes, I'm glad I've found you, very glad indeed," he said, his lip twitching downwards at the corners now, as well as the center.

I hadn't asked a yes or no question and, despite his bullet-like stare directed at me, wasn't sure if he was actually speaking to me or into the Bluetooth hanging on his ear.

"Is there something wrong?" I asked, not that I cared.

He laughed, a high-pitched, frantic sound. "Wrong? What could possibly be wrong? I found Mrs. Paalmann's phone number, no thanks to you, and managed to contact her."

"Oh?" Shit. Well, guess he was talking to me. I could see I was going to have to apologize to Andrea. I hoped she didn't think I'd given him her number.

"And you'll never believe what she told me."

I'd never believe she'd tell him she would send him a check. "I can't imagine."

"She said there was no way she would consider investing in my organization. That high and mighty friend of yours accused me of money laundering! I'll have you know I run a registered social welfare organization for special needs children. Do you understand me? We do our best to influence local and state lawmakers to pass legislation that will help the children but, thanks to you, she calls it bribery and accused me of buying politicians for personal gain. I have never been so insulted in my life. She is a small-minded, avaricious woman with no right to manage the wealth she possesses. I have a mind to sue."

I considered counting to ten, but got to three before my icy stare demanded words. "You do that, Mr. Fulton. I can't wait to find out how right she is. Won't your other investors just love that." I spun on my heel and stomped off. Question my friend's integrity? Freaking ass. The only thing I'd do for him was applaud Andrea's decision to do research and ferret out the truth.

The door to Max's tack room, closed when I'd passed a minute earlier, stood ajar. Huh. He'd likely gotten an earful. Fine with me. I'd be happy to rip him a new one, too, if he so much as opened his little mealy mouth. Before I could pause and give Max a chance to show his face, Blackie whinnied again. He was the only male in my current orbit not due a good kick in the ass.

Man, did I need to ride my horse. I didn't care if the skies opened up and poured buckets of cold rain on me. In fact, I had half a mind to head for parts unknown and get away from all the people in my life intent on causing problems.

Blackie was usually happy to see me, but today he seemed ecstatic. He pressed against his stall door and all but popped out like a jack-in-the-box when I opened it. If he hadn't stood still once he'd gotten into the aisle I'd never have managed to buckle his halter. Once in the grooming stall, he nudged me constantly with his nose as I put his saddle on, then he dove, open-mouthed, into the bridle when I held it up. If he'd had thumbs he would have dressed himself. It wouldn't be accurate to say I led him from the barn. He jigged sideways down the aisle to the door, dragging me along like an inadequate anchor.

"I take it you're in a hurry," I said. "Do you think there's much chance of standing still while I get on? I'd hate to do a face plant because you couldn't be a little patient at the mounting block."

I got lucky. He held onto his manners long enough for me to swing a leg over his back, but was off at an energetic walk even as my butt hit the saddle. I patted his neck and we headed for the trail.

It wasn't the power my horse's stride produced that satisfied me today. Today, the illusion of control he allowed calmed me. Particularly since I was losing it everywhere else.

I'd have had a smile on my face by the time we returned to Copper Creek if my stomach hadn't started to churn anew, anticipating my talk with Delores. I rode up through the parking lot to the office, but it was still dark. My foray to her house yielded the same result as before. I still didn't see Max anywhere.

With my horse now cooled out, thanks to our search for Delores, I returned to the barn, groomed him and dressed him in a clean stable blanket. I stuffed the dirty blanket into a large plastic bag. The horse laundry would pick it up from the bin outside Max's office next time they came by.

I took Blackie back to his stall, gave him a sugar, and watched him nose around for any hay he'd missed. He'd figured out, when he'd first been stabled here, that sometimes there'd be a few wisps hanging from the hay-drop hole in his ceiling. If he reared a little, he could reach and pull down a small mouthful. I waited while, lifting himself in a levade, he inspected the hole with his nose. Nothing today. Miguel had likely swept the loft.

To delay my departure and satisfy my own curiosity, I peeked in on Elf, Agnes' injured horse. He was munching hay in a corner of his stall, his right front leg wrapped neatly from knee to hoof in a heavily padded bandage. Poor guy. I could only guess what kind of injury he'd sustained, but I knew for a fact it could not be Delores' fault. Having spent years on the hunter-jumper competition circuit and many more training and teaching, she knew the dangers of sub-par and unmaintained footing. This was not her fault. And Max needed to be told.

Max's office door was still ajar and, after I dropped my bagged up blanket in the bin, I knocked. If he was there, I'd ask if he'd seen Delores. But, no one answered.

"Max?" I pushed the door wider, and scanned the room. Empty. A couple of bridles hung from the cleaning hook at the back, and the desk light was on. He'd been here, probably still was, somewhere. I began to shut the door and stopped. The picture over his desk captured my attention. I stepped further into his office unable to take my eyes from the painting, my heart thumping against my ribcage. I hadn't recalled the artist when I'd seen it before, but it had to be Stubbs – a British painter, renowned for his oils of anatomically correct horses. The painting looked old and expensively framed. An original? A good print?

For a long moment I hesitated, gnawing my lip. Could this be the picture Dave was looking for? That would be unbelievable. Totally and completely unbelievable. How in the world would it get from a private collection in a Seattle home to the tack room of a hunter-jumper trainer in Snohomish? Yup. Not only unbelievable, but unlikely.

I shook off the shiver of excitement that stirred my gut, closed the door softly and headed for my car.

But ... what if?

What if it was and I said nothing?

What if I accused him and I was wrong?

The answer popped into my mind the moment I headed my trusty, aged Ford Escort home: Ask Dave to email me a photo and the particulars of the stolen painting then compare what he sent with what was above Max's desk. If I was wrong, then no one would know – except Dave, and he wouldn't care. And yes, the irony of having just told Paul not to call him wasn't wasted on me.

But, if I was right ....

A grin fixed itself to my face and refused to go away even as I parked in front of my house, hurried up the walk and entered the den of the snarling lion. He was my snarling lion and I could handle him.

# Chapter Twenty

I closed the door behind me, shouldered out of my barn coat and found a hanger in the hall closet. "Paul!" My bootjack was nowhere to be seen, so I stepped on the heel of one boot only to pull it half way off. "Paul!"

The chair in the office squeaked, and he came into the front hall, somewhat subdued in appearance.

"You want some help?"

"Please." I sat on the floor and held up a foot. He slid the boot off and held out his hand for my other foot.

"Sorry for being so short tempered earlier," he said, freeing me of the last boot.

"It's okay."

A corner of his mouth turned up, briefly, and he held a hand out again, this time for my hand, and helped me off the floor. I scooped up my riding boots and stashed them in the closet.

He studied me. "I take it you had a good ride?"

The excitement of my discovery almost had me forgetting I'd ridden. "Yes, but there's something I need to tell you."

"Wait." He slid his hands into his jeans pockets. "Let me finish apologizing first."

I blinked. "Okay."

"I should have listened to you about calling Dave. He didn't feel he could get involved, and I respect that. I also shouldn't have argued with Phil."

"Did you call Thurman?"

"No."

"Well, don't." I struggled to hold down a smile and tried to turn it into a playful gaze from beneath lowered lashes. "I'm glad you stuck up for our theories. Maybe we're wrong, but maybe we gave him something to think about, too." I went to him and slid my arms around his waist. He rubbed a warm hand up my back. "And besides, you know something? You're darned sexy when you get determined."

His eyes narrowed. "Really. I'll remind you of that sometime in the near future. What's going on? This is sounding like purposeful flattery."

I leaned back in mock horror. "Can't I give you a compliment? Why, you sound as if you don't trust me."

"'It is a wise man who knows his own wife.'"

"I think it's one with good eyesight and a decent memory, Mr. Shakespeare."

"Are we going to continue to play this game or are you going to tell me why you're being so cagey."

"You're ruining all my fun." I pinched his side and he twitched, but didn't take his eyes off me. "All right." I sighed for dramatic effect. "I believe I may have found Dave's stolen painting."

"Within the time since I saw you last?"

"Yes."

"I'm impressed."

"Well, I possibly discovered it several days ago -- but I didn't know at the time."

"Nevertheless, I'm very proud of you. You've ridden your horse and recovered stolen art in less than ..." he looked at his watch, "... two hours. You beat the pros at their own game. Did you leave it in the car? Shall I go bring it inside?"

"You don't believe me, do you."

"What gave me away?"

"Possibly the sarcasm, although I can't be sure. Could have been the difficulty you were having speaking with your tongue in your cheek." I punched him lightly in the chest. "I'm serious. I think I found the painting."

He scratched the back of his head, and regarded me with narrow, undisguised skepticism. "So, what are you planning to do about it?"

"The only sensible thing: call Dave and have him email me a picture of the painting and the particulars – size and whatnot. If it looks like what I saw in Max's office, then I'll go check it out before I call Dave back with the hot tip."

"It's in Max's office?"

"Above his desk, in plain view."

He snorted. "And if it is, by some remote chance, the stolen painting, do you think he's going to let you in there to examine it?"

"Of course not. We'll go over this evening after everyone's left and sneak in to look."

"We will? And what are you going to do if the door is locked?"

"Try and find a key. Delores might have one."

His mouth set in a firm line. "You will not get her involved in this."

"Or I could try and pick it. Somehow. You could help."

"You think I know how to pick locks?"

"It wouldn't be the first time you've surprised me." I batted my eyelashes at him.

He frowned -- for a long time. Finally, he sighed. "Call Dave. If he sends you the picture and you're ninety-nine percent positive it's a match, we'll see what we can do."

I threw my arms around his neck, kissed him on the jaw and dashed to the phone.

"How long do you suppose we're going to have to wait?" Paul whispered.

"No idea. Agnes shouldn't even be here at this hour. In fact, Max should have been long gone, too." Both their cars were parked off to the side of the Big Barn and within sight of where we waited near Miguel and Maria's house, hunkered down, in Paul's car. We'd done a reconnaissance of the area, as Paul insisted, when we arrived at nine o'clock, and discovered both vehicles. In order not to arouse suspicion, we parked close enough to the house to encourage the idea we were there visiting.

"It's possible they've both gone off with someone else and left their cars here, isn't it?" I asked.

"I suppose."

"How about we walk through the barn and see if anyone is here? We can check on Blackie – if we need an excuse." And it sure beat the heck out of sitting in the car on stake out and waiting for an opportunity that we might already have.

"That'll work."

Paul slipped an arm across my shoulder as we strolled toward the barn. Blackie whinnied as we approached. Great. I hadn't thought of my horse announcing to the world we were here. Once in the barn, we had no trouble seeing. Miguel always left every third light in the aisle on, in case of an emergency.

Sure enough, Max's office door was closed. I knocked and when there was no answer I looked around and tried the knob. Locked, of course.

"Try not to look so suspicious," Paul hissed.

"And you're not?" I shot back.

He stood casually off to the side, hands in his pockets. No, he didn't look suspicious. Bored, but not suspicious. Hopefully, he'd have no trouble picking the lock. I stepped back to give him some room and checked my jacket pocket for the twentieth time to make sure the printout of the email I'd gotten from Dave was still there.

But instead of crouching and pulling out the tools he'd rounded up for the job, he took my arm, and pulled me along with him down the barn aisle, settling into a casual stroll.

"We have company," he whispered.

Halfway to Blackie's stall, headlights swept the inside of the barn. Paul stopped and turned as the sound of tires on gravel and a diesel engine grew closer and came to a stop outside the Big Barn. I wanted to run and hide -- a grooming stall was nearby -- but Paul wasn't moving, and I stopped struggling. That would certainly look suspicious. A truck door slammed, and in a moment a man strode into the barn. He carried a fairly large shopping bag, went directly to Max's tack room and tried the knob.

"Oh, hey." He waved at us. "Either of you folks seen Max around?"

It was Rick, Don's partner. "No," Paul said. "Sorry. We just stopped by to check on Blackie."

"Oh, say," he said, gesturing at me. "You're Thea. Sorry, I didn't recognize you. Don did all your work, didn't he?"

"That's right. This is my husband -- to-be. Paul Hudson."

"Nice to meet you." Rick strode over and the men shook hands. "If you need a vet, give a call. I'm trying to make sure Don's clients aren't left in the lurch." He addressed Paul.

"Thanks, I appreciate that," I said.

Rick's eyes flashed to me and Paul's mouth twitched in an amused way. "Are you going to be hiring another vet at your practice to handle the client load?" he asked.

Rick laughed. "You looking for a position?"

Paul chuckled politely. "You're out of my league, I'm afraid. I'm a PhD, not a DVM."

"Can't use you then. What I really need right now is

someone to run the office to replace Willa. If you're interested, Thea," he said, finally looking at me, "or know anyone who is, give me a shout."

"I'm busy with my accounting business, but I'll spread the word."

"Well, hey, good talking to you. I'm going to check on Elf and leave this stuff for Max. You think it'll be okay if I hang it on his door?"

"What's in the bag?"

"Bandaging material, Legend, Banamine and some Ace."

Expensive stuff. I sure wouldn't leave it lying around. "I can give them to Miguel, if you like. We're going to his house to visit for a bit after we say hi to Blackie. Did Elf bow a tendon?"

"Yeah. It's a shame. He's a nice horse. We'll do an MRI this week, I think, to see how bad." He handed Paul the bag, then dug in his shirt pocket and passed him a business card, as well. "See you folks around. Call if you need me."

"Sure thing," Paul said.

Rick turned and went back to Elf's stall. Paul tipped his head toward Blackie. We strolled the remaining distance to his stall. I slipped in and fussed with his blankets just for effect. When we walked back down the aisle, Rick was still with Elf.

"Looks like we need to go over to Miguel's after all," Paul whispered once we were out of the barn. "Good thing we've got an excuse."

I glanced up at Paul. "You know, Rick could have motive for the murders."

"I was thinking the same thing."

"We should mention it to Thurman -- after we check out the painting."

Paul smiled. "Planning on it."

We mounted the couple of steps to Miguel and Maria's front porch door and, since my hands weren't full, I knocked. After a moment, Maria answered the door in her bathrobe. Her eyes widened when she saw us.

"*¡Válgame Dios!* There is something wrong?"

"No, sorry to bother you," I said. "Rick left these for Max."

Maria took the bag from Paul and peered inside. "Dr. Rick? *Bueno.* Maybe I give you Miguel's key and you put this in Max's office?"

"Sure! We'd be happy to do that," I said. Paul shot me a disapproving look. Perhaps I was a bit too enthusiastic, but this was perfect. A legitimate way to get into Max's tack room and take a look at the picture.

"Come in out of the cold. I will go get it." She handed the bag back to Paul and hustled off toward the kitchen. We stepped into the living room, closing the door behind us.

"This is perfect," I whispered to Paul.

He nodded, but didn't look nearly as pleased as he should have been. Maria's rapid Spanish to Miguel and his response prompted Paul to cut me a wry, I-told-you-so look. Why he thought I'd understand was beyond me since, except for a few phrases, he knew I didn't speak the language. Miguel came out of the kitchen, wiping his mouth and moustache with a napkin.

"Paul, Thea," he greeted us, "you are here late. There isn't a problem, is there? I can take the supplies over with me when I do barn check at ten."

Now I knew the reason for Paul's lack of excitement. "Oh, uh, no --"

"To tell the truth, Miguel," Paul said, "the reason we're here is to check on the painting in Max's office. We just happened to run into Rick and told him we'd bring this here so he wouldn't worry about someone walking off with it."

Miguel nodded. "There is a painting in Max's office? Do you mean the photographs on the wall?"

"No," Paul said, and continued to spill the beans.

Miguel and Maria listened with rapt expressions.

"I hope it is the painting," Maria said. "Then he will become arrested and we will be rid of him. Delores will have him off her head."

"Back," Miguel corrected.

"Yes. Delores will have him off her back. We should go over and look right now."

Paul grimaced. "Probably not a good idea. Rick is still there, and it will look pretty suspicious if we all go marching over. Besides, we told him we were coming here to visit."

"He's still there?" I asked.

"I haven't heard his truck start up. It's hard to miss that diesel."

I went to the window by the front door and looked. Sure enough, he was right.

"You sit down and wait," Maria said. "I'll make us a ... ¿cómo se dice –."

"Dessert," Miguel said, his dark eyes flashing with delight.

"Yes. Sit, all of you. I will be quick."

Maria hustled into the kitchen while Paul and I followed Miguel to the living room. Paul eased onto the sofa and stretched out his long legs. I perched with the bag on my lap, eager to go, once Rick had left the barn. I didn't have to wait long. In less time than it took for me to wonder which of Maria's special treats I would have to abandon in order to check on the painting, the unmistakable rumble of Rick's diesel engine reached my ear. I was on my feet the next instant.

"I'll just run over and take a quick look," I said and held out my hand for the key.

Miguel dug into his jeans pocket, produced a key ring and sorted through them. "This one, I think. If it doesn't work, try the one next to it."

"Right." I made for the door.

"You might want to wait until he's actually out of the parking lot," Paul said.

"Oh. Right." I hugged the bag to my chest and chewed my lip, all the while listening for the retreat of the truck's engine. Finally, after what seemed ages, the pitch of the rattle and grumble changed. Rick was on the move, the sound growing fainter by the moment. I reached for the door knob when I was certain he'd gone. "Okay, I'll be back in a minute."

I all but jogged off the porch, down the steps and across the yard. The night wasn't pitch dark, courtesy of the yard lights, so I had no trouble seeing where I put my feet. When I reached Paul's car, I also had no trouble seeing the man coming from the doorway of the Big Barn.

Bart.

He looked furtively in the direction Rick had disappeared then hurried toward the side of the barn where Max and Agnes had parked their cars. Under his arm he carried a rectangular object. It looked to be the size of the painting I was on my way to examine. What was he up to? No way could he know my suspicions. Did he think he was he was stealing from Max to cause him misery? Wouldn't that be a laugh.

A far more sobering thought crossed my mind. Had he actually been in the tack room when we, and then Rick had tried the door? What a surprise that would have been. I couldn't even peek at that scenario playing out without my stomach twisting.

But, more to the point, how was I going to get a look at that painting now? Considering his recently expressed feelings toward me, there was little chance he'd voluntarily allow me to examine what it appeared he was stealing. I'd have to tackle him. Sure he wasn't a very big guy, but he was bigger than me.

I glanced back at the house and calculated how long it would take me to run back and get help. If he hopped into Agnes' car, I'd haul ass back to the house and grab Paul. We could at least follow him to wherever he was going, and call Dave on the way. Oh, yeah, I could hear it now: "Dave, I think Bart may have just taken the painting you might be looking for, but I'm not sure."

That was not going to go over well.

I crouched by Paul's car and peered over the hood. Bart opened the trunk of Agnes' car, and put the object inside.

Then he slammed the lid. There went my idea of sneaking a peek of it in the backseat.

Again, Bart cast a quick look around then dug around in his jacket pocket. What he pulled out was small. A key? A pack of gum? I quit speculating when I saw a tiny flame. A lighter. He was going to have a smoke?

No.

He strode purposefully back toward the barn, flicking the lighter several more times. Was he out of his mind? He couldn't really be planning on fooling with that thing in a barn full of hay and horses, could he?

I left the bag of supplies for Elf by Paul's car and broke into a trot.

"Bart! Bart! Mr. Fulton, wait up!"

He paused, glanced my way, then was back in motion, faster than before and headed for the barn door. I reached the entrance in time to hear the quick rhythm of his footsteps ascending the last of the wooden staircase to the hayloft.

# Chapter Twenty-One

Blackie whinnied loud and frantic. He crashed against his stall walls and door, his distress rippling out to spook his close neighbors into a noisy clatter and cause the other horses farther away to become restive. I stopped at the base of the hayloft stairs and cast a begging look in his direction.

"Please stop, Blackie," I whispered. "I should have gone for help, but there's a good chance Bart's just not thinking, like when he walked up behind you. I'll get the lighter. I'll be careful." I had to be, and successful. My horse's life and every other horse's in the barn depended on it.

Stupid Bart. A fire could catch and spread in a heartbeat. I took the stairs to the hay loft two at a time, tripped, scrambled and proceeded with more caution.

In the inky blackness at the top of the stairwell I felt around for the door and found it unlatched and ajar. The memory of his anger when I'd threatened to persuade Andrea to ignore his plea for sponsorship of his "social welfare" organization turned my gut cold. Could he be laying a trap for me? No. That made no sense. He had no idea I'd be here. He was here for the painting.

Blackie screamed.

The painting.

Bart knew about the painting. He wasn't stealing it from Max. He was saving it.

His words to Agnes echoed through my mind. "You are done with the damn horses." Once simply a comment of high emotion in the midst of a spat, now it ran thick with intention.

The sick bastard was going after the horses.

Rage propelled me forward through the dark. Throwing hesitation aside, I flung the door open and barreled inside.

Light streamed up from the hay-drop holes in the loft floor. Now able to see, I swung in a full circle. No Bart.

Nothing but the half empty loft with hay bales, stacked in tall islands down the length of the barn. Multiple islands. With black, man-sized shadows. Crap.

I sniffed for smoke.

Nothing. Nothing but sweet hay and the earthy scent of horses and Blackie's continuous, desperate slams and kicks against his stall walls vibrating the loft floor. His screams obliterated all other sounds, including any noise Bart might be making that would lead me to him.

Damn it all. Where the hell was he? I clenched my fists wanting to pound something, anything. I had to find him.

Nerves singing with the tension, I dashed to the shadows. I'd surprise him, grab the lighter, run for the house. I could outdistance him. If he escaped, I didn't care. Someone else could catch him. I had to prevent a fire, and act immediately.

Heart pounding, I peeked around the corner of the first stack of bales, found nothing but a wide broom and a pair of hay hooks, their sharp points safely buried deep into a bale. I scurried to the shadow of the next stack. Again, the same frustrating results.

I moved farther into the loft. Like pale, immobile search

lights, the additional illumination through the hay-drop holes provided better visibility, but robbed me of hiding places and the potential of surprise. Sweat traced rivulets from my armpits, down my sides. Where the hell was he?

I sniffed the air again. Still no smoke.

Swallowing against the dryness in my throat, I assessed the next stack of hay. A quick glance around one corner told me I had yet to locate Bart. I darted forward, peered around the side of the new stack and stopped short.

On the loft floor in a pile of loose hay lay two bodies. I sucked a breath and pulled back into hiding, flattened against the hay bales.

Crap.

More bodies.

Blackie's hysteria hit fever pitch. My heart rate hit flight mode. Bart had to be the killer all along. He wasn't an idiot with a lighter and a bad idea, he was a cold-blooded killer. He wouldn't hesitate to murder me, too.

My courage fled. I had to get out of here, get help, go to the stalls and turn all the horses loose.

I wheeled, but a vise-like grip on my arm swung me into a tighter turn. A solid jar to my jaw jerked my head back. I went airborne, slammed against a stack of hay bales, bounced to the floor. Hands seized me, flipped me face down. A weight crashed onto my back, drove the air from my lungs. A yank on my hair jerked my head sideways.

Bart's face, distorted with fury pressed within inches of my own.

"Bitch!" he screamed. "Fucking bitch! I'm going to kill you. You've ruined all my plans."

He wrenched my hair again. Desperate, I threw movement in the same direction. His fist grazed my cheek and thumped against the wood floor. He yowled, released my hair, cradled his own hand.

"Bitch! Bitch!"

In his howling, his weight lightened on my back. I pushed

hard with my feet, bucked him forward and scrambled, twisting to break free. But with a heavy thud he was on me again, pinned me to the floor on my back. His knees crushed my shoulders.

I swung my legs, kicked at him, missed, twisted, until he grabbed my face in one hand, dug his fingers into my cheeks, forced me to look at what he held in his other hand.

He aimed a syringe, needle uncapped, at my neck.

Horror slowed time.

I watched a spurt of clear liquid eject from the tip, hang in the air before it wet my face and dripped down my jaw.

I watched a familiar hand land on Bart's shoulder and fingers curl deep into jacket and flesh.

I watched Bart's eyes widen.

In a wild effort, Bart jabbed at me an instant before Paul pulled him off.

The needle pierced my jacket, sank like a punch into the soft muscle above my collarbone.

Icy cold rushed into my flesh.

Paul threw Bart as if he weighed nothing into the stack of hay. The bales toppled at the same time the syringe fell from my body to the floor. With my heart pounding as if to escape my chest, I picked up the empty syringe and stared, hopeless, from it to Paul, unable to speak.

My husband stared back, his head tipped in an unaskable question. I clamped my lips against a sob and nodded.

Recognition of my unalterable fate, the fate that claimed both Don and Willa, transformed his savage expression to slack-jawed despair.

He dropped to his knees beside me, scooping me into his arms. "No, no, no, baby, God, no." He choked out the words, rocking me against his chest.

I held on to him, as tight as I could, while I still lived.

But ... Don, I knew, had gone fast. *My* heart still beat. Air moved in and out of *my* lungs. *My* head was clear. "Paul, Paul, I'm okay. I'm --"

His sharp grunt cut me off. I slipped from his grip as, lips compressed, eyes squeezed in pain, he reached a hand over his shoulder for something I couldn't see.

What I did see was Bart, too close, arm raised. At my gasp, Paul pivoted on his knees and pushed to his feet. My eyes fastened on a hay hook embedded in his back. Horror pulled a scream from my throat as, with one hand, he yanked it free and flung it aside.

Unfortunately, the twin to it was in Bart's grip.

Bart, the man I'd dismissed as ineffectual, weak, mildly clumsy, now moved with the confidence of a trained fighter. Paul, no stranger to a fight, shifted to the balls of his feet. Bart roared and lunged. To my relief, Paul slipped easily out of his reach.

I scooted backward, to stay out of the way, and fumbled to my feet. A small hitch in Paul's next dodge drew my attention to a thin dark streak running down the right side of his faded blue jeans. Blood. Strength left my legs. Paul had ripped the hook, sharp enough to securely penetrate into a bale of hay, out of his own flesh. My knees buckled. Only intense determination to help him and rage kept me upright. I reassessed his posture. His right arm, pulled tight against his body, seemed all but useless. I had to either be his right hand or guide Bart to Paul's left. I wanted to tell him, but didn't dare distract.

They sidled left then right. All the while Paul kept himself between me and Bart, maintained his distance, waited.

I had to do something, anything, to help, but the best my terrorized mind could manage was to dodge along with Paul, stay out of his way, not give Bart any opening.

Bart feigned attacks, rushed forward, then back, waved the hay hook in a figure eight, tossed it from hand to hand, laughed a high, thin titter. His gaze jumped between Paul and me. With a cold squeeze to my heart I realized what Paul obviously knew: if Bart managed to get around him he'd come for me.

Then, as Bart's eyes slid in my direction again, Paul dove for a tackle. The two men rolled on the loft floor. But Paul was bigger and, despite his useless right arm, pinned Bart. Relief nearly dropped me to the floor -- until the little bastard swung a leg and kicked his heel into the wounded side of Paul's back. He woofed in pain and tipped over. Bart wiggled free and swung the hay hook toward Paul's head.

Bart was fast, but Paul was faster. He rolled out of the way and gained his feet as Bart attacked again, aiming for Paul's midsection.

My husband jumped backwards, avoiding the lethal swipe, and fell into me. I staggered, tangled with the legs of the two bodies and fell. The momentum sent me skidding across the floor to the edge of a hay-drop hole. I dangled over the edge, clawing at air, my heart racing with another dimension of fear.

Briefly and forever I hung over the ten-foot drop to the stall floor. My grasping hand found the rough wood edge of the hole. I sucked air, pushed and rolled to safety.

Behind me came growls and thuds as the two men grappled once again.

Below me, Blackie screamed and plunged, kicking the walls with earthquake force. Determined to help, I scrambled, got my feet under me and looked directly into the terrified gaze of Agnes Fulton. My jaw dropped.

No dead body here.

Although trussed up and with duct tape over her mouth, she was definitely alive. A quick look at the other body confirmed it was Max – and there was no doubt he lived, as well. He squirmed frantically out of the way of Paul and Bart, now circling each other, jockeying for an opening to attack.

Paul breathed heavily through his mouth, face set in intense concentration, lips pulled back. I shoved to my feet, searched for something, anything I could use to bring Bart down, but I couldn't even find the damn broom. This had to be over soon. Paul had to best him.

As I looked on, helpless, useless and frantic, Bart sprang, swinging the hook like a windmill. With Paul's sideways move to the left blocked by hay bales, his only evasion lay to the right. He leaped as Bart closed in. From the arc of my husband's arm, he probably meant to drop him with a blow to the back but Max, duct-taped and wriggling for all he was worth, could not get out of the way fast enough. Paul tripped over him and slammed to the floor with enough force to shake the boards.

I dashed for Paul, avoiding Agnes and fallen hay bales, intending to help him to his feet. But instead of attacking Paul, Bart pulled the lighter from his pocket, set a pile of loose hay alight and then charged at me.

Untangling himself from Max, Paul yelled my name, and then a louder, "Run!"

I responded too late. Bart grabbed a handful of my jacket and propelled me backwards. I swung at him, but he kicked at my feet and delivered a vicious shove. The step I took to gain my balance met only air.

I flailed for a handhold.

Bart whooped, triumphant. "Get trampled, bitch."

Slamming hard against the edges of the hay-drop, I plummeted to the stall below.

To my surprise, the fall was short. I landed on the broad, unlevel back of my horse and slid to the ground. Blackie continued to circle his stall. I scooted through the bedding to the wall. I had to get out, get Blackie out, get help for Paul.

But Blackie had plans. He continued to scream, stopped his frenetic motion and stood directly under the hay-drop. In a short moment, with a whoosh and a grunt, Paul dropped through the hole, landed ungracefully on my horse and slid to the ground. He struggled to rise and I hurried to help, not knowing how badly he was hurt and afraid my horse would tread on him.

Blackie quieted immediately, nuzzling first me and then Paul, his heavy breathing the only indication of his extreme anxiety. He stood directly above us, as if guarding us from further danger.

"Are you all right?" Paul asked cupping my face with his left hand.

"Yes," I whispered. "But you're not."

"I'm good enough to get out of here and get help. The fire he started is smoldering. We don't have much time."

We helped each other up, although Blackie continued to hover.

Then he shifted, hunkering back on his hindquarters as if he were going to leap.

"Where are you two? Where are you?" Bart's voice came through the hay-drop.

Paul pushed me behind him, toward the stall door just as Bart stuck his head through the hole. Blackie bounced on his front legs, shaking his head, ears flattened to his neck.

"Dammit, dammit, I'll make him trample you." He disappeared for a moment before reappearing – head, shoulder and arm now precariously dipping through the ceiling. In his hand was a small pistol.

The report from the gun was not as loud as my horse's bellow.

Blackie lunged upward, mouth open, teeth bared. Faster than a snake-strike he had Bart by the arm, yanked through the hay drop and hurled against the back wall.

Bart bounced to the floor, face down in the shavings and didn't move.

Shaking, I reached through the stall bars, unhooked the latch, and shoved the door wide. Blackie trotted out into the aisle.

"Go," Paul said and pushed me through the doorway.

I only had time to grab a handful of Blackie's mane as we took off as fast as I could run.

With each step my legs became less cooperative, less willing to support my weight. My mind dipped and spun along with the shifting ground. At the barn door Blackie stopped.

"I'm not feeling so good," I said, groping for something more on my horse to hang on to.

"I've got you," Paul said, wrapped a heavy arm around my shoulders and gestured vaguely toward the parking lot. "Help's coming." In slow motion he sank to his knees, dragging me with him. I grabbed onto my husband trying to save us both. Blackie nickered, but didn't move.

"The police are on their way," Miguel shouted.

Paul's breathing labored. "Good," he called back and tipped against me. "Shit. What'd that asshole do, stick a hot poker in my back? My side is on fire."

"It was a hay hook." The words came thick, difficult.

Paul sagged, sat on his heels, and with an effort laughed, shallow and short. "I thought he punched me then got his pocket knife stuck in my jacket. Hey," he scrutinized me from a couple inches away. "You don't look so good."

Then his eyes rolled back and he toppled onto me. We crumbled to the ground like a teetering stack of books.

Blackie's soft, dark brown muzzle pushed at Paul's inert form. I tried to call out for help, but lifting my hand to Paul's heavy head required more concentration and strength than I possessed. Despite knowing I'd been drugged and would lose the battle, I fought to stay awake. Miguel called to his son Jorge before his big, square hand pushed Blackie's nose away from my face. Cold night air replaced warm, sweet horse breath, but did nothing to counteract the drug.

Paul's weight came off me, and another wash of cold air caught me like a slap, making me shiver. Another set of hands slid under my armpits pulled me upright then lifted me into strong arms.

"Agnes and Max," I said, then willed the rest to come out. "In the hayloft. Help them."

"Okay," Jorge said, his face now close to mine. The concern on his face aged him. I'd not have recognized Miguel's son, if not for his voice.

I made another herculean effort at speech. "Fire. There's a fire."

Jorge's eyes went wide and flashed toward his father. "Dad. Thea said there's a fire in the hayloft."

Thank God. He'd understood.

More voices surrounded us. I thought I heard Detective Thurman, tried to look, but my eyes wouldn't open.

# Chapter Twenty-Two

My recollection of the next few hours was spotty. Once, I knew I was on Maria's sofa and then somehow in a brightly lit hospital room with no sensation of time passing. Each time consciousness swam by, the memory of Paul collapsing in the gravel sent a jolt of panic through me. Though I fought it, the drugged blackness returned each time and fear twisted my heart into a painful knot. Dreams spun wild, disjointed images, both upsetting and confusing. I woke briefly in a dim, chilly, unfamiliar room with a vague antiseptic smell, and whimpered for Paul. A strong, warm hand grasped mine and a light blanket settled over my shoulders. Tears stung my eyes. I turned my face into barely yielding, sterile-scented crispness and slept.

With a sudden certainty, I knew it was morning. A different kind of light suffused the room creating a warmer, less complete darkness behind my closed eyelids. The silence that met my ears was absolute, like the quiet that only comes in the early hours before anyone stirs. I moved a bare foot, exploring the limits of the lightweight covering over me. The unfamiliar stiffness of the sheets and firm mattress had to be hospital-issue. That fact alone deepened my sadness despite the fact I knew myself to be alive and, with the exception of some soreness, unharmed.

The events of the previous evening did not come flooding back. Neither did they arrive in bits and pieces.

They'd never left.

The only new information I possessed was the certainty that, but for those hellish memories, I was alone. I knew nothing of what had happened to the barn, to Agnes, to Max, to the horses and, with tears leaking from still closed eyes, my husband.

Not knowing twisted at my gut and tightened an iron band around my chest.

With more resolve than energy, I opened my eyes and threw back the sheet and light blanket. If it was going to be bad news I had to know. I would not wait for someone to eventually show up and tell me.

The creak of a chair jerked my attention to my right. Paul, haggard and fully dressed in his usual T-shirt and jeans, was on his feet and reaching for me. A blanket slipped to the floor from his shoulders. I managed a squeak of surprise, then threw myself into his arms.

And burst into tears.

"I was so worried," I was finally able to sob out, after I'd kissed him enough, touched him enough, assured myself he was real and alive.

He continued to hold me tightly, kissing my face, my lips, the side of my head, stroking my hair, wiping at my tears. "Shh, it's okay. It's over," was all he said, and he repeated the words like a litany, as if trying to convince himself as well as me.

I could not stop crying, pressing into him until, at long last, I was able to take a normal breath. Reluctantly, I untucked my face from his neck and glanced around the hospital room. There was a second, unused, bed, a recliner chair pulled close and no one else. The clock on the wall above a sink said five. I sat up a little, sniffed and scrubbed at my tear-soaked eyes. "How long have you been here, next to me?"

"All night."

"They let you stay?"

"I wouldn't leave so they brought me a chair."

My heart overflowed. "Oh, Paul, I do love --" and then I remembered his wound. The one that bled all over his jeans, the one he'd gotten when he thought I was dying, the one I'd feared Bart managed to kill him with. "Your back!" I slid off the bed, and examined his T-shirted back. There was no hole in the shirt. I eyeballed his jeans. No blood. "I thought ...."

"Vi brought me clean clothes."

"So ...?"

"So I got stitched up and bandaged. You can look when we get home, if you like. It was nothing."

"I find that hard to believe.".

I eased his shirt up. A good portion of the right side of his back was swathed in thin, white padding and tape. Nothing, my ass. I patted his left shoulder and smoothed his shirt down before climbing back onto the bed. This time I sat facing him, instead of on him. He took both my hands in his and raised them to his lips.

"I thought he'd killed you," my husband whispered.

I touched his face. "I thought he had, too -- for a minute. Then I felt okay and figured I'd be fine. Then I thought he'd killed you. Why am I here?" I gestured to the room in general.

"Observation. Bart injected you with a sedative of some sort. Not fatal, obviously, like Don and Willa, but the doc wanted to be sure you'd come out of it."

"Is that what he did to Agnes and Max, too? Shot them up with a sedative?"

"Apparently, but they were both recovered from it enough when the ambulance got there. Bart had them in the hayloft since late afternoon, drugged and duct taped. According to Agnes, he was going to start a fire and have them die of smoke inhalation."

I scoffed. "I'd think that duct tape on a couple of bodies would tip off the police there was something amiss. What an idiot."

"He was going to remove it -- after he'd given them each a final dose of sedative and was sure they were out -- then set the fire. Make it look like Agnes and Max had met in the loft for a little tryst, had a smoke and, whoops, burned the place down."

"Agnes told you all this?"

"Agnes and Max told Thurman. Thurman told me and asked me to tell you when you woke up."

I nodded. "And Bart? Did they catch him?"

"Yes and no." He grimaced.

"What? What does that mean?"

"He's dead. They found him in Blackie's stall, and the gun as well. Thurman said he probably died when he fell from the hay-drop."

I bit my lip and studied my husband. Why hadn't he mentioned Blackie's role?

He rested his hands on my shoulders and, without breaking eye contact, inclined his head until almost touching mine. "I didn't see him fall, I told Thurman that. I was too busy protecting you from getting shot."

True enough. He'd thrown himself over me. I may have been the only witness to Blackie pulling Bart through the hay-drop, but Paul had to be aware of what happened.

"Blackie's okay, isn't he? Bart didn't shoot him?"

"Blackie's fine. Henry had a look at him, gave him some Banamine just to be safe, and told me he's acting as if nothing at all happened."

I ran my hands down my husband's chest, smoothing the wrinkles in his shirt. "I want to go home."

"Me, too.".

We'd had to wait for the okay from the doctor before leaving, and on the way home we detoured by Copper Creek. A hand-lettered sign at the entrance said "Closed for the day." Paul steered around it and into the driveway. The parking lot was empty of all cars. Stacks of hay bales took up much of the space. Apparently the loft had been emptied.

We parked the car and got out. Blackie, out in his paddock, whinnied at our approach and trotted to the fence to meet us. I ducked between the rails and wrapped my arms around his neck. Paul stroked his face and ears, and the three of us kept a silent, grateful companionship until my horse sighed and moved back to his breakfast. Paul ushered me back to the car, and we went home without talking to any of our human rescuers.

When we finally walked through our front door I felt I'd been away for a month. I made quick phone calls to Delores, Miguel and Maria, and my aunt and uncle, telling them we were fine, and wanted to rest a bit. Then we headed for the bath tub.

I filled it, added some lavender bath salts and we both eased in, soaking our bruises, helping each other wash. I was careful not to get Paul's bandages wet, and did not peek at the wound. I simply couldn't do it, not yet. I'd have a look later, when the memory of the hay hook buried in his back was not so fresh. Maybe.

When our bath was done, we made love.

Carefully and gently, and then in celebration of being alive.

Afterwards we slept, twined together until the doorbell woke us. It couldn't be anyone we knew -- none of them used the bell. Paul groaned, swung out of bed and pulled on a pair of jeans and his robe. I rolled over and looked at the clock as he clomped down the stairs. Eleven-fifteen. On a Monday. I'd call it a sick day. I hoped someone had telephoned the university for Paul. He'd already missed a class.

"Thea," Paul called.

I slid out of bed and pulled on my flannel robe. Paul was in the hallway when I came down the stairs, showing Agnes to the living room. She perched on the coral wing chair, twisting the strap of her purse.

"I'm so sorry to bother you," she said, her eyes darting between me and Paul. "I wanted to thank you for saving my life last night, and tell you a few things."

"Would you care for some coffee?" I asked, hoping she'd say yes, because I really needed some.

"No, no thank you. I can't stay."

I sat on the edge of the sofa, wrapping my robe a little tighter around me. Paul sat next to me, leaning forward, forearms resting on his thighs. We waited. Agnes looked down, and cleared her throat.

"I think I know why Bart did what he did." She raised her gaze to us, and when neither of us made a comment, she continued. "You, um, probably know that Bart is -- was -- a good bit younger than me. I guess I knew all along that he was more interested in my bank account than me, but at the time, I thought …." She laughed, a small strangled sound, her hand pressing against her chest, and she shook her head. "Sorry. I was foolish. Everyone saw it but me." She took a breath and set her purse on the floor. "Maybe, if you don't mind, I'll have a glass of water?"

Paul patted my knee and got up. From the amount of water running in the kitchen, I suspected he was also fixing a pot of coffee. Agnes, eyes downcast, fiddled with her hands until he returned with a tall glass of water, handing it to her along with a napkin. She murmured a "thank you," took a sip, and continued.

"A few years ago, Bart created his social welfare organization. He immersed himself in it right from the start and became more and more obsessed. He went on endless business trips to various state offices in Olympia to meet with different politicians, law-makers, special interest groups. He planned dinners, hosted parties – all catered. And he spent enormous amounts of money on what he called 'necessary courting of political influence.' I started riding out of loneliness, at first, then found I loved it. I met Max, and ...." She shrugged.

Paul and I exchanged a glance. I half expected him to appear uncomfortable with her confession, but his features were composed, his shoulders relaxed.

I leaned forward. "Agnes, you don't have to tell us all of this."

"I want you to know." Her gaze moved from me to Paul and back. "I thought you might understand. Max gave me purpose."

I reached for Paul's hand, nodding. He twined his fingers through mine and settled our hands on his knee.

She took several swallows of water, then held the glass on her lap. "I began to get worried about how Bart was spending my money, so I restructured my trust, and gave him an allowance. It was generous -- I thought -- but Bart was furious. That's when the abuse started to escalate." She laughed a little in her gravelly way. "Do you know I didn't realize for the longest time how abusive he really was?" She paused, seeming to think, then sipped some water before she continued. "I found the Stubbs painting stashed in the back of his closet. I figured it was a nice reproduction and something he didn't want, so I gave it to Max. After all, it was in Bart's closet, he couldn't have wanted it. The funny thing was, I never made the connection between Bart's anger and his discovery of the painting in Max's office even though that's when his abuse became ... physical. I didn't know until I talked to Detective Ross that the painting was stolen from one of the people Bart had tried to solicit contributions from."

"You didn't think Bart might want to sell it?" Paul asked.

She shook her head. "Not until Detective Ross said it was likely his plan once the investigation was shelved."

It was somewhat gratifying to know I'd been right about the painting, but my flash of insight had less to do with that than other doings at Copper Creek. At last I understood the source of all the accidents that had made Max so mistakenly furious with Delores. "Bart was responsible for the broken mirror in the arena, the hole in the footing that made Elf fall and everything else, wasn't he."

"I believe so. Bart wanted me to give up horses and stem the 'waste of money that could be used for more important pursuits.' The accidents began shortly after I restructured my trust to stem the hemorrhaging of money into his organization. I didn't make the association at first, but the more upset Max became, the more I started to suspect Bart. It was why I started to spend so much time at the barn -- I thought if I was there, watching, I could prevent anything more from happening ... or catch him in the act."

"Why didn't you tell Max instead of allowing him to suspect Delores?" Honestly, I was a tad miffed at her logic.

"I was afraid if I told Max, he would break off our relationship, consider me too much of a liability. Silly of me, I know, but his dream is to be a successful international competitor and while I'll always take second place to that, he needs me to help him. That's why I bought Rum Runner. Obviously, that only provoked my husband. First, he tried to convince me riding was too dangerous, and then he tried to kill the horses." Her face flushed with anger and she swallowed more water.

"So Don's death was an accident?" I asked. "And Willa? Was her's an accident, too?"

"No." She looked me directly in the eye. "When the asshole injected me with the last dose of Valium up in the hayloft, he went into great detail about how unhappy Willa was working for Don and Rick, how unappreciated she felt, and how I'd been responsible for connecting him with her when I'd sent him in to pay a bill. Can you believe it?"

I could, but opted for a sympathetic shake of my head.

"He cultivated a relationship with her and she helped him substitute the euthanasia solution for the vaccine. And *then*," she chugged half the glass of water, "and then, when she nearly gave him away twice when he was hiding in the bathroom, he said he had no option but to kill her, too."

I gripped Paul's hand. Holy crap. It hadn't been a clogged toilet she was keeping Rick from, but Bart. His presence there had no doubt accounted for her jittery behavior when I'd stopped by for the Banamine, too.

"I hate him for the affair, for him killing Don and Willa, and trying to kill me. But I hate him more for trying to kill the horses. I'm glad he's dead. I'm sorry if that shocks you, but the horses never did anything to deserve it. They are innocents and depend entirely on us for their care."

I reeled at her dismissal of Don's and Willa's deaths. They were innocents, too – particularly Don. Poor Willa had been played and duped by an expert. She never stood a chance. A low rumble came from my husband.

"You suspected Bart when Don died."

Paul's terse statement propelled my righteous horror into words. "Good God, Agnes. Why didn't you go to the police when Don died? Why didn't you tell someone? So much of what happened could have been prevented."

Her fingers tightened around her water glass and she seemed to sink into the chair. "I had no solid proof, only suspicions, and mostly I thought I was being the delusional, stupid old woman Bart told me I was. I thought I was only trying to find excuses for the hateful way I was feeling toward Bart after ... I know someone like you, so full of self-confidence, finds this hard to understand." She raised a pleading gaze to me. "I tried to get help. I came to you."

My jaw sagged. Crap. Could I have prevented much of the tragedy by doing what she'd asked?

Paul straightened. "Don't lay this at Thea's feet, Agnes. I'm sorry for what you've been through but, the fact remains, you should have gone to the police." He stood, took a couple of steps toward the front door and waited, a muscle flexing in his jaw.

She chewed her lip, eyes wide at Paul's anger. "I'm sorry. I didn't mean to imply .... I'm sorry." She scooted forward in the chair and awkwardly rose to her feet. "I think I've taken up enough of your time."

I stood as well, and she handed me her glass. "I hope neither of you will think too badly of me after all of this. I am grateful for what you've done, and so is Max. I know he plans to stop by later." She walked quickly to the door. Paul and I followed. The goodbye was brief and distinctly uncomfortable.

I didn't want to talk to Max, but I supposed we didn't have much choice. We locked the door behind her and went back to the kitchen. Paul poured coffee while I pulled a package of Aunt Vi's cinnamon rolls from the freezer and slid them into the microwave. We ate our "breakfast" in peace, but not half an hour after Agnes' departure there was a knock on the front door.

"It's probably Max," I said, and sighed. "Can we just let him go away?"

Paul collected our empty mugs and plates from the table and took them to the sink. "I'll talk to him. Why don't you go put some clothes on? I don't think he'll be our last visitor this morning."

He was probably right. I trotted up the stairs, planning on taking enough time dressing to allow Max to say "thank you" and leave.

"Thea," Paul called. "Phil's here."

Detective Thurman. Once again he'd come to us. Time to tie up the loose ends. I threw on my sweats and hurried back downstairs. Thurman was sitting at the kitchen table and Paul was measuring out coffee for another pot.

We exchanged a few pleasantries and, in response to his inquiry, I assured the detective I was fully recovered, then listened as he repeated a short version of what I'd already heard from Paul at the hospital. My husband filled more mugs with coffee and handed them out. When Thurman concluded his update, he drained his mug then put it down with care.

"Now, your turn. How did you two come to be in the hay loft last night?"

Oh. Right. "Paul didn't tell you?"

He looked at my husband. "Paul was not especially cooperative last night. When he wasn't passed out, he was belligerent as hell. Wouldn't leave you even to get that hole in his back cleaned up and stitched."

My heart swelled and I turned to my hero and touched his face. "That's so sweet."

Paul kissed my finger tips.

"Sweet nothing. You were a damned nuisance, Hudson." Then he glared at me. "And that horse of yours stood on Miguel's porch while you were inside the house and wouldn't budge. Everyone had to squeeze around him. Pain in the ass to try and get a stretcher past him. He even followed you to the ambulance and would have climbed right on inside if Maria hadn't removed him."

"She 'removed' him?"

"Hollered something at him in Spanish then slapped her thigh like she was calling a dog."

I laughed at the image. "He went with her?"

"Yup. Turned around and followed her off, just like … well … a dog."

I grinned at Paul. "Did you know?"

He chuckled and shook his head.

Thurman didn't express any amusement. "So, are you going to tell me how you got to be in the hay loft?"

Oh, right. I told him and, in the process, reminded myself about the Stubbs painting.

"I take it Dave got the painting back?"

"He did. He told me you'd called and thought you'd found it. Lucky for him you have a sharp eye. He hated that assignment. Told me he got married and went to Hawaii to avoid it. Pretty drastic if you ask me."

I was so going to kick Dave's butt. I wanted to see Andrea,

though, since she was probably worried about us and I doubted she'd allow any butt-kicking.

Paul rubbed a hand over his mouth, but didn't do an awfully good job of getting rid of his grin.

"Just so you know," the detective said, "Michelle is off the hook." He pushed away from the table. "Gotta go and have a chat with Agnes Fulton now about her nut-job of a husband and finish up all the damn paperwork. Wanted to talk to you two first, though."

We saw him out, and not five minutes later there was another knock on the door. My aunt and uncle, Delores and Maria filed in. Each carried containers or bags. My sister trailed along last, empty handed.

"Food," Aunt Vi said with a stiff smile. "We thought you'd be too tired to cook." Taking Delores' and Maria's bags from her, she marched past me to the kitchen. Everyone else went to the living room and sat down. No one said a word, and they all looked mildly annoyed, except my sister. The hang-dog expression she wore was so unlike her.

I scanned the room for Paul only to find him hanging back and watching the lot of them as if he wasn't planning on sticking around. We should have stopped and talked to everyone this morning on our way home from the hospital, but he'd hustled me home, only allowing our brief visit with Blackie. I'd chalked it up to his not feeling well. Now I wasn't so sure.

"I'll just go put some clothes on," Paul said.

"Oh, don't bother for us," Aunt Vi said, returning to the living room, chin raised and with a pointed look for Paul then me. "We're just *family.*"

Paul swallowed, tightened the belt on his robe, and slid a quick look in my direction. Crap. I knew it. He'd caved. My question wasn't, what had he done, since that full-blown conclusion was obvious from my aunt's tiny remark and his guilty look, but rather, "what possessed him?"

"Let's all have a seat in the living room, shall we?" my

aunt said, although it was apparent Paul and I were the only ones not seated.

Aunt Vi settled primly on the sofa next to Uncle Henry. He scooted over, without losing the frown or the crossed arms, closer to Maria and her dark-eyed disapproval. Delores studied us from the coral wing chair Agnes had occupied earlier. Only Juliet wasn't giving us a stare down. She sat on the rug by the fireplace, fiddling with the embellishment on the top-most layer of her colorful shirts.

With a sigh, Paul gestured to the remaining chair, his leather recliner, for me.

"Thank you, no. I'd rather stand," I said.

He sat, and cleared his throat, but didn't speak.

"I understand from your sister," Aunt Vi said, casting a severe frown in her direction before leveling the same look at me, "that Paul's insistence last night at the hospital that you were his *wife* was not a desperate fabrication simply to get his own way, as I originally supposed."

Paul sat a little straighter. "The nurse was *trying* to toss me out. And she was getting ready to call security."

"You were covered in filth and blood and acting like a mad man with all that shouting and cursing. You're lucky they didn't throw you in the clink. She would likely have allowed you back into Thea's room if *you'd* allowed her to do her job and change Thea into a hospital gown, instead of acting like a toddler about to lose his favorite toy."

"Wow, auntie," my sister muttered, "that's tactful."

"My dear," Aunt Vi snapped, "we Brits are known for our forthrightness with manners, not our spineless tact."

Uncle Henry closed his eyes, briefly.

My sister rolled hers. "Oh, right, like Monty Python. I forgot." She swept a wide, imperial gesture at Paul. "'Throw him to the floor!'"

"That will be quite enough. I'll be getting to your part in this chicanery in a moment."

Juliet slouched and stared at the floor. No need to throw

her to it. She was already there -- literally and figuratively. How could I be angry with her? She'd been right about Michelle all along. She'd been the only one to have the guts to do what it took to save her.

My anger at my husband dissolved, too. After all, he was my hero. I laid my hand on his shoulder to let him know.

"Now," my aunt's gaze flicked from me to Paul and back to me. "I understand from your sister that the two of you saw fit to get married in Las Vegas while you were there for Andrea and David's wedding."

I nodded, my mouth dry.

Paul cleared his throat and laid a hand over the top of mine. "That's right. It was my idea."

I squeezed his shoulder. "Mine, too."

"Well, of course," my aunt sniffed. "It seems to me that's a two-person decision. I doubt you clubbed her over the head to get her to cooperate."

"Of course I thought it was a good idea," I said, a bit defensively. "The getting married part, that is. We discussed the pros and cons of waiting and having our wedding here and decided to avoid all the problems and take advantage of being in Las Vegas."

"What 'problems' might you be referring to?"

Paul and I exchanged a nervous glance. I didn't dare look at Delores since she was related to some of the major ones. "Um, well, you know. Mother would probably turn the whole thing into a huge deal."

"Circus, you mean," Juliet said.

"Rubbish," Aunt Vi said.

Delores laughed. "She has a point, Vi."

"Hardly. A wedding most certainly is a 'huge deal,' as you say, Thea, and don't you forget it. Too many people take a casual approach to marriage these days and end up in the courts getting a divorce. At least you two were smart to live together first and get to know each other, make sure you could get along. Your mum wants what's best for you, and she has some experience you don't –"

"Not any more," Juliet said, and was immediately shut down with an icy glare from our aunt. "Sorry," she muttered.

Paul straightened and took a breath. "My family is opposed to our marriage."

"Oh, pish posh," Aunt Vi waved her hand. "Henry already told me. They'll come around. My sister did when Thea and Juliet's mum and dad got married. Besides, once your family meets Thea, they'll love her. And, since you're already married, it rather a moot point, isn't it."

Paul squeezed my hand and I looked at him. He shook his head very slightly.

"Do you two realize I thought you were expecting? I was terribly upset you didn't feel you could confide in me." I had no idea if Aunt Vi was talking to me or Paul – not that it mattered. "Why did you keep your wedding a secret? You haven't given one good reason for that bad decision yet."

"We didn't want to hurt everyone's feelings."

"So you were just going to pretend and have another wedding in … June? Or was it August … I think you might have said … April?"

"April," I said.

"Mercy."

Maria leaned across Uncle Henry to my aunt. "That does not give us much time."

I grimaced. "Well, uh, I've got Mrs. Cunningham working on it." Juliet sat a little taller, watching me with big eyes and a somber, expectant expression from her place on the floor. I caved. Completely. "And Juliet is making my dress."

My sister beamed. Aunt Vi's eyebrows shot up her forehead and Delores laughed. Uncle Henry uncrossed his arms.

Maria nodded, obviously pleased. "She will do a good job. You wait and see."

Juliet heaved herself up from the floor and looked out the front window. "If you guys are done with me, I've gotta go.

And Paul, I'll bring those dress designs by tonight."

I opened my mouth to point out how unnecessary it was to run them by him now.

"A deal is a deal." She smirked.

I swallowed. We'd revisit the discussion later. "Are you going to take your motorcycle?" It was still parked by the front porch, right where Paul had left it.

"Yeah, I'll be by tomorrow and get it." She waved over her shoulder and skipped out the front door.

Maria looked over the back of the sofa and out the window, then tsked a couple of times. "It is as I thought."

"What's that?" My aunt asked, craning to see, too.

"She is again with Eric. We will see how that works out." She sighed and shook her head.

Lucky us, the interrogation seemed to be over and Juliet's exit the signal for everyone to leave.

Delores paused at the front door and watched my aunt, uncle and Maria go down the walk to the car before she turned to us. "Maria wanted to ask, but it looks like she was too shy."

Maria shy? "What did she want to ask?"

"If you were married by Elvis."

Paul grinned. "No, all the Elvises were busy. We got Dolly Parton."

Delores threw back her head and howled. "I'll tell her. I think she'll be satisfied."

She reached the porch steps, stopped and turned around, her expression suddenly serious.

"I know about Jan's boy," she said.

Paul said nothing. I took his hand.

"Is he yours?"

"No," my husband said.

"You're sure?"

He nodded.

"Leave your mother to me," she said. "Good thing you got married in Vegas."

She turned to go, but I caught her arm. "Why didn't you tell us you knew Sybil?"

She sucked her lips in for a moment, then shook her head very slightly. "There was no need. She wasn't involved."

"But you could have told us. We'd have believed you."

She tipped her head, regarding me briefly before answering. "Yes, you would have -- but you'd have gone to talk to her, anyway. And she'd have told you the same thing she told me when she came charging into my office after Michelle was arrested."

Her pause prodded me to prompt her. "Which was what?"

She sighed. "That she wished I'd been the one to die instead of Don."

I gasped and she patted my hand, still clinging to her arm.

"She was angry and needed to defend her daughter. She's no threat to me or anyone else. You two take care of each other. It's been a rough time."

My hand dropped from her arm and she walked slowly down the steps to join everyone else at my uncle's car.

With the exception of making a call to Andrea to reassure her we were fine and ask if she and Dave could be available to be in our wedding, we talked to no one else for the remainder of the day. Perhaps all our issues weren't settled, but I could deal with what remained -- probably.

After dinner, Paul finally gave up pretending his wound wasn't bothering him, took a pain pill and went to bed to wait for the medication to work, but he didn't sleep. After worrying myself into a state, I gutsed-up and took a peek under his bandages to check for a possible infection. There wasn't one, and it didn't look nearly as horrible as my imagination claimed it would.

I cried anyway.

I cried for this man whom I nearly lost, whom I loved with every ounce of my being, who saved my life. I cried myself to sleep in his arms.

Despite the flood of emotion, or maybe because it, I slept

soundly. Paul said he did, too. The evidence of such somnolence was on the kitchen table when I went down to make coffee in the morning: the large manila envelope could hardly have walked itself into our house and parked itself on the table.

A hastily scrawled note in my sister's handwriting was attached. "Finished this last night and dropped it off this morning. Didn't want to wake you guys up. I hope you like it." It was signed with a smiley face.

Paul came into the kitchen, yawning, before I could open it.

"What's this?" He took the envelope from my hands, read the note, and pulled out two sheets of paper, examining them both without even a flicker of an indication of his opinion.

Anticipation had me hopping on my toes. "Let me see."

"In a minute." He held the pages away from my view and kept rotating so I couldn't even get the barest glimpse. Finally, I grabbed his arm to hold him still. Laughing he turned the pages toward me. "Looks like she can draw."

My breath caught. Yes, my sister could draw. I never knew. The woman in the gown even looked like me, hair style and all. And the dress ... white, simple, with a draped neckline and cap sleeves which, from the back view, proved to actually be wide ribbons that came together, along with two more from the side seams, to form an elaborate bow in what would be the middle of my back – my bare back – with the ends trailing to the floor.

"Do you like this?" I asked my husband.

He nodded. "Do you?"

"I love it."

SPECIAL BONUS SECTION

# EXCERPTS FROM THE FIRST FOUR

# THEA CAMPBELL MYSTERIES

# Death by a Dark Horse
## ~ The First Thea Campbell Mystery

Half way to the west-side paddocks the slow crunching of car tires on gravel caused me to step to my right. A black Nissan Z eased alongside, and the smooth whisper of the passenger-side widow lowering caught my attention.

"Hey, BC! Thea!"

I bent slightly to see the driver through the open window. Greg Marshall. I should have known. Although I'm an accountant, no one else calls me BC—Bean Counter. How original. He hadn't called me that last night, but then he hadn't been sober, either. I didn't want to talk to him right now. I wanted to find my horse. I wanted to forget last night. If I could forget both him and Jonathan that would be okay, too.

"Hi, Greg." I kept walking.

He kept pace with his car. "Hang on a sec."

My shoulders sagged. I stopped and looked in the window again.

He appeared very Abercrombie & Fitch casual this morning, instead of the GQ businessman of last night. He flashed his ever-handy thousand-watt smile. I flashed a forty-watt one back. Then my gaze dropped to the passenger seat of his spotless Z. It overflowed with red roses. Hastily, I returned my attention to my jacket's balky zipper, hoping I'd jumped to the wrong conclusion. The relentless pain in my head tightened up a notch. He needed to run along now.

"Beautiful day," he said.

I turned the urge to roll my eyes into a glance at the cloud layer. "About time for some rain, though." Okay, enough of this. The pointed look I meant to toss at him got sidetracked by the roses again. He laughed softly and I felt myself flush.

"Don't worry." The teasing smile was still there. "They're for Valerie."

Thank God. "They're stunning. She'll love them."

He held my gaze for a fraction of a moment. The intensity of his smile flickered, like a kid waiting for a much anticipated event, but didn't want to act overexcited and uncool. "They're, um, to go with this." He leaned across the passenger seat and I caught the spicy scent of his expensive cologne through the open window. From the glove compartment he produced a small, light blue box tied with a white satin ribbon.

A Tiffany & Company box.

"Oh. Nice."

Jonathan, my boyfriend, had given me one like it last Valentine's Day. I'd been sick with apprehension until I discovered the tasteful pearl earrings instead of a diamond ring I would have handed right back. I doubted Greg's box held earrings of any kind. He's a financial planner, so I expected the box held an investment—the kind Valerie would wear on her left hand. Why was he showing all this to me?

Greg's smile turned apologetic. "Listen, about last night...." His words glued me to his gaze. "I'm kicking myself for my behavior. All the traveling and meetings wore me out. I wasn't keeping track of the number of beers I'd had. Forgive me?"

Kicking himself? He could have chosen better words. Well, fine. "Don't worry about it. I've had to fight off worse." I aligned my zipper again and yanked. No luck. Was he really afraid I'd taken his sloppily executed, unasked for kiss as a serious invitation? Idiot. I started walking, again, but the car rolled along beside me. I stopped. What now? I slid a look at him.

"Hey...." He hung his head, and half pouted. Despite

knowing the remorse was fake I couldn't hold down a tiny chuckle, and shook my head when it snuck out. He should have known better than to worry. I knew my five-foot-two-inch self was no competition for Valerie. Leggy and graceful, she was the personification of the elegant dressage rider. Women either envied or hated her. Men fell over each other to get next to her. And that's before taking into consideration her net worth.

"Thanks," he said, giving me a you're-a-pal wink. "I'm going to drive around back and surprise Valerie. I expect she's parked in her usual spot."

That would be the spot behind the New Barn, where her horse was stabled. Where no one was supposed to park— including her. He wouldn't mention last night's blunder, would he? That'd just make my morning.

My head throbbed.

Now, not only did I have to find my horse, I had to avoid Valerie just in case he was dumb enough to say something. He was egotistical enough to twist things and brag that I'd been the one to make a pass at him.

"See you later." He lifted a hand in a casual salute. "Oh, the top half of your zipper-pull is up by your collar."

I shifted my focus. Huh. No wonder it wasn't working.

I wiggled my fingers good-bye and watched his car disappear around the corner of the Big Barn before continuing my trek to the paddocks. I hoped Valerie was at her gym instead of here at Copper Creek. Even if Greg kept his mouth shut I had good reason to avoid her. She never missed an opportunity to fire some salvo at me designed to point out her superiority.

I was perfectly aware of her superiority.

She was my age, twenty-nine, and had been long-listed for the last Olympic Dressage Team. It would surprise no one if on the next go-round she made the short-list. She had a long career ahead of her. Goody for her. Showing held no appeal for me, despite my famous uncle. Sure, I was several levels below her and I'd catch up eventually, but my goal was to be the best dressage rider I could. I had a fabulously talented horse I loved, and wanted only to do right by him. She could keep her competitions.

I dismissed Valerie from my thoughts. I had other, more important issues in my life. And, arriving at the west paddocks, eyes squinting against the pounding in my head, I could see I also had a long search ahead of me.

Blackie wasn't in any of these paddocks either.

When I got my hands on Jorge I was going to wring his neck. I turned around and strode back toward the Big Barn, gravel flying out from under the heels of my boots.

Ten minutes later I stood in the doorway of the last of the three barns, having checked the occupants of every stall. I had located neither Jorge nor Blackie. Jorge could be on break in the house, but Blackie ….

It shouldn't be this hard to find an eleven-hundred pound horse.

# LEVELS OF DECEPTION
## ~ THE SECOND THEA CAMPBELL MYSTERY

After returning the first fossil to its proper shelf, I located the next one and repeated the process. As I was setting up the third specimen there was a whoosh and thump as the big storage room door opened then closed. I didn't expect to be the only one doing work but was a little surprised when the echo of footsteps came closer. A young man, probably a few years short of my twenty-nine, dressed in khakis and an almost white short-sleeve shirt, rounded the end of the stacks and approached. His aquiline nose found the perfect accompaniment in the unrestrained, enthusiastically curling brown hair that brushed his shoulders. However, an aggressive scowl trumped any potential friendliness his appearance might have produced.

"Hello," he said, and crossed his arms.

"Hi." I lowered my camera and smiled.

His gaze barely touched my setup before snapping back to me. "Taking pictures?"

Wow. What a masterful command of the obvious. In the pause before I answered, a flush crept up his neck and he shoved his hands into his pockets. Poor guy. He really didn't have a firm grip on "man-in-charge."

"Yes. Dr. Hudson asked me to take some photographs and e-mail them to him. I'm Thea Campbell, by the way." I held out my hand.

"Scott Loch." He extracted a hand from his pocket and

gave mine a damp, cursory shake. "I'm surprised the web site photos aren't sufficient." His gaze went to the list of fossils sitting on the table. "Is this yours?" He picked up the e-mail printout.

"Yes. The web site shows only one view of each fossil." I was surprised he didn't know that. "Are you part of the Paleontology Department staff?"

Instead of replying, he took a long look at the e-mail with my name and Paul's in the heading. Call me crazy, but I was willing to bet he hadn't shown up out of curiosity. He was checking on me, and I suspected Mrs. Peabody had put him up to it. The woman wasn't going to give up. He put the paper down before he answered my question.

"More or less. I'm a grad student and Dr. Whitaker's secretary for the summer. Are you an undergrad?"

"Dr. Whitaker?"

"Department head."

"Oh, right. Actually," I said. "I'm a friend of Dr. Hudson's. I'm just running this errand for him."

A hank of his hair fell forward. Frowning, he pushed it back, briefly snagging his fingers. "He could have asked one of us. Why didn't he?"

"I'm sure I don't know." And as much as I hated to admit it, he had a point.

"Are you sure you're able to manage this?" He picked up the copy of Paul's e-mail again. This time he seemed to be reading the instructions. He kept glancing at my setup. "Pat should have gotten in touch with me."

"Pat?" I asked. The name wasn't familiar.

"She's Dr. Hudson's graduate assistant this summer."

My molars slammed together with enough force to send a sharp pain through my temples. Paul's graduate assistant out in the wilderness with him was a woman? Was there a reason he had not told me his assistant was female, had not corrected me when I'd commented on how pleased he seemed to be that he had gotten *him* for an assistant? This was phone call material. E-mail was too easy to evade. Not that I was jealous. Just cautious. And not stupid.

"The camera? Can I see it?" Scott's hand extended toward me and flapped in a give-it-to-me gesture. I guess I missed the first request.

Although I tried to think of one, I couldn't find a reason why he shouldn't see my photographs. Irritated, I passed the camera to him and waited for him to ask me how to operate it. He scanned the shots I had taken with the assurance of a techno-geek, then returned it to me.

"Don't let me keep you from your work," he said. "Nice to meet you."

Right.

Within two undisturbed hours I'd relegated Pat to the status where she belonged -- an academic necessity -- and photographed nearly all the fossils. There were four I couldn't locate, although I spent a good deal of time trying. Paul needed them. Maybe someone had checked them out, like library books. I rolled my shoulders and sighed. There was only one thing to do. Get help. I would have to go back to the dragon.

She wasn't there, but Dr. Fogel was. My jaw unlocked.

He stood, absorbed in some papers, and didn't notice me walk up.

"Excuse me," I said.

He paused in his reading, gave me a blank look, then a congenial nod.

"Miss Campbell, done already?" He pushed his glasses up his long thin nose.

"No, I'm afraid not. I ran into some problems and wondered if you could help."

"I can try." Although the man was all straight lines and angles, his expression held soft humor.

"I'm having some trouble locating some fossils on my list." I handed it to him. "I circled the catalogue numbers of the ones I couldn't find."

All at once his edges and angles sharpened. "Ah yes, I see. How's everything going at the dig?"

He should know. Paul told him I was coming, he must have told him why as well. A zing of warning spiked up my spine. It was the same feeling I got whenever a horse I was riding telegraphed his tension when sensing a possible threat. Instinct kicked in; minimize my reaction, and divert attention. "He hasn't said much. So, the fossils I couldn't find -- I was wondering if someone might have checked them out."

Affable once again, his warm brown eyes regarded me with amusement over the top of his glasses. "No, all specimens remain in the archives. Although it's possible someone might have put them back on the wrong shelf. That happens sometimes." He perused the list, his eyebrows making journeys up and down his forehead as he read. "Well, let's go see what we can find."

He preceded me down the hallway at a brisk pace, my list fluttering in his grasp. I sprinted, catching the storage room door just before it closed behind him, slipping once again into the chilly, dry-earth-scented repository.

Dr. Fogel had already reached the first fossil location and was scanning the shelf above and below its assigned spot when I caught up. He made an about-face and examined the shelves on the opposite side of the aisle, just as I had done. He harrumphed, consulted the list, and hustled to another aisle. This he did twice more with the remaining specimens while I followed anxiously waiting for an exclamation of success that never came. With a shake of his head, he headed to the computer, pulled up a search screen, and typed in the catalogue numbers, his large hands moving with surprising dexterity over the keyboard. Then he repeated the search using the Latin name of each specimen, and again with other search criteria. With each effort his frown grew more pronounced, and the furrow between his eyebrows deeper. He consulted my list again, then headed for the stacks. Again. I listened to his rummaging as he moved from one area to another, checking areas of the storage room I hadn't. My worry grew right along with my irritation at being left uninformed. After several long minutes he returned.

"Let me check something else."

I chewed my lip and traipsed after him to the computer. He clicked on a couple of links, and stared at the screen, one hand resting on his hip and the other covering his mouth and chin. The blue and white screen cast an eerie reflection on the lenses of his glasses, making him appear eyeless.

"At least I can get the rest off to Paul." I tried to sound unworried.

"What? Oh, right, yes. Good idea." He lightly tapped his jaw.

"Maybe the photographs I have already will be enough."

He nodded as though he were responding to the sound of my voice rather than the words, then shut down the computer and walked away. He stopped and turned, his index finger touching his lips before pointing at me. "Perhaps the specimens you found will be sufficient."

"Thank you for your help," I said to his now-retreating back.

I combed my fingers through my hair and massaged the back of my neck, rolling my head. There was nothing to do but go home with what I had. The idea didn't make me happy. I should be able to do better than this. Giving up never sat well with me, whether riding my horse, working on my clients' books, or anything else. Paul was fast becoming the most important person in my life, yet I had to give up on something that was important to him. But, dammit, what else was I supposed to do?

I packed my camera and supplies in my bag and left. I'd found and photographed eleven of the items on Paul's list. I paced, distracted, down the now-familiar, long hallway flogging my memory for some clue, some approach I'd missed that would help me get the remaining four fossils.

Paul was efficient. Every photograph would have a

specific purpose for his lecture, and he was missing better than a quarter of them. If I'd planned the presentation my list would ... include back-ups -- duplicates, or near duplicates, just in case there were problems.

I stopped. Why hadn't I thought of that earlier? That was it!

Had he thought of that -- to include back-ups?

My excitement sputtered. How was I going to find out? Why hadn't I asked Dr. Fogel before he left? The dragon was probably back at her desk. Now I'd have to ask her where I could find him. Damn.

I hiked my bag more securely on my shoulder. Okay, then. I'd faced her once. I could face her again. As I rounded a turn in the corridor Dr. Fogel's voice echoed softly ahead, coming toward me but still some ways away. Hope I could avoid Mrs. Peabody again quickened the pat-pat of my sneakered feet until Scott's angry, strident pitch cut off Andrew Fogel's quiet tone, halting my rush.

"If you don't do something I'll --"

"You'll do nothing. I'm certain he already suspects me. If you're found out it will --"

"I won't jeopardize our plan." Scott's tone was a sneer. "But I'm telling you we have to do something about her."

Her? Her who? Her me? What had I done? Crap. Their voices were getting closer.

There was nowhere to hide.

# AN ERROR IN JUDGMENT
## -- THE THIRD THEA CAMPBELL MYSTERY

Rumors of Andrea's marriage in September broke my heart. It hurt to hear the information fourth-hand, but worse was learning who she'd married: Sig Paalmann, an exceedingly wealthy horseman. I knew him by his reputation as a dressage judge harshly critical of those who struggled with the sport. There were two habits of his that created the lion's share of responsibility for this reputation. The first was the demoralizing verbal commentary he fired at many a hapless competitor at the conclusion of their test, and the second was his custom to write additional, more callous edicts on the test sheet itself. Trainers and coaches carried packs of Kleenex to hand out to their unfortunate students who couldn't escape the arena soon enough at the conclusion of their ride, or who foolishly insisted on reading the scored test sheet at the end of the show.

Unfortunately, Sig's presence at the awards dinner was a given. Every local judge had been invited to this premier equestrian gala.

Andrea, of course, was with him.

I had to talk to her, no matter how painful. If I could find the courage. If I could get her alone.

After dinner was my best chance.

Pre-meal socializing was not going to work in my favor, if one could call the tense scene before me "socializing."

Lips drawn tight against his teeth, Paalmann spoke in a

rapid burst to my great uncle, Henry Fairchild. In his mid-sixties, close to Sig's age, Uncle Henry had an unfailingly kind character that couldn't be more different from Sig's. But now, even from a distance, the flash of anger in my uncle's eyes was impossible to miss. Sig, punctuating his words with small chops of his hand, either didn't see or didn't care. He was engrossed in vehemently expressing an opinion my uncle found distasteful.

I doubted my uncle had said anything to provoke him. I'd heard from show organizers and volunteers like my aunt that even when in a cooperative mood, Sig was unpleasant. The world revolved around his desires.

He'd obviously desired Andrea. Who could blame him? She was elegant, intelligent and generous. What had my friend seen in this sarcastic, egotistical bastard twice her age?

My sister prodded me with my purse, jerking my attention back to immediate company. "Andrea's put on weight since last time I saw her."

"She looks beautiful. Don't be so critical." But Juliet had a point. Although far from unattractive, Andrea wasn't her usual stylish self. Maybe the shapeless gray dress was to blame.

More likely it was her listless expression.

A horrible possibility crept into my mind. What if Sig had forbidden Andrea to contact any of her old friends … like me?

An elbow gouged my ribcage. "Hey," Juliet snapped. "I said I'm not being critical. Besides, I hear everybody puts on weight after they get married." She looked down, flicking a slender hand over the red-sequined curves every male had ogled on our way in. "Man, I hope it doesn't happen to me." She flashed Paul a wicked smile and reached across me to pat his stomach. "Aren't you kind of jumping the gun?"

Paul started, then stood up a little straighter. "I need to start running again," he muttered.

But he'd noticed Andrea, too, and I knew he was thinking. If he hadn't been, Juliet wouldn't have surprised him. This "thinking" of his concerned me. He'd chided me more than once for leaping to conclusions -- which I wasn't. He was wrong. And as surely as I knew how each and every Sunday would begin and end, I knew exactly what he was doing at this moment. He was sizing up an opportunity to prove to me that Andrea would be delighted to see me. My gut told me I needed to approach Andrea privately. Paul needed to be distracted.

I pressed against him, as close to face to face as I could manage while still holding his arm, and gazed up at him with as much ardor as I could self-consciously pull off in a crowd. Heat crept up my neck and scalded my cheeks.

"You look perfect," I purred, ignoring my embarrassment and praying I was subtle.

A corner of his mouth turned up. Tapping into his libido was a sure thing. Worked every time. I brushed against him and felt his long, slow intake of breath. His arm tightened, pressing my hand into his side.

"Gagging here, you two," Juliet groaned. So much for subtle.

"Let's go say hello to Andrea," he said, and took a step in her direction, spinning me on my too-high heel.

My heart slammed into my ribs while my "sure thing" dragged me toward the exact situation I wanted to avoid. Damn, damn, damn. What was wrong with him? Couldn't he take a hint? I hauled at his arm.

"No. I'll say 'hi' later." I said. "We should look for our table and Aunt Vi."

Paul urged me along. "Come on. They haven't even started serving the salad yet. She'll be happy to see you, and I know you want to talk to her."

"I do -- did -- do want to talk to her. But not right now. Later. When she's not with her husband."

"Why?" Juliet asked.

Great. I'd forgotten she was still with us. The short answer might save me from looking any more foolish. "Because he's a jerk."

"I thought he was a dressage judge. He's not nice?" Juliet said.

Paul's mouth twitched, but a small snort escaped anyway. However, the fear that Sig might be deliberately keeping Andrea from me scared off any levity I might have felt.

"'Nice' is not a prerequisite for a dressage judge," I said.

"Well, no duh." Juliet crossed her eyes, implying I'd been the one with the dumb remark. "Isn't he a friend of Uncle Henry's?"

"Passing acquaintance."

"Well, you must be wrong, Miss Know-It-All. Uncle Henry saves his stern lectures for friends and family, so the old guy next to Andrea who looks like he has a stick up his --"

"Juliet! And no, I'm not wrong. That's him, Sig Paalmann."

Paul tipped his head in interest, then looked again toward Andrea.

Juliet's brow furrowed. "He has to be as old as Uncle Henry. And the conversation seems pretty intense for a couple of guys who barely know each other."

"Oh, they know each other. They're just not friends. Uncle Henry has no patience for someone as deliberately nasty as Sig." At that exact moment my uncle shook his head once and walked away from Sig and Andrea. Not surprised, I continued. "And yes, Sig has to be around sixty."

She shivered. "Eww. Andrea's what -- thirty?"

"Next month."

"Sorry, but even if he was worth bazillions, it just doesn't make up for the ick factor."

"He is, in fact, worth bazillions," I said.

"Whoa. No shit. Well, I'd never let the flash of cash blind me, but looks like your BFF has." She wiggled her fingers, palm up.

I scowled at Juliet's insult. Could my friend really have changed that much? The Andrea I'd known since grade school wasn't a money-grubber. She regularly worked more *pro bono*

cases than anyone else in her firm, and championed the Great
American Small, Struggling Business. Unfortunately, her track
record with men hit the "also ran" lists -- due to her tendency
to get doe-eyed over a handsome face and ignore the warning
signs of a man-looking-for-a-sugar-mama. She had made
consistently bad choices and ended up getting used. Sig, while
distinguished, was not her usual well-built, testosterone-
dripping, needy fare. To the best of my knowledge he did not
require any rescuing and was, by reputation, an emotional
deep freeze.

My heart lurched. Had she thought she was breaking her
old pattern with him, only to overlook warning signs more
dire? A cold certainty made me shiver. Andrea's cocoon of
silence since her hasty September wedding had not been of
her own making.

Juliet narrowed her eyes as she continued to study my
friend and her husband. "Sig Paalmann ...." She tapped a long
red fingernail on her chin. "Isn't he Paal Toys?"

I nodded. "Makes those cute dolls. You know the ones."

"Apple Cheek Babies? Wow. Who'd have thought the guy
who makes the doll on 'every little girl's Christmas list,'" she
had deepened her voice to a good approximation of the TV
announcer's, "would look so opposite of Santa Claus? Well,
except for the gray hair."

Paul tipped his head again, first at Juliet, then me. "Wait a
minute. Did you say Sig *Paalmann*?" He pronounced his last
name differently than Juliet and I. "That's who Andrea
married? *The* Sig Paalmann?"

I eyed him. "I suppose so. How many of them could there
be?"

"He's got one of the most extensive private collections of
dinosaur fossils in the world -- that's public knowledge,
anyway. Not that any of my colleagues have had any more
opportunity to view them than I have."

Juliet rocked her head side to side. The conversation had
veered to the uninteresting -- for her. If there wasn't loud

music and louder laughter, she'd find something else to do. However, the increased animation in Paul's voice alarmed me. I had to keep him talking or this time he'd succeed in dragging me to them.

"I know he owns an impressive art collection and antique cars, but I'd never heard about the fossils."

"The rumor is he limits access. To a paranoid degree. Most paleontologists would give their left -- um, would really like to be invited to inspect the collection."

"Including you?"

"Yeah. But I draw the line at giving over body parts I use." He grinned. "So, let's go say hi. I'll lay you odds he'll be so busy bragging to me about how much he knows about my area of expertise that you and Andrea can do some catching up."

Damn. No way was this going to work out well. "No, really. I don't think ...."

"Come on." He patted my hand, which was still clutching his arm.

I'd encountered that man-on-a-mission spark in his eye before. Short of throwing myself on the ground and shrieking, my chances of turning him aside were zero. I'd have to ditch Plan A and go with Plan B -- whatever that was.

"Have at it, you guys," Juliet said, peering through the crowd in another direction. "I'd love to tag along and find out what Andrea sees in the old fart, but I need to protect my sweetie from all the dressage queens. They lust after that god-of-a-man. Can't say I blame them. Eric dressed up is almost as delicious as Eric naked." Her voice dropped to a sultry timbre with the last sentence, and she flapped her lashes at Paul.

He reared back.

Her mouth curved, cat-like. "I must go remind them all they don't stand a chance. You know how I hate waving this ring, and other things, under people's noses." She held her hand out, examined the modest diamond, and gave it a quick polish on her sleeve. "Sometimes one must sacrifice." She flitted off, left hand pressed delicately to her bosom.

"I could have lived my life happily never hearing any of that," Paul said, grimace still in place.

I'd wanted to chuckle, but my throat constricted the moment he moved off in Andrea's direction. I hoped she, in realizing the attraction of the fossil collection for Paul, would introduce him as Dr. Hudson, professor of paleontology at the University of Washington. Then, while the men talked shop, the two of us would shift around making inane, self-conscious chit-chat and I'd figure out how to arrange to meet with her later.

Perhaps Sig would show a kind side. Perhaps Andrea would be glad to see me. Perhaps she'd understand I was still her friend, if I could untie my tongue enough to explain how the murder investigation and nearly losing Paul was a wound too private to share at the time, even with her.

And perhaps Paul would luck out and Sig would invite us to view the famous private collection.

Then again, sometimes you never get a chance to find out.

# BushWhacked
## ~ THE FOURTH THEA CAMPBELL MYSTERY

Even as loud as it was, the diesel tractor's grumbling did not drown out my sister Juliet's scream. I whirled and spotted her across the yard, by my house, partially concealed by the big rhododendron. Her second scream, a prolonged howl, set my pulse into a panicked lick in a single beat. The shovel I'd been using, to improve a temporary home at the back of the garden for the big old rhody, flew from my hands with the force of a home-run swing.

Blood, and a lot of it, was my first thought.

I booked it, straining to see as I ran from the end of my yard toward the house. Unfortunately for me, the half-uprooted rhododendron hid most of Juliet. From sixty feet away all I could see was the flashing of pink parka and red Wellies in a frantic, blurry motion that took her nowhere. No way could I determine what had gone so wrong -- and with my twenty-three-year-old younger sister, assuming the worst was always the safest bet.

However, the jerky, marionette-gone-berserk leaps accompanying her continual high-pitched shrieking had me reconsidering after a few frantic strides. I cut my pace to a walk.

Mice, and a lot of them, was my second thought.

No doubt we'd uncovered a nest of the little critters (previously) sleeping through the cold, wet December, doubly protected in their cozy burrow by the dense evergreen branches of the rhody and the foundation of my house.

Without warning, Juliet's panic found a forward gear. Unfortunately Paul, my fiancé, was also by the house -- and standing directly in her path. With the speed of a fat man on a zip line, she slammed him onto his back in the sodden grass and kept going. The shovel he'd held arced gracefully through the air and pierced the center of the kitchen window, shattering the glass with Hollywood drama.

Juliet's fiancé, Eric, driving the borrowed tractor and finessing the heavy lifting of the rhody, took a slow minute to notice her hysteria -- understandable, since he was practically sitting on the noisy engine. He made up for the oversight with the speed in which he abandoned the machine and rushed after her. They both disappeared around the corner of the house without a backward glance.

I hot-footed it to Paul, although he'd regained his feet before I was half-way there.

"Are you okay?" I asked, ignoring my sister's still audible, though incoherent, babbling.

"Yeah." He snagged his knit cap off the ground and pulled it back on over his dark hair, then brushed plant debris and dirt-on-the-verge-of-mud off his butt. I helped. "Looks like we've got another window to replace. What the hell was that all about?"

"Probably a family of mice who thought they were hibernating. She was practically standing on the rhody while Eric lifted it out of the ground. The poor, groggy little things probably ran laps around her feet."

"Mice don't hibernate, Thea," he said, striding the few paces toward the rhody before I was done brushing him off. I trotted after him and took another couple of swipes. "In Western Washington, the winters are so mild they probably don't even --" He breathed an oath with religious overtones -- a new habit I noticed a few days ago when he'd returned from his Christmas visit with his family in Minneapolis. Crouching by the base of the plant, he pushed the leafy branches aside.

With my line of sight cleared, there was no need to ask what had grabbed his attention. Dangling from a root was a dirt-colored human skull.

# From the Publisher

All Thea Campbell Mysteries are available in trade paperback and e-book format at your favorite retailer, both online and in bookstores.

Thank you for reading!

# About the Author

Susan Schreyer lives in the great state of Washington with her husband, two almost-on-their-own children, a couple of teenaged cats and the ghosts of a number of family pets of various species. Her horse lives within easy driving distance. Occasionally, Susan makes a diligent effort at updating her blogs "Writing Horses" and "Things I Learned From My Horse," and writes articles for several worthy publications. Mostly, she works on stories about people in the next town being murdered. As a diversion from the plotting of nefarious deeds Susan trains horses and teaches people how to ride them and, when the weather gets to her, works in a veterinarians' office. She is a member of the Guppies Chapter of Sisters in Crime and is co-president of the Puget Sound Chapter of SinC. When she has a minute she cleans her house and does laundry.

Susan can be run to earth at the following locations:

**Website:** www.susanschreyer.com

**Facebook:** Susan Schreyer Mysteries -- www.facebook.com/pages/Susan-Schreyer-Mysteries/161359303906634

**Twitter:** @susanschreyer

**Blog:** Writing Horses http://writinghorses.blogspot.com

**Blog:** Things I Learned from My Horse http://thingsilearnedfrommyhorse.blogspot.com

**E-mail:** susan@susanschreyer.com